IGNI FERROQUE

A DARK MM PARANORMAL ROMANCE

TENNEBROSE
BOOK TWO

ASHLYN DREWEK

FOX HOLLOW BOOKS

Cover design by Teresa Conner at Wolfsparrow Covers

For Stefka,
This one's for you, bish. I can't be there in person to tell you how amazing you are, so let this book be a reminder.

A NOTE ON CAPITALIZATION

Since the overall theme of this book deals with religion, specifically the Christian religion, I wanted to take a moment to point out something in regard to the various capitalizations in the story. While writing as Phelan, our pious Necromancer, I capitalized religious nouns, such as the Bible, and the pronoun(s) for God (in this case, the standard "He/Him/His") to show Phelan's respect.

While writing as Remiel, our demon, I did not, and for the same reason—to show his disdain for Heaven and all it entails. God is capitalized in Remiel's chapters as a name only, not because of any respect on Remiel's part. He has none.

Choosing to capitalize "Devil" and "Hell" also depended on the context. Hell, in this story, is a literal location and is therefore capitalized. And "Devil" is used when referring to *the* Devil, as in the king of Hell and the Christian personification of evil. All of the other "devils" running around are just figures of speech.

TERMS & PHRASES

Latin terms & phrases

Deo adjuvante — By the help of God

Desistas — Stop/Quit/Give Up

Igni Ferroque — With fire and iron

In nomine Patris, et Filii, et Spiritus Sancti. Amen — In the Name of the Father and of the Son and of the Holy Ghost, Amen.

Mors ad caelos — Through death to Heaven

Mors omnibus — Death comes for us all

Necās — (You) Kill

Pater noster, qui es in caelis — Our Father, who art in Heaven

Reperio — Unlock/Open

Ubi amor, ibi dolor — Where there's love, there's pain

Vade retro daemonium — Go back, demon

Hebrew terms

Bĕlīya'al — Worthless

El ʿ āzār — 'God has helped'

A WARNING TO THE READER

This book contains references to or scenes depicting: somnophilia, **noncon between MCs** and other graphic descriptions of sexual situations, **on-page torture between MCs**, off-page child abuse, blood play, strangulation and breath play, **on-page suicide**, mental illness and institutions, parental estrangement, extreme religious views and criticism of said views (there's a heavy focus on Christianity/Christian mythology due to the demonic aspect), and religious self-harm. **Reader discretion is greatly advised as this book is NOT for everyone and most will probably find it offensive.** Please heed the warnings.

CHAPTER ONE

PHELAN

Unearthly screams tore through the North Woods, dampened only slightly by the patter of steady rainfall. It was an unseasonably cool night for late August but the chill air helped with the smell. So much sulfur was always nauseating, no matter who you were or how many demons you killed.

I closed the tome in my hands and secured the clasp, watching the demon writhe in agony on the ground. Green and black flames licked all over its body until its charred remains crumbled to ash, hissing and popping as the rain put it out.

"Good job," Marcus Ambrose said to me as I dragged my heel through the various circles of sand and gravel, disrupting the lines and dispelling the magic.

Acknowledging the praise with a slight incline of my head, I nevertheless felt a wave of nausea roll through my stomach. Summoning and trapping demons so other Necromancers could kill them shouldn't be something I was praised for, but I was. It was the one thing I *was* good at, therefore it became the crux of my identity, no matter how awkward I felt about it.

With our duty finished, the small gathering of witches collectively nodded and began the trek back to our respective vehicles.

"That's the third demon we've killed this month," Temperance said quietly as we made our way through the darkened forest, mindful of the gnarled tree roots and uneven terrain.

"I am well aware," I replied, tucking the aptly-named Book of Damnation into my messenger bag, out of the rain. Bob Winslow might have been the official archivist for the Congregation, keeper of the grand Book of Transactions, but he wasn't the only one recording events. The Necromancers of Winslow kept our own book and it was my responsibility to record any and all interactions with demons, including when we ultimately dispatched them from our realm. It was the only way to ensure future generations of Necromancers had the necessary information to keep our Congregation safe.

"I know you're aware, Phelan." Temperance didn't even bother hiding her huff. "The question I've been wondering is 'is it enough?' Is it even wise to begin with? The Book of Lazarus gave us a list of demons to control, demons that would benefit our families. I know they're scared about what happened with the marquis last year, but should we really be wiping out one of our best resources without considering all of the costs? Not to mention the fact the demons are bound to figure out we're working off a hit list and then what? We could be starting a war, which is the exact opposite of what anyone in this town needs."

"All fine questions that should be directed to one of them," I replied, nodding toward our more distant kin,

Marcus and Caius Corbin. "They're the ones with active powers. You and I are just..." I shrugged, not knowing which word to use for our relatively trivial standing in the witchy community.

While I was perfectly content with my role within our dark little enclave, it was obvious where we ranked in the grand scheme of things. I came when called, cast the necessary protective circle or triangle, and spoke the Latin required to summon the demons to their death; Caius and Marcus were the executioners in the family, along with Warren Simms. The rest of us merely did as we were told.

"What we do is nothing to be sneered at. It's the bedrock of necromancy," my cousin snipped. "Besides, without us and our studies, they wouldn't have half of the ability to do what they do. They may have the power, so to speak, but we have the knowledge."

I slid her a pointed look. "Knowledge which we're not sharing with the rest of the Congregation..."

"Do you think the Congregation would be happy to hear the dark families are out traipsing through the North Woods every other day, summoning and killing demons before the creatures get the idea to start picking off freshmen coeds? It would be a witch-hunt all over again and our families would be at the center of it. We finally have a modicum of peace thanks to Cassius and Graeme's engagement. As much as I don't agree with annihilating every single demon in the Book, I also don't want to go back to three hundred years of senseless murder."

I made a noncommittal noise in return. If history taught us anything, peace was a relative term. The Corbins had been restored in the eyes of the Congregation at the expense of the Hewitts' downfall. The Olivers, meanwhile, continued to lay low regardless of who was the top dog. It was our trademark move since 1667 when one pesky in-law tarnished our name forever. Even the mortals in town gave us the side-eye when they heard our name, like we were going to suddenly sprout warts and boil their children alive in a cauldron. *She was a Corbin!* I wanted to scream, but that name meant nothing to people who were raised on scary stories involving the infamous Winslow Witch.

"I'm going to Boston tomorrow," Temperance said, abruptly changing the topic and subsequently darkening my mood even more. "You want to come with?"

I stole a glance at her before replying, grateful she wasn't a mind reader from a distance. "No, I'm good, thanks."

"Phelan."

Ignoring the sigh in her tone, I fished the keys out of my pocket and remotely unlocked my SUV, hoping she'd take the hint.

"When's the last time you've been to see her?" she asked, elbowing me and completely derailing my plan of pretending I didn't hear her over the steady rainfall. For a moment I debated whether or not I should play dumb, but it would only draw out this conversation longer than I wanted it to.

"It's been... a while," I replied, looking away from her. Seventy-four days, precisely.

"Phelan!"

I winced and ducked my head, letting the cool rain run down the back of my neck to chase away the sudden flash of hotness. "I've been busy."

"Bullshit."

"It's the truth. You know the rare books department has been turned completely upside down with this whole cataloging nightmare. I haven't had the time to make it down there."

"I can't believe Hester has let you get away with that excuse. Didn't she demand you come see her every Wednesday night for dinner or something?"

"She did. And she has no room to talk. She's the reason my mother is there in the first place."

"It's more complicated than that," Temperance said softly.

No, it wasn't. But I wasn't going to stand around getting soaked to the bone just to argue with her.

"I'll see you later," I said, yanking open my door. "I have to dry this book out."

"Don't forget to request those demonologies from the Bodleian for me," she said as I closed the door.

Waiting until she disappeared into her own car, I exhaled a sigh and turned the engine on. Rain plinked off the windshield, streaking down the glass and pooling in larger tracts the closer they got to the bottom.

Guilt gnawed at me the longer I sat there, replaying Temperance's admonishing tone in my head. Seventy-four days. It had been seventy-four days since I saw the woman who birthed me in the flesh, but how long had it been since I saw a lucid version of her? The answer was never.

Bridget Oliver may have been listed as my mother on my birth certificate, but I felt no ties to her other than pure societal obligation—especially as a Winslow witch. Here, family was supposed to be everything. Except, Temperance was more of a mother to me than Bridget ever was. I was eternally grateful to my cousin—she made growing up under the stern gaze of Hester Colburn Oliver bearable. But none of that helped when it came to dealing with Bridget, a woman who had been in and out of my life in the form of photographs and weird, disjointed letters with the occasional visit thrown in to make it all the more confusing. Hester had her committed when I was a baby and then threw away the key, yet *I* was the one expected to be a dutiful son. For what? To assuage Hester's own guilt? Or to show me what happened when witches dabbled with demons, to remind me that anything less than perfection may result in insanity?

Tamping down my resentment, I turned the wipers on and finally shifted the car into motion, trying not to think about mothers and demons and how the two were often conflated. I suppose there was a reason for that.

CHAPTER TWO

REMIEL

"This town is turning into an absolute nightmare," Melech said, surveying the ring of scorched earth in the early morning light. The rain had washed most of the evidence away but there was enough energy left to piece together what happened while the mortal world was sleeping. "I thought we put all of this behind us in the seventeenth century."

"First Nadav. Then Ronove. Now Jabez." I swept up a handful of black, sulfurous dust and glowered at it. Fury raged inside of me so hot wisps of pale green flames flickered around me, singeing the nearby blades of grass.

I threw the black dust onto the ground in disgust, scattering the remnants of my most loyal duke. The damage was done; his body was gone. Nothing I did now could bring him back, but I would happily slaughter everyone who played a role in his death. "Three of my best lords and countless other creatures in my legion. You say this has been happening for *months* but you're just *now* telling me?"

Melech cleared his throat. "Jabez said not to. He was

looking into the others' deaths. He didn't want to worry you until he had more information."

"Worry." Blowing the dust particles off my hand, I swiped my palm across my thigh, dislodging whatever might have remained on the fabric of the long, black shendyt I wore as I stood slowly, coming eye-to-eye with him again. "Am I to believe this is merely a coincidence? A stroke of bad luck? Divine retribution, perhaps?"

"No. It would seem *they* are hunting us," he admitted with a growl.

"If they are, you'd better deal with it, General, or I'll make sure you're the next pile of ash."

Melech stiffened, his black, reptilian eyes narrowing.

I wasn't intimidated, nor was I concerned with hurting whatever little feelings were bubbling up inside his massive chest. "The next time I'm summoned here, it had better not be to clean up another one of your mistakes. Find whoever is doing this and end them. Now."

"I hardly think this qualifies as *my* mistake."

"I don't care what you think. As Jabez noted sometime before his untimely death, I have enough to 'worry' about with Hazael trying to overthrow my rule. The last thing I need to deal with are witches assassinating members of my court one by one!"

"It won't happen again." Melech inclined his horned head. His hand flew to his sword suddenly as he dropped into a half-crouch. "Sire!"

I halted immediately, spotting the danger for myself as clear as day.

A witch was coming down the pathway, straight for us. My invisibility powers were enough to shield me in most situations unless this one had some form of magic that was attuned to demonic presences. Still, he didn't appear to see me *or* hear my armor as I drifted away from the mound of dust that used to be Jabez.

The witch moved forward without hesitation, stepping into the clearing—and right past me—without giving any indication he knew I was there.

The scent of him washed over me in his wake, a combination of musk and cedar, blended with rosemary and citrus. A protection spell? Something for his memory? Whatever its purpose, it was positively mouth-watering.

I turned and followed him, shadowing each step in silence.

The witch stopped at the edge of the charred dirt and dug around in the bag that hung from his shoulder.

Melech had his sword at the ready, hovering near the witch's neck on the opposite side.

My gaze cut to him sharply. When he caught my eye, I shook my head once. My curiosity had been piqued. I wanted to see what this wayward witch was doing out here, all alone.

Melech cocked his head but lowered the sword and retreated backward, giving the witch room.

Like a rabbit sensing a wolf, the man froze suddenly. The sound of his heart rate picked up, but he stayed exactly where he was, as still as a statue, listening with his head canted.

After he incorrectly determined the threat was gone, he resumed scrounging in his bag before unearthing a small, battered bible and an aspergillum. A strand of dark red beads tumbled from the hand that held the palm-sized book, a little silver cross swinging back and forth like a pendulum.

Not just a witch—a *Necromancer*.

Desire swelled so strongly within me that my chest

spasmed. He represented the best of both worlds, two of my ultimate cravings. Separately, witches and those with extreme religious devotion were both amusing to play with. But combined? I shivered with anticipation. In light of the ongoing war with Hazael, I could use something to distract me, alleviate my stress. A Necromancer was just the thing I didn't know I needed until I set my sights on *him*.

At that moment, I didn't care who or what tried to intervene. I was going to make that Necromancer mine in every conceivable way until I corrupted the entirety of his being.

Murmuring in Latin, he sprinkled holy water over the scorched earth and bowed his head to finish the prayer. When he was done, he crossed himself and pressed the rosary beads to his lips before all of the religious items disappeared back into the bag only for another book to emerge, this one larger.

He scribbled something inside, noting the time on his watch.

I shifted behind him, peering over his shoulder. From the looks of it, he was documenting Jabez's demise for posterity, including blessing the spot where the demon had been vanquished so we wouldn't be able to piece him back together like a cracked egg. Little did he know, Jabez was gone for good. By reducing him to ash, the witches had eliminated him from existence. He'd gone to an abyss where neither God nor the Devil could call him back again.

The Necromancer froze in front of me, the pen stopping abruptly on the page, his muscles tense. I was so close to him now I could hear the uptick in his breathing, the way his heart hammered against his ribs. He knew he wasn't alone, but he didn't seem to have enough power to sense, what, exactly was lurking nearby. Perhaps he thought what he was feeling was a lost spirit, drifting around the woods in search of salvation. If he was aware of how close two high-ranking demons were standing to him, I doubted he would have been as calm.

Before I realized what I was doing, my hand lifted and brushed along the top of his short, dark hair. Power rippled into my palm, sending a shiver down my spine hard enough to make my feathers rustle. Instinctively, the witch ran his own hand through his hair, glancing around warily.

Snapping the book shut, my new plaything shoved it into his bag and set off at a brisk pace, back the way he came, casting cautious glances over his shoulder every now and again.

I exercised what little restraint I had and let him go, throwing my wing in front of Melech when he started to chase after him, his sword still unsheathed.

"What are you doing? Why didn't you let me kill him?" Melech asked, torn between looking at me for answers and watching our adversary leave.

"Because I decided I want him."

"But sire." When I looked at him with an arched eyebrow, silently daring him to say more, Melech continued with a sneer. "He's a witch! I could smell the stench on him from here."

"Do you know how long it's been since I've had a witch as a pet? Besides... He could prove to be useful to me."

"How?"

I cut a dismissive glance in his direction and disappeared back into the depth of the underworld.

In the days following my run-in with the Necromancer in the woods, I spent as much time watching him as I could—never too near, in case he could sense me, but close enough to observe him in his daily routine.

I was particularly keen to see if he or his fellow witches were in any sort of communication with Hazael. It didn't take long for me to conclude Phelan Oliver was, without a doubt, one of the most boring creatures I'd ever hunted. In the twenty-first century, that was saying something.

His days were spent working in the rare book section of the university library, either in his office or down in the archives. He was polite to students and staff, soft-spoken and unassuming. It was easy to overlook him and he seemed to prefer it that way. He ate lunch—the *same* lunch, I might add, except for Fridays—at the same time every day, either in the sunken garden outside the library if the weather was good, or in his office if it wasn't. He declined requests to dine with coworkers and seemed unaware of the females who circled him like sharks in the water, sighing and batting their lashes.

His evenings and days off weren't much more exciting. His time away from work was just as regimented, just as predictable, just as painfully boring. If he wasn't at the massive black house in the woods, a remnant from his colonial ancestors no doubt, then he was at the meetinghouse in town. If he wasn't congregating with other witches, he was on his knees in church. Frankly, it was the only appealing part of the mass, other than when he opened his luscious mouth to accept a piece of bread the stupid humans claimed had divinity. I could think of plenty of other things he could put on his tongue and I guaranteed they would taste better than a stale wafer.

True to his profession, Phelan filled the quieter parts of his days with his nose stuck in a book or transcribing ancient religious texts from one language to another. For *fun*. I nearly fell asleep just watching him.

His only other form of amusement was the afternoon he spent rock climbing by himself in the abandoned quarry on the north side of town. I'd been tempted to take him then, while he clung to the jagged granite by his fingertips, muscles straining, sleek with sweat, but some part of me held back. I suppose I wanted to see him up close, to see how he'd react when he could see me in the flesh. Well, as much as he could see anyway. There was no way I could possibly reveal my true appearance until I had him exactly where I wanted him.

For curiosity's sake, I followed some of the other witches in town from time to time to see if I got the same feeling from them that Phelan evoked in me.

I didn't.

While their day-to-day lives may have been more interesting, comparatively speaking, they were completely and utterly mundane. None of them elicited the same spark within me.

He was truly an anomaly. And one of these days, he'd be mine.

CHAPTER THREE

PHELAN

A rustle of movement in my periphery drew my attention upward, away from my computer screen to the door of my office. A figure lurked there, watching me. I jumped, realizing a split second later it was Veronica, looking at me expectantly.

"I'm sorry. Did you say something?" I spit out quickly, hoping she didn't realize how on edge I was. Ever since my trip to the North Woods the other morning to cleanse the ritual space a second time, I'd been... unsettled. The weight of unseen gazes pressed against me, phantom fingers brushed through my hair and against my skin no matter where I went. If it was Mary Oliver coming to harass me about being in "her" woods again, I was going to make the Corbins banish her once and for all.

"I said we're going to lunch if you want to come with us," Veronica repeated with a smile.

"Oh, no thank you. I brought something."

"Let me guess. Ham and cheese?" She grinned. While I was busy casting about for something to say, she let me off the hook gracefully. "If you change your mind, we'll be at the bistro."

"Thank you." I inclined my head, even though I had no intention of taking her up on her offer. Forced socialization was not something I was keen on, even if they were fellow book lovers.

As soon as she left, I resumed my work, losing myself in ordering rare books from other libraries for our various professors and grad students, making sure the restoration of other archival documents was going according to plan, and, when time allowed, keeping abreast of news from medievalists around the world and anything promising coming from Biblical scholars. Even though we guarded our secrets like ill-tempered dragons instead of trying to combine our collective strength, one never knew when a new grimoire or artifact would pop up and shake the witchy world.

Such had been the case with the Combermere Codex.

Sealed up in a manor wall in England, it was only discovered in the 1800s when the home was being restored. It made its way to America during World War II because the witches at the University of Ashbourne feared its capture, should England be invaded. Given Hitler's fascination with the occult and the book's evil disposition, it was a very real concern.

It came in an iron cage with strict instructions on how and when it should be used. In short, never. Since then, the Codex, while invaluable to Necromancers, had been sealed up, safe and sound, beneath my very feet in the library basement. Other than observing it from afar when I was entrusted with the keys to its prison, it was one of the few books in Tennebrose's extensive library that I hadn't actually read—nor did I plan to.

A sudden chill ran down my spine. The feeling that I was being watched again weighed on my shoulders.

I looked up, glancing out at the library behind my office windows, but no one was there.

Turning to my watch, I blinked when I saw the time. I switched off my computer and gathered my things, heading out of the rare book section and toward the main part of the library, turning off lights as I went.

I'd just reached the door that sectioned off the restricted area when it opened inward and someone stepped inside.

Drawing up short, I caught the edge of the door, remaining firmly in the way of the man trying to enter. He nearly crashed right into me but pulled back at the last second with a head-to-toe glance.

"Sorry about that," he said with a slow smile. "I guess I didn't see you there."

"It's ok. I was just—" The moment the stranger's icy gaze locked onto mine, a rush of heat flooded through me and my hands started to tingle. My fingers tightened on the door for support. I hoped he didn't notice any sort of shift in my demeanor, even though I cleared my throat and stumbled over the rest of my words. "Um, on my way out for the evening."

"Well, then I won't keep you," he said with a long, considering look that seemed to drift between my mouth and my eyes. "Unless you want me to."

"I'm sorry, this section is closed for the night."

"Oh, I wasn't talking about the books." His voice was like silk, but there was a glint of something in his pale blue eyes as they swept over me lazily. Something predatory. Something that made a droplet of sweat trickle down the back of my neck.

"We open again at eight tomorrow," I said, trying to size him up more subtly than he was with me. He didn't look like the usual sort of person who came to the rare books section. Quite honestly, he didn't look like any sort of scholar I'd *ever* seen.

I chided myself silently for making such snap judgments. Sure, he was wearing a black leather jacket with tight gray jeans slung low over his slim hips. And yes, his long blond hair was currently tied up in a messy sort of bun at the nape of his neck. But his striking looks didn't mean he was brainless. Clearly. He was here for something, after all. Although I couldn't shake the feeling in the back of my mind that he had zero interest in rare books and that my first gut reaction was the correct one.

"I don't suppose you'd let me grab one thing?" he asked, tipping his head forward slightly and lowering his velvety voice, like we were co-conspirators. I could imagine listening to him speak at length, getting wrapped up in each sensuous syllable that fell from his full mouth.

I gave myself a mental slap, eliminating the ridiculous scenario from my head immediately. Where it came from, I had no idea. Well… I did have one idea but that was *not* happening. That wasn't even on a list of possibilities of happening. Aside from the fact he was a complete stranger, appraising me like his last meal, I wasn't interested in any sort of sexual encounter. With anyone. Ever.

"I, um…" I licked my lips, forcing myself to hold his gaze even though my insides twisted together sharply the closer he came. "I'm sorry. The system is already turned off for the day and I was on my way out, as I said."

A half-smile quirked the side of his mouth, drawing my attention once more to his full, pouty lips. He let his gaze drop from mine before flicking up a second later, sending another spasm through my stomach. "I guess I'll see you tomorrow then."

"Eight o'clock," I repeated, flashing him a polite smile.

He hooked his thumbs in his front pockets and raised a pointed eyebrow at me, making no effort in hiding his open perusal. Like a live butterfly being skewered to a specimen board, I squirmed under his gaze.

Finally, the stranger spun on the heel of his boot and strolled away with preternatural grace.

Closing my eyes, I exhaled a few slow breaths, willing my heart rate to return to a normal speed. To help that endeavor, I pulled the damp collar away from my neck and fanned it a bit, hoping to circulate some air across my skin.

Objectively, I could say the man had been attractive if that was your type, and even though I was beyond inexperienced when it came to relationships, I was pretty sure he'd been flirting with me. I could also safely say I'd *never* looked at another man the way he looked at me. Even the most aggressively flirty woman had never looked at me like a lion about to devour a lamb. I might have been flattered, but that was the least concerning part of the whole encounter.

I waited until the stranger was out of sight before I closed and locked the door. Throwing a glance over each shoulder, I made sure the coast was clear before casting a quick ward over the lock. Despite the fact my magic was on the pathetic end of the spectrum, I hoped it would be enough to deter any would-be thieves until the morning. Or at least until I could make a phone call to a more powerful witch.

A spider descended on a silken strand from the top of the door frame, hovering at eye level.

"Do you mind?" I asked, nodding at the door.

The creature bobbed for a moment before continuing its descent to the doorknob. Once it landed, it scurried around the handle a few times, securing the silk before jumping off again. Swinging itself like a pendulum to the doorframe, it attached a nearly invisible line from one side to the other—a harmless measure that would alert me if someone had, indeed, made it inside overnight.

"Thank you."

Hitching my messenger bag up onto my shoulder, I proceeded to the main exit trying to appear as nonchalant as possible. Avoiding the large, tiled Tennebrose seal in the library foyer more out of respect than any genuine fear that my soul would be trapped at the university forever, as the rumors went, I lifted a hand in farewell to the student at the circulation desk on my way by.

The stranger was nowhere to be found. Thank God. I was *still* sweating.

Once I was outside, I slipped my cell phone out of my pocket and dialed Temperance's number.

"What's up?" she asked as soon as she picked up.

"We have a big problem."

"What's that?"

"I'm pretty sure a demon just came into the library."

"Are you absolutely sure?" Temperance asked, pacing back and forth in my spartan living room, wearing a hole in the already well-worn rug. Though, I wasn't about to remind her it was an antique.

I nodded, running my thumb in absentminded circles

back and forth over the crucifix on my rosary. I'd replayed it again and again in my head. It was the only thing that made sense. The sudden heat, the nerves, the wildly inappropriate and out-of-place fantasy of him exploring every inch of my body with his mouth...

"But he didn't sense what you were?" Temperance interrupted my ruminating, her blonde brows drawn together. "He didn't realize you were a witch?"

I shook my head, trying to blink away the image of him in my mind. "I don't think so. The perk of not really having much magic, I suppose. I'm not that detectable."

"Stop it," Temperance huffed and sat on the couch next to me. "Did he say what he wanted?"

"No. Just that he would see me tomorrow."

She snorted. "Yeah, *that's* not happening."

I furrowed my brows at her. "What do you mean?"

"There's no way you're going to work."

"But I have th—"

"I don't give a shit *what* you have! A demon says something cryptic like 'I'll see you tomorrow'? Guess what? You're not going to work tomorrow!" She stared at me with piercing blue eyes, a shade lighter and icier than the watery blue-green color I inherited. "Got it?"

"Maybe I was wrong," I protested lamely. "We should tell the others. They can come to the library in the morning and see if it really was a demon or just some art student, or something, and I can keep going with the cataloging project. He said he was there for a book. Maybe he's working on an illuminated manuscript. Or... something."

"I really wish you would trust yourself," she said with a sigh, leaning forward to brush her fingers through my hair. "And I wish you'd reconsider your living situation. I'd feel a lot better if you were in town, not all the way out here in the sticks by yourself."

"I'm not a child anymore, Temperance." I shrugged her off and smoothed my hair back into place. My living arrangement was yet another argument I didn't want to have with her. Housing was notoriously expensive in Massachusetts, even in a small town like Winslow, which is why I preferred to live in our family's historic saltbox house—for *free*. Plus, it got me out from underneath our grandmother's hawkish gaze. Sure, the electricity was spotty sometimes and the roof leaked when it rained, but it was quiet and as far from people as I could get when I wasn't required to be around them.

"I know. You're a grown-up pain in my ass. But I worry about you. You've taken your necromantic duties a little too literally." She glanced around my living room as if the sparse furnishings spoke for themselves. "It's not the fourteenth century anymore. You don't have to live like a monk to practice your magic."

"It's not about the magic," I replied tightly.

"You're not your mother."

I got to my feet quickly, putting some distance between us under the guise of retrieving a book from the built-in bookcase across the room. A black spider tiptoed out from behind the books, creeping along the edge of the shelf toward me, its tiny pinchers moving rapidly. Frowning at the arachnid, I gave a slight shake of my head. As considerate as the offer was, I did *not* need a spider biting my cousin on my behalf.

If spiders could huff, I'm sure it did, right before it scuttled back to the shadows.

"One day, Phelan," Temperance said behind me. "Just take one personal day off of work. Please? I'll see if Marcus can meet me at the library in the morning and if it turns out to be nothing, then you're back at work the day after."

Leafing through a book without actually reading anything, I glanced over my shoulder. "And if it *is* something?"

"Then I guess another sigil will magically appear in the Book of Damnation once we vanquish the demon." She slapped her hands on her knees and got to her feet. "Ok?"

I closed the book and shoved it back on the shelf. Turning to face her, I crossed my arms over my chest, watching as she traversed the distance with a knowing look.

"Fine," I said at last. "I wouldn't hold my breath though. It was probably nothing."

We said our goodbyes and Temperance made her way out the front door, leaving me alone with my thoughts and the silence of the empty house around me, finally able to exhale.

I was about to head upstairs for the night when my cell phone rang. It was Peter Simms.

Glancing at my watch, I answered with a furrowed brow. "Hello?"

"Hey. It's Peter. Can you come to the house?" Well, *that* was never a good start to any conversation.

"Is everything ok?"

"Um, yeah. No. I don't know. Amber and I were talking. I could really use your advice. It's about Isla."

"Ok. I'll be right there."

"Thank you."

I disconnected and went to the kitchen for supplies. At this point in my life, I didn't have to ask any more questions—there was only one reason people would call me looking for "advice." Particularly after sunset.

Untying a bundle of dried lilacs from the low-hanging beam across the ceiling, I snagged a cluster of lavender too and carried everything to the counter. Plucking a few of the buds off of each flower, I sprinkled them into a mortar and added some lemon balm leaves before grinding them together with the pestle.

I shook the herbs into a sachet and tied it off, moving down to the cupboard at the end of the kitchen. Sifting through the crystals, I grabbed a piece of rose quartz and fluorite. The very last thing I took out was a pink crocheted spider, about the size of my hand. Items in tow, I headed out the door.

About twenty minutes later, I pulled into the Simms' driveway and parked. Glancing around the quiet neighborhood, it all seemed so perfectly normal it was hard to imagine what sort of evil was lurking in quiet suburbia. But this was Winslow, after all. Evil didn't need a reason to exist. It just did.

Peter opened the door before I could even lift my hand to knock. "Thanks for coming," he said, pulling me inside and closing the door, as if he was afraid the neighbors might see me. Mortals might be generally clueless, but other witches would know exactly why I was there and no one wanted to be accused of having demons in their home.

"What's going on?" I asked, glancing around the quiet house. Amber and Isla were nowhere to be found.

"It's Isla," he said, shoving his hands in his pockets and rocking back on his heels. "She's been having dreams. Nightmares. For weeks. Amber thinks it's normal, that it's part of her development and whatnot, but..." He swallowed whatever else he was going to say and cast a cautious glance toward the stairwell.

"But you think it's something else?" I prompted.

He nodded. "I can't take it anymore, Phelan. No one is sleeping. Isla used to go down so easy and now she screams when we try to put her down. We even tried co-sleeping and she still wakes up screaming in the middle of the night and won't go back to sleep. I wanted to get her something from the pharmacy, but Amber freaked out and accused me of trying to drug our baby."

"She's a Green, right? Amber?"

He nodded again.

Divination plus the dark arts. My heart broke for the little girl already. Who knew what her genetics had inadvertently subjected her to? But at least we *knew* both sides of her lineage, which meant we knew what the potential fix was, unlike me and the other bastard witches of the world. Your powers were a crap shoot. Or you were pretty much a dud. Like me.

"Don't worry," I said, squeezing Peter's shoulder. "I'll fix it."

Peter let out a shaky breath and gestured toward the stairs. "They're up there."

I went first, making my way up the steep stairs of the old house. The closer I got to the nursery, the hotter I grew under my collar. Literally. Beads of sweat gathered at my hairline with each step. As much as Amber didn't want to believe what was in front of her very eyes, Peter was right to call me. A house this old? Inhabited by witches with their powers? It was like a homing beacon for demons and children were always the most susceptible.

It wasn't hard to guess which room was Isla's—the purple butterflies on the door were kind of a clue.

Rapping my knuckle on the cracked door, I waited until Amber told me to come in before pushing it open the rest of the way.

She was rocking Isla in the corner next to her crib. Everything appeared to be in order. Books and toys were stacked neatly on the bookcase by the door. A mobile with butterflies and crystals hung above her crib, turning slowly with gentle music playing.

Amber's glare darted from me to her husband and her arms tightened around their toddler. "Oh my God! She's fine, Peter! Night terrors are normal for kids her age."

"I'm assuming she's been to her doctor?" I asked, skipping right over any attempt at small talk. Amber clearly wasn't in the mood and I wasn't any good at it, anyway.

"Of course she has!" she snapped. "She's perfectly fine! She's not sick. She doesn't have an infection. It's just bad dreams. He shouldn't have called you."

"Have there been stressors in the family lately?"

Amber's glare hardened. "Like what? Like, are we getting divorced? I know that's what everyone keeps asking!"

"Amber, calm down," Peter sighed. "That's not what he meant."

"It's exactly what he meant! I've read the studies too, Peter! Death, divorce, major illness—all reasons for night terrors, especially in children. So either we're stressing her out or you're saying a demon has possessed our baby!"

Isla's face scrunched and even from across the room I could see the tears well in her eyes.

Rather than tell her parents this was exactly the sort of thing they should avoid in front of her, I walked over to Isla and crouched down next to her and her mother, pulling out the pink spider. "Hey, angel. I brought something for you," I said softly, holding it out to her. "I made it. Isn't it cool?"

"A spider?" Amber scoffed behind Isla, muttering, "Typical."

Isla, on the other hand, had zero hesitation in taking the crocheted creature. She squeezed one of the stuffed legs before turning it over and running her finger over the fuzzy body, completely unperturbed by the animal and what it represented to most people.

"They ward off evil during sleep," I said to Amber, making sure to smile brightly and keep my tone light for Isla's sake. "And the eyes are made out of jet, for more protection."

"So that's all? A stuffed animal is going to fix everything?" Peter asked.

"Maybe," I replied, straightening slowly and running a hand over Isla's silky red curls. "But I'll stay with her tonight to make sure there isn't something... else... happening."

"Stay with her?" Amber interjected. "No, I don't think so. I don't care if he's your family," she said, glaring at her husband. "He's not staying in our daughter's room, alone, for the whole goddamn night!"

Peter scoffed and threw his hands up. "Oh, Jesus Christ! What do you think he's going to do to her? He's basically a fucking priest!"

"He's an Oliver!"

"And I'm a Simms, yet you married me!"

"Well, maybe that was a mistake after all!"

Isla burst out crying.

"Oh, perfect," Amber sighed, kissing Isla's head, trying to undo the damage, but it was too late.

"Forgive me for saying this, but you two look... exhausted. At the very least, let me take care of her and give you two a break." I glanced between the parents, hoping that statement was put at delicately as possible. Sadly, I'd seen it before—parents who were particularly sensitive to any possible critique of their child or parenting skills. But this sort of thing wasn't a criticism. The sweltering heat in Isla's nursery, her reaction to the discord around her, mixed with so-called "night terrors"? The signs were clear. There was a demon lurking nearby, feeding on all the misery like a leech.

Peter and Amber engaged in a staring contest for several moments while Isla wailed, clutching the little pink spider in her fist like her life depended on it.

"Fine." Amber caved first, standing abruptly and walking over to me. "But I'm watching on the monitor."

"I would expect nothing less." I gave her a small smile, taking Isla from her arms and settling the toddler against my hip. I tugged on one of the spider legs to get Isla's attention on me and not her parents. She snatched it backward, cuddling her new possession to her chest and sniffling, but no longer screaming.

"Let us know if you need anything," Peter said from the doorway.

"I will. Goodnight." I waited until they left, closing the door behind them, before turning to Isla. "Let's get rid of that demon once and for all. Ok? Ok." I carried her to her crib and set her inside, humming softly and preparing for another round of screaming to start.

While I hoped she'd lie down on her own, I also knew that probably wasn't going to happen. As soon as her feet touched the mattress, Isla sprang upward and held onto the railing, staring up at me with wide eyes, her lower lip quivering.

"I know, baby girl. We're going to take care of it. I promise."

Slipping my rosary beads out of my pocket, I crossed myself and then Isla. I kept them wrapped around my hand while I fished the crystals out of my pocket and slid them underneath the mattress. Next came the herbs. I sprinkled a ring around the bed, murmuring a prayer as I went.

"Now, it's time to sleep, angel." I slipped one hand behind her back and pressed the palm of the other to her forehead. Her eyelids sank shut and she crumpled, falling backward onto the hand supporting her. I eased her down onto the mattress and positioned her in a relaxed pose, the pink spider between her hands on her stomach.

Retreating from the crib, I sat in the chair Amber had been in earlier and started my vigil, my fingers moving over the rosary slowly with each new prayer.

I was on the second "Glory Be" when the shadows started to shift, twisting and curling along the wall toward the crib.

Closing my eyes, I exhaled a slow breath.

Here we go...

As my heart rate lowered, the real world faded away.

Entering the dreamworld, I took a moment to acclimate myself to the darkness of Isla's mind before I began searching for her, opening a variety of doors only a child could think of—big ones, small ones, ones straight out of *Alice in Wonderland*. Every shape and color imaginable, the doors represented memories and dreams alike inside her head. It was a frustrating game of hide and seek. Children always were. Despite their age, or perhaps because of it, their minds were infinitely more complex to navigate. Adults tended to compartmentalize, making it easier to get in and out, as it were. But children? It was like entering a maze designed by someone on an acid trip.

A giant brown teddy bear appeared at the end of a long hallway in Isla's mind, its fur dirty and matted. A red bowtie hung limply around its neck, torn and stained. It was reminiscent of an antique toy, a testament to its age and how well-loved it was by its owner. But something about it felt... off. It was completely unlike the other toys littering Isla's mind, which were all colorful and new.

I cocked my head, watching it, trying to suss out what I was sensing.

It stared back at me with one black button eye and a look I could only describe as sinister.

"I don't think you belong here," I said, starting toward it, grasping my rosary beads tighter.

The teddy bear tilted its head slowly, giving me a moment's pause. We continued to stare at one another, frozen in time and place, waiting to see who would make the next move.

The teddy bear broke first.

It turned and sprinted down another hallway.

I darted after it, chasing it down the hall to a white door with purple butterflies. Isla's bedroom door.

The bear crashed through the door and slammed it shut. On the other side, Isla screamed. It echoed in reality, which meant I didn't have much longer before her parents busted through the real door.

Without opening my eyes, I threw a ward at the bedroom door in real life, hoping it would buy me some time.

Back inside the dream world, I turned the knob for the nursery door, but it wouldn't open.

Isla's screaming continued, accompanied by a high-pitched laugh that made my skin crawl.

"*Reperio*," I growled at the door.

It swung open and the screaming stopped abruptly.

The replica of Isla's nursery was completely covered in cobwebs. Thrashing wildly, the teddy bear was caught up in the sticky silk, trying to reach the crib. It stopped when it realized I was in the room.

"You think your tricks are enough to stop me, witch?" the teddy bear hissed, its head spinning slowly to look at me.

"Looks like you're stopped to me," I replied with a smirk.

"You can't protect her every night."

"I don't need to."

I ducked beneath the silver strands, weaving my way through the web like a labyrinth, careful not to touch any of it and disrupt the magic my familiars had created.

Frantic pounding echoed through the room. The teddy bear wailed, nearly drowning out the sound of Amber screaming in the real world. It was a mimicry of Isla's cry, a desperate attempt to get her parents to intervene on its behalf. But if they managed to wake Isla in real life, they'd set that thing free and I couldn't let that happen.

Isla's gaze darted back and forth, around the room at dizzying speeds—from me to the door to the teddy bear and back again, terror on every part of her little face.

"Hi angel," I said as I came closer to the crib. "Everything's going to be ok from now on, I promise. Just keep looking at me, ok? Don't look at that ugly bear."

Isla blinked up at me, tears glinting off her cheeks in the soft yellow glow from her moon-shaped nightlight. She stretched her arms up and reached for me, still clinging to the fuzzy pink spider.

"Oh, you still have her!" I gasped in faux delight, scooping up Isla and the spider. "Can I show you something really cool? I need to borrow her for a minute then you can have her back."

Behind me, the teddy bear snarled, clawing through another swath of cobwebs.

In the real world, Amber screamed at me to open the door—something I was *not* about to do, no matter what she threatened to do to me, or whom she threatened to call, from the Deacon to the police.

Plucking the spider from Isla's hands, I leaned in close and whispered to it. "*Necās.*"

The crocheted creature twitched in my palm, morphing into a living spider right in front of us. It started growing immediately, swelling in size until it dwarfed the teddy bear.

As soon as the spider leapt off my palm, I turned Isla away from the demon bear and spoke softly in her ear, nothing more than a prayer but hopefully enough to distract her from what was going on behind us.

The giant pink spider rushed down the web, headed straight for the teddy bear, its fangs gleaming.

"Very soon, witch, you'll meet a fate worse than this," the bear shouted, still trying to free itself from the silken strands. "Your own screams will drive you to insanity. Just like your mother!" The demon's cackling resumed, even after the spider launched itself at its throat and bit deep. The bear's maniacal laugh turned to caterwauling, mirrored by Amber's banging on the bedroom door.

The spider made short work of the demon, wrapping the immobilized body in a silken bundle in no time at all.

"Get it out of here," I said, waving a hand at the window. It slid upward silently, revealing a pitch-black void beyond.

Pinching its prey between her palps, the spider hoisted the demon teddy upward and scurried out the window with it, chittering proudly on her way out.

Slamming the sash shut, I exhaled a breath as the door to Isla's nursery flew open in the real world.

Amber and Peter rushed in as I turned around slowly, mentally closing the door on the dreamworld and facing their wide-eyed gazes with as much calmness as I could muster.

"What the hell did you do?!" Amber shrieked.

"What was all that yelling?" Peter asked.

Isla yawned and rubbed a hand over her face, her head resting against my shoulder, exhausted from her last nightmarish adventure.

"Uh-oh. We dropped this," I said to Isla, ignoring her parents' questions as I stooped to retrieve the pink spider from the floor. Isla took it from my hand and cuddled it to her chest. "There we go. Let's go say goodnight to Mommy and Daddy, hmm?"

I handed Isla off to Amber with a polite smile. "I'll get out of your hair now."

"Wait," Peter interjected. "What was it? Was it a demon?"

"Just a nightmare," I replied with a shrug, quickly avoiding Peter's suspicious gaze.

On my way to the bedroom door, I sidestepped him, snagging a worn, one-eyed teddy bear off of the top of the bookshelf. "Where did this come from?" I asked quietly, tossing a glance over my shoulder. Amber was putting Isla to sleep again and neither seemed to be paying any attention to us.

"It was Amber's, I think. Her mother found it in the attic and brought it over a couple weeks ago."

"When the nightmares started." It wasn't a question and I didn't pose it as such. To drive home my point, I raised both brows, waiting for him to make the connection on his own.

"Let me walk you out," Peter said, a bit too loudly to be nonchalant, but Amber didn't even turn to look at us.

I waited until we were in the foyer, well out of earshot, before I held up the ratty bear. Still, knowing how old houses echoed, I kept my voice low. "This, right here, was the issue. I'm taking it and I'm destroying it. Make up whatever lie you have to for your wife, but you might want to think long and hard about your mother-in-law and why she gave your daughter this bear."

"Are you saying she did it on purpose? Knowing there was a demon in it?"

I shrugged. "Maybe. Maybe not. But I saw how you two were up there and that's in front of company. I can only imagine what's been going on behind closed doors." I held up a hand to stop him from explaining. "Babies are stressful. I get it. Marriages take work. I get that too. But you've had problems with your mother-in-law from the beginning. Maybe this was her way of throwing a match into a powder keg, hoping the added stress of not sleeping and fighting about why would be enough to get you two to divorce."

"That fucking bitch..." Fury twisted every line on Peter's face.

"Recharge the crystals under Isla's bed during full moons and don't let Amber take the spider away," I said calmly, hoping to redirect his anger into something more useful than plotting his mother-in-law's murder—justified or not. "That demon is gone for good. The spider will make sure nothing else can get close to her again."

"And what am I supposed to do about Eileen?"

I squeezed his shoulder gently. "Boundaries. Really firm boundaries."

"Can't you give me a spider to keep *her* away?"

"If only it was that easy," I replied with a smile. I turned to go, but Peter snagged my elbow.

"Phelan?"

"Yeah?"

"Thank you. And I'm sorry about Amber. And all that up there. She didn't mean it. You know she didn't."

I nodded, giving him my best attempt at a reassuring smile. "I know. You guys should all get some much-needed rest."

He nodded glumly.

Slipping out the front door, I pulled it shut behind me, keeping a tight hold on the teddy bear. I was more than ready to go home and destroy the poppet once and for all and then take a long, hot bath.

At least now I could officially say one perk of vowing to remain celibate was the fact I'd never have to deal with a mother-in-law. There was enough crazy in my own family without marrying into it.

CHAPTER FOUR
PHELAN

A week passed without incident since the demon came into the library. Temperance and Marcus had hung out there all day in different sections, but whoever he was, he never showed. I went back to work the day after, keeping an eye out for him, but there was no sign of him. That didn't mean I had stopped thinking about him, though.

Tennebrose was supposed to be a safe place for witches. More than Winslow itself, I considered the university my home. So to have a demon—well, *possibly* a demon, since the jury was still out...—come to my "home"? It set me on edge, even more than the unnerved feeling I'd been carrying since we defeated the last demon in the woods. But *that* demon, the duke, looked nothing like the one who'd come to the library. The duke had leather wings and curved horns. So was the blond stranger even a demon, then?

Thoughts of the maybe-demon invaded my head so much I began seeing him everywhere. Pacing me on the opposite side of the massive library bookshelves, his pale eyes tracking my every move. Standing across the quad on campus, close enough that I could see him but too far for magic to have any effect. I even saw him in the woods outside my house, wisps of silvery blond hair moving through the trees or strange shadows darting past my windows.

Even my dreams were no longer safe. Night after night, I was trapped inside my own head with only *him* for company. The dreams were usually the same: we were in the library again, reenacting our first meeting. Except he wasn't there for a book. He was there for me. Sometimes he was polite and charming, like he was in real life, though his flirtation was ramped up by a thousand degrees, making me blush from head-to-toe in the morning when I recalled our "conversations," imagined though they were. Other times he burst through the door to my office and kicked it shut, seizing my face between his hands and kissing me so hard and rough it made my head spin. After *those* dreams, I usually woke with a hard-on, regardless of the fact I'd already experienced a release sometime in the night, as evidenced by the ridiculous increase in laundry I'd undertaken.

Beyond the kissing and fervent groping (on his part), nothing sexual ever happened. Despite him begging me to take them off, my clothes remained firmly in place and my dream-body remained free of sin... regardless of what my dick might have been doing in the real world while I had no control over it.

The whole thing left me confused and overwhelmed, to say the least.

I couldn't tell Hester about him and I refused to tell Temperance. I couldn't tell anyone in the Congregation for that matter unless I wanted a one-way trip to the looney bin just like my mother. So I went to the one person I could confess anything to—Father Sullivan.

Quiet creaks and squeaking noises filled the old confessional booth as I waited for the priest to appear on the other side of the screen. After several minutes of the unnerving sounds, I realized all of the noise was because of me. Pressing my rosary beads into my thigh to stop their clacking, I chided myself to stop fidgeting so much in my chair.

The last time I'd been this nervous about a confession was when Hester found Peter's porn stash under my bed and dragged me to church. I didn't even have to confess—she did it for me, reminding me each and every step of the way that lust was a sin. Father Sullivan had heard the entire scolding before she shoved me into the confessional. My penance from the priest was a month of nightly prayers and daily volunteer work, so I'd be too tired for any wickedness.

It might have been twenty years ago, but what if Father Sullivan remembered that embarrassing summer and thought I'd invited the demon into my life with my lack of discipline? What if he thought my sins were too great to overcome this time and the demon was my punishment? Worse—what if he thought I was going crazy, like my mother?

The red velvet curtain slid open on the other side and I sat up straighter, clutching my rosary beads. Once the priest was seated, I bowed my head and crossed myself. "Bless me, Father, for I have sinned. It's been a week since my last confession.

"I've been having dark thoughts, Father. I've been seeing a… person… everywhere I go. When I'm awake. When I'm asleep. They're in my dreams, making me feel things I shouldn't feel. I wake up with questions and confusion. I worry I'm on the wrong path, that something is trying to lead me astray."

"Some*thing*?" the priest said. Based on the smoothness of the voice, I knew it wasn't Father Sullivan, but that wasn't a cause for concern. The priest on the other side was simply a stand-in for Christ himself—at the end of the day, it didn't matter *who* heard my confession, simply that I made it.

Even though he couldn't see me, I nodded. "The Devil. Or one of his agents." Outside of the Congregation, the Church was the only place I could speak freely of demons, although I didn't want to get into too many specifics about my witchy lineage. The Church and witchcraft were still at odds with one another, even though the Necromancers in my family were born from those priestly sorcerers and it was a tradition I'd fully embraced.

Thankfully, the priest didn't sound disturbed. "Hmm... go on."

I tried to study his profile through the screen, but the whole point was anonymity so I couldn't discern much, other than the fact he was young. Perhaps Father Sullivan was training a new priest.

"Did I do something to cause this?" I asked, trying to get my brain back on track. "I've prayed. I've fasted. I've begged God's forgiveness for whatever I might have done, yet he continues to follow me every single day. I don't know what else to do, Father. Even my own thoughts are no longer a refuge. He's everywhere."

"He?"

I swallowed thickly and hung my head at the slip-up. Honestly, I didn't know which would be a worse confession—admitting I thought I was being hounded by a demon or that I spent my days obsessively looking over my shoulder for a man with long blond hair and a wicked smile.

"Yes, Father," I murmured. "The person I've been seeing is a man. Or at least looks like one."

"Have these thoughts about him been immoral?"

Heat rushed down the back of my neck and my cheeks burned. I licked my lips, trying to retain some moisture in the sudden inferno. "Sometimes… but only in my dreams. I don't have those thoughts when I'm awake and in control." Ironic that my magic centered around dreams and yet I was powerless to stop my own from spinning *out* of control. More than once I'd woken, flushed and sweating like I'd run a marathon, with fragments of indecent dreams lingering in the back of my mind. I cast spell after spell to sleep without dreaming, but even that failed to stop them.

"Do you like what he's making you feel in your dreams?"

"I…" My brows knitted together, the answer stalling on my tongue. Did I? No. I mean, the obvious answer was no. It must have been a trick question because while the Church didn't view homosexual orientation as a sin in and of itself, they condemned the act and same-sex relationships. But I wasn't gay. Or bi. Or pan. Or *anything*.

I didn't think about sex with *anyone* because that wasn't in the cards for me. To practice the level of Necromancy I did, I needed to remain as pure of mind and body as possible. It was one thing to summon a spirit like the Corbins, it was another thing entirely to summon a demon *and* successfully control it. Medieval priests had been the last Necromancers to bend demons to their will and if I wanted to emulate even a fraction of their competence, I was resolved to follow the strict rules they laid out. While I never did it for my own gain, I needed to be ready for the dark families whenever they required my services. Temperance might have known the history of summoning demons, but I was one of the few who knew the proper techniques for casting complex circles and had the Latin to command the creatures. Aside from my dream magic, *that* was my true power—knowledge. And I wasn't going to risk it by engaging in meaningless sex.

"I don't know," I said at last. "I don't know what I'm feeling. I've never faced this problem before. Tell me what I need to do to fix it, Father, to make him go away."

"You can't."

"Father?" Hope plummeted inside of me like a lead balloon. I knew it. I was too far gone that even the Church couldn't save me.

"This is a test of your faith. You'll either overcome it or you'll give in."

"I'll overcome it," I said quickly.

There was a soft laugh on the other side of the screen and the shadow shifted. "Pride is a sin, too."

"I know. Forgive me."

"You're forgiven. Go in peace."

"Wh-what about my penance?"

"Oh, yes." The priest fell silent for a moment. "Three Hail Marys."

I couldn't help but make a face. "That's... all?"

"Thoughts alone are not sins. Until you give in to temptation, your penance doesn't need to be severe."

Nodding, though thoroughly confused, I wasn't going to press my luck. "Yes, Father."

He said the prayer of absolution quickly. As soon as "Amen" fell from my lips, the curtain on the other side slid open. I crossed myself and stood, waiting for a beat before exiting the confessional.

I genuflected before the cross, then dropped onto a kneeler in the back of the pews, hands clasped and head bowed toward the giant crucifix above the altar.

Three Hail Marys later, I crossed myself again and got to my feet. I wasn't sure if I felt better or not. Despite the confession and the absolution, my soul still felt heavy, like this was a temporary fix to a long-term problem. A bandaid on a gunshot wound, as it were. How long before my soul bled out?

On my way toward the front doors, Father Sullivan appeared with a smile. "Phelan! Good to see you. Have you come for confession this morning?"

I nodded, mustering as much of a smile as I could. "I've just finished my penance."

Father Sullivan's gray eyebrows furrowed. "I don't follow."

I furrowed my brow right back at him. "The penance after Confession?"

"But you haven't confessed yet."

"I did. With the other priest." I gestured toward the confessional booth.

He glanced around, the confusion never leaving his wrinkled face. "I'm the only priest here, son."

"Then who...?" I scanned the near-empty church, skipping past the little old ladies with their veiled heads bowed in prayer. The only other man I saw was the elderly custodian, quietly mopping the floor. Turning back to Father Sullivan, I shook my head, blinking through my own bewilderment. "I have to go."

"Are you alright? You look pale. Maybe you should sit down."

I didn't answer him as I bolted to the front door, squeezing my rosary beads for dear life.

I blew across the top of my mug, watching the tendrils of steam dissipate across the small, circular table between Peter and I. The coffee shop was quiet this time of day, in the lull between the mad dash of the morning and the lunch rush in the afternoon. Thankfully, Peter was able to meet me right after I left the church. The perk of being your own boss, I suppose.

"I'm glad you called," he said. "I wanted to let you know that Isla is doing great."

"That's good. I'm happy to hear it." Somehow, the steam seemed to curl backward, circling up the back of my hand and caressing my wrist. I rubbed my forearm, trying to dispel the feeling. It didn't seem to matter. The sensation snaked its way around my arm, winding upward to my throat and then up to my ear. A droplet of sweat slid down the back of my neck, disappearing into my collar, which suddenly felt two sizes too small.

"And that demon is gone for good, right?"

I nodded. "Banished from our realm, never to return."

"You didn't kill it?"

The phantom feeling stroked along my cheekbone. I ran a hand over my face, glancing around our immediate vicinity. The two college kids behind the counter weren't paying us the slightest bit of attention, nor was the elderly patron seated in the corner with her nose buried in a bodice-ripping romance novel. And if none of them were paying attention to us, then none of them were casting any spells our way.

“Are you ok?” Peter asked, his brow furrowed. “You seem... distracted.”

“I am. I mean. Maybe. I don’t know. I don’t know what’s going on. My imagination has been running rampant lately. I was wondering if, perhaps, you could help me this time?”

“Of course. Anything. What do you need?”

“I don’t know.” God, why was this so hard? The words wouldn’t even come to me. If I managed to think of something coherent, then they jumbled on my tongue, refusing to come out. It had to be sleep deprivation. That was all. And a creeping paranoia I was following in my mother’s footsteps. “I’ve been seeing this... thing. Everywhere. I’m afraid it’s a demon, but I don’t have any proof. I went to confession today and I imagined an entire interaction with a priest! I either nodded off in the confessional or maybe I have a tumor...” I worried my lower lip, racking my brain in the desperate search for another answer—anything but the obvious.

Peter didn’t look particularly concerned that I was one arson away from turning into Bridget. “Are you sure it wasn’t Father Sullivan?”

“Positive. I didn’t see him until after I was finished. And it wasn’t his voice.”

“Do you know whose voice it was? Like, have you ever heard it before? Another librarian? A professor? Someone from the Congregation?”

Ghostly fingers carded through the shorter sides of my hair, just like they had that morning in the North Woods. I squeezed my eyes shut, trying to ignore it. “It’s the same one from my dreams.”

“Your dreams?” Peter cocked his head at me. “But you—”

“I know! I know how ridiculous it is. I’m a

Dreamweaver and I can't even help myself. That's the problem!"

"It's ok. We'll get it figured out. What do you need from me? Some sleeping pills?"

"A potion."

Peter leaned back, glancing around warily. "Are you asking me as a pharmacist or as a—"

"You know what I mean. I've tried everything I have on hand. Herbs. Crystals. Tea," I huffed, gesturing emphatically at the mug in front of me.

"Yeah, hence why I suggested a pharmaceutical. Not everything has a demonic origin."

"I'm afraid this does," I said quietly. "Thus far, nothing commonplace has helped. Neither has anything religious. Fasting and praying. Not even—"

He frowned at me before I could even finish my sentence. "Don't tell me you're doing that bodily penance shit again."

In lieu of answering, I wrapped my hands around the mug and stared at the bits of chamomile floating on the top. This was my second mug and I wasn't feeling calm in the slightest. The feeling of fingers stroking my thigh didn't help. At all.

Peter sighed. "Phelan... Why do you do this to yourself?"

"I was raised to follow the old ways. You know that."

"I know, but sometimes I wish you wouldn't."

"Now you sound like Temperance."

"Well, it's true. She might be the other cheerleader for the old ways and following tradition and whatnot, but you don't see *her* starving herself or wearing hair shirts. She just lords it over the rest of us whenever shit goes sideways in this town and tells us to read a fucking book."

"About the potion?" I reminded him, forcing myself to meet his gaze before he continued on a tangent.

He stared back, unimpressed by the plaintive look on my face, before sighing again. "What do you want it to do?"

"Sleep," I said quickly. "Sleep *without* dreaming. If I could just clear my head and break whatever hold this thing has over me, I can figure out how to get rid of it once and for all."

He nodded, resignation etched in his features. "I'll get the ingredients later today and I'll let you know when it's ready. Give me about a week. Think you can manage until then?"

"I can. Thank you. Oh, one more thing. Do you have any monk's pepper on hand?"

He chuckled. "PMS problems keeping you up at night? Boobs feeling a little swollen?"

For once I managed to crack a smile, even though I rolled my eyes at him. I was glad that's where his mind went instead of to the real reason I wanted the plant—decreasing libido. "I've been feeling a little queasy with all of the fasting. Figured it could help with the dual headache and nausea."

"Yeah, I've got some. I can drop it off tonight after work. Just put it in the mailbox?"

I nodded. "I'll look for it. Thank you. I'd appreciate it if you didn't tell anyone else about this, though."

"Of course not. What's one more secret in a town like Winslow?" He gave me a small smile, tinged with sadness and sarcasm alike.

CHAPTER FIVE

PHELAN

Crossing myself one final time, I unbuttoned my shirt and shrugged off the fabric. Peter's disapproval rang in my head as I folded it, setting it to the side. He didn't understand, but I didn't blame him. There weren't many who did, especially in today's secular world.

I picked up the scourge from the small shelf in front of me, hefting the weight of it in my hand. Closing my eyes, I grasped onto the top of the kneeler and adjusted my grip on the long handle.

Exhaling a slow, steadying breath, I slung the leather straps over my shoulder.

The sting of the tiny leather balls bit into my skin. Heat bloomed across my back and I gritted my teeth, preparing for the next hit.

I couldn't go back to confession. Not for this, anyway. I had to take care of this maybe-demon problem myself. I was beyond Father Sullivan's help. And I couldn't risk having another hallucinatory confession and word getting out that I was seeing things like a crazy person.

The second strike was harder. The initial heat spread from the new source, growing in intensity.

But to truly be close to Christ, to cleanse myself of whatever evil had attached itself to me, I couldn't shy away from the pain. I would suffer as Christ and the early martyrs did. I had to. Anything to restore the balance I'd somehow disrupted.

I flung the scourge across my other shoulder. The leather caught the lower side of my back, near my ribs. Pain shot through my skin. I gasped but managed to stifle the majority of the noise.

My fingers curled tighter around the edge of the kneeler, trying to steel myself.

The fourth blow landed in nearly the same area as the first. I couldn't help the cry that escaped that time. My back burned everywhere, even without the scourge marks. Something even hotter trickled down my skin.

Forcing my eyes open, I held the discipline aloft. Blood glistened on the dark leather tips dangling in front of my face.

"Three more," I whispered to myself. Three more strikes to reach the magical seven. Seven deadly sins. Seven heavenly virtues. One early priest called for the self-flagellation to last as long as it took to recite forty Psalms, but I'd settle for seven. Although, if this didn't work, I'd reconsider doing it his way.

As the pain from the fifth whipping radiated across my back, my mind drifted to the maybe-demon from the library. If he truly was a demon, then he was my first brush with one without any sort of protective circle. The fact I'd walked away unscathed was a miracle. But none of that explained why I couldn't get him out of my head.

The sixth blow caused me to slump against the kneeler's shelf. I tried to breathe through the pain, ignoring the sweat and the blood sliding down my fiery skin, but it was hardly working. Just like it wasn't working to rid myself of my maybe-demon. He was still present in my mind no matter what I did. That velvety voice. The way he looked at me, making my insides knot together.

I should have eaten something other than monk's pepper before I submitted myself to this ritual. I don't know why I thought I could fast *and* successfully undertake any mortification of the flesh.

Pride. That was why. My greatest sin. Salvation was the reason I sought to punish myself here on earth, in the hope of sparing myself punishment in the next life. The endorphins didn't hurt, either. It was like running too far or climbing too long. My body screamed in protest and I pushed it regardless, riding a wave of pain-laced bliss... all because of pride. Because I had to do better, *be* better. I had to be perfect. If I wasn't perfect, then I left myself vulnerable to the insanity that claimed my mother. *That's why we don't dabble in demonic necromancy,* Hester always said. So I *didn't* dabble. I lived and breathed it until I had no other identity.

The room around me was sweltering. I would have sworn a demon was present, except that was impossible. The house would never allow it. Would it? No. Generations of Olivers had left their mark, warding the structure against demons and other witches. Only those who were invited could cross those magical boundaries. And there's no way I'd invited a beguiling blond with a sinful gaze into the house, no matter how much I might have been losing my mind.

One last strike. One last moment of suffering. Hopefully it would be enough.

Summoning the strength I had, I flailed the scourge over my shoulder.

The leather slapped against my tender skin, slicing through it like claws.

Sickness swelled inside of me.

Between the heat and the pain, I could barely breathe. It felt like I was suffocating. I dropped the scourge and stared at the crucifix above me, praying for strength, for guidance, for a bit of peace.

Jesus remained silent, gazing down at me with sad, knowing eyes.

It was too late.

I was already damned.

Swaying on my knees, I collapsed.

CHAPTER SIX
PHELAN

Friday afternoon campus became a ghost town. While everyone excitedly rushed home to embark on their weekend plans, I dragged my feet until the last possible minute before locking up the rare books section of the library and trudging to the parking garage. Normally, I would have been one of them, except my usual Wednesday dinner plans had been pushed to Friday and I was in no mood for a lecture from Hester.

The September sun was warm on my back despite the chill in the air, soothing away the soreness left after last night's flogging. A storm front was rolling in by the looks of things as dark clouds chased away the blue sky. That would make driving to and from Boston especially aggravating.

The trees were changing colors and in another week or two, all of Tennebrose would be ablaze in reds and oranges and dark purples. I supposed that's one reason our mascot was a phoenix. That, and the university was founded by the two fire families. It had always seemed a bit pretentious to me, but considering the Oliver family history, I hoped I could be forgiven for not broadcasting my lineage as proudly as those two did.

William Hadder, a professor from the history department and a bit of a town legend in his own right, tried to corner me one time to ask about my connection to the historic Olivers, namely Mary, the infamous Winslow Witch. I didn't know what to say to the man who'd spent the last fifteen years railing against Black Mary to anyone who would listen, so I sputtered through some awful defense that Mary wasn't even a real Oliver and I had no idea what he was talking about.

Thankfully, Temperance turned the corner shortly thereafter and dragged her colleague away, talking loudly about an upcoming conference and what keynote speaker they were soliciting.

If only I knew who my father was, I would have opted to take *his* last name. Surely it couldn't be worse than "Oliver," at least not in this town. Mather or Hathorne might get me some wary looks but that was hardly any different than what I had now.

I was still pondering the identity of my missing sperm donor even after I arrived at Hester's, twenty minutes late, for my weekly penance. I mean, dinner.

"She's in the dining room," the maid said, closing the front door behind me.

"Thank you." Shrugging out of my coat, I handed it to the woman with a faint smile and made my way deeper into the historic Federal-style house.

Hester was seated at the head of the table, a roaring fire in the marble fireplace behind her. From the way the flames illuminated her ornate chair from behind, she looked like she'd sprouted horns.

"You're late," Hester said flatly.

"There was traffic."

"It's Boston. There's always traffic."

"Well there was more traffic than usual," I said as politely as I could manage while easing into the chair beside her, mindful to keep my back off of the rigid wood for fear of busting open one or more of the scabs. I'm sure she'd be more put out that I bled all over an antique than concerned for my welfare.

"I assume that means you came from work?" She arched a gray eyebrow at me and sipped her wine.

I snapped the cloth napkin open and draped it over my lap. "I did."

"Visiting hours will be over by the time we're through," she continued, watching me like a hawk.

"Then I'll visit another time."

"She's your mother."

"I am well aware of the familial relationship."

"So why haven't you been to see her in months?"

"How would you know the last time I saw her? Are you having me followed?" I scoffed, taking a large drink of ice water and wishing it was something much, *much* stronger.

"No," Hester replied smoothly. "I merely inquire at the front desk and they tell me."

"I've been busy," I said, sliding my gaze in her direction, returning her unimpressed stare with one of my own. "And it's not like she'd know if I was there or not anyway."

"She's still your mother."

"Do we have to do this every week?"

"Of course not. You could always go see her."

"She gave birth to me and then tried to burn down the house with me still *in* it. Not very motherly, if you ask me."

Hester drummed her polished nails on the table. "You're in a foul temper tonight. Did you skip lunch?"

"No," I huffed.

"Well, I hope you're hungry. Silvian made lamb chops."

I stared at her, looking every bit like a guppy while waiting for the punchline. Except, my grandmother was *not* a jokester. When she didn't respond, I blurted out, "But it's Friday!"

"And?"

"I can't eat meat on Fridays."

She sighed before sipping her wine again.

"You *know* I can't eat meat on Fridays," I continued, clenching my hand in my lap, under the table and out of view. "*You're* the reason I'm Catholic!"

"Yes, Phelan, Catholic. Not a monk! It's not Lent, for God's sake."

"The law of the Church still states—"

"Are we really going to have *this* argument again?"

"I am a Necromancer who specializes in demons!" I said under my breath, leaning closer to her in case any of the staff were within hearing distance. Since she hadn't practiced magic in thirty years, it was safe to assume they were not aware of the family history. "It is my *one* contribution to this disaster of a family. If that means I have to fast for forty days or flog myself or refuse to eat Silvian's lamb chops, then so be it! I will *not* end up in a mental institution like my mother!"

Hester's eyes narrowed, but her reply was trapped behind her pursed lips and the fact the door to the kitchen swung open.

"Here we go," Silvian said as he bustled into the dining room, bearing a salad plate in each hand. "The first course."

I leaned back and cleared my throat softly. "Thank you," I murmured to the chef.

"I'll be back with the bacon-wrapped scallops," he said, disappearing again.

I shot my grandmother a scowl.

"Pick it off," she said, stabbing a tomato with her salad fork. "It's not like it'll kill you."

Thunder rumbled outside, mirroring my worsening mood. I know Peter said the potion would take a week, but I truly hoped it would be sooner than that. Just one night of peaceful sleep. Was it too much to ask for?

"Would you rather I was a losel?" I leaned in again, lowering my voice. "To have no magic at all versus the minuscule amount I *do* have? Or would that be preferable for you? Then you wouldn't have to worry about me turning into Bridget at all."

"Would you stop using words from the fourteenth century?" she sighed, her fork clattering on the edge of her plate.

"Forgive me for putting my extensive education to work. I want to make sure you feel like you're getting your money's worth out of my Ph.D.—something most families are proud of, by the way. I realize half the town is connected to the university, but am I really such an embarrassment to you? Magical abilities aside, does my work at the library mean nothing?"

Hester covered my hand with hers, her expression softening. "You're not an embarrassment and you're not going to end up like your mother. Alright? Your mother is sick. You're not. End of story."

I pulled my hand away from hers, returning it to my lap. "Then why do you always look at me like that?"

"Like what?" Her shoulders straightened and there was a flicker of something on her face, the very look that needled me each time I saw it. A look I could point out when it was present, but that I couldn't articulate in the moments afterward.

"Like you don't trust me. Like you're... scared of something."

"I am scared, Phelan. I think you're too hard on yourself. The fasting, the praying, and especially the self-flagellation. You're missing out on the best parts of life. I don't want you to get to my age and regret not truly living or having a family of your own."

"That's not what God wanted for me."

"How do you know?"

Silvian came through the swinging door again, the smell of bacon preceding him.

I ground my molars together, trying to ignore the fact I was practically salivating by the time he set the plate between us. Perhaps it would have been better if I went full vegetarian, then I wouldn't have been so tempted to break the rules involving prohibited foods. But, no. I wouldn't give in. I was stronger than bacon, even if my growling stomach said otherwise.

"Bon appétit!" Silvian said, leaving us to it.

"So... how is work?" Hester asked, helping herself to a scallop and clearly shifting the direction of the conversation.

"It's fine. Busy. It usually is the first few weeks of school." I pushed some of the lettuce around on my plate but didn't make an effort to actually eat anything. There was no way anything green or leafy was going to compare to the crispy bacon sitting right in front of me.

"I heard you helped Peter's little girl. Any idea where the demon came from?"

I furrowed my brow at her. "Where did you hear that?"

"I might not live in Winslow anymore, but that doesn't mean I'm outside of its web."

Secrets. Always secrets with her, including the fact she could never give *me* a straight answer about anything. I shook my head, spearing a piece of cucumber. "It, uh, was in a toy. Someone gave it to her."

"On purpose?"

I shrugged. "I would hope not."

"You're not a convincing liar, dear."

"Then tell me—as a grandmother, how could you intentionally terrify and traumatize your granddaughter like that? Just to ruin your daughter's marriage?"

"Perhaps Eileen thought she was saving her daughter."

"At the expense of her granddaughter?"

"Sometimes you have to make a choice."

"So why did you choose your grandchild?" I asked, even though it felt like a wad of cotton was suddenly wedged in my throat.

Hester took a moment, holding my wary gaze before she finally answered. "Because my daughter was beyond saving."

"Was she really trying to kill me?"

"She was out of her mind, Phelan. I don't know what she was trying to do. Now, eat your salad before the lettuce wilts."

I nodded and dutifully took a bite, the vinaigrette sharp on my tongue. No matter how much I wanted it to, it did *not* taste like bacon.

Dinner was mostly quiet after that. A superficial conversation about superficial topics, both of us dancing around the elephant in the room that was Bridget. I had questions. So many questions. But after years, *decades*, of having them ignored, I knew better than to ask for details. Most days I tried not to think about it—or about her.

Finally, Hester walked me to the front door and gave me a kiss on the cheek. "Drive carefully. This rain doesn't look like it's letting up anytime soon."

"I'll be fine. I'll see you next week." *You*, I wanted to reiterate. *Not Bridget.* But there was no point in beating that dead horse.

I was almost home when my cell phone rang, Marcus's name flashing across the screen.

"We're meeting at the old quarry in an hour. Can you make it?" he asked as soon as I answered.

Lightning tore through the sky overhead. The rain fell in sheets, blurring the windshield even with the wipers working at full speed. The wind slammed against the side of my SUV, buffeting my car as I headed northbound.

"Are you serious? Have you even looked outside?" I asked.

"The next one on the list is a fire demon," Marcus replied, as if that solved the issue of the torrential rain.

I stifled a sigh. All thoughts of being warm and dry in my bed curled up with a book went right out the window. "Yeah. I'll be there."

"Why does it always have to be raining?" I grumbled, setting my messenger bag on a fallen tree before hauling myself over it.

"Because we're focused on fire demons," Marcus replied, shooting a pointed look over his shoulder.

"It was rhetorical." I slung my bag back on my shoulder and kept moving, my booted feet sliding now and again on wet leaves and mud. "My main concern is for the books. They shouldn't be out in these conditions."

"Well, there's only a few of these demons left," Caius added from the front. "After that, we can move on to another sort of demon. Earth or something."

"Considering some of us come from fire families, do you think it's a good idea to eliminate that type of demon entirely?" Temperance asked. "I mean, they're in the Book of Lazarus for a reason. Maybe their names were put there to help us."

"Yes, help us eliminate them when they got out of hand," Warren Simms said darkly.

Temperance and I exchanged a look. The only problem with that mentality was that the demons hadn't gotten out of hand. Yet. But killing them left and right was bound to draw unnecessary demonic attention to Winslow sooner or later.

Once we reached the old quarry, the others huddled under clusters of trees and umbrellas, watching me set up the protective circle.

Since the rain hadn't let up, I used sand instead of chalk to line the rings, murmuring the appropriate prayer for each concentric circle.

As soon as it was complete, I looked over at the Selectmen from each family, waiting to see if they were going to call this off. From their grim expressions, the answer was no.

Withdrawing the Book of Damnation from my bag, I flipped through the pages until I got to the summoning spell and began the long, drawn-out incantation.

"*Come, Abriyah,*" I continued in Latin, trying not to rush

through the spell as I neared the end, *"for I command you by the eternal glory of God. Amen."*

The center of the circle glowed. Orange flames sparked to life in a circle before they darkened and turned black, highlighted with an eerie green that added a sinister glow to the area.

I closed the book and stepped back, making room for the others as a vaguely humanoid shape appeared in a cloud of putrid smoke. A piercing shriek ripped through the night air, sending the sulfurous green cloud gusting in our direction.

Caius fisted his hand, crushing some unseen part of the demon's anatomy while Marcus and Warren generated huge orbs of fire and shadows, respectively.

The inhuman screaming intensified, slowly morphing into a female wailing. The figure, likewise, shifted from a red form, covered in scales, to a naked female. The leathery wings melted onto her back, sliding down her skin into the form of a dress, the same color her scales had been. Clawing at the ground, she looked up at the three Selectmen with tears in her eyes.

"Please," she choked out. "I came when you called. I don't want to die. I'll do your bidding." Her gaze turned to me, flashing like burning coals. "It's *you*."

I couldn't help but frown at her visceral reaction to seeing me. Even though I had no idea what she was talking about, it felt like a threat. Maybe word of what we were doing had finally spread throughout the underworld.

I murmured the start of another prayer in Latin at the same time Marcus hurled the ball of blazing orange at her. Warren's swirl of shadows came next.

The masses of orange and black exploded against her

body and disappeared, affecting her no more than a gust of hot air would.

She laughed, pushing herself up onto her hands and feet, crawling closer to the edge of the circle to stare at me through Warren's legs. "Come here, little witch. I need to tell you something."

I ignored her and kept praying, shooting an exasperated look at Temperance and hoping she'd be my translator since I couldn't stop what I was doing.

"You need to hurry," Temperance said. "We have to close the portal."

Marcus and Warren responded with more magic, but just like before, it had no obvious effect on the demon.

Caius unsheathed his family's ritual knife and moved closer to the circle, looking for a way in to deliver a fatal blow without breaking the circle.

"*May Jesus Christ, the King of glory, help us,*" the demon hissed in Latin, sidestepping in a crouch to keep me in her sight, "*to make the right use of all the suffering that God sends.*"

Her prayer interrupted my own. My mouth ran dry and I tripped over the words. It wasn't a prayer I was familiar with, but nevertheless, it struck a chord in me, stirring a tingle of dread in the pit of my stomach. Usually, when demons prayed it was to mock God, but I didn't get the sense that's what she was doing. It felt akin to déjà vu, like I should know the prayer, but I didn't.

"Phelan!" Temperance shouted, but I could hardly hear her over the demon's cackling.

"*Mommy's good boy.*"

"Don't listen to her," Temperance said, running over to me and trying to turn my face away. I couldn't. My gaze was fixated on the demon's coal-black eyes.

"*May the Holy Cross be my light!*" the demon shouted.

While Abriyah was distracted, taunting me, Caius lunged, driving the blade into her chest.

The center of the circle exploded, knocking everyone backward and blowing the lines of sand to oblivion.

A host of demons rushed out, punching through what was left of the invisible barriers and flying off in a hundred different directions. There were too many to count, in varying shapes and sizes, with scales and fur and feathers. Clawed hands grabbed at the witches on their way by, inhuman jeers and laughter drowning out the screams of the Necromancers being tossed around like dolls.

Magic flew back and forth, orange and black bursting like bombs. Green fire swirled through the darkness, engulfing Necromancers and demons alike, eliciting a cacophony of screaming.

I scrambled to my feet, searching for Temperance, but the second I was vertical something slammed into me from behind. Sprawling across the rocky ground, I sucked air back into my lungs and rolled over just as a set of black talons slashed downward, scraping against the ground where I'd been laying.

Before I could get away a second time, another demon seized me from behind, crushing my ribs in the process. A forked tongue flicked against my cheek.

"Mmm. A priestly one," the demon hissed. "I can taste the myrrh. So sweet."

I tried to ignore the creature behind me, muttering a banishment spell under my breath.

"Sweeter than its blood?" the first demon asked, squatting in front of me and cocking its scaly head to the side so it could stare at me with a red, reptilian eye.

Struggling against the claws that held me, I tried to lean away from the black talon looming closer to my face.

A voice I didn't recognize shouted clearly above the din, yelling something in a language I didn't understand.

The demons all froze and turned toward the noise. The one holding me started trembling, meanwhile, the one in front fell to its furry knees and bowed its horned head.

Suddenly, the demon behind me was gone, ripped away with a yelp. The sickening sound of flesh being ripped apart and bones snapping followed, ending in a wet gurgle and a distinctive *splat*.

I didn't dare turn and look at the carnage behind me. I'm sure I didn't want to see any part of it. Besides, I was too busy trying to locate the rest of the Necromancers, to make sure they were safe. Interspersed amongst the cowering demons, the rest of the witches were still there, frozen, although their immobility looked like it was being controlled by something not of this world. None of them so much as blinked or tried to fight back, even as the demons bowed and scraped at the unseen thing behind me before they turned and fled into the night.

The demon in front of me stole a glance upward, its red eyes darting back and forth in a panic. A second later, it burst into green flames, twisting and screaming and seeping through the ground like it was water.

I crossed myself quickly and pressed my hands together in prayer, squeezing my eyes shut. "Grant unto us, we beseech Thee, O almighty God, that we, who seek the shelter of Thy protection, being defended from all evils—"

A blinding white light burst behind my eyelids.

Then, I was falling.

And I wasn't stopping.

CHAPTER SEVEN

PHELAN

My head throbbed with the worst migraine I'd ever had in my life. I must have fallen and hit my head against a rock or something during the ritual. It was raining, I remembered that much. And a fall like that would explain why my entire body ached, like it had been crushed. It probably didn't help that I seemed to be laying on the hardest surface known to man instead of my bed. Why wasn't I in my bed?

Even after I opened my eyes and blinked a few times, the world remained a strange shade of dark green and the edges were fuzzy. I couldn't make out any of the shapes around me, not my dresser or a door. Nothing. That was odd. Was I in the living room? No. There would have been windows and my bookcases.

I remembered the oh-so-lovely dinner with my grandmother. Getting the phone call from Marcus, the long drive back to Winslow in the rain, and tromping out to the North Woods to do my duty. I'm pretty sure I set up the protective circle but that's where things went dark.

I had to have tripped and fallen on something. That

would explain why nothing seemed familiar. But I didn't smell rain or damp leaves, not to mention the fact I was sweating despite the forecast calling for low temperatures.

I tried easing myself up into a sitting position but got nowhere.

"What the—?" I yanked hard on a metal cuff attached to my wrist, trying to bring my arm back down over my head. It didn't budge. I don't know why I tried the other one, but I did anyway, with the same result.

This couldn't be happening. I wasn't important enough to be kidnapped. I was literally a nobody. No one important at the university. No one important in the Congregation. Although, witch hunters probably didn't care. God, please don't let it be witch hunters...

I willed the cuffs to open, even though I knew it was pointless. The iron negated whatever magic I had. I hoped it was a mere coincidence and that my kidnapper didn't know about my lineage, that the iron cuffs were just a sturdy, albeit outdated, means of restraint.

"You're awake," a voice said from somewhere behind me. It was male and vaguely familiar, though I had no idea from where. With my pulse racing, it was hard to keep my current thoughts straight let alone my fuzzy memories.

I craned my head to try and see where he was but between the darkness and the angle I couldn't make out anything.

Then it hit me, like waking up from a dead sleep because someone threw ice water on you. That velvety voice from the library; the priest from confession. The voice that was seared into my memory whether I wanted it or not, that had been whispering incessantly in my dreams for weeks.

"What am I doing here?" I asked, even though I was

pretty sure I knew the answer. He *was* a demon and now I was his prisoner.

"You're here as my guest."

"Guest?!" I yanked against the chains, suddenly feeling even more vulnerable being stretched out on display with no possible means of defending myself. Not that I stood a chance against a demon anyway. In the time it would take me to pray for God's assistance, he'd probably eviscerate me.

"Careful, pet," he said soothingly, soft footsteps drawing closer. As he moved, the lights in the room brightened. Except, they weren't lights—they were candles, set into iron sconces on the black stone walls, flickering with bright green flames. "I don't want you to injure yourself before the real fun has started."

"I swear to God, if you don't let me go—"

He laughed, a soft, melodic sound that filled the room. "Oh, God's not going to save you. No, I'm afraid no one is. You're mine, Phelan Oliver, until the end of days."

"End of days?" Something in the way he said it made my skin crawl, prompting me to reassess my surroundings. The first clue should have been my sense of smell. The smell of fire. Brimstone. And underneath those, a spicy scent reminiscent of the incense used in Mass. The second clue was the oppressive heat. The *green* fire. "Oh my God..."

One thing was certain—I wasn't in Winslow anymore.

That meant it wasn't bad luck or a random demon kidnapping an ordinary human out of boredom. This one knew my name which meant he knew full well what iron would do to me. I kind of wished it was witch hunters now. I'd have stood a better chance with them. At least *they* wouldn't have dragged me to Hell.

"Clever little thing." The demon appeared, at last, completely transformed from the image he'd presented at the library. Gone was the effortless look of a model in skinny jeans and a t-shirt. The only clothing he wore now was a long black skirt, barely clinging to his hips by the looks of it. An ornate silver sash hung even lower, accentuating the taper of his waist. His right bicep was adorned with an intricate silver band but that appeared to be the only sort of jewelry. Not that he needed any more embellishment.

Long, silver hair reached the center of his bare back where a pair of giant white wings extended. The tips of the feathers were as black as tar, like he'd accidentally dipped them in an inkwell.

"Let's see just how clever you think you are," he said, practically purring.

He was breathtaking, even more so than he had been at Tennebrose when he was trying to pass as human. Arguably, he was the most beautiful thing I'd ever seen. And without a doubt the most dangerous.

A dazzling smile curved his lips as he moved closer with the grace of a dancer. The black fabric parted on his thighs with each step, while the jewels on the sash winked mockingly in the unnatural firelight, drawing my attention to it periodically.

"You're not just a demon," I said lamely, my body frozen with fear and disbelief. A lifetime of studying and I still wasn't prepared to comprehend the creature in front of me. His beauty, his wings… he was one of the fallen. There wasn't a shred of doubt in my mind.

He ran a hand along my fingers, my palm, down my arm, and finally spread his own fingers out over my chest.

In one swift motion, he grabbed a handful of my shirt and tore it open, scattering buttons and fabric alike. Feeling even more like a sacrificial lamb about to be devoured, I watched his hand warily as he resumed stroking my chest and the faint patch of hair in the center. Goosebumps fanned across my skin wherever he touched me, accompanied by a deeper feeling in my blood I couldn't describe. I didn't think I wanted to.

"Who knew you'd be this delightful?" he said with another smile, biting his lower lip as his gaze raked over me, like he was trying to decide which part he was going to rip off first.

I swallowed thickly. "What do you want from me?" His hand didn't stop moving, nor did that strange warmth inside of me. It went down my abdomen, following the trail of dark hair from my navel to the top of my pants. Instead of stopping, his hand dipped inside, skimming through the hair below. When his fingers wrapped around my shaft and squeezed, I shut my eyes, bracing for an unimaginable pain that never came.

"What do all demons want?" His fingers released and his hand reappeared before drifting further. Curling around my balls on the outside of my pants, he tightened his grip on them until I opened my eyes to glare at him.

"Then kill me already and take whatever power you think I have. Hate to break it to you, but I doubt it will do a prince of Hell any good."

Fire danced in his silver eyes, like molten iron. His fingers splayed again, running up my abdomen and seizing my jaw, squeezing mercilessly. "You do not issue commands, pet. Besides, it's not your power that I'm after."

I wisely kept my mouth shut that time, molars grinding

together against the pain and indignation of being touched like that.

"Learning already," he said with a malevolent smile, running the pad of his thumb across my lips before pushing it inside. He slid it past my teeth and dragged it along my tongue in languid strokes. "If you behave, tell me what I want to know, I might keep you around a century or two."

Any sense of self-preservation was destroyed by his intrusion. Apparently, my pride meant more to me than avoiding pain, so I didn't even think before I bit his thumb, gnashing my teeth against his knuckle until the taste of copper filled my mouth.

Instead of flinching away, like I'd hoped—like any normal being would—the demon surged forward and clamped his other hand around my throat. I had no choice but to let go if I wanted any attempt at sucking air into my lungs. As soon as I did, he laughed, painting his blood across my lips despite my attempt to thrash my head back and forth to avoid it.

"You should know better than to try and inflict pain on a demon. We live for it. You, on the other hand... we'll see how long you can hold out. Which do you think will go first? Your body or your mind?"

I licked my lips and spit his own blood back at him. Most of it landed on his bare chest, but a few speckles managed to hit his sculpted jaw.

His backhand was swift, sharp and stinging against my cheek. My eyes watered so quickly I squeezed them shut to keep the tears inside. It was bound to be the first of many bruises, given who my captor was. Part of me wished I knew what he really wanted; what, exactly, I was suffering for. But the other part of me didn't care. As horrific as it was, I'd already accepted this was my fate now and it would take a miracle to save me.

"*Pater noster, qui es in caelis,*" I whispered, keeping my eyes closed while I finished the prayer.

When I opened them again, the demon was gone.

CHAPTER EIGHT

REMIEL

"Now that you have him here, what are you going to do with him?" Melech asked, flipping a knife in his hand leisurely as I sifted through the papers Jabez left behind, looking for any clue that would tie my new pet to Hazael's war efforts.

"Whatever I feel like," I replied blithely. And whatever *that* was, I certainly wouldn't be gushing to Melech about it. He might have liked to think he had my confidence, but he would be sorely mistaken. The only one who had ever come close to that was Jabez and now he was gone forever. I was certainly not looking for a replacement.

"The witches will come for you. You can't kidnap one of their own and not expect them to retaliate."

"Let them. Then we'll know what they're planning and if Hazael has anything to do with it."

"Jabez was a duke," Melech continued, his tail twitching as he took a step closer. "If they can kill him, they can kill you."

Throwing the handful of papers down, I stalked over to Melech and seized him by the throat. I slammed him into the wall and hoisted him upward along the black, craggy rocks with one hand until his feet dangled helplessly off the ground. "Your concern for my welfare is touching, Melech, but I neither need nor want your counsel. If one more word escapes your mouth, I'll rip out your tongue and feed it to the dogs. Do you hear me?"

When he nodded, I dropped him unceremoniously in a heap and stepped over his lashing tail. "If you want to be useful, make contact with the other princes and see if they've been having similar problems with witches in their domains. Do *not* tell them about my guest and do not mention Hazael's name outside these walls."

Melech grunted out a "Yes, sire," as he got to his feet.

"Also, try not to let on that we're under siege from two fronts now. Unless you want even more enemies clamoring at the gates. If I fall, you fall. Remember that." I gave him a pointed look before exiting the room. I'd had enough of his unsolicited opinions today. It was high time I returned to check in on my new toy and make sure he wasn't doing anything foolish, like gnawing through his wrist like a trapped fox.

Entering my chambers quietly, I paused at the threshold, taking in the sight of Phelan in the flesh. It was still strange he was here. After watching him for so many weeks, memorizing every move and every gesture, it almost seemed too good to be true, to be able to touch him when and where I pleased. And touch him I would. Repeatedly.

From a distance, Phelan looked like he was asleep, but the second I appeared at his side, his eyes flew open, narrowing in the candlelight. He looked like he was dying to speak, to curse or yell, but he simply gritted his teeth, the muscle in the side of his jaw clenching furiously.

Waving a hand over him, the iron cuffs around his

wrists and ankles disappeared, only to be replaced with a heavy collar around his throat. I tugged him forward by an equally weighty chain and pulled him off the table and onto his feet.

Normally, I wouldn't have to take such extraordinary measures with my pets, but Phelan was different. He could be dismissive of his powers all he wanted, it wouldn't hide what I knew was true. Power thrummed through his blood at a steady rate, strong enough that I felt it the very first time I saw him in the woods. Besides, I couldn't have my new pet escaping just yet. I wanted to play with him first.

"Where are you taking me?" he asked, rubbing the red marks on his wrists. Each step was more of a limp, undoubtedly sore from lying in the same unforgiving position for so long.

I ignored him, leading him across the room to the massive fireplace. Shoving him down onto a pile of pillows tossed on top of a blanket, I seated myself in the only chair, keeping the chain wrapped around my hand. A tray of food magically appeared on the table next to me, though I had no intention of eating. "Hungry?"

He glanced between my face and the tray but said nothing, nor did he make any move toward it.

"Come here," I said, tugging the chain for effect.

He didn't budge. "I'd rather starve."

"But where's the fun in that?" I yanked him forward onto his hands and knees, keeping the chain taut. "Crawl to me."

Again, he refused and even had the audacity to pull back as hard as he could without completely strangling himself on the iron collar.

Wrapping more of the chain around my hand, I pulled him forward, slowly, watching him do exactly as I said even though every movement was against his will. He looked so good like that—submissive but absolutely furious—it was all I could do to stop myself from throwing him backward on the pillows and taking him right there.

I didn't stop reeling him in until he was between my thighs. Clad only in my usual, a long black shendyt, I spread them wider to accommodate him as well as my hardening cock and jerked him up into a kneeling position.

"Was that so hard?" I asked, leaning forward to stare into his eyes, a brilliant color that shifted between blue and green with the lighting. Even now, they were so full of fire. And hate. It sent a thrill right through me. No, he wasn't weak at all. It was merely a ruse.

The anger never left his face. He was going to be harder to break than I thought but I lived for the challenge. It made the reward that much sweeter.

Picking up a piece of steak from the plate, I held it out to him between two fingers. "Now eat. You'll need your strength for what I have planned."

"Eat food in the underworld?" He snorted, his upper lip curling. "I thought you knew who I was, what I am. No scholar in their right mind would eat anything you offer, let alone a witch with half a brain."

"Listen, Persephone," I growled, yanking the chain upward so the collar stretched his neck even more despite his attempts to stay away from me. "Whether you stay or go is entirely at my pleasure, not whatever paltry morsel I shove between those luscious lips. If you keep testing me, I'll make sure our time together is pure agony. So for your benefit, I suggest you cooperate."

Surprisingly, his gaze dropped and he leaned forward, biting off a chunk of the steak. I'm sure his compliance had nothing to do with me and everything to do with the stupid hope he'd survive this whole ordeal.

Still, I couldn't help but smile triumphantly when he leaned in again and took the remainder of the steak gently between his teeth, careful not to have any contact with my fingers.

The victory was short-lived.

His hand shot out, snatching the knife from the plate. Without hesitation, he plunged it into my chest, ramming it between my ribs and into my heart. He gave the blade a vicious twist and ripped his metal leash out of my hands, jumping to his feet. As soon as he was vertical he bolted for the door.

I hissed through the pain, pulling the knife out slowly and tossing it to the side. Challenging, indeed.

Before he got to the door, I shimmered across the distance and reclaimed the chain, yanking him back to me like a toy. Seizing him under the jaw from behind, I turned him slowly, enveloping him in my feathered wings and keeping him pressed close to me.

"That was very brave and *very* stupid," I said, walking him backward to the giant, four-poster bed. "You think it's that easy to run from me? That I would actually let you go?"

He clung to my wrist with both hands, his chin tipped up in a struggle for air. Still, the defiance never left his eyes.

"What did I tell you earlier?" I tilted my head, my gaze locked on his. "I live for pain. Stab me a hundred times if you want, witch. All it does is fuel the hunger in me to hear you scream."

"Then get on with it," he said through gritted teeth. "If you can."

I unfurled my wings and threw him backward onto the bed. As soon as he landed, iron manacles reattached themselves to his wrists and ankles, pulling his limbs to each corner of the bed.

"I'm afraid this is going to hurt, pet," I said with a malicious smile as I climbed on top of him, straddling his waist. "But trust me when I say it's for your own good." I seized his left hand in my right and slotted my palm against it tightly until there was no space between them.

His brows furrowed a split second before the rest of his face twisted in pain. An unholy fire spread from my hand to his, flames shifting between black and dark green, swirling between our palms and searing into his skin. He gritted his teeth but a scream tore out of him regardless. Writhing beneath me, his body remained held in place by my weight and the manacles.

When the arcane flames subsided, I pulled my hand away, admiring the charred black mark etched forever in his palm. A series of lines and circles, they were meaningless to anyone unless they were familiar with demons' sigils. And now Phelan wore mine—for eternity.

"There is no escaping me now, Phelan. *Ever*," I said, wiping the beads of sweat from his forehead. "And you're going to tell me what I want to know. Do you understand?"

Jerking away from my hand as much as he could, he squeezed his eyes shut with a grimace. Before his breathing even returned to normal, his lips started moving frantically as he whispered another prayer in Latin, as if it would undo the dominion I now held over his soul.

Laughing softly, I draped myself along his side. Still exposed from where I'd ripped his shirt open earlier, I let my fingertips trace up and down the lines of his abdomen, wishing the whole while that it was my tongue instead. "That's not going to save you, you know. No one is going to save you. Least of all your god."

He didn't stop praying. In fact, the words picked up as my hand dipped lower, slipping beneath his waistband. I circled his groin, sliding my fingers into the thatch of hair above his cock and along the crease of his thigh and pelvis, near enough but never quite touching it. Instead, I focused on the other sensitive areas he had, ones he probably didn't even know about. Poor lamb. I'd be happy to teach him, though.

"Tell me, do you like that?" I asked, dragging my tongue along the shell of his ear. If it was possible, he closed his eyes even more and turned his head to the other side as far as it would go, as if it would matter. I simply closed the short distance, nosing the underside of his jaw and around his throat, kissing and licking his skin. The minty citrus I'd smelled in the woods was still there, as alluring now as it was then.

I felt his swallow beneath my lips, the faintest bit of his dark stubble scratching my face. Each breath was sharp and quick and his pulse hammered against the side of his neck.

"Not all torture is painful," I said, leaving a trail of soft kisses down his chest before swirling my tongue around his nipple, delighting in how quickly it hardened in my mouth. While he was distracted, I let my hand venture to the top of his pants, unbuttoning them and pushing the material out of the way to expose his swelling manhood.

He sucked in a surprised gasp and tried to shift away from me, but the iron didn't let him get far.

"Have you ever laid with a man?" I asked, using the tips of my feathers to caress along the length of his shaft. It twitched right before Phelan jerked his hips away with a soft curse.

"No, of course not," I murmured, nuzzling the side of his face and breathing in the scent of him. Not the remnants of his cologne or whatever soap he'd used—but the scent of fear radiating off of him. It flooded my cock until it was so hard it wept in anticipation. "I venture to guess you've never been with *anyone* like this. So virtuous, so *good*. You're a priest in all but name. I'm actually glad you resisted me before. In the library. At church. Even in your dreams. All those times I offered you temptation, but you never succumbed. It's going to be so much better like this. Taking you apart, piece by piece, making you mine completely."

At last, he opened his eyes. Torment was written all over his beautiful face, mixed with resignation. He thought he knew what was coming, what devilish plans I had in store for him. He had no idea.

"If I ever get out of here," he said quietly, "I will kill you if it's the last thing I do."

Offering him a fleeting smile, I seized his jaw in one hand and crushed my lips to his. He tried to pull away, but my hold was too strong. I wasn't the least bit surprised when his teeth sank into my lower lip, piercing the delicate skin. Rather than back off or let him go, I squeezed his jaw until his mouth popped open with a small cry. As soon as his lips parted, I thrust my tongue inside, letting my blood and saliva mix with his as I swirled our tongues together.

No matter how many furious noises he made or how hard he tried to free himself, I didn't give him a moment of peace. In addition to kissing him roughly, I grabbed his cock and stroked him, grinding myself against his hip to show him what his struggle did to me. His mind may have hated every second of it, but it wasn't long before his cock lengthened in my hand and he was as hard as I was.

Pulling away with an evil smile, a strand of bloody

saliva dribbled down his chin. He turned his head and spat out a mouthful before glaring up at me. "You're vile."

"I'm going to enjoy every minute of this," I said, sliding between his legs and raking my nails down his stomach. "Ripping apart that so-called righteousness of yours. Dirtying you up and letting you feel how good it is to sin. I haven't played with a real Necromancer since the Middle Ages. I can't believe I forgot how delicious your kind is."

He closed his eyes again, his bloodied lips moving in silence. Another wasted prayer. Another unanswered plea. One of these days he'd learn.

I breathed across the head of his cock, chuckling darkly when his hips thrust down into the mattress as if he could avoid what was inevitable. Dragging the tip of my tongue over the slit, I watched with utmost fascination as his dark brows furrowed and his jaw clenched impossibly tight.

Swirling my tongue around the crown, I traced the ridge and followed the vein down and up again, slurping and sucking along his shaft. Since he didn't give me the reaction I wanted, I swallowed him whole, all the way down to the root, massaging his balls. They were so heavy. I could only imagine the release I'd get from him.

Exhaling sharply, Phelan jerked against the chains, his body twitching beneath me. Mmm. Finally.

I was desperate to know what he was thinking, with his eyes screwed shut and his teeth on the verge of cracking. Was this really his first time? His entire body was so tense, it had to be. But it wasn't just his resistance to *me*, hating the idea of a demon pleasuring him. No, it went much deeper according to all the little cues his body was giving off. He was at war with himself, his piety clashing with a primal need he didn't yet understand.

The realization filled me to the brim with excitement.

I'd be his first. His last. His everything. He *was* mine, completely.

While I worked along his length, sucking and lapping at his hardness, teasing his balls with my fingers, I used my power to tiptoe along the edge of his mind, looking for a way to slip in through the cracks. Except, there weren't any cracks to be found. Since he was awake, his mind was like a fortress. Still, there had to be a vulnerability somewhere.

The second he noticed what I was trying to do mentally, a sharp pain shot through my mind. It knocked me back with so much force my physical body felt the blow as hard as if he'd punched me.

"You'll never get inside my head, demon."

My eyes flew open, locking on his. He was more incensed by the mental assault than the physical one. How curious.

I was also intrigued by how strong he was. He was so much stronger than I'd ever known a witch to be, yet he kept the power almost completely undetectable. It seemed he was full of surprises.

Would he be so strong in the throes of ecstasy? He could pretend he didn't want it, but he couldn't fight his body's natural desire for release. Could he wage a war on two fronts? I know I could. I'd been doing it since time began.

"We'll see about that," I replied with a smirk. "I have all the time in the world. You, on the other hand..." Tugging open the black fabric around my waist, I tossed it to the side and crawled onto his lap, relishing how wide his eyes got as I straddled him. Rocking my cock against his, I watched another wave of goosebumps spread over his skin. "Let's see how long your conviction holds out."

I grasped both of us in one hand, stroking our smooth skin together with practiced ease. Did he even indulge in self-pleasure? I doubted it, considering how devoted he was to the necromantic arts. The Church said pleasure was dirty, sinful, and priests needed to be pure. Phelan might as well wear the Roman collar for as much as he followed the old ways.

But faithful as he was, he couldn't fight nature.

Slowly, he began to blink a little too long, his dark lashes fluttering a little too much, matching the uptick in his breathing. Oh, he hated me. Even without the bond of my sigil, I could feel it burning inside him. But he hated himself even more. He hated how his cock throbbed in my hand and unnatural lust coiled in the pit of his stomach, desires he'd kept buried for the entirety of his life. Hate and lust—there was a reason they were among the deadliest of sins. But there was another sin he had in spades; pride. How beautiful it was going to be to watch him fall.

I let a mouthful of saliva drip from my lips, coating the head of his cock. A small gasp escaped him when I smeared it all around, rolling my palm over the crown to make sure it was nice and wet.

Rising up on my knees, I shifted forward, angling it beneath me. Before he had time to protest, I sank down again, taking him inside in small increments. It wasn't for my benefit—it was merely to prolong the tortured look on his face, a fascinating mix of euphoria and disgust. He didn't bother closing his eyes anymore, nor did any prayers fall from his lips. Instead, he watched me with unbridled hatred, every muscle in his body so tight I was sure at any second he'd snap like kindling.

Swiveling my hips, I ground myself against him, taking him as deep as he could possibly go with a satisfied groan.

"That's perfect." I licked my lips and stroked myself

while I began to rock on top of him. "You're perfect, pet. Everything I hoped you'd be."

He didn't say anything. Instead, he tightened his grip on the chains binding him and clenched his teeth harder. Fighting. Always fighting. I couldn't wait to watch him surrender.

"Give in to it, Phelan," I said, rocking faster. The tips of my feathers stroked along the column of his throat and down his chest, drifting over his nipples until they pebbled.

He shook his head, not daring to break eye contact with me again, it seemed. If he thought I'd be entreated to stop by the look in his eyes, he was mistaken. I was too far gone to stop now.

I clenched around him as hard as I could. His eyelids sank shut and he bit his lower lip. His body trembled beneath me as the war raged inside of him. I could feel it in his blood, hate and desire embroiled together. A lifetime of following arbitrary rules set down by mortals who lived a millennia ago now collided with his new reality—one in which he didn't have to follow "the" rules; he only had to follow *my* rules. And I had none.

"You can't fight this," I said, riding him harder, impaling myself on his cock again and again.

But fight he did, until I wasn't sure if I actually would win this particular battle. The longer he fought, the longer I fucked myself on top of him, the less certain I was I'd be able to breach his defenses. That in itself was deeply unsettling.

Phelan ground his molars together so hard they had to be aching. His body flinched under my hands as they ran up and down his body, caressing the outline of his muscles. I dug my nails into his chest, part primordial urge, and part frustration. He gasped, glancing down at the crescents dotting his skin. Heat flared in his pale cheeks and his breathing quickened. So he liked a little pain. *That* was a useful tidbit to discover.

"Give in, pet. Give in to me." I reached behind me and toyed with his balls as I rode him, tugging and massaging, meanwhile, my wings continued to caress the rest of his body until he was overwhelmed by the sensations.

He closed his eyes and shook his head.

I pinched one of his nipples until he bucked beneath me, squirming helplessly against the feeling.

After that, it wasn't long until his orgasm broke, like a wave against rocks. He cried out, straining against the chains as his cock pumped frantically, emptying his release deep inside of me. I seized my chance. For a split second, his mind was mine for the taking.

I sifted through his memories, his knowledge, his power, everything that made up a man, searching for any sign of the witches' plan or Hazael's influence.

A ritual diagram flashed into view before I was knocked backward with another blinding pain. I closed my eyes and held my head, trying to catch my breath. He was *so* strong. The potential of his power sent a chill down my spine. If I wasn't already aroused by him, the challenge he presented would have had no problem getting me there.

Laughing softly, I raked a hand through my damp silver hair and pushed it off my forehead. "Are you still going to deny how much you enjoyed that?"

"Go to Hell," he said between his teeth, glaring up at me.

"You forget where you are." I eased off of his softening cock and tucked it back inside his pants, buttoning them again before crawling up his body and draping myself on top of him so we were nose-to-nose. "You think you hate me now? This is only the beginning for you. You don't even know what hate truly is."

He swallowed thickly. "Tell me your name and I'll show you how deep my hatred goes. I have a spell I'd like to share with you."

I tsked him, wagging a scolding finger beneath his nose. "You know I'll never tell you that, witch. But if you feel inclined to cry out a name next time, call me Remiel." I pressed a chaste kiss to his lips and climbed off of him.

Even though I only managed to get a glimpse inside his head, it was time to let Phelan's body rest while his mind agonized over our sexual encounter. Knowing him, he'd be praying for the next century. And maybe after he realized his god wasn't going to answer his desperate pleas, I'd be able to unlock more of his secrets.

CHAPTER NINE
PHELAN

As soon as I was alone, I yanked against the iron chains as hard as I could, again and again, until the metal bit into my skin and threatened to tear through it completely. But it was pointless. If I was going to get out of here, I couldn't do it alone.

Closing my eyes, I inhaled a deep breath and exhaled it slowly. Even if I could still feel that demon all over me, touching me, tasting me, I couldn't dwell on what had happened or what any of it meant in the long run. I had more important things to do, like surviving.

Ever since I woke up, my memory started coming back, a piece at a time. I remembered most of it clearly now. The circle. The summoning. And the explosion. He must have grabbed me during the chaos. It was still cause to hope, though, because that meant the Congregation would be looking for me. I'm sure with their combined strength and the right spell, they'd be able to pull me back to safety in our realm. They just needed to know where to look. Except my power could only access the dreamworld, a foggy space with liminal ties to the aether and spirit realms. Unless my would-be rescuer(s) actually fell asleep during their search, I wouldn't be able to reach them...

It didn't matter. I had to try.

Relaxing each part of my body, one by one, I slowed my breathing as much as I could—my heart rate along with it. I had no idea what time it was in the mortal world, or if time existed at all in Hell. Could my magic even reach beyond this place? The iron meant I couldn't conjure any in my own reality, but did the limitations extend to the dreamworld, too?

Flitting through the darkness in my head, I sought out any other flash of light, any sign of another mind I could tap into. But there was nothing. How long had I been down here? Surely *someone* had to be looking for me, searching for any sign of where I'd gone, clues as to what had happened to me...

Like a lost ship at sea, I drifted in total darkness, waiting. Praying.

I'd nearly given up hope entirely when a blinding light enveloped me out of nowhere.

Temperance's mind seized mine with a vengeance, as crushing as her hugs tended to be. "Phelan! Oh my God! You're not dead. Where are you?"

"Hell," I answered truthfully. "It was the demon from the library. You have to help me get out of here."

"How?"

"I don't know!" I forced myself to swallow, to keep from falling into hysterics now that I knew help was close at hand. "He's bound me with iron. Do you know if there's a way around that?"

"Not off the top of my head. I'll have to look in some alchemy texts, see if anyone ever wrote anything down."

"While you're at it, look for a demon named Remiel. I doubt that's his real name, or at least not all of it, but maybe there's something in the Book of Lazarus that can help us. Or even the Combermere Codex."

Temperance drew in a sharp breath. "The Combermere? Really? You think he's that important?"

"He's a prince," I said quietly, a fact I knew but hated having to admit out loud. In the hierarchy of demons, princes were notoriously hard to control and even harder to kill. Now that I'd apparently been taken as his "pet," the odds of me returning to the mortal world were slim to none.

"Shit..."

"I know..."

"Ok. It's ok. Everything is going to be fine. I'll find a way to get you out of there."

"Do you think Hester would help?" I was stupidly hopeful, even though my gut told me I knew better.

Temperance hesitated and I had my answer before she actually spoke. "You know she refuses to practice magic anymore. Not since..." Since Bridget was committed and Hester declared demonic necromancy was too dangerous for anyone in the family to "dabble" in. And this was exactly why I didn't *dabble*. I studied and studied and studied some more; dedicated my life to mastering the knowledge and practices those priests laid out. I followed every rule and restriction I had to in order to make sure I *didn't* end up like Bridget and now I was somewhere even worse.

"I was hoping she might make an exception. But even if she won't do it herself, maybe she'll tell you how?" I asked quietly, the flicker of hope sputtering out regardless of my question. "Or maybe one of the nature witches knows similar magic? Maybe a water witch? Water can sometimes be a portal. Or, or an earth witch? One who works with energy? Oh! Better yet! Nathaniel can simply pull the instructions out of Hester's head and tell you how to do it."

She interrupted my babbling abruptly. "Try not to worry. I'm going to figure this out. Just... hang in there."

"I know. Just know that I love you."

"Don't even start with that."

"I want to be prepared. For the worst."

"Phelan, you've been preparing for the worst since you were a kid. Where's that never-ending supply of faith?"

A demon prince destroyed it with one full-body orgasm —something I could never, *would* never, admit to her or anyone else as long as my soul retained any sort of cognizance.

"I should go. I don't want him to catch me," I said weakly.

"I'll reach out to you as soon as I can."

With nothing else to say, I severed the link between us.

Alone again, I stared at the rough stone ceiling overhead, trying not to imagine what lay beyond these walls. While this room hearkened back to an ancient castle, I'm sure the rest of the landscape was... grim. But who really knew? Maybe demons lived apart from the pain and suffering of the other tormented souls. I hoped I'd never have to find out.

Remiel's sigil flared hotly in my hand, mocking me.

A shudder racked my body, as much from the pain in my palm as from the memory of what just occurred.

Inhaling through my nose, I exhaled even slower through my mouth, hoping to quell my rising nerves. Except all that did was give me another whiff of Remiel's particular scent. The spicy muskiness was all over me, even stronger now than it was before.

I squeezed my eyes shut, staving off the tears before they had a chance to form. It wouldn't do me any good to lose it. I had to keep my wits about me, especially with a demon who'd stop at nothing to torment me for the rest of my life—however long, or short, that would be.

Out of nowhere, something seized me in the dark. Claws scrabbled at my limbs, yanking me off the bed and hurling me across the room. I landed hard and rolled across the rough stone floor, heavy iron cuffs still attached to each wrist. Before I could even get my bearings, the shadowy creature seized the chain between my restraints and dragged me along like I was nothing more than a sack of potatoes.

I twisted and yanked, trying to free myself from its clutches. The creature slapped me across the face with a thick, lizard-like tail and kept walking, as unbothered by my struggle as a horse was with a fly.

Blinking hard, I tried and failed to clear the tears from my eyes.

"Where are you taking me?" It was probably pointless to ask, but I had to try.

The creature snarled in response but didn't speak.

I tried to see where it was dragging me but it was impossible in the near dark. The torches flickering along the walls were too few and far between to see much of anything in their eerie green light. From the echoes all around us, it sounded like we were in a tunnel of some sort.

Any time I managed to get my feet under me and attempted to stand, the creature yanked me off balance. I crashed to the ground, again and again, until my thighs were scraped and bruised, despite the fact I was still wearing pants.

The demon pushed open a heavy door and stomped into another chamber, straight out of my nightmares.

A putrid smell hit me immediately. The spicy fragrance from Remiel's room was gone, replaced with blood, vomit, and urine. It all mixed together in a noxious combination with the ever-present smell of brimstone and smoke. If there had been any food in my stomach, it would have come up again from the revolting odor.

Chains and metal cages were scattered around the room. One or two still held the remains of... something. Human. Demon. I couldn't tell from the rotting gray lumps beyond the iron bars.

The floor was sticky with something I was sure I didn't want to know the origin of and I was grateful when the lizard-demon finally let me stand.

Little did I know it was only so the creature could throw the chain over a post high above my head and anchor it to a peg on the other side. It didn't stop me from jerking on the restraints immediately, trying to pull them down again. The demon ignored my struggling and snatched one of my ankles, clamping another manacle to it and yanking the chain taut before doing the same thing to the other one.

Once I was immobilized in the center of the room, trussed up like Sunday dinner, the lizard-thing trudged out again, slamming the door shut.

I let out a steadying breath, trying to assess my new situation. While I didn't appreciate what transpired between Remiel and I, I had a feeling my day was going to get infinitely worse.

Turning my attention to my ankles, I tested each of them, but there wasn't much give in the metal. I could stand normally, with my feet spread, but the chains were anchored so I couldn't bring them together or lift them more than an inch off the floor. There would be zero chance of escaping while I was like this, let alone fighting off anyone who came to torture me.

Heavy footsteps echoed to the left.

I turned toward the noise, trying to see into the pitch-black corner of the room.

The footsteps kept coming, but I couldn't make out anything beyond the limited circle of emerald light until, finally, another creature emerged from the darkness.

A demon. Higher-ranked than the last thing that brought me here, but nowhere near Remiel's status by the looks of him. This one was the traditional nightmare—twisting black horns, dead snake eyes, and a slender tail that twitched back and forth.

Lifting a clawed hand, the demon stopped in front of me and unfurled a whip, letting it dangle inches from my face.

"You will answer my questions," the demon said in a low, gravelly voice, "or you will suffer greatly."

"What questions?"

"What your Congregation is planning."

"We're not planning any—" My head whipped to one side from the impact from his backhand. Stars burst behind my eyelids and the world moved in slow motion. I clenched my teeth before opening my mouth again, testing to see if he'd actually managed to break my jaw with just one blow.

"Tell me the next step of the plan."

"What plan? There is no—" His large fist rammed into the center of my stomach, driving all the air out of my lungs and radiating pain through my torso. Now I *really* wanted to vomit, but I was too busy trying to gasp for a full breath.

Growling, the demon moved behind me, dragging the whip along the ground.

I was still wheezing from his punch, waiting for the next question, when he cracked the whip. The strip of leather slashed across my back without warning. I couldn't help but cry out, half in surprise and half in pain.

The intense stinging didn't subside, it simply spread across my back until the next lash, and then *two* places on my back were screaming in agony. I was used to the scourge, with its seven lashes and hardened tips, but this whip was different, wielded by one who wasn't seeking to sanctify me and who would happily strip the flesh from my bones.

He didn't ask another question until he'd whipped me five times. I could barely catch my breath. My whole back felt like it was on fire. A scorching wetness dripped down my skin, splattering all over the dirty stone. I could only assume it was blood.

Trudging up to me, the demon seized a handful of hair and wrenched my head backward. "What are your elders planning?"

"I don't know," I said, squeezing my eyes shut and waiting for another punch. Instead, he shoved my head forward with a growl and returned to his place behind me. A second later, the sting of the leather sliced across my skin again.

The question was always the same—centering on "the plan." The plan that didn't exist. Nothing else about magic or witchcraft or Winslow. Simply "the plan." And each time I didn't give a satisfactory answer, he dealt out another round of whipping.

As much as I tried not to scream, I couldn't contain it. Tears sprang to my eyes and spilled down my cheeks as blood dripped from the wounds on my back. At least, I hoped it was blood and not swaths of skin.

I eventually lost count of how many lashes he was up to. All I knew was that my shirt hung in tattered strips, soaked by blood and sweat. Despite my best efforts to control it, my body shook violently. The chains that held me rattled, betraying each tremble. At that moment, I felt more connected to my ancestors than I ever had—bound and tortured before an inquisitor who would stop at nothing to hear what they wanted.

"Tell me!" the demon snarled.

"Enough, Melech," came the voice of my nightmares, every bit the smooth purr it was the first time I heard it in the library.

Remiel appeared from nowhere, shimmering into view in the corner of my eye.

"Yes, sire." The other demon threw the whip on a table and disappeared back into the darkness.

"Oh, my sweet lamb. Look at you. You could have ended this at any time," Remiel said as he walked up to me. He caressed my cheek before tipping my chin up with one finger.

I could barely keep my eyes open, let alone tell him to go fuck himself.

"You have the power," he continued, letting my head

drop again as he circled around behind me. "All you had to do was answer him truthfully."

I didn't even try to see what he was doing. The only thing I could think about was the pain. Now that it had stopped, I tried to imagine all the ways it was going to get infinitely worse as Remiel's hands slid over my shoulders, ripping what was left of my shirt off of me.

"Simply tell us what your Congregation is planning and you can go home." Something cool and wet glided across my back.

I jerked away from the sensation, but Remiel clamped a hand on my shoulder, keeping me still.

"Shhh. It'll help with the pain." The fingers of his other hand moved across my back, smearing more of whatever it was. It smelled herbal.

"If you're so concerned about my pain, why let him torture me at all?" I asked, fighting the urge to dry heave from the relentless nausea.

He continued his ministrations in silence, because he wasn't concerned. Just like there was no way he'd ever let me go home. It was all a ploy. Good demon, bad demon, as it were.

My eyelids started to droop, growing heavier with each second that passed. After such brutality, the salve was soothing, chasing away the pain and quelling the blistering fire in my skin. I let my head rest against my arm, hoping he'd at least unchain me when he was finished. I'd long since lost feeling in my hands from being strung up and every muscle in my body was screaming for rest.

The second I thought to hope, I felt him slithering around in my head. It was the same feeling as when he forced me to have sex with him, like a silk ribbon slipping along my skin. And now I knew *exactly* why he let his creature have at me.

Gritting my teeth, I threw up a mental shield as quickly as I could. He hissed behind me, his fingers digging into my shoulder where he'd maintained his grip. I might not have been able to physically hurt him, but I felt a twinge of happiness knowing I could at least wound his mind.

"Stay out of my head," I snarled over my shoulder.

"You can't hold out forever."

"Shows how little you actually know about witches. I'm beginning to doubt if you're even a prince at all." It was foolish to antagonize him, but what did I have to lose? My life? It was over the moment I woke up in this miserable place. Maybe if I harassed him enough, he'd lose patience with me and end it quickly.

He laughed darkly and seized a handful of my hair, yanking my head back so his mouth was right next to my ear. "I'm going to enjoy breaking you."

"Do your worst, demon."

"Oh, I shall." He dragged his tongue along my ear before shoving my head forward again. Licking along the side of my neck, he bit down on the tender slope above my clavicle so hard I yelped. "That's it, pet. Scream for me."

Knowing it was what he wanted, I bit my lips in an attempt to stifle any future sounds.

His hands slid down my sides and over my hips, pushing my pants downward until they pooled at my feet. He grabbed my ass in both hands and squeezed, hard. "So perfect."

For some reason, it didn't occur to me what he was doing until I felt his hardness press against me from behind. Any fatigue was instantly erased by a new wave of dread.

"Tell me what the plan is," he said, alternating between kneading my ass and caressing it, all the while rubbing his cock against me, "and I promise I'll let you go."

No matter how much I wanted that to be true, I knew it was all a lie. Demons couldn't be trusted no matter what they promised you or how sincere they sounded. Necromancy 101. "Even if I knew, I'd never tell you."

His finger dipped between my cheeks and pressed against my hole, circling the rim and tapping out a warning. I couldn't help but gasp, torn between being concerned over what his hand was currently doing and what it was going to do next.

"Do you think your Congregation would applaud your sacrifice, little lamb? Do you think any of them would care that you're willing to die for them? They despise Necromancers. Why should you suffer for *them*? Tell me what I want to know and I'll stop. Unless you don't want me to."

I tried to ignore what he was doing, even after he pushed his finger past my rim, but it was impossible. An unfamiliar burning swept through me, along with an occasional spark whenever he'd crook it inside, touching parts of me I didn't know I had.

"I'm not willing to die for them," I replied through clenched teeth, "but I will if it means stopping you."

"You know what they say about pride, pet—it goeth before the fall."

I bit my lips again, preventing myself from speaking, but I couldn't help whimpering as he worked one finger, then two, and eventually three, in and out of me. His other hand carded through my hair, scratching along my scalp and sweeping down my neck before going back up. A shiver raced down my spine each time he did it and I hated him even more.

After his fingers withdrew from inside me and his other hand slid down my waist to my hip, I hoped that was all, that we were through with this battle of wills. I truly didn't know what he was asking so I couldn't even lie to try and save myself. The demons kept talking about a "plan," but how was I supposed to convince them there *was* no plan?

Gripping my hips with both hands, Remiel yanked me backward as much as I could go with the chains holding me in place, his cock slotting between my cheeks.

Oh fuck! Fuckfuckfuckfuck.

"Anything to say?" he murmured, alternating between kissing and biting my neck, his tongue swirling hungrily over my skin. "Hmm? Anything at all?"

I wanted to shout, cry, swear, beg. Anything to stop what was coming next. I didn't. He'd only enjoy it more. Pride *was* my greatest sin but I'd be damned if I let him get the better of me.

My heart pounded in my chest as his hands roamed over my torso, making a point to twist my nipples, before skimming down to my hips.

The iron around my wrists rubbed my skin raw, a painful reminder I was helpless to do anything—except give him answers I didn't have.

"No?" His teeth grazed along my ear again. "Have it your way."

A hot, steady pressure pushed against my entrance until it gave way. Fire flared from that spot and spread throughout the rest of my body. It felt like I was being split in two. His fingers were nothing compared to his cock.

As much as I willed myself to stay silent, I couldn't. I cried out when his hips slammed into me from behind, seating himself inside completely.

"Good boy," he purred, gripping my hips tightly. He slid

out part of the way and thrust in again. "Open up for me. Scream if you have to. Cry. Beg. Swear. Let it all out."

I didn't give him the satisfaction, but I couldn't contain every sound as he drove into me over and over. The physical pain eventually subsided but the humiliation was worse. Even if my body made it through this ordeal, the shame alone threatened to suffocate me from the inside.

A gentle caress slipped through my mind as his cock rammed into me again and again. So *that's* what he really wanted. This wasn't simply to torture me, to degrade me, to have one more thing to taunt me with. He thought he could replicate the other day when he actually got inside my head while he got me off. I'm sure he thought it would be infinitely easier given how distressed I was, but he was wrong. It *wouldn't* happen again. Not if I could help it. And I would rather die before I gave in to him.

I tried to focus on the sensation in my mind, to make sure my defenses were firmly in place, but each thrust battered against them. The whipping had already weakened me, mentally and physically, and now I had *this* to contend with. The line between pain and pleasure was thoroughly blurred, a strange combination that left my insides hot and knotted together in confusion.

How long could I possibly hold him off? What if *this* was truly Hell? To be violated for eternity, my mind plundered as much as my body, used for his own filthy desires? But if it was Hell, why did I feel any pleasure at all? It seemed contradictory. Unless it was part and parcel of his ongoing manipulations.

His breath was hot on my neck as he leaned in. "Just remember you can stop this at any time. Just give me what I want. Unless you like it, you like being used by me. If that's the case, I'm going to fuck that guilt right out of you until you're screaming my name."

His hands slid over my body again, clawing and caressing until goosebumps spread across the whole area. One arm wrapped around my waist while he seized my throat with his other hand, jerking me back against him. The lash marks on my skin burned with the contact and a whimper fell from my lips.

"Well?" he growled against my ear. "Do you? Do you like getting fucked like this? Do you want me to stop? Do you want to be a good boy and tell me everything I want to know?"

Despite the fact he was holding my throat, I shook my head. I didn't have the words to answer him. I didn't even know what question I was trying to answer in the first place. All of my rationality melted away, scorched from the inside out by the fire in my blood and the steady pressure building in the bottom of my stomach.

He held me tightly, one hand clenched beneath my jaw, constricting my airway, while he drove into me in furious thrusts. He licked and kissed my neck, biting and sucking at the sensitive skin until I was sure every inch of me would be marked by him, one way or the other.

I couldn't tell if he was still in my head or not. I felt him everywhere. All around me. Inside of me. I didn't know what was physical and what was mental anymore, where he stopped and I began.

He loosened the hand from my throat, only to claim my cock with it, sliding up and down my shaft with an embarrassing amount of pre-cum. The added sensation threw a new wave of gasoline onto my internal fire. The expert way he stroked my dick while he pounded into me, filling me up, pushed me toward a precipice I desperately tried to avoid.

Until I couldn't.

The tension inside of me snapped.

"Holy shit!" I cried out as an orgasm tore through me, jetting over Remiel's hand in thick, white spurts.

"There it is," Remiel sighed, still thrusting in long, deep strokes. "That's what I wanted."

I was still trembling through the aftershocks when he buried himself inside of me one final time, muffling a cry of his own against the back of my neck. His chest rose and fell quickly against my back, each of us breathing hard, covered in a sheen of sweat from the perpetual heat and the exertion of what we'd just done. No. What he'd done *to* me. There was no "we" in this equation. There would *never* be a "we."

"So perfect," Remiel whispered, holding me in a perverse embrace as he nuzzled against my skin.

A strange feeling took root inside of me, seeping out of my chest and filling the void left in the aftermath of my climax. Is this what it felt like to be broken? Did he succeed after all? I couldn't be sure. I'd never felt anything like this in my life. The few times I'd given in to self-indulgence didn't feel like this and I thought nothing would top *that* amount of guilt. How wrong I'd been.

"One of these days, demon, I'll kill you for this," I said, though I doubted the truth of my own words. It wasn't a lack of desire on my part—if given the chance again, I would do everything I could to kill him. I simply doubted my ability to see it through, unmatched as our powers were.

"I love the way you lie to me." Sliding out of my body, he nevertheless tightened his arms around my torso and pressed his lips to my ear. "Rest easy, pet," Remiel purred.

"Melech will be back for you later to continue your conversation."

As the sinking dread coiled in the pit of my stomach, I was suddenly whisked away through time and space. One moment I was standing in a torture chamber, chained to the ceiling, and the next I was lying facedown on Remiel's bed—chained, of course, and completely naked. I didn't know whether to cry, scream, or pray. In the end, it all seemed pointless.

CHAPTER TEN
REMIEL

Leaving Phelan to tend to princely matters was not something I relished. As soon as I was able, I returned to my chambers to see if he'd had a change of heart since our last conversation. At the very least, I'd settle for another glimpse inside his mind, which I *hadn't* been able to accomplish, to my growing irritation.

Fast asleep on his stomach, nestled amongst the pillows on my bed, Phelan looked like an angel with his perfect mouth, slightly pouty, and his dark lashes fanned out over his cheeks. He was so beautiful it made me want to lock him away and keep him as a precious treasure that only I was able to enjoy. The rest of the world didn't deserve him.

Easing onto the bed next to him, I studied the soft lines of his body—the slope of his shoulder blade, the taper of his waist. And of course, the deep lash marks Melech left all over his skin.

Curiously, beneath the fresh gashes, there were a series of crisscrossed lines and scarred divots. I traced one of the older scars with the tip of my finger, the realization dawning on me. He was a flagellant. Of course he could handle the pain of a whipping. It was part of his damnable religion—sacrifice and torment in the vain hope God would love you.

I should have healed the wounds. *All* of them, old and new. A better person would have. But I didn't. If I ruined him, no one else would want him—except me. Then maybe I wouldn't have to fight so hard for his affection, he'd give it willingly, grateful to have any at all.

Never mind the fact no one would be able to touch him again, anyway. He was mine now. Marked. Claimed. For all eternity.

My fingertips skimmed along his bare thigh, coasting over his hip and dipping back down to caress the curve of his ass. I was hard within seconds, dying to possess him again. The way his left knee was hitched up, exposing a glimpse of his manhood, made me want to push his leg up even further and devour every inch of him.

While my fingers traced featherlight tracks on his skin, I slipped into the crevice of his mind again. He wasn't dreaming, but he certainly wasn't awake either. Whatever was going on inside his head remained a mystery to me, even though he was unconscious. For the briefest moment earlier I thought he would let the drawbridge down, but he didn't. Even if he capitulated to the bodily pleasure, the fortress in his mind was sealed up tight. I could creep around as much as I wanted and I wouldn't get inside again. I'd lost my one and only chance during our first encounter because I'd made the mistake of underestimating him. It wouldn't happen again.

What I needed to do was to truly break him, but that was proving more challenging than I'd anticipated. I couldn't remember the last time a witch had given me such trouble. They generally put up more of a fight than humans did, but none of them had ever lasted as long as Phelan. I didn't know what that meant for him—or me.

He exhaled in his sleep and turned his face slightly into the pillow. My hand stilled, resting on his backside, waiting to see if he was awake. I couldn't see his expression from where I was, but I imagined there was a crease between his brows. Always so pensive, even when he assumed no one was watching.

When he didn't stir again, I resumed stroking his soft skin. Along his marred back, over the smooth tightness of his ass, and down his muscled thigh. On the upward return, I caressed the inside of his leg, letting my fingers skip to his balls and massage them lightly where they lay.

Since that didn't seem to disturb him, I dragged one finger upward over his taint and touched the place where I'd truly staked my claim. It was still swollen but that didn't stop me from pressing the pad of my finger against it.

Phelan sucked in a sharp breath as a dribble of sticky liquid coated my finger. He was still full of my release, a realization that sent a new wave of lust coursing through my veins.

"Don't," Phelan said, not even bothering to pick up his head. "Please, I can't. Not again."

"Are you willing to tell me why your Congregation is hunting demons?"

Silence, save for his teeth snapping shut.

"Then there's no reprieve," I murmured, pushing my finger in the rest of the way.

He buried his face in the pillow, muffling a cry. His body was trembling by the time I slid my finger out, thoroughly coated with the evidence of our earlier tryst. I smiled at the glistening wetness and shifted myself behind him, pushing his legs open and forcing his hips to lay flat.

"Give in, Phelan," I said, gripping his backside and spreading his cheeks, feasting on the sight of him. "Stop fighting what you really want."

Not surprisingly, he didn't answer. I moved back a bit more before leaning down and dragging the flat of my tongue across his ravaged entrance.

He whimpered, jerking the chains on his wrists so hard he was going to scrape the flesh from his bones if he wasn't careful.

My fingers dug into his tense muscles, massaging them and spreading him wider as I lapped at the swollen skin, swirling my tongue around and pressing it in just as I had with my finger. He was already delicious, but the added taste from my release made me practically feral, desperate to devour every bit of him.

Phelan's whimpering continued, muffled by the pillow until he forced himself to come up for air, gasping and panting, straining against the manacles on his wrists.

Licking and sucking and kissing like mad, I consumed every bit of him, along with his sighs and gasps, until my cock was on the verge of bursting.

Moving upwards, I straddled the outside of his thighs and covered his body with mine, letting my cock glide along his crease, giving me some of the friction I was desperate for.

"No," he moaned, shaking his head.

"Yes." I captured his earlobe between my teeth and sucked on it. Squeezing my legs, I forced his together and thrust downward in the tightness between his thighs. I didn't try to push inside of him again; instead, I aimed my cock along his balls, already slippery from saliva and evidence of my arousal.

He pulled on the chains as I lifted my hips and thrust

down again into that tight warmth between his legs. Phelan squeezed them tighter around my cock and it was my turn to whimper.

"That's so good," I whispered before biting the back of his neck. He cried out and hissed in pain, but I didn't let go. Meanwhile, I kept fucking against him as hard as I could, my cock slipping between his thighs, along his taint and sac.

Every time I thrust down, his own cock was pushed against the mattress. From the gasps and aborted moans, I knew he wouldn't hold out forever. The friction was too good to ignore, no matter how pious you were.

"Give in, pet," I said, slipping one hand around his throat and squeezing. "Surrender to me."

He gasped, trying to shake his head despite my grip.

I ground my pelvis against his ass every time our bodies slammed together. He tried not to buck his hips, to keep them planted as firmly as he could to the mattress, but it was impossible with how hard and how fast I rutted against him.

His fingers clawed the air, twisting around nothing, and his breathing came in short pants. Even after I loosened my hold on his throat, his cheeks remained flushed.

"You want to, don't you?" I asked, letting my words ghost over his ear, followed by a flick of my tongue. "You're so close. On the very edge of release. I can feel it."

He shook his head again.

"Fall with me, Phelan." I forcibly turned his face toward me and captured his lips with mine. My tongue plundered his mouth while my cock continued to work against his balls, slipping and sliding in the heat between his thighs, a feeling almost as blissful as actually being inside of him.

He cried out against my lips and his body quaked

beneath mine. His thighs clamped together even harder as the scent of his climax filled the air. I swallowed each moan and whimper, kissing him ruthlessly until my own release spilled out of me, further ruining the bedding beneath us.

My wings draped over both of us, cocooning us like a blanket as our ragged breathing returned to normal.

"You disgust me," Phelan muttered.

"You disgust yourself," I replied, pressing wet kisses along the back of his shoulder. "It's simply easier to blame me."

"I suppose you want me to be grateful you didn't force me, like before?"

I slid one hand around his waist and wedged it between his body and the mattress. When I pulled it out again, my fingers were coated with proof of his orgasm. "Don't pretend it didn't feel good," I said, pressing two fingers inside his mouth and swiping the cum over his tongue.

His head jerked back at the same time he bit down on my knuckles, but there was no escaping the taste of himself. As soon as I pulled my fingers free, he spat over his shoulder. I couldn't tell if he was aiming for my face or not, but he didn't succeed. Most of it ended up on my wing.

I chuckled, ruffling the dampened feathers to flick it away before I stretched out on my back next to him, folding one arm beneath my head. "One of these days, pet, you're going to come around. You'll find there are worse things in this universe than me."

When he didn't answer, I cracked an eye open. Of course, he was watching me with a baleful glare. I wouldn't expect anything less.

"Don't believe me?" I asked, raising my brows at him.

"I will never see you for anything other than the revolting monster that you are."

"Never say never, lamb."

He clenched his teeth and turned away from me, seething into his pillow.

I rolled onto my side again, tracing the edge of the lash marks on his back. Some of them had opened again; weeping blood mixed with the sheen of sweat on his skin.

Dragging the flat of my tongue along the salty mixture, a delighted purr rumbled in the back of my throat. I didn't miss the way Phelan's back tensed, like he was trying to stave off the goosebumps spreading over his skin. His power was so potent, it tingled over my tongue. No wonder I'd barely managed a glimpse inside his head.

Before I could taste him again, an obnoxiously loud clamoring erupted in the hall outside my chamber, a sound I'd, unfortunately, know anywhere. Armored soldiers moving at a rapid pace.

"Sire!" Melech bellowed as the chamber door flew open. "Hazael's legion is attacking the river gate!"

I swore under my breath and climbed out of bed. "Did you send reinforcements to the black gate then?" My armor materialized into place with each step I took. By the time I reached the door, I was fully dressed and thoroughly irate.

"No, I said—"

"I know what you said! Now, do as *I* say. Stay here and guard this room." I threw a pointed glance over my shoulder at Phelan, watching me from the bed with a furrowed brow, curiosity replacing all earlier contempt. "I wouldn't want anything to happen to my pet in my absence."

I shut the door on Phelan's parting scowl and made my way toward the black gate to put a hasty end to this latest attack.

CHAPTER ELEVEN
PHELAN

As soon as Remiel was gone, I yanked on the chains binding my wrists. I didn't expect them to break, but maybe the black bedposts they were attached to would snap with enough applied pressure. If I could be so lucky.

After several minutes of struggling, I concluded the intricately carved wood wasn't going to give no matter how hard I pulled from this new position. Short of crushing the bones in my hand, there was no way I could get the cuffs off. I didn't even see a lock I could pick if I was somehow given the means and opportunity.

Burying my face in the pillow, I unleashed a furious scream until my throat was raw and scratchy.

It didn't help.

By the time I was done, I was drained—emotionally, mentally, physically. With the ghost of Remiel's body pressing against mine, making it do things I didn't want, I couldn't think clearly.

Closing my eyes, I tried to ignore the scent wafting up from the bedding as I worked to slow down my whirling thoughts and my rapid breathing. It was frankincense, I told myself. Or myrrh. The same incense used in thuribles the world over to cleanse one's self in the presence of God. Except that incense didn't also smell like cinnamon or musk...

Damn him! He'd wrapped himself around every single thought for weeks and now even God wasn't a safe subject!

Once I calmed down enough, I was able to slip into the dreamworld again, even though I expected to be waiting awhile for my cousin's return. We were quite similar in that regard—once she got a bee in her bonnet for a particular research topic, she lost all sense of time until she was finished with her task.

To my surprise, though, she wasn't hard to find.

"Do you have a way out of here yet?" I asked the moment I felt a connection to her.

"No," Temperance said glumly. "I couldn't find a single alchemical reference to defeating the properties of iron, short of actual transmutation. But I don't think gold will help you in your current situation, anyway."

"What about a portal? Another summoning? Anything?"

"Not that I could find."

"Did anyone else in the Congregation have any suggestions?"

"I'm doing everything I can, ok?"

I tried not to feel utterly defeated, but each negative response felt like a ton of bricks smashing on top of a little glass bubble of hope. "Anything on Remiel, then?"

She took entirely too long to answer, obliterating the speck of hope I'd been desperately clinging to like a buoy in the ocean. "You're going to have to get into his mind, Phelan. If you can't get out of the chains yourself, that is your only hope. Persuade him to free you."

"How am I supposed to do that? My power is only active in the dreamworld—not the waking one."

"He doesn't sleep?"

"If he does, it's not around me."

"You have to try *something*. I need more time."

"Time for what?! Every minute I'm down here is another minute I'm closer to death, which after everything that's happened, I would frankly prefer."

"Do not say that! Do not even think it. I'll get you out of there. Just stay strong and have faith."

"Do me a favor, then."

"Anything."

"Look into someone named Hazael. I know he's another demon, but find out everything you can. He's apparently in some sort of war with Remiel. Maybe I can use that to my advantage."

"I'll get started right away."

"Shit! He's already coming back!" I didn't know how I did it, but somehow I was able to sense Remiel's approach. It was like a weird tingling erupted over my skin before I even heard his voice echoing in the hall. I was hoping that whatever siege was happening would have kept him occupied for longer. Unless it had already been long enough? How long had he been gone? It was hard to tell. It seemed like minutes, but time moved so differently in the underworld, much like it did in dreams.

"Remember he's just a demon, Phelan," Temperance said quickly. "They don't trust anyone or anything. Manipulate him the way he'd manipulate you."

Slamming the door on the dreamworld, I returned to literal Hell on Earth just as the door to his room opened and shut again.

I kept my eyes closed and made sure my breathing

stayed even as his footsteps approached the bed. Not that sleeping was any sort of a deterrent to him. Nothing was. He was a fiend of the worst sort and I hated myself for the plan that formed in my head.

As I could have predicted, Remiel crawled into bed, sans armor, and pressed himself along the length of my body. He traced designs over my bare skin with both his fingers and his wings, smelling like smoke and blood on top of his usual spicy scent. It wasn't long before I felt something light caress my balls and sweep across my ass. It was hard to tell what it was, but it didn't really matter. He'd take what he wanted regardless of what I did or didn't say.

"Melech?" I asked, feigning a sleepy inhale. I figured if it was long enough for him to thwart a siege, it was long enough for me to have fallen asleep again.

Remiel stopped immediately. In the next instant, he gripped my shoulder and rolled me over as much as the iron manacles would allow without ripping my limbs off. "What did you just say?"

I blinked and looked around, as if I was trying to get my bearings.

"Did he come in here while I was gone?" Remiel seized a handful of hair and yanked me forward so we were nose-to-nose. "Answer me!"

Outwardly, I acted confused and made sure my expression matched. Inwardly, I was delighted. While I didn't know if Melech was the source of his irritation specifically or if it was the idea that *anyone* had been to see me, I nevertheless took joy in seeing him so furious. If I could keep him angry, it could either buy the time Temperance needed or increase the chances of him making a mistake and I could escape myself.

"I don't know what you're talking about," I lied, literally

through my teeth as my scalp screamed in protest under his vicious manhandling. "One moment I'm asleep and the next you're yanking me around like a doll."

"You were dreaming of him then?" Remiel's silver eyes flashed in the firelight, like the glint of a knife. His possessiveness thrilled me because it gave me something to exploit, which meant I still had a fighting chance, small as it was.

"The only thing I've dreamt of since I've been here is my inevitable death," I replied. "Unless you're ready to give it to me, get out. I have nothing to say to you, now or for the rest of this damnable eternity."

"I have been lenient with you thus far, but make no mistake—I will push you to the brink of death, again and again, unless you tell me why you said his name."

"Jealous it was his?" I smirked at him. "Or that it simply wasn't yours?"

Fury flashed across his face and his eyes literally darkened, the silver shifting to pewter and then to black, until I couldn't differentiate the pupil from the iris.

I decided to press my luck, continuing to goad him. "Perhaps I should call out to Hazael while I'm at it and see if another demon wants to come claim me. After all, you're so covetous of one another. Always wanting what you can't have. Wasn't that why you fell, Remiel? Jealousy? Because God didn't love you?"

He released his hold on my hair, exchanging it for one around my throat. Jerking me forward, I thought he was going to kiss me, but he forcibly turned my head at the last second, whipping it the other way just as fast. From what I could tell, it looked like he was... inspecting me. For another mark? Some telltale sign someone else had played with his toy in his absence?

"Whatever you're looking for, you're not going to find it," I said smugly.

Tension released from the chains; they seemed to lengthen right before Remiel pulled me up into a sitting position. "You can make things easier on yourself, you know. Tell me what happened while I was gone and I can make you feel so, *so* good," Remiel whispered against my neck, his fingers clawing through my hair before he pulled my head back sharply, his teeth bared. "Or I can make sure you're begging for death by the time I'm done with you."

"If I lie, you'll punish me." I matched his glare with one of my own. "If I tell the truth, you'll still punish me. Not much of a choice."

"This isn't a democracy."

"No, this is Hell and I'm at your mercy. So do whatever you're going to do already and then leave me alone. I won't fight you."

"You're yielding?" He pulled back slightly, his brow furrowing. Maybe it was a coincidence, but his eyes changed color again, like a blacksmith knocking fire scale loose to reveal the glimmering metal beneath the dark flakes.

I pretended to hesitate before nodding.

Suspicion lingered in his now-silver eyes and he made no move to release me.

"Will you at least undo the chains first?" I asked, making sure I jangled them lightly for effect. "You've already marked me. There's no need for them, is there?"

Remiel considered me for a moment, his gaze locked on mine, no doubt searching for an ulterior motive. I must have been convincing. With a wave of his hand, the chains disappeared. I'd barely had time to process that revelation when one hand clamped around the back of my neck and he kissed me roughly.

I pulled away, shaking my head. "No. Not like that."

He arched an incredulous eyebrow at me. "No?"

"No," I repeated. Just because I was acquiescing didn't mean he had free rein to abuse me however he wanted. "I want to touch you first," I said before he could chain me again. Raising one hand slowly as I spoke, I brushed the silky strands of hair off of his cheek and pushed the mass of silver over his bare shoulder. "You're the only one I've been with... like this. I want to see what it's supposed to be like without all of the pain."

Once the side of his neck was exposed, I traced the blue ribbon beneath his pale skin down to his clavicle. He shivered as my fingers swept over his chest, mapping out the array of faint silver scars like a constellation. How many battles had he fought in his lifetime? How many beings had he killed? The answer was unfathomable.

I slid my hand over the newest scar, a white line above his heart where I'd stabbed him. He might have marked me with his sigil, but he wasn't going to escape unscathed, either. For some reason, that realization made the corner of my mouth lift into a smile. If given the opportunity, I'd scar him again. In a heartbeat.

Forcing myself to move on, I let my fingers trail up to his shoulder. Biting my lower lip, I reached hesitantly for his wing. Surprisingly, he unfolded it and curled it forward, making it easier for me to reach.

The hard bone structure beneath contrasted with the soft downiness of the feathers. They were even more brilliant up close, the purest white I'd ever seen, glistening like new-fallen snow, except for the blackened edges. Had they always been that way? Or was the black a punishment from God? A flaw on an otherwise flawless creature?

I stroked the feathers languidly, watching the iridescent sheen dance over them in the green firelight.

Remiel stretched his wing to its full extent and ruffled the feathers before folding it onto his back again.

Apparently done with his wings, I went back to studying the perfect planes of his face. Humans may have been created in God's own image, but Remiel was breath-taking. I didn't think it was another illusion, disguising a scaly, grotesque face beneath, like I'd seen on other demons. His beauty was entirely real, as was his cruelty—something I could never let myself forget even as I was about to sin against God and everything I'd been taught my entire life.

Tracing my fingertips along his sharp cheekbone, I followed the slant of his jaw back to his mouth. His lips parted when I took his face between my hands and leaned in.

God forgive me.

My eyelids sank shut as I pressed my mouth to his softly. He stayed still under my hands, letting me kiss him. Slowly, lightly, with growing confidence.

It wasn't... terrible. In some ways, it was better than kissing Emily Ainsworth behind the meetinghouse in high school. Neither one of us knew what we were doing and even though I was still pretty clueless on that front, Remiel knew exactly what to do with his mouth. He might not have moved, but he sucked my lips, gently, in a way that made me moan in spite of myself.

The next thing I knew, his lips parted and his tongue slipped out, coaxing my own lips open. He alternated between licking into my mouth, swirling his tongue with mine, and that gentle sucking sensation that made my toes curl. All without even using his hands.

Over the course of my life, I'd had other people question my devotion to medieval Necromancy and all that it entailed—the monk-like lifestyle Temperance accused me of. I never did. I knew adherence to the strict rules and requirements our ancestors laid down was what kept me safe. Dabbling in dark arts without the proper knowledge is what led to Bridget's insanity, according to Hester, and I refused to end up like her.

But now, with Remiel turning me into a blazing inferno with just his mouth, I wondered if my solitary existence was ultimately worth it.

Tearing my mouth away from his, I exhaled sharply, trying to screw my head on straight. Of course it was worth it! Necromancy was the defining feature of my life. Without it, I was nothing. This was just a ruse. A means of getting in a demon's head, using his own methods against him. That's all. An attempt at claiming some power in a situation where I inherently had none.

Remiel chased after me, kissing my cheekbone, my jaw, all along my throat. His hands were in my hair, on my skin, pulling me back to him, overwhelming all of my senses like he always did.

I planted my hands against his chest and pushed him out at arm's length. "Wait. Wait, just a second."

"What?" he breathed, barely masking a growl.

"My back," I said quickly. "Can you help?"

"Can I help?" He repeated my words slowly, raising both brows. I found some minuscule amount of comfort in the fact I was confusing him as much as he was confusing me—not that I'd ever admit it to him.

"You were an angel once. There must be some goodness

left inside of you. Please. I want to... to enjoy this as much as I can." I closed my eyes against the lie, hoping the promised end would motivate him if my request alone wouldn't.

He ran his fingers through my hair in a surprisingly intimate gesture. When I looked at him, he tipped his chin toward the bed. "Lay down."

Swallowing, I nodded and turned, laying on my stomach as carefully as I could. The whip marks burned with each movement, threatening to tear open again. If I was ever going to get out of here, there's no way I could do it with injuries like this.

Remiel shifted forward on his knees and something featherlight skimmed across my back. I didn't know if it was his hands or his wings. Ultimately, I didn't care as long as he healed what his minion had done.

His hair tickled my skin when he ducked his head. Something warm and wet traced over one of the lashes near my shoulder and he groaned. It was his tongue. "So fucking delicious. I could savor you for an eternity."

Before I could say anything, his tongue made contact again, licking along my skin while his hands caressed other areas of my back. I didn't mean to shiver, or sigh, but I couldn't help it. Relief flooded through me, replacing the pain completely.

He pressed kisses down my spine, all the way to my ass.

Before he could spread me open again, I rolled onto my side, facing him, and shook my head. "I'm not done with you yet."

"You're only prolonging the inevitable. Unless you plan on fucking me?"

Did I plan on that? Would I even be able to? I had no idea. I was winging this entire encounter. It's not like I had time to think anything through. After all, which was the worse sin? Being the transgressor or an unwilling participant? But how unwilling was I when *I* was the one who brought it up?

Remiel raised his brows, clearly waiting for an answer.

"I don't know..." I said truthfully. "I don't know what to do." I shifted onto my knees in front of him and moved closer, laying my hands on his chest lightly and stroking his pecs. Lord, his body was perfect. Everything was hard and smooth, like sculpted marble.

One of my hands drifted to his stomach. I held my breath as I let it graze over the bulge beneath the black fabric wrapped around his waist. Increasing the pressure, I cupped my hand around it as he groaned and thrust against my palm. "Will you show me?"

Hunger flashed in his eyes and suddenly I felt more like a lamb than ever before. Instead of pouncing right away, Remiel ran his hand through my hair again, stroking the back of my neck and dragging his fingers across my shoulder slowly, gently. "Take it out."

My heart about leapt to my throat with the command. Nevertheless, I nodded and reached for the silver belt. Unfastening it, I tossed it to the side and turned my attention to the black skirt. It was tied together on his hip; one tug of the lace sent it pooling on the bed.

As the material fell away, his cock came front and center. It was long and thick and harder than anything I'd ever felt. Sliding my hand up and down his shaft, I marveled at how hot and silky it was, how heavy it was as it lay in my palm. Seeing another man like this, *touching* another man like this, it was... surreal. But it wasn't awful. It was simply something I had to endure.

Remiel let me stroke his dick for a moment before he

reclined backward on the bed, propped on his elbows with his thighs spread. “Lay with me.”

I did as he said, laying along his side and waiting for the next instruction.

He took my hand in his and wrapped it around his cock, thrusting upward while pushing our joined hands down. Once we fell into some sort of rhythm, he let go of my hand and slid his fingers into my hair, pulling my mouth against his.

I didn’t fight him. I opened my mouth willingly and swept my tongue against his, sucking it gently when it probed inside. A moan reverberated between us. I wasn’t even sure who did it. Remiel inhaled, twisting his fingers into my hair, as if he could possibly pull me any closer.

I was practically panting when I tore my mouth away from his. He didn’t miss a beat, reeling me in by the back of the neck, straight to his lips. He kissed and bit my throat, alternating between sucking and running his tongue over the assaulted skin. By the time he was done, I could only imagine the amount of bruising I’d have.

“I’m supposed to be doing this to you,” I managed to say, hissing in another breath as his teeth nipped my shoulder.

“Kiss me then,” he said, tilting his head to the side and exposing his throat.

I leaned upward, pressing my lips to the soft skin under his jaw. The roughness of my five o’clock shadow left faint patches of pink along his completely smooth skin, but he didn’t seem to mind.

“Now bite.”

Once again, I obliged the order, sinking my teeth into his neck until a low rumble sounded in his chest. He squeezed my ass with one hand, pulling me forward so I was pressed along his side, my dick rubbing shamelessly against his bare thigh.

"Perfect. That's perfect, pet."

I bit him again, moving down his throat like he did to mine. When I got to his chest, I went back to kissing his skin, blazing a trail downward. I had no idea how far I was supposed to go. I mean, the answer was probably pretty obvious but he didn't expect me to... did he? Laying there being used by him was one thing... An excusable thing. Something entirely out of my control. But actively trying to make him feel anything other than excruciating pain was something *completely* different. Was I really prepared to go that far?

As if sensing my moral dilemma, Remiel threaded his fingers through my hair and tilted my face upward as soon as my lips passed his obliques. "Are you ready for this?"

"No," I admitted. "I'm not ready for any of it." I had no idea why I was being honest with him. Did I think it would have any effect on his black heart? Not for one second. Maybe I just couldn't keep track of the lies anymore. Or maybe I wanted him to put me out of my misery and take charge, spare me from having to make the decision for myself.

Remiel's knuckles skimmed the side of my face, almost tenderly, which was even more confusing. "You really haven't been with anyone, have you? Man *or* woman."

Heat flared in my cheeks and I shook my head, preparing for more humiliation or mockery. It was bad enough I got it from my family—I didn't need to hear it from someone who'd lived a thousand lives, indulging in whatever depravity he wanted. I'm sure the word "abstinence" wasn't even in his vocabulary. Or "restraint"—except in terms of kidnapping and torture.

A slow smile spread across Remiel's face. He gripped the point of my chin between his thumb and forefinger and sat up, leaning closer, his silver gaze drinking me in with barely-concealed delight. "You want to be good for me, don't you?"

I nodded, even though my stomach twisted into knots.

"You'll do as I tell you?"

Another nod.

"You won't resist?"

Fighting every instinct I had, I shook my head.

"Open your mouth."

Swallowing, I did as he said. His fingers slid into my hair again, cupping the back of my head and pushing it downward with surprising gentleness.

Right before my mouth enveloped the head of his dick, I closed my eyes and prayed for the strength to see this plan through. It wasn't even a plan. It was a half-cocked idea. A desperate attempt at clinging to hope. And if it failed, I didn't know what I'd do except be a demon's plaything for the rest of my existence.

"Use your tongue. Just like when we kiss." Remiel sucked in a breath through his teeth, his hips rolling upward, sliding more of himself into my mouth. "That's it. You're doing *so* good. All the way in."

His cock was hard and soft all at once, smooth and slippery but unyielding as it moved into the back of my throat. The act itself was surprisingly... ok. No, it was weird. Beyond weird. I felt like a snake, unhinging my jaw to accommodate his size. The taste was much like the rest of his skin, faintly salty but with a honey sort of undertone? I didn't know how that was even possible, but admittedly it wasn't as gross as I thought it would be.

My gag reflex kicked in out of nowhere and I pulled

myself off his cock, despite the fact his hand was still in my hair. Gasping in a breath, I blinked through the haze of tears when Remiel seized my face with both hands. He kissed me fiercely, using his thumbs to brush the dampness from my cheeks.

"Do it again," he said, guiding my head back to his hard-on. "I want to feel every inch of your throat close around my cock."

My throat protested that idea very much, but I opened my mouth regardless and inhaled a breath before diving down once more. I made it farther than I did the first time before I gagged, dripping tears and spit all over him as I reared back.

"Oh, fuck, Phelan," Remiel rasped, stroking himself with my saliva. "Look at what you do me. I'm so fucking hard for you."

Despite the ache in the back of my throat and the fact my jaw was killing me, I was oddly proud of my small accomplishment.

No. No, no, no. I was *not* proud. I was horrified by myself and how easily my body adapted to him, how quick I was to preen my feathers seeing the lustful look on his face. If I ever made it out of here, I'd have to go to confession twice a day for the rest of my life and it still wouldn't be enough to make up for what I was doing now.

"Stop it," Remiel growled, rolling onto his knees quickly. His fingers encircled my throat and he pushed me backward, forcing me to lay on my back. "Stop letting some profane dogma dictate what you feel."

For a moment I was worried he'd managed to get inside my head, that he heard my conflicting thoughts, but I didn't feel him slinking around up there. It must have been the look on my face that gave me away.

He slapped a hand against my cheek, rubbing away the sting slowly. "Stop."

"I didn'—"

Another slap, this one a degree harder. "I said stop."

A flutter of nerves rushed through me and I nodded.

"Kiss me."

For once, I didn't hesitate to press my lips to his. Threading my fingers through his hair, I held him by the back of his head and kissed him. Harder and harder, until my lips were bruised and the critical voice inside my head had ceased talking.

Remiel ground his pelvis against mine, rubbing our cocks together. I didn't even know when I got hard, but I tried to tell myself it was a natural reaction. It didn't mean anything—just like all of the times before. It was entirely out of my control. If anyone was to blame for this, it was Remiel. One thousand percent.

Pulling his mouth from mine, Remiel nosed beneath my jaw, biting and kissing along my throat, his hands caressing every inch of me.

I gasped when his teeth grazed my nipple, sending a spark of pain and pleasure right through me. He sucked on it gently while he toyed with the other one, rolling it between his fingers and pinching it so hard I squirmed beneath him.

"That's what I thought," he murmured against my skin, licking his way down my abdomen while the tips of his wings brushed my cheeks, my shoulders, down my arms.

"What?" I asked, hating how breathy it came out.

"You like a little pain. Deep down." He licked me from my balls all the way up to the crown of my dick, flicking the underside with his tongue.

I didn't even know what I liked or didn't like but I

wasn't going to argue with him, especially not when his whole mouth enveloped my cock and slid all the way to the base.

As soon as my eyes rolled upward, I squeezed them shut, chiding myself for liking what he was doing to me. But no amount of silent scolding stopped the feeling of his mouth on me, licking and sucking and biting anything he could reach. Not just my cock, but my balls, my thighs, my abdomen.

Even the feeling of his hair against my skin was driving me crazy, tempting me to reach out and touch it. No, not just touch it. Grab it and yank him around like he always did with me. Except, that would definitely be crossing a line... beyond the line I already crossed.

The warmth of Remiel's mouth disappeared and I heard him spit. The moment I opened my eyes to see what he was doing, my lids slammed shut again as his finger slid inside of me.

"No, not this," I said with a grimace. "It hurts too much."

"Only for a moment," he replied, nipping the inside of my thigh before lapping at the skin. "Then you know it gets better."

"I don't want any pain this time. You sai—"

"I know, pet. Just breathe and let it sit there. I'm going to make you feel so good. I promise."

I exhaled a shaky breath, trying to focus on Remiel's mouth and the way he used every part of it to tease my cock. His lips, his tongue, even his teeth. It all combined in a wave of pleasure I was no longer fighting. The pleasure made it easier to ignore the burning from his fingers as another joined the first, the way they curled and twisted inside of me. All until he brushed against one particular spot. A surge of unexpected tingling replaced the pain, so much so that a moan escaped from me before I could help it.

He groaned around my cock, sucking it with vigor. His fingers crooked again and I couldn't help but thrust up into his mouth. Swallowing as much of my shaft as he could, he worked his fingers in and out faster, obviously pleased with this new discovery.

All of a sudden, I didn't know what I wanted more, to bury my dick in the back of his throat or impale myself on whatever part of him I could. Whatever I chose, it didn't feel like it would be enough to sate the deviant desire he unleashed in me. I felt like I was on fire, burning from the inside out.

"I need more," I panted, rolling my hips to try and get whatever it was my body wanted, whether it was from his mouth or his hand. Or both.

He looked up at me with a wicked grin, his tongue swirling in my slit. "Yeah?"

"Yeah." I nodded frantically.

"What do you say?"

"Please, Remiel. I want it to feel good." I couldn't believe I was actually asking him to fuck me, but I was. I'd officially lost my mind. Or at least greatly over-committed to this plan.

The hungry gleam in his eyes almost made me combust on the spot. No one had ever looked at me like that before. Or, maybe I'd been too oblivious to notice.

Grabbing a pillow, he wedged it under my ass and tilted my hips a second before he buried his face between my cheeks, licking and probing every inch of me with his wicked tongue.

It felt so much better this time around, maybe because I

kind of knew what to expect. Or maybe it was because I *wasn't* fighting him.

Once he deemed I was ready, Remiel slid between my legs and lined his cock up against my hole. Then it seemed like time almost... stopped. Like he was waiting for something. His silvery gaze locked onto mine like a magnet, refusing to let me look anywhere else.

Before I could ask him what he was doing—or God forbid, beg him to keep going—the head of his dick pressed against me, pushing inside with relative ease.

My lashes fluttered and I felt myself arching to get away from the very thing I'd asked for.

Remiel's hands came down on my hips, holding me in place. "Don't run away from it. Just breathe and open up for me."

I tried to focus on breathing in more than a gasp at a time. I was so... full. I was afraid even the smallest movement from either of us would end up tearing me to pieces, which was stupid, considering I'd survived the first time intact and he'd been anything but gentle.

He ran his hands up my sides and fanned them out over my chest, stroking me gently. "Just relax. You're going to feel so good."

I'd barely nodded before his head ducked low and he sucked my cock into his mouth again.

"Oh my God!" If it wasn't for his hands planting firmly on my chest, I might have come off the bed. To have him inside of me, blurring that line between pain and pleasure, was one thing. But to add his mouth back into the mix? It was the greatest feeling I'd ever experienced. I should have been sickened by guilt, but then he would roll his hips, moving in and out gently while lavishing attention on my dick and I stopped caring about anything other than the rush of pleasure coursing through me.

Without thinking, I reached for his head, lacing my fingers through his hair and pulling it away from his face. The sight was absolutely unreal. His perfect lips wrapped around my dick, the unbridled lust in his mercurial eyes.

He dragged one hand down my stomach and gripped the base of my shaft, stroking me in time to his steady thrusts while continuing to circle the crown of my dick with his tongue.

A strangled cry left the back of my throat. All of the sensations were... I didn't even have a word for it. I couldn't think. I couldn't even see clearly, despite the fact I was watching Remiel's mouth with rapt attention. The world around me was hazy, like I was drunk on the lasciviousness of it all.

Remiel grabbed my arms and pulled me forward into his lap without warning, burying himself inside completely. My yelp of surprise was muffled by another one of his searing kisses. I tangled my fingers in his long hair, stroking his tongue with mine. His hands ran up and down my back, clawing now and again as he thrust up into me. Each sting made me shiver, ratcheting up the tension inside of me until I was matching Remiel's thrusts from below, grinding myself against him.

"Are you going to come for me?" he asked, biting my shoulder.

"Yes," I panted, tightening my grip on his hair.

"Good." He grabbed my hips again, fucking into me so hard I saw stars.

It only took a couple more thrusts and the dam inside of me broke. A pathetic mixture of moans and grunts came out of me as I shot my release all over the both of us.

Remiel swore under his breath before crushing his lips to mine. He held me close, mess and all, and kept kissing me until he came too. I felt him spill, his cock pulsing inside. In a way, it was somehow satisfying to know I'd caused it. Satisfying and so *very* wrong. Sinful. Beyond sinful.

When his hips slowed and the rocking stopped altogether, he tore his swollen mouth from mine and met my heavy-lidded gaze with his own. "You're so fucking perfect, Phelan."

Burying my face in the side of his neck, I closed my eyes, letting out a ragged breath.

I never knew what to say when people complimented me, but I was even more tongue-tied when it came to Remiel. As crazy as it was, at that moment a small part of me believed him.

God help me.

CHAPTER TWELVE

PHELAN

Laying in Remiel's bed in the aftermath, I stroked his feathers idly, marveling once again at their softness. He didn't seem to mind since he made no move to stop me and it was easier to focus on something trivial like that than dwell on what just happened. How good it felt, but how wrong it all was.

"It doesn't hurt you to lay on them?" I asked quietly.

"No," he replied. Since he was on his side, he had one wing folded on his back, but the other was stretched out over the top of me, like a blanket.

"Can you feel this?" I brushed my fingers backward and forward over the feathers, making sure not to touch the wing structure itself.

"Yes," he murmured, lifting his steely gaze to mine.

I ran the tip of my finger over the black edges. "Were they always like this?"

"No."

"Did it happen when—"

"Since your mouth is so bored, why don't you put it to

use elsewhere?" He drove his question home by taking my hand and pressing it against his cock, hard once more.

"Again?" I blinked. "But we just..." Glancing down at him, I gaped at the fact he was, indeed, ready to go for another round.

"Consider it a compliment." He ran his hand over my chest, raking his nails across my skin on the way back.

"I don't think I'm flattered." I'm sure it had absolutely nothing to do with me and everything to do with the fact he was insatiable.

"You should be. After all, I did kill two of my soldiers for you." He rolled on top of me, using his knee to spread my legs wider, making room for himself, while he kissed my neck.

"That *was* you." The final piece of my memory from that fateful night slid into place. I remembered it all, now. The summoning. The way the demons broke through from the other side. The way they cowered before him. Even though I hadn't seen Remiel at the time, I saw the fear he inspired in creatures wrought from nightmares. It was mesmerizing, in a way, and utterly terrifying.

A flutter of nerves ran through me at the realization. Never in a million years did I imagine a demon that powerful, that fearsome to his own kind, would set its sights on me. While the devout tended to be prime demonic targets, I couldn't remember the last time I heard of a Necromancer being abducted, let alone taken by a prince.

Remiel swirled his tongue over my pulse point, rolling his hips against mine. He was clearly done talking, but I hoped to distract him a little longer. I didn't think I could handle him forcing another orgasm out of me, especially not so soon after the last one.

"Why?" I asked quickly. "Why did you do it?"

"Because you're mine, pet." He practically growled his reply, locking his narrowed gaze on me, as if daring me to challenge his statement. "And no one touches what's mine without permission."

"I don't understand." Dragging my fingertips along his sharp cheekbone, I brushed his hair behind his ear, giving me a clearer view of his face and the way his jaw shifted irritably. "Why me?"

"What is there to understand? I saw something I wanted and I took it."

"That's it?"

The corners of his eyes tightened, but I couldn't tell if it was amusement or annoyance. "Don't look for a deeper meaning. You'll only disappoint yourself."

"When did you first see me? That night?"

He groaned, definitely in the annoyed sort of way, and went back to kissing my throat.

I caught his face between my hands and lifted it toward me again. "Please talk to me. Then we can do… whatever it is you want to do."

"Fine." He rolled his beautiful eyes, pulling out of my hands with a curled lip, but not actually climbing off of me. "The woods. The morning after you killed a duke."

"Oh." Shit! I *knew* I'd felt something that morning, some uneasiness stirring in the pit of my stomach. I thought it was Mary Oliver or some other cantankerous spirit trying to scare me off. That explained a lot, though—the surge of power I felt, the way my life turned upside down in the weeks that followed, the sense I was never alone.

"Yes, 'oh,'" he said with a smirk. "I claimed you as mine before you'd even left the clearing. Your fate was sealed. And now you belong to me."

"Forever?"

"Until the end of days."

I nodded, caressing the side of his face again. "Thank you for answering."

The second time I reached my hand upward, I pressed my palm against his forehead and spit out a command in Latin. "*Sleep*."

Remiel crumpled on top of me, unconscious.

"Fuck." It took everything I had to shove his dead weight off of me. Guess I hadn't thought *that* part through.

As soon as he was clear, I sprang out of bed and ran for the chamber door. Tearing it open, I flew into the darkened tunnel in the opposite direction the lizard-demon dragged me the other day. There had to be a portal somewhere, a literal way out of this hellhole, I just had to find it before Remiel woke up and before any other demon spotted me. The problem was, I had no idea how many demons there were here or what any of them would do to me if they caught me.

But I couldn't think about any of that.

This was my one chance at escape. If I failed, I knew I'd never get a second one. If he didn't kill me outright, Remiel would never trust me again and I could only imagine the punishments he would dole out.

When the tunnel turned and the uneven ground beneath my feet started going higher, I picked up my pace and rushed to the end, colliding with a heavy door in the dark. I swore under my breath and fumbled for a handle. My fingers found purchase on a large, metal bar and I yanked it to the side. The door swung inward with a low groan and I darted through the opening to the world outside.

Fear propelled me out into the darkness, through gusts of freezing air and clouds of sulfur. The castle was perpetually warm, but outside? I was surprised how cold it was. It wasn't how I pictured Hell at all, which was both a relief and a surprise.

Wrapping my arms around myself, I moved past gnarled trees with claw-like branches and rock formations that looked like people had been trapped inside, screaming in pure agony. I wished desperately for clothing I didn't have, but the adrenaline pumping through my veins kept my limbs in motion. And if I kept moving, eventually I'd find my way. I *had* to.

"God, grant me the strength to make it through this," I whispered to myself. "Please don't let me die down here."

CHAPTER THIRTEEN

REMIEL

As soon as Phelan pushed me off, I blinked myself awake.

"Well, that's interesting," I murmured to myself, watching Phelan's backside as he fled from my chambers without so much as a backward glance.

Since I had no need for sleep, I was surprised his magic even had an effect on me. It wasn't long-lasting, but it was obviously enough to give him a slight advantage—something that *wouldn't* happen again, no matter how doe-eyed and sincere he looked. I knew now it was all a ruse and I couldn't believe I was stupid enough to fall for it.

Shimmering from my chambers to the top of the battlements, I watched from the darkness as Phelan made his way down the central pathway, ducking into shadows of his own every time a sound echoed through the dark stone labyrinth.

Eventually he'd reappear, pressing onward. Determined as ever.

I'm sure he had no idea where he was actually going, but his innate sense of direction was fascinating to watch.

At every fork in the road, he picked the correct one—climbed the right hill, avoided the traps, slowly making his way toward escape.

Melech crept up next to me, growling low. "You're not stopping him?"

Stop him? No. I wouldn't be stopping him. His tenacity made him all the more appealing. Besides, it was one of the easiest ways to figure out what the witches were planning. No doubt he'd run straight to them, regaling them with his horrendous ordeal and basking in their sympathy for a change. If they were in league with Hazael, there would have to be some sort of communication between them and I'd make sure someone was in place to intercept it, even if that meant I had to watch over Phelan myself until the truth was revealed.

I threw Melech a bored glance, irritated that he couldn't see the bigger picture for himself. "Make sure he makes it back to his people unharmed. I don't want any of those creatures down there harrying him on his way. If they get within three feet of him, destroy them. Painfully."

"What about the Land of the Dead? The forest?"

"Make sure he makes it back to his people unharmed," I reiterated slowly. "If you can't fend off a few angry spirits, then what good are you to me?"

"Sire." He inclined his horned head and drifted down the battlements, keeping his insulted growl to a minimum.

"Oh, and Melech?"

The demon paused, looking back.

I met his gaze and held it, so there'd be absolutely no misunderstanding me. "If I find out you touched him without my permission, I'll crucify you." It wasn't an empty threat. I would personally tend to his misery, enjoying every second of it if he or *anyone* so much as laid a finger on what was mine.

Melech's tail whipped back and forth, but he was wise enough not to reply. He merely grunted acknowledgment of the promise and carried on.

Phelan was already scaling the craggy walls, making his way slowly but surely toward the sliver of silver light at the top of the rocks. Once he crested it, he'd realize he reached the gated walls of my domain and the Land of the Dead lay beyond them, a place I'm sure he was intimately familiar with as a Necromancer. But first, he'd have to traverse the Forest of the Damned, where even the bravest witches hadn't ventured in all my years on earth. If he could survive the horrors there, he could survive anything.

My gaze lingered for another moment, admiring my feisty little pet all the more as he rested at the top of the wall, peering at the shadowy vastness beyond. He was full of surprises, a fact that thrilled me to no end. I couldn't wait to see what he did next. But for now, I'd have to content myself with memories of our brief time together until the next time I could see him.

CHAPTER FOURTEEN
PHELAN

Literally climbing out of the pits of Hell was never something I imagined myself doing. But it was only the first leg of the journey home.

The next was the Land of the Dead.

At least... I thought it was the Land of the Dead.

As soon as I scaled the outer walls protecting Remiel's castle, I landed none too gracefully on the cold, damp ground beyond. The syrupy scent of pomegranate and frankincense replaced the smoke and brimstone I'd just escaped. I exhaled a relieved breath and forced myself to my feet to carry on.

Like all Necromancers, I'd had my share of crossing over and wandering the dark, misty landscape. But this place was different... It smelled like the spirit realm I was used to, except with an underlying rot and sense of dread.

I wasn't in the Land of the Dead, then. Or at least not the one I was used to. I had no idea what this place was or what fresh terror awaited.

Skeletal trees soared upwards, disappearing into the darkness above, while rivulets of dark crimson ran down their ghostly trunks. Claw marks slashed into the bark here and there, like wild creatures had treed their prey and then tore them to shreds. If I looked closely, I could see strands of hair and chunks of flesh caught on some of the jagged, broken branches.

I shivered as something hard crunched under my bare feet, but I didn't dare look down. I was too busy glancing from side to side, mindful of every shriek and howl and agonizing scream in the distance. Screams that ended in gurgles and wet slapping sounds, like hunks of meat being prepared for a barbecue. Sounds of something gnashing. Something eating.

Something bumped my head and I ducked instinctively. Looking up, I gasped and stumbled backward, catching myself against a tree.

Dozens of corpses floated overhead in various stages of decomposition. They bobbed on an invisible wind, knocking into one another and against the trees, but never drifting off, like they'd been lassoed together by some unseen force.

The foot that had touched me dangled from a woman's leg, attached by a scrap of skin and tendon. It faced the wrong way, along with her head. Half of her face was missing, the skin ripped clean off so the glistening bone glowed eerily in the darkness. She grinned at me, her dislodged eyeball swaying as her body floated with the others.

"God help me," I whispered, crossing myself.

"God doesn't exist here," the woman whispered back.

Backing away slowly, I didn't dare turn my back on her or her floating companions until they were nothing more than grayish-green blobs in the distance.

The floating corpses gave way to a slew of mangled bodies, twisted and hardened into stones lining the path.

Beyond that, the trees shifted and moved, turning toward me and swaying closer. I thought it was my eyes playing tricks on me until I saw a hand clawing at me from *inside* the tree. The bark stretched but never broke, keeping whatever it was contained. Ghastly faces pressed against the white and gray trunks, contorted into horrible screams, but no sound came out except for a low moan, like the wind in the trees.

I hurried onward.

I didn't know how long I wandered. Each second felt like an eternity.

All I knew was that I couldn't give up, nor could I sit still. Who knew how long I had before Remiel woke and sent his horde after me. There had to be a way out, like his castle, and I'd keep walking until I found it.

Dry leaves scraped my ankles and I paused. Despite the multitude of trees, there hadn't been any foliage before now.

A glimmer of hope struck me and I followed the leaves at a quicker pace.

The ghostly forest faded into a regular one, complete with the smell of damp earth and dark berries. The smells of home.

In the distance, a pair of trees grew together near a rocky outcropping, their branches intertwined in an arch.

"The North Woods," I whispered, stumbling toward it.

We'd all been warned as children not to venture near portals in the woods for fear of what might be lurking. Hester, in particular, had been adamant about it, and as one of the few witches who could move easily between realms, we believed her.

But there was a reason the original Winslow settlers chose *that* spot for their village—the natural portal was a source of magic in the land, magic that could be tapped into and harnessed to keep their community safe from the natives, other settlers, and demons alike. It made the original witches stronger, no matter what sort of magic they practiced.

And now, God willing, it would be my ticket home.

Hurling myself through the space between the trees, I landed hard on the ground with a grimace. Pain radiated from my face, where it smacked into the damp, leaf-covered ground, all the way to my toes. But as much as my body ached, I couldn't let myself lay there.

Scrambling to my feet, I took a second to get my bearings, to see if I'd managed to escape at all or if I'd merely made a fool of myself. But I had the answer, deep in my bones. The smells, the birdsong, the way the splashes of sunlight through the leaves warmed my bare skin. I'd made it back.

Offering my thanks to God silently, I hobbled toward Norwood Bridge, trying to ignore the pain and the renewed sense of fear that at any moment, a legion of demons would rush out of the portal behind me and drag me back to Remiel.

The Corbins were the closest refuge, so that's where I went.

Showing up on my kinfolk's doorstep, naked and dirty, was also on the list of things I never thought I'd do, but I swallowed my pride and rang the bell, immediately pounding on the door to make sure someone heard me.

I was still knocking when the front door swung open. Cassius took one look at me and yanked me into the house, eyes wide.

"Oh my God! What happened?!"

"Is your father home?"

He shook his head, leading me to the parlor and wrapping a chenille throw around my shoulders. "He's gone to D.C. for a conference. He won't be back until next week."

"What day is it?"

"It's Saturday, the Eighth."

I stopped abruptly and looked at him. "What?!" I'd only been gone a day?! But my time with Remiel felt like... forever. No wonder they hadn't rescued me. There hadn't been enough time. That's what Temperance kept talking about.

Cassius raised his brows at me, clearly not comprehending my confusion. "Phelan, what's going on? What happened to you?"

"I need you to call Temperance for me."

"Ok. I will. Let's get you cleaned up first. You look like Hell."

A hysterical laugh threatened to spill out of me at the same time my eyes welled. Truer words had never been spoken. And the relief I felt at being home, being safe in the Corbins' mansion, was overwhelming.

Cassius and I didn't speak again until after I'd showered and changed into the clothing he left out for me. I stared at myself in the bathroom mirror, working up the courage to face whatever family members had been assembled downstairs and trying to decide if I still looked the same. I suppose I did. Tired and bruised, but essentially I looked like the same person who'd literally been to Hell and back while the rest of the world carried on without me. But inside, I was irrevocably changed. A thousand showers couldn't erase what Remiel had done and no amount of clothing could mask that I'd sinned against God in the worst way.

Pain flashed across the black mark on my palm, like it

was agreeing with me. I winced and closed my fist, stuffing the offending hand into my pocket before exiting the bathroom and descending the stairs.

I followed the voices to the kitchen, fully expecting to walk in on half of the Congregation.

Surprisingly, there were only three people—Cassius, Temperance, and Marcus.

They stopped talking immediately and Temperance flew out of her seat, hugging me fiercely. "I knew you could do it."

"I'm sure you would have found a way," I replied, easing out of her embrace with a wince.

"What's wrong?" She didn't even give me a chance to answer. Her hands immediately went to my temples, to see for herself what had happened. Her eyes widened a split second before I knocked one of her hands away, silently cursing her for smothering me and cursing myself for not thinking to have my mental barriers in place. God only knew what she saw. Hopefully whatever glimpse she caught pertained to my escape and not anything that happened during my captivity.

"I'm fine," I said quickly, moving away from her and sitting in the empty space between Cassius and Marcus.

Temperance resumed her seat, her blue eyes clouded with suspicion. My cheeks burned under the weight of her stare, the unspoken judgment washing over me. Did she know what I did to escape? Did she see what transpired between Remiel and I? What I'd begged him for?

"Welcome back," Marcus said. "As I'm sure you know, we have questions for you."

I nodded. "As soon as I get home, I'll document what happened in the Book of Damnation." Mostly... There was a lot that would never see the light of day if I had any say in it. As much as it pained me to edit the historical document in order to save face, I also didn't want my humiliation written out for all of eternity. Hopefully I'd find a way to kill Remiel and no other Necromancer would suffer at his hands again. "How are the others?"

"What others?" Cassius asked, glancing between Marcus and I. "What happened?"

"There was... an incident during last night's summoning," I replied.

"What summoning?"

Instead of answering, I deferred to Marcus. Cassius also turned to his uncle, his dark brows raised expectantly.

Marcus shrugged and spread his hands. "I suppose you're old enough to know. Ever since last year, we've been slowly eradicating the demons in the Book of Lazarus."

"Why?" Cassius blinked.

"That's a very good question," Temperance said, shooting Marcus a glare.

He ignored her. "We're trying to keep Winslow safe, after last year. If there are no more demons to command, then hopefully no one else will do what Claudia and Lennox did. Except a group of demons broke through the barrier last night. Phelan was captured. No one else was seriously hurt, thank God, but before we can proceed with anything we have to locate and banish the demons who managed to escape."

"Well, we know they're connected to the demon who took Phelan," Temperance said, glancing in my direction. "But we couldn't find any records of anyone named Remiel. He's not in any of the main demonologies we have access to."

"Or the grimoires," Marcus added.

It was times like these that it would have been helpful

for witches around the world to share their knowledge with one another through the wonders of technology. But, historically speaking, that never ended well for anyone. Our survival depended on secrecy, even if it circumscribed the information we had to work with.

"His name might not be real, but this is," I said quietly, withdrawing my left hand from under the table and laying it flat, palm up, so they could see.

A collective gasp went around the table.

"His sigil should be enough to find out who he really is. And once we know what kind of demon we're dealing with, we'll know how to defeat him," I said with more confidence than I actually felt. Finding information on a prince was like finding a needle in a haystack. They didn't maintain their position for millennia by being easy targets.

"What else do you know about him?" Marcus asked.

"He's one of the fallen; a prince of Hell. He has some level of telepathy but that's it. That's all I know." It sounded so pathetic that *that* was all I was able to glean from our time together, but it was true. I was sequestered from anyone else, except his henchmen. There was nothing else to indicate what sort of demon he was, what powers he might have, or what (if any) vulnerabilities we could exploit.

"In the meantime, what are we going to do about this?" Temperance asked, gesturing to my hand. "We don't even know what this means for you, what sort of control he has."

Marcus cleared his throat. "Do you feel any different?"

"No." I glanced between them, watching the incredulity on both their faces. "I'm not under his influence! I swear!"

"But how do we *know*?" Marcus continued, choosing his words carefully.

"I don't know," I huffed. "How am I supposed to prove

something like that? Has anyone else in the Congregation ever been marked by a demon? In all the histories I've read, the answer is no! This has never happened in the four hundred years of Winslow's history. Hauntings? Temporary possessions? Yes. But someone actually wearing a demon's mark?" My hand burned all over again, pain and a strange tingling radiating from the center of my palm.

Marcus and Temperance exchanged a long glance, as loud as if they'd told me directly they didn't believe a word out of my mouth.

"I could get some holy water," Cassius offered, interrupting the silent conversation happening across the table.

"Holy water won't work," I said, sliding an irritated look at him. "I'm marked, that's all. I didn't suddenly turn *into* a demon."

"But if you're possessed, wouldn't your body react violently?"

"It would. As much as if you held up a cross or said the name of God... which clearly isn't the problem since *I* just said it."

"Well, there has to be a way to get rid of that thing," Temperance said, glaring at Remiel's sigil. "A banishment spell or some sort of ritual cleanse?"

"What about a binding spell?" Cassius asked.

"No!" The shout came from all three of us, so quickly Cassius shrank back in his chair, blue eyes wide.

"Binding spells are *not* to be used on other witches," I explained, making sure my tone was more pedantic instead of scolding. "It's unethical, to say the least."

"It should be forbidden," Marcus agreed.

"Sometimes they're necessary," Temperance said, patting Cassius's hand, "but not in this case."

"What did the Deacon have to say?" I asked warily.

Peregrine and I had always gotten along well enough, but I'm sure he wasn't going to be happy with what happened. After all, it was his job to keep the Congregation safe, which was almost impossible to do when half of those people were sneaking around behind his back. It was like herding cats.

Marcus and Temperance shared another look that made my stomach twist into knots.

"What?" I glanced between them, looking for the weaker link, the one I could press for the truth they seemed intent on hiding. "What aren't you telling me?"

"We didn't tell him," Marcus said.

A flash of heat radiated from the mark on my hand, my anger or Remiel's amusement? I couldn't tell what all the strange sensations meant and I hated that he might have a perpetual link to me, but right now I was more concerned with what Marcus said. I shoved my hand under the table again, clenching it out of view. "Wh-why not?"

"We couldn't let them find out what happened, what we were doing when it happened," Temperance replied hesitantly.

I cocked my head, staring at her. "I'm sorry? You couldn't what?!"

"It wouldn't be good for the Necromancers," Marcus butted in. "If we told them you were taken by a demon after a group of *other* demons escaped from the circle, they'd start asking questions. Things are finally peaceful in the community. We don't want to reopen old wounds. So, we'll handle it ourselves."

"Old wounds?" I repeated, blinking hard, as if it would help me process what he said. I knew we were hiding this information from Peregrine before, but that was *before*!

Before I was fucking kidnapped by a prince of Hell! I must have still been in Hell...

I glanced around, trying to determine if anything was out of place in the Corbins' kitchen. Even if I couldn't find anything wrong with my surroundings, this must have all been a sick mind game. It was the only explanation for their complete and utter disregard for my well-being.

"The Congregation doesn't need to know about the extent of our dealings with demons," Marcus continued. "News of your capture, unfortunately, would not be received favorably. You *know* that. Outside of the dark families, no one else knows what happened—about you *or* the demons on the loose. It's best for everyone if we kept it that way, especially until we can remove your mark."

"You didn't tell Hester?" I let my gaze settle on Temperance, watching for any minute tic on her face for the real answer. When she lowered her lashes, avoiding me, I knew. "Did you even *try* to find a way to bring me home?" I turned my attention to Marcus next. "Or was I some sacrificial lamb to save face with the nature witches?"

"Of course I tried," Temperance snapped, drawing my ire back to her. "Summoning a demon is one thing, but I've never opened a gateway to Hell, Phelan. And even if I had managed it, there's no guarantee you wouldn't have brought all of Hell with you like before."

"Wow..." I tried to swallow my anger, but it lodged in my throat, choking me. One summoning gone awry in all the years I'd been practicing and suddenly I was a complete failure to them, despite the numerous demons I'd successfully commanded over the years. "Now you sound like Hester."

"It's not like that," Temperance countered, softening, trying to undo the damage she'd already caused.

"The fuck it's not." I stood and pushed my chair in as calmly as I could. "Thank you for your help, Cassius."

He nodded, his arms folded over his chest, trying to make himself as small as possible in the midst of our family feud.

Marcus also remained absolutely silent.

"Phelan, wait." Temperance stood as well, but I ignored her.

I kept ignoring her as I made my way through the house and out the front door. So much for being home, for being back with my family. Remiel was right. I couldn't fucking believe it. I was nothing to them, except a pawn to be sacrificed. A scapegoat if there ever was one.

Temperance caught up to me in the driveway and yanked me to a stop. "Where are you going?"

"Where do you think? Back to Hell where I apparently belong!" I snapped, ripping my arm away from her.

"I tried, Phelan! I did every spell I could. Cast every circle. I even summoned another demon to try and fetch you. I just couldn't get to you!"

"No, but Hester could. You know damn well she could!" I shouted, coming nose-to-nose with my cousin. "She could have brought me back before her goddamn tea got cold! But you didn't tell her! And why is that, I wonder?"

"She hasn't cast anything in decades! Let alone done any sort of astral travel!"

"That's a bullshit excuse!"

"Fine!" Temperance threw her hands in the air. "Because you know she would have left you there, citing the same old 'greater good' bullshit she uses whenever someone brings up Bridget. One person isn't worth risking the safety of the entire Congregation. Right? But I *wasn't* going to abandon you! I was going to keep trying. No matter what. Just like I'm going to find a way to get that mark off of you."

"Leave it," I snapped, shaking my head. "I've been branded my whole life as Bridget Oliver's son—the bastard child of the craziest witch Winslow has ever seen. Everyone always watching, waiting for me to go insane just like her. Now I have a physical mark of shame to go along with it. Too bad it's not a B in the middle of my goddamn forehead!"

"What has gotten into you? The Phelan I know doesn't get angry, doesn't swear, let alone bring God into it."

"Well, the Phelan you knew is as good as gone. He stayed in Hell while this thing in front of you is all that's left and with the way you're looking at me right now, I might as well have not come back at all. I'd serve the Congregation better as a martyr, right? At the very least it doesn't challenge the oh-so-innocent narrative you and the other Necromancers are spinning to cover my apparent fuck up!"

"You didn't fuck up! But you know how complicated things can be."

"Let me *un*complicate them for you." I stormed away from her, heading down the driveway again. Temperance called my name a few times, but she didn't chase after me. It was just as well. I'd always felt like an outsider, even amongst the dark families. Now, there was no doubt.

CHAPTER FIFTEEN
PHELAN

In the days following my return, I couldn't shake the feeling that Remiel was still nearby, watching me. It was the same feeling I had before, the sense I was never truly alone even in my thoughts. I vacillated between being unnerved by the idea he could snatch me away at any time and, more alarming, nonplussed at the prospect.

His mark remained as black as ever. No amount of scrubbing, praying, or spellwork would remove it. I practiced hiding it for when I inevitably had to be near people again, but when I was alone I found myself staring at it, tracing the lines, wondering what he was up to. He *had* to know I was gone. So, why hadn't he come for me? Perhaps the house's magic was enough to shield me from him. Three centuries' worth of sacrifice and protection spells had to be good for something. Right?

But I couldn't hide in here forever. Eventually, on the most basic level of survival, I'd have to restock my pantry. Plus, I had a job and responsibilities to the rest of my family, even if the majority of them had hung me out to dry. Temperance and Peter had left the most messages—one checking on me to make sure I was ok and begging me not to be mad at her, and the other to say the sleeping potion was finally ready. Not that it would do me any good at this point. Potion or not, there was no way I could get Remiel out of my head, not with his sigil flaring hotly at the most inopportune times.

So, no, as much as I wanted to live inside my tiny bubble, playing with the spiders and catching up on all of the menial tasks I'd been putting off, I knew I'd have to leave the house sooner or later and I'm sure the demon prince would be outside, waiting to run me down like prey.

A steady dripping filled the otherwise quiet house.

Sighing, I set my crochet project to the side and ventured to the stove, taking down one of the pots that hung overhead. I followed the sound of continuous splatters to the living room and set the pot beneath the newest leak, making a mental note to crawl up there and check the roof whenever I made it outside again.

Thunder rumbled in the distance and the rain picked up, pattering against the windows with an increased staccato. Lightning flashed, illuminating a face in the window.

I jumped and squeezed my eyes shut, willing my heart to slow down before it burst. It was *my* face, reflected back at me. Nothing more.

Since I was seeing things that weren't there, I took it as an indication I needed sleep—desperately—despite the fact that's all I'd more or less done since holing up in the house. If I wasn't doing mindless tasks or chores, I was curled up in bed, wondering what God's plan was for me now, especially after I'd thrown away thirty years' worth of discipline and sacrifice. All because I wasn't strong enough to hold out for a rescue that was probably never coming in the first place.

Turning out the lights in the kitchen, I headed up the narrow staircase to my room, leaving my problems and rising resentment for another day.

The house creaked around me, shifting as the wind blew through the crevices. It wasn't alarming until a rush of cold air swept down the staircase.

I paused mid-step, listening.

Hearing nothing but wind and steady rainfall, I shook my head and carried on, although the chill air continued to swirl around my ankles as I moved into my bedroom.

The window was open.

Furrowing my brows, I glanced around before crossing to it. I pushed the sash down and turned the lock, taking a moment to peer out into the inky blackness in the yard. Nothing moved beyond the wavy glass. Nothing shimmered. And nothing revealed itself with each lightning strike. Why was I looking for something that wasn't there?

I moved away from the window, unbuttoning my shirt while I wandered over to the armoire in the corner. As I shrugged out of the garment, something whispered across my skin, chasing the material as it slid down my arms. It wasn't a spider. It was moving too fast to be one of them. Whatever it was, I ignored the wave of goosebumps and tossed my button-up in the hamper.

It was harder to ignore the caress over my ass and down my thigh as I slipped out of my jeans.

"Stop it," I hissed, turning abruptly and heading straight for my bed, swatting the light switch downward on my way by.

First I was seeing things, now I was feeling them.

My mind was playing tricks on me, that was all. My body was unable to draw a line between the memory of what happened in Hell with something innocent and perfectly explainable in the present. It was always worse at night; I knew that. It was best not to pay any attention to it, so that's what I did. Ignored it. Stuffed the feelings into a bottle and cast it as far away from me as possible.

I crawled underneath the quilt and settled onto my side, facing the window. Lightning streaked behind the wall of clouds, a faint crack of light in the black sky, much like the sliver of light that guided me to my freedom from the underground.

How had I even managed to escape? The journey itself still seemed unbelievable, that the creatures who growled and hissed at me from the shadows never actually tried to stop me. I'm sure it had nothing to do with me and everything to do with my sadistic captor. Maybe they smelled him or sensed his mark and decided it was best to steer clear of me altogether. In a way, I suppose I should have been grateful.

I closed my eyes, unwittingly thinking of Remiel.

Who was I kidding? He was all I could think about now. Before, when I hoped he was a figment of my imagination, I could find a way to distract myself for periods of time. That ceased being an option the moment I woke up chained to a table in Hell as his personal plaything.

Something warm slid around my throat, constricting my airway. A soft, even hotter sensation pressed against my ear, my cheek, the side of my neck, hungry and insistent like his kisses had been.

"It's not real," I whispered, refusing to open my eyes, even a peek. The pressure increased on my throat and I gasped, fingers digging into the sheets. It wasn't real. It couldn't be. Demons couldn't come into the house.

The warm sensation continued, memories of Remiel's hands roaming over my bare skin. The feeling invaded my own hand, making it skim along my waist and straight to my dick, palming it over the top of my boxer briefs. A wave of sparks rushed down my spine.

Not nearly enough friction, apparently, my hand slipped beneath the waistband. I sighed as my fingers wrapped around my semi-hard cock and gave it a few lazy tugs.

I shouldn't. I knew I shouldn't. I should fight the ghostly hand guiding mine, stroking my shaft as it grew rigid in my fist. Remiel already took so much from me. I couldn't let him take my discipline, too. My restraint. My... fuck. My self-control.

With an irritated huff, I rolled onto my stomach and shoved my traitorous hand under the pillow, trying to get comfortable in a positively uncomfortable situation.

Falling asleep had been difficult since my return, as was the actual sleeping part, despite the many hours I spent in bed. I found myself jerking awake with every little noise, then tossing and turning for the remainder of the night. So trying to fall asleep with a hard-on certainly didn't make things any easier.

A faint, wispy feeling floated across my shoulders, like feathers.

Just the wind again, seeping through the cracks in the window frame, I told myself.

It traveled downward, along my spine, to the small of my back.

It was just goosebumps. From the cold air. Making the sensitive hairs stand on end. Nothing more.

I ground my hips into the mattress, simultaneously trying to relieve some of the ache and shimmy deeper under the quilt to block the draft.

Breathing hard, I was vaguely aware that my mouth

had gone dry. Beads of perspiration gathered on my upper lip and I would have sworn the temperature in the room raised by a thousand degrees. I threw the quilt backward and peeled off my underwear, tossing them to the floor. Resuming my position, I bunched the pillow under my cheek and tried to clear my head so I could actually get some sleep.

The wind came back almost immediately, curling over my shoulders, down my spine, brushing along my hips, all the way to my feet and back again. Such a feather-light touch, I wondered if I truly felt it at all.

Closing my eyes, I gloried in the cool air for just a moment before willing it to stop, even though I knew I had zero air abilities. Rolling one shoulder back, as if to tell the wind to knock it off, I nestled into the pillow again.

It didn't matter. The breeze kept dancing over my skin, sending shivers down my spine despite the scorching temperature in the room. Or was it just me? Was I suddenly feverish? It would explain the hallucinations I seemed to be having.

"Stop," I repeated, trying to banish any and all thoughts of the silver-eyed demon.

Absentmindedly, I swiveled my hips, rubbing my persistent hard-on against the mattress. Had they always been such a problem? Before Remiel came into my life, I'd had that part of myself on lockdown. If an erection happened to occur, it was ignored with the same amount of willpower required for any other mundane task. Sadly, things required a great deal more effort these days. Perhaps it was God's punishment. He knew what I did in Hell and He wasn't about to let me forget.

The ache in my dick spread to my balls. The only relief was to shift my hips again. The friction ignited a trail of fire through my body, loosening the knots I'd been carrying for... ever?

I couldn't help but groan as some of the tension lifted.

The warmth from before returned, securing my wrist in its strange snare and pulling it from the safety of the pillow.

"No," I moaned, shaking my head even as my hand slipped beneath my body, stroking my cock again. "No, I shouldn't. I shouldn't..."

My fingers tightened on my shaft, disobeying me.

"Give in," Remiel's voice whispered in my ear. It was easy to imagine he was the one stroking my cock, faster and faster. It was certainly easier to blame him.

But *he* wasn't here.

Still, it didn't stop me from imagining he was. The solid weight of him on my back, his wet kisses along my shoulder and my neck, his knees spreading my thighs open. Even the feeling of his cock pressing inside me, my body stretching to accommodate his size. It was a feeling I could never forget—the way it burned as it filled me up, blurring a line between pleasure and pain I never even knew existed, until it was nothing but total bliss.

I drew in a ragged breath, pushing my hips back to meet the imaginary partner behind me. The memory was so strong a moan fell from my lips as I felt him sink into me all the way, his thighs tight against mine and his hands kneading my ass.

"This is what you wanted, isn't it?" his voice whispered.

"No," I rasped, squeezing the base of my cock to try and stave off the heat gathering in my groin. The memory of Remiel was overpowering. Even now, I could feel the soreness from his relentless thrusting—a delicious burn I never imagined experiencing, let alone wanting.

"Liar." His voice sounded so real, like he was right

behind me, his breath hot on the back of my neck and his fingers clawing through my hair. "I feel you tightening around my cock. Already so close to that release you're so desperate for. Let me give it to you."

Thrusting down into my hand and the mattress, I squeezed my eyes shut, trying not to roll my hips. I didn't want him to be right, even if it was all in my head. He'd forced me to sin before. God could forgive that if I showed enough penance. This? This was all on me and I had to stop. But I couldn't.

I pushed myself up onto all fours, effectively removing the temptation of my hand *and* the mattress. Remiel's memory, however, I couldn't shake. Phantom caresses swept over my back, my hips, gliding along my muscles. An intense pressure dug into my ass so hard I gasped, like he really was there, grabbing onto me.

"Mmm, that's perfect, pet. Right where I want you."

He was everywhere all at once, and yet I was alone, filling the room with my torrid moans and whimpers. God, I *was* desperate. And I was angry. I hated him; hated what he did to me, hated that some depraved piece of me wanted it. I mean, that's what was happening. Right? Why else would I think of him so vividly? Remembering the smell of cinnamon in the curve of his neck, the taste of honey on his skin. I should have forgotten it all, forced it from my mind. And yet...

"Are you going to come on my cock?" Remiel's silken voice broke through my haze of thoughts. "Hmm? Such a needy little sinner already. I bet I don't even have to touch yours. You're so close. Just listen to you. That ragged breath, trying so hard to be good when you know deep down you're not. Deep down, you know this is what you want."

"Oh, God..." I squeezed my eyes shut, trying to block out

his voice. It was impossible with my ass in the air, as vulnerable now as I'd been before to his ravaging. The memories of his cock inside me were so real I could hear the sound of our skin slapping together. I could feel each thrust, angled just so in order to maximize the fire burning inside of me, stroking and gliding along some part of me that begged for more.

I clawed the mattress, panting, trying to stop myself from combusting on the spot.

"Come on, pet. Give it to me. Give me that release. I want to feel you tremble beneath me."

"No," I moaned, even as my body hurtled toward the rapture he was offering.

"Yes," he hissed.

Something curled around my throat again and squeezed, pulling me up onto my knees. I gasped for air only to pant it back out, my labored breathing matching each thrust. The sting of teeth sank into the back of my shoulder and I was done for.

I came with a cry, hands-free as my inner demon taunted, jetting cum onto the mattress in wave after wave until I collapsed in a heap on top of it.

The world around me spun. The solid weight on my back remained, absorbing each shudder as the aftershocks rolled through me, twitching through my exhausted muscles.

In my delirium, I remembered the feeling of Remiel's climax as well—a satisfied groan, followed by his silvery laughter. "So perfect, pet. You feel so good when you're being so bad."

My eyelids drifted shut, overcome with exhaustion on too many levels to count. I'd deal with my sinfulness in the morning. For now, I just needed sleep.

I didn't remember picking the quilt up off the floor, but when I woke in the morning it was there, draped over my shoulder.

Rubbing my eyes, I forced myself up into a sitting position. Despite the restful sleep, every muscle in my body ached. It felt like I spent the whole day climbing when I knew I hadn't.

The sheets beneath me were stained with… something. I picked up the edge of the quilt and glanced down at myself, swearing silently. Guess that explained *that*.

Scrambling out of bed, a wince marred each movement. Still, I did my best to ignore the unusual pain as I stripped the bedding and wadded it up into a ball. On my way to the hamper, something white fluttered in my periphery. I stopped abruptly and took a breath before I turned to face it.

A single white feather lay on the floorboards, its tip an inky black.

Stooping slowly to try and accommodate the screaming protest in my body, I picked up the feather and twirled it between my fingers.

It couldn't be.

There was no way he could get into the house. Even if he had, there's no way he'd leave again without me. The feather had to belong to a bird. An exceptionally large bird… with markings unlike any I'd ever seen in these woods. *That* was the logical explanation. It had to be because I refused to believe in the alternative.

My gaze dropped to the bundle of soiled linens gathered in one arm as my dream from the night before replayed in my mind. The twinges in my body paralleled the events unfolding in my memory. Remiel's hands, his mouth. His voice...

I want to feel you tremble beneath me.

I shook my head, refuting the evidence in my hands.

"No. It wasn't real," I said, standing again and marching across the room to the fireplace. I struck a match and threw it inside the hearth, the sheets right after it. Holding the feather for a moment longer, I glanced between it and the steadily rising flames.

If it was a regular feather, I had nothing to lose.

If it was one of Remiel's... maybe I could use it to remove the mark. Transfer it, somehow, or use it as part of a banishment.

Erring on the side of caution, I cracked open the decorative box on the mantel and slipped the feather inside. Until I did more research, it would be foolish to get rid of something that could potentially benefit me. Kind of like burning my sheets.

My shoulders sank as I looked at the mound of regret smoldering in the fireplace. I'd have to buy another set the next time I went to the store, whenever I managed to work up the nerve to leave the house again.

CHAPTER SIXTEEN

REMIEL

Screams echoed off the dark, windswept stone around me.

I gazed down at my realm from my lofty perch, taking in the suffering that stretched across the horizon. It used to give me pleasure to hear those screams, to know that the agony all around me could be stopped with a snap of my fingers if I so chose. At the very least, I took satisfaction from a job well done. Now? It had lost its appeal. Not for any moral purpose, since morality had no place in Hell.

No, I was simply... bored.

Without Phelan around, the days had grown increasingly dull. Spying on him from afar no longer held the same thrill, not when I'd had him all to myself to play with. The only reason I hadn't reclaimed him immediately and dragged him back to Hell was that I was still waiting on him or someone in his precious little Congregation to make contact with Hazael so I could finally learn what they were really planning. But so far, that plan had led absolutely nowhere. Either they weren't communicating with him, or they'd found a way to do it without leaving a trace. I didn't know which was more frustrating.

Unfortunately for me, the mere thought of my redheaded nemesis brought a snarl to my lips along with unwanted visitors to my gate.

Before the guards could so much as move to raise the massive iron portcullis, my wings snapped open and I leapt off the stone ledge, gliding over the wall and landing on the other side. If these unwelcome emissaries thought I would receive them *inside* my castle walls, they were dead wrong. I'd never allow another demon's servants to enter my realm, even under the guise of peace.

Hazael's stench invaded my nostrils, but he wasn't amongst the small army of minions bowing and scraping at my feet with nervous huffs and snorts. "What do you want?"

"A message." A lump of mottled brown flesh and fur limped forward, holding out a scrap of paper to me.

Snatching it out of the proffered claw, I unfolded it. Before I could so much as read the first line, Hazael's cretins attacked. They swarmed me from every angle, claws and fangs ripping into me, blades stabbing as deep as they could.

Behind me, the guards stationed at the wall shouted. The heavy portcullis clanked and groaned, lurching upward a little at a time.

I flung a pair of Hazael's imps to the side, conjuring my armor and sword. Once I was equipped, I hurled a ball of black flames at another. The creature howled and thrashed about while I stabbed one of its compatriots and proceeded to rip it in half, freeing my sword from its ribcage.

The winged demons in my legion soared over the rampart, dispatching any ghoul that stood in their way. I appreciated their efforts to try and clear a path for me, but the task was impossible. For every fiend we managed to slay, two more appeared to take its place, popping up out of the barren ground like invasive weeds.

The original messenger appeared in front of me, throwing a vial of liquid in my face. It burned my eyes on contact, blurring my vision and filling the air with the smell of my own scorched flesh.

My outraged yell morphed to one of pain as something sharp and heavy slammed into my back, puncturing deep beneath the back of the protective collar I wore.

Whatever it was, it dropped me to my knees.

I slashed outward, blindly, with my sword while trying to reach behind me and dislodge whatever it was they'd impaled me with.

Unable to reach it, and with the sound of Hazael's reinforcements on the way, I had two options: bleed out before the portcullis could finish raising or flee.

I hated both prospects.

Even if my soldiers could reach me in time, I'd have to rely on another demon to actually help me instead of seizing the opportunity to advance their own position by handing me over to Hazael, weakened as I was.

But where would I flee? I was still a target inside my own castle, especially with Melech away, following up on the information Jabez had made note of before his murder.

No, there was only one place I could go—one place no one, in *any* realm, would look for me. One place I could take the time I needed to heal from whatever weapon Hazael managed to procure. One place I would be safe from him or any other opportunistic demon.

Using the little strength I had left, I sought out Phelan

across time and space. Like a light in the dark, I found him and latched on.

I meant to materialize in front of him calmly, take stock of the situation and assume command as I always did. But when I came into view in his living room, I collapsed in a heap at his feet, unable to maintain my posture let alone any pretense of superiority. My vision was slowly coming back, but it was fuzzy at best, and he was more of a blur than anything.

"What the—?!" Phelan jumped out of his chair, dumping a book on the ground as he danced back out of reach. "How did you get in here?"

"You have to help me," I panted, pushing myself into an upright position on my knees. Once I was vertical, I unhooked the shoulder guard on my right and let it clatter to the floor. The left fell a moment later, leaving only the breastplate in place. I stupidly lifted my arm, trying to unhook it from behind my neck. A wound in my side split wider, releasing a fresh wave of blood.

Phelan grabbed a poker from the fireplace and brandished it like a weapon. "The hell I do! I should be grateful to whoever did this and finish you off!"

"You can't." I pressed my hand against my ribs, but it did little to staunch the flow of blood. Even if it had, I was still bleeding in other areas. I could feel it dripping steadily down my back with each ragged breath.

"God makes exceptions!"

"You'll die too."

"What?" The poker lowered slightly.

"You and everyone else I've marked. I die, you all die. And then you all belong to Beliar. No redemption. No forgiveness. Eternal damnation in the darkest pits of Hell." Hopefully I painted enough of a picture for him that he'd come to his senses. With each second that passed, my vision got a little darker around the edges.

"You're lying," he said through his teeth.

My laugh ended in a grimace. "Am I?"

With a frustrated growl, he threw the poker to the side but still made no move toward me. "I'm not a healer! What do you expect me to do for you? Call 911?"

I shifted on my knees with a wince, trying to widen my stance and bow my head so he could see what the issue was. Unfolding my tattered wings, I revealed whatever it was that had been rammed into my spine, right where those ghouls knew I couldn't reach it.

"Oh my God…" Phelan circled me warily. "What is that?"

"Take it out and I'll tell you all about it."

"Is this why you're not healing?"

"Phelan," I whispered, trying to keep my breathing even. "Come here."

Surprisingly, he knelt next to me, the crease between his brows deepening.

I seized him by the throat and hauled him closer. "Take the fucking thing out or I'll make sure we both die in agony."

"You don't want to die," he tossed back with a smirk. "Of all the places you could have gone, you came here. You could have crawled off into a hole somewhere or gone to anyone else, but no. You came to *me*, thinking I would save you to save myself." He shook his head. "I've been ready for death since the age of thirteen. So you're going to have to give me a better incentive."

"What happened to your sense of Christian charity?"

"I don't know. I think it disappeared right around the

time you held me against my will. Not to mention everything *else* you did against my will."

I rolled my eyes, trying to ignore the pain radiating through my body. "What do you want? An apology?"

"Wouldn't hurt."

My eyelids grew heavier. A tremble rushed through my limbs and I knew he felt it in my hand, my grip weakening with each word. "I'm sorry."

"No, I mean a *real* apology."

I gritted my teeth. "All's fair in love and war, pet. I make no apologies."

"We're not *at* war."

"Then why is your family killing mine?!" I didn't mean to shout it, but I did, after which I couldn't even catch my breath again.

Phelan's expression softened. "Those demons were your family?"

I opened my mouth to answer, but the answer never came. The world blurred over completely and went black. The last thing I saw was Phelan's wide eyes before my head smacked into the ground.

CHAPTER SEVENTEEN

PHELAN

Add taking care of a demon to the list of things I never envisioned doing in a million lifetimes.

After Remiel passed out, I stared at the jagged hunk of wood sticking out of his back, trying to decide what the best option was. I wasn't lying. I *wasn't* a healer by any stretch. The only medical knowledge I had came from fourteenth-century monks and *that* was based on the concept of the four humors which went out of fashion as soon as the Western world discovered germ theory.

Unhooking the piece of black armor from around his neck, I slid it out of the way and undid the lacing on the back of the breastplate. That, however, I couldn't move, since he was essentially laying on it. I'd worry about his comfort once I figured out what had injured him so badly.

Remiel's wings were surprisingly easy to maneuver. I unfolded them gently and pushed them open, exposing more of his back. Brushing the bloody feathers out of the way, I leaned in to assess the thing that had impaled him up close. It looked like a stake. Or a spear. Hell, it could have been a tree branch for all I knew.

I went for the simplest method of extraction—wrapped a towel around the wood and yanked as hard as I could. It dislodged after a couple of forceful tugs but the wound didn't heal, so I spent the next twenty minutes using tweezers to pick out the splinters left behind. Rather than waste something that could obviously harm a demon, I stashed the larger piece of wood in a ziplock bag and deposited all of the little pieces in a glass jar. To be on the safe side, I stored them on opposite ends of the house in case Remiel went looking for them.

By the time I came back to his unconscious body, a handful of spiders had come out to investigate the body on my floor. They inched closer and closer to Remiel, like they were testing the waters in case he suddenly woke.

"Shoo." I flapped my hand at them, clearing the way so I could kneel without squishing them all.

The gaping hole in Remiel's back had finally closed, along with the multitude of gashes and puncture wounds. There was still blood all over the place, but his breathing evened out and some of the color had returned to his skin.

Nevertheless, I was glad I brought a bowl of warm water and a rag back to the impromptu surgical site on the floor. The reddish-brown splotches came off his skin easily enough, but his feathers were still discolored. Maybe I should have used soap too.

Soap?! What was I? His caretaker? No. I helped him on the most basic level possible. That was all. Something I would do for anyone, friend or foe. Clearly.

I scoffed at my own stupidity and tucked his wings back into place before rolling him over. Whatever had blistered his eyes was gone now, leaving zero traces for me to analyze. He looked different in the pale yellow light from the fireplace, though. Less... evil. Maybe I was just struck by his mortality. I knew demons could be killed, obviously, but until this moment he'd seemed too powerful to succumb to something as humbling as death.

Removing his ornate breastplate, I added it to the pile of discarded armor and retreated to the kitchen for more supplies. The *important* supplies, more important than worrying about trying to get his feathers clean again, anyway.

I retrieved the things I'd need to scrub his blood out of my floorboards quickly and set about my task before it had time to really set in and stain. I'm sure I could have tried to salvage some of it for a spell or something, but blood wasn't really my thing—not like the Corbins at any rate.

Once everything was clean and put back in its place, I picked up the book I'd inadvertently dropped earlier and resumed my seat.

I read the same page about half a dozen times before I snapped it shut and set it aside, staring at Remiel and the steady rise and fall of his bare chest.

Why was he *here*?

How was he here? Even if my magic wasn't really strong enough to do anything in the waking world, the house had so many wards on it he shouldn't have been able to get in uninvited. I'd never had a demon show up *inside* the house. No Oliver had in the three-hundred-and-fifty years the house had been standing. Yet here he was.

Had we been living with a false sense of security for all these centuries? Could demons really come and go at will in our house, or was Remiel the exception? I mean, there was the whole feather... thing. But I still wasn't entirely convinced it was real. It was a demon's mind trick. That was all. It had to be. Or some sort of PTSD. *That* was the logical explanation, as I'd proclaimed the morning after, and I wouldn't be swayed from it.

My gaze drifted to my palm and his mark. Was this an all-access pass for him? If so, what else did this mark give him access to? Me and "everyone else"? Who was "everyone else"? Did he mark every witch and human he came into contact with? Would I recognize one of his other victims if I came face-to-face with them? Would I inherently know the same demon had laid claim to both of us? Was he off torturing them when he wasn't with me? Stalking them and disrupting *their* perfectly ordered lives?

Clenching my hand into a fist, I forced my attention to the fireplace. Fire was one of the few things I hadn't tried yet. What would happen if I shoved my hand into the flames? Would everything else burn except his mark? Or would the sigil protect me? As tempted as I was to test that theory, I didn't relish the idea of smelling my own flesh burn, no matter how desperately I wanted it gone.

There was another theory I could test, though, especially while he was unconscious...

Kneeling next to Remiel, I leaned over him and laid my palm against his forehead.

Slipping into his mind was easy enough, but navigating the vast darkness was another matter entirely. I had no idea where he'd squirrel away the sort of information I'd need to remove his sigil. Plus, I had to be careful I didn't inadvertently stumble into a trap.

Creeping along, I did my best to tune out the screaming and crying, shrieks and howls of unimaginable pain. At least I couldn't see anything. Thankfully the source of the sounds, as horrible as they were, remained out of view, in the shadows, much like they had in Hell.

A green glow in the distance attracted my attention, so I made my way to it carefully.

As soon as it came into view, I was both surprised and somewhat disappointed.

It was a book. A very old book, by the looks of it, opened to one of the center pages.

A crude drawing of a baby was featured in the middle of the page, the vellum brittle and stained with age. From the faded brownish color, I could only assume the choice of ink was actual blood.

Around the infant was an elaborate circle, ringed with demonic sigils and other strange symbols. The word at the top of the page, however, was unmistakable: *sacrificium.*

Remiel's eyes flew open.

Before I could dart away, he grabbed me and threw me to the side. Instead of letting go, he rolled with me, pinning me beneath him on the hard floor.

"Looking for something?" he snarled.

I strained against him, trying in vain to free myself from his grasp. "Afraid of what I'll find?" Or should say, *found.* I didn't know why a demon would have a spell to sacrifice children in his head, but I had a pretty good idea and I hated him all the more for his callous disregard for innocent lives.

He must not have realized what I saw, since he smiled and leaned closer, his silver eyes shimmering. "Oh, I've missed you, my pet. Life is so boring without you around, pretending you hate me."

"I'm not pretending." I pushed against his bare chest, but he didn't budge. "Get off me."

"I rather like this position." He shoved his knee against my thigh and wriggled closer between my legs, not so subtly pressing himself against me in the process. I'm sure he'd be hard within seconds. He always seemed ready in that regard. Blood loss probably wasn't much of a deterrent. "If memory serves, I think you like it too."

"That's where you're wrong. I don't like anything when it comes to you."

"Lie after lie after lie. My little sinner." He chuckled and brushed his lips over mine. "But since you helped me, I'll give you a respite."

He climbed off slowly and got to his feet, holding out a hand to me.

I looked at his proffered assistance, trying to decide if it was a trick or not, before ultimately slipping my hand into his. He pulled me upward with hardly any effort and let go as soon as I was vertical. Maybe blood loss *was* a deterrent. This was the first time he hadn't tried to maul me since he revealed he was a demon.

"How did you get in here?" I blurted out the question before I could help it, just in case he changed his mind about the mauling.

A slow smile spread across his face and he held a finger to his lips. "Trade secret."

"Were you here before?"

He canted his head, his smile never wavering. "Was I here when?"

"Whenever," I huffed, folding my arms over my chest, suddenly feeling stupid for even trying to get an honest answer out of him.

"You mean, did I come to you in the night?" He swayed forward, circling me slowly like a cat toying with a mouse. "Did I haunt your dreams and put all of those wicked thoughts in your head?" When he stopped behind me, out of sight, his wings unfolded and wrapped around me. A moment later his lips caressed the curve of my neck, but that was all the contact he made. "Did I make you touch yourself? Wishing it was me? Is that what you're asking?"

I squeezed my eyes shut, not wanting to believe a word out of his mouth despite the fact I asked the question. "What do you want from me? Honestly. You could go after any Necromancer. You could take out the whole Congregation if you wanted."

"I could." His hands slipped around my waist and pulled me back against his chest. "But it's you I want."

"Why? Haven't you tortured me enough?"

"Is that what I've done?" His fingers crept beneath the hem of my shirt, splaying across my abdomen. Heat bloomed under his hands, somehow managing to send goosebumps fanning across my skin.

"You know you have. And you said I'd have a respite this time." I pushed through his wings and stormed forward, out of his reach. "We're not in your realm anymore. You don't get to show up here, making demands and forcing me to do what you want. You may have marked me, but that doesn't make me your slave." I mean... it probably did, once I thought about it. But that didn't mean I wasn't going to try and preserve some sense of dignity.

He practically pouted, which I suppose was better than the alternative. "You're awfully moody tonight."

"I wonder why!" I didn't even try to soften the glare I shot in his direction. "I have an archdemon in my living room and there isn't a damn thing I can do about it! I'm glad you're not dead for all of the innocent souls you've apparently laid claim to, but make no mistake—I would be more than happy to cut the black heart out of your chest this very second if I could."

"You're always welcome to try." He extended his hand

toward me, an ornate silver knife flickering into existence on his palm.

Tempting though it was, I pointedly crossed my arms over my chest. "And condemn how many other souls in the process?"

A smirk twisted his lips. "You sound jealous, pet. Are you jealous?" When I didn't deign to answer his question, he bit his lower lip, giving me a once-over before continuing. "Rest assured, you have my fullest attention."

"I don't want your attention. I don't want anything from you except my life back!"

He scoffed, wagging the knife at me like a scolding finger. "Your life. What does that even mean? 'Your life.' This miserable existence? Is that what you call a life? Your Congregation didn't even try to rescue you, little lamb. Your only value to them is being their sacrifice. I told you you shouldn't have been so eager to die for them. I've seen it time and time again, yet you chose not to believe me."

"At least I don't have people running around stabbing me with giant pieces of wood. Doesn't seem like your life is too charmed, either." It was his turn to glare and I smirked in triumph. "What was that, anyway?"

"A giant piece of wood, as you already deduced. Congratulations." He rolled his eyes and sauntered to the bookcase, lazily trailing a finger along the book spines. The knife seemed to have disappeared again, but who knew how easily he could recall it.

I pivoted, tracking him as he moved around the room. "You were bleeding when you got here but when I stabbed you in Hell, you'd already healed by the time you caught up to me. Is it the place that matters? No... because if that were true you would have stayed in Hell. It's the wood, then. What makes it so different?"

He stopped perusing my bookshelf long enough to throw a contemptuous look over his shoulder. "You expect me to answer that?"

"You said you would."

"I lied."

"I figured as much. Doesn't change the fact that I helped you, even after everything you've done. I'd say you owe me something in return."

"Oh really?" He spun to face me again, his arms and his wings spreading wide. "And what is it you'd like, lamb? The world is yours. All you need do is ask."

"Remove your mark."

"Never," he growled, his wings snapping shut.

"Why not? As you've pointed out, I'm nothing! I can't get you power. I can't get you information. What do you want from me?"

"I take joy in watching witches suffer, and you suffer so beautifully, Phelan. You have tragedy in your blood."

"What is that supposed to mean?" I watched him warily as he laughed, crossing back to me with unhurried steps.

His gaze raked up and down my body, half-predatory and half-amused. "You know what it means. You don't belong here and you know it. Deep down, in the darkest part of you that you've tried so hard to forget."

"I suppose you're going to tell me I belong with you, sitting at your feet like a dog for the rest of eternity?"

"Not at my feet—in my bed." He seized me by the back of the neck and pulled me forward, pressing his forehead against mine. "And on the floor and against the wall and anywhere else I can have you. In return, you can have whatever you want. Books. Jewels. Just name it. I'll give you the world."

"I would never give myself over to you like that. You're

loathsome. You represent everything Necromancers stand against."

"You've already yielded," he said, his silken tone taunting. "Willingly. As I recall, you even asked for it. Damn near begged."

"That was part of a larger plan. It wasn't real." I tried to pull away from him, but his fingers dug into the base of my skull, keeping me right where I was.

"Every time you lie to me, your heart beats a little faster. Did you know that?" Remiel slid his fingers up into my hair, twisting hard enough to make me gasp. His lips hovered over mine, a dark smile curving the corner of his mouth. "Just like when I do this. Pull you close. Make you submit. You hate what I make you feel."

"And what is that?" I gritted my teeth, trying to maintain my composure in the face of his relentless assaults. How could he put a label on it when *I* didn't even know what I felt? Except revulsion. I could identify that feeling well enough.

"Blasphemy."

The word had barely registered before his mouth was on mine. I braced my forearms against his chest and tried to push him back, but his other arm snaked around my waist and kept me more or less pinned to him.

When he finally tore his mouth from mine, I gasped fresh air into my burning lungs. He didn't seem similarly afflicted, since he moved on to kissing my throat and biting the side of my neck, his hands roaming all over my body. It was only a matter of time before he got what he really wanted from me. I needed a distraction, something, anything, to throw him off course.

"Tell me about the demons," I spit out, the plan only half-formed in my brain. "The ones you say we killed."

Remiel jerked back, his brows slanted sharply. "What?"

"You said they were your family. Before you passed out. Were they really?" I swallowed thickly and held his silver gaze, waiting to see what his next move would be.

He released me roughly, anger hardening the planes of his face. "What game are you playing at now, Necromancer? Searching for more information to try and use against us?"

"No," I answered honestly. "I'm trying to understand you."

He snorted, his upper lip curling. "There's nothing to understand." He spun on his heel and turned his back, the tips of his wings dragging on the ground as he moved across the room, away from me.

"I don't believe that. I don't think you do, either. What makes an angel fall? What makes a demon care about anything other than himself? Why not just kill me already so there's no escaping you? There's so much to understand about you, Remiel, I don't even know where to start."

He turned suddenly. Something large and dark flew toward me from where he stood. I threw my arms up to shield my face, but nothing ever collided.

A heavy book slammed onto the ground right in front of me and slid to a stop at my feet. The Oliver Family Bible.

"Everything you need to know, witch, is right there," he snarled, stabbing a finger at the Bible. "You don't have to dig any deeper."

"You of all people know this isn't the whole truth," I said, stooping and picking up the fragile book. Though the letters were faded to the point of being illegible, the impression from the embossing was still there: *Oliver Family Bible, Blackbury House, Bayfield, Norfolk.* Carrying it safely in both hands across the room, I returned it to the shelf next to him.

He tilted his head, searching my gaze, the corners of his own eyes narrowed with suspicion.

"Maybe I can help you somehow," I continued softly, mindful of my tone and my heart rate. Now that we were actually getting somewhere, I didn't want anything to spook him. "We can strike a bargain. Something that benefits us both."

"You want to make a deal with the devil?" He arched a brow, a trace of amusement on his lips.

"In a manner of speaking."

"Let me guess, you want me to remove my mark?"

I nodded. "Yes. And in return, I'll help you find a way to defeat Hazael once and for all."

"And if I decline your offer?"

I shrugged, hooking my thumbs in my pockets casually. "Find someone else to save you next time."

"If I die, *you* die."

"So you said. But we both know demons lie."

"Why would I give up what is already mine?" he asked, stepping in front of me and using his body to maneuver me backward against the wall. His wings formed a cage on both sides, cutting off any chance of escape.

"What do you want more?" I tipped my chin up, meeting his gaze without flinching. "One worthless Necromancer or destroying your enemy?"

He licked his lips and leaned in, bracing a hand on either side of my head. "What makes you think I need your help defeating Hazael?"

"If you could have done it by yourself, I imagine you already would have." I didn't shy away from him, even as his lips whispered over mine. I'm sure he could hear my heart stuttering or sense it somehow like he always did.

"And somehow *you're* going to find his weakness? A worthless Necromancer, as you say."

"I'm a research librarian. Gathering information is what I do."

"We'll see about that," he mumbled against my lips, barely even a kiss. His hands caressed the sides of my face as he stepped backward, shimmering out of view.

The temperature in the room dropped by about twenty degrees and I knew I was alone once more.

Exhaling sharply, I closed my eyes and let my head thunk backward against the wall. God help me.

CHAPTER EIGHTEEN

REMIEL

"Hello, lover," I said, appearing out of nowhere next to Phelan in the library. He'd been at it for hours, dragging out book after book and poring over the pages. Now he was in the chained section with the oldest and rarest books Tennebrose had to offer, leafing through a text in Hebrew. I'd popped in and out periodically but my boredom couldn't take much more of this.

Phelan startled and dropped the book on the small table at the end of the row of massive bookshelves, as far as the chain would let the reading material go.

"What are you doing here?" he hissed, glancing around quickly at the same time he grabbed my t-shirt and yanked me around the corner of the bookshelf. He shoved me against it roughly, the old chains rattling over the spines of the aged books.

The fact he didn't spurn the new nickname made me smile, along with how assertive he was being. "Isn't it obvious? I've come to help."

"I don't need your help. I don't want your help. I want you to leave. Now. Before someone sees you."

"Then you're going to have to let go, pet." I slid a pointed glance at his hand, still fisting the front of my shirt. "Unless you like keeping me close." Leaning forward, my lips grazed the corner of his mouth as he jerked backward.

"I don't have time for your games right now."

"Implying you have time later."

"No! Not now. Not later. Not for the rest of eternity. Now would you please go?"

"What's wrong, lamb? I thought you liked having my undivided attention. You sounded *so* very jealous the other day at the thought I'd given anyone else my sigil." I grabbed his hips and pulled his pelvis against mine. The unforgiving denim that was so popular in modern society frustrated me. I hated all of the layers of fabric between us. I wanted to feel him, *all* of him, as much as I wanted him to feel me.

"You're delusional." He stiffened in my arms, craning his neck to glance out at the main section of the library again.

I laid my palm over his heart, tsking him softly. "There it goes. That rapid flutter I've missed."

"If you don't mind, I have work to do. Helping *you*. Remember?" He scowled at me for emphasis.

"I don't mind one bit." I dug my fingers into his hip and slid my other hand up over his shoulder, cupping the back of his neck.

"I said no." He turned his face away, huffing a sigh of sorts when I proceeded to kiss his jaw instead, breathing in the scent of him. Mouthwatering as always and begging to be bitten. "I'm serious, Remiel."

"You're always serious." I traced the shell of his ear with my tongue, just to feel him shiver.

"Do you know how many witches work at Tennebrose?

Not to mention the students. If anyone with any sort of real power sees you, we're both dead."

"I look human," I countered, glancing down at the white t-shirt and gray skinny jeans I'd manifested for the occasion.

"Barely."

I frowned, more than a little put out he didn't appreciate the effort I was making to blend in for him. "What does that mean?"

He gestured at me impatiently, as if the explanation was obvious. Before he could actually verbalize what he was trying to imply, a female voice called out from the other side of the bookcase.

"Phelan? Are you in here?"

"Who is that?" I tried to peer past him as he shoved me farther down the aisle, inadvertently rattling the chains again.

"I'll be right there!" he yelled, slapping a hand over my mouth at the same time. "That is no one," he hissed at me with a glare. "Now you need to go! For real this time!"

I swatted his hand away from my mouth. "And if I don't?"

He clenched his teeth, preparing for a rebuttal no doubt, but the sound of heels approaching stopped him. He tried to shove away from me as fast as humanly possible, but the woman turning the corner still saw something since her eyes about doubled in size.

"Oh. I'm—" She blinked and glanced between us. Wrinkled shirts aside, guilt was plastered over every inch of Phelan's face, along with a crimson stain on his cheeks. His heart hammered in his chest and a fresh wave of fear rolled off of him. "I'll come back."

"No, I was—we, umm. What did you need?" Phelan

took a step toward her, folding his arms over his chest; trying and failing to look nonchalant.

"I had a student ask for the Bayfield Manuscript but it's marked as unavailable. Do you know anything about it?" she asked, stealing another glance at me though she was pretending to be one-hundred percent focused on her colleague.

She wasn't a witch; one glimpse inside her mind told me that much. The thing I did *not* like was how many memories of Phelan were tucked away in the little gray squiggles in her head.

I dug deeper into her subconscious while Phelan sputtered through some excuse or another. He squeezed his eyes shut and rubbed his forehead. "I, um, think that was one of the ones we sent to restoration. The binding was coming loose if I remember correctly."

"Oh. Ok. Do you know when it'll be back?" She snuck another glance at me about the same time I unlocked a treasure trove of touching moments between the two—working side by side, the occasional lunch, and so many long, wistful glances it left me nauseated. *That* was coming to an end that very moment if I had any say.

I sidled up behind the object of her painfully obvious affection and wrapped my arms around Phelan's waist, brushing my lips across his cheekbone, while fixing her with a challenging stare. "Are you alright, lamb? You look ill all of a sudden."

"You do look flushed," the woman agreed hesitantly, forcing her gaze away from me.

A nervous laugh escaped him and he grabbed my hand as it drifted along his abdomen. Crushing it in his, he forced a smile to his face that looked more like a grimace. "I'm fine. Six to eight weeks. It'll be back in six to eight weeks, Veronica."

"Ok. I'll let him know."

"Ok. Great."

The spastic beating of Phelan's heart didn't slow at all, even though I rubbed my thumb in small circles beneath his restricting hand, trying to calm him. If she didn't leave soon, he was either going to suffer some medical malady or I'd throw him over a table and claim him right there in front of her. Maybe both.

"Is this your boyfriend?" the woman asked after an awkward beat.

We answered in unison.

"No!"

"Yes."

"No," Phelan repeated firmly. "No. We're not... together."

"Ok," she said, drawing out each letter. "Well, I will leave you two alone to talk that over. Thanks for your help, Phelan." The woman lingered for another moment before finally turning on her heel and walking away, her shoulders slumped in defeat.

I smiled victoriously.

If I didn't have my arms wrapped around him, Phelan probably would have wilted to the floor the second she was gone. A rush of air left his lungs and his posture crumpled.

"What's wrong, lover?" I said into the curve of his neck. Pulling the collar of his shirt to the side, I dragged my tongue along the newly-exposed skin, licking a droplet of sweat that trickled down from his hair.

"Stop! And stop calling me that!" he snapped, throwing my hands off his waist and darting away from me. He spun with a glare once he was well out of arm's reach. "You cannot just show up here whenever you feel like it an-and get all handsy and tell people we're together!"

I glanced around the vacant aisle. "But we *are* together."

"Not in a literal sense."

"No, a literal sense would be much more fun." I rushed up to him so quickly that he backed himself into the bookshelf, chains jangling as loudly as his rapid heartbeat. I caged him in with my arms, flicking my tongue over his lips. "Oh, I could most certainly fuck you right here. Tie you up with these chains and desecrate all of your precious little books."

Clawing the front of my shirt, he tried to shove me away, using the giant bookshelf as leverage. "You could have cost me my job just by *being* here! Fucking me at work would definitely get me fired and then hauled in front of the Selectmen!"

I rolled my eyes and forced myself to retreat, leaning against the bookshelf across from him. "You say that like it's some great loss."

"It would be to me! I know you don't think much of my life, but it's still *my* life. I don't need your help messing it up any more than it already is."

"You could have a different life."

He snorted. "With you?"

"Naturally."

"No, not 'naturally'!" He strode across the distance I'd just created, keeping his voice low. "There is nothing 'natural' about you. You represent everything dark and hateful and repulsive about the world."

"You mean about humans," I corrected with a smug smile, "and little saintly witches like you."

"Mock me, mock God for what it's worth. I don't care

what you do as long as you do it as far away from me as possible."

"Why? Afraid I'm going to corrupt you?" I slid forward, tilting my face toward his, our lips a breath apart. "Turn your heart as black as mine? Get under your skin? What if you can redeem me, lamb? Don't you want to be my salvation? My way back to the light? You could save me from myself, if that's what you really wanted. Imagine the triumph."

He held his ground, scowling and refusing to take the bait. "You might want to drag out this little game as long as you can, but I don't. The sooner I get you what you want, the sooner I'll be rid of you."

"Oh, Phelan..." I stroked his cheek before seizing either side of his jaw so hard he winced. "You'll never be rid of me. I might remove my mark. You might even manage to kill me. But you'll *always* belong to me. And you know what?" I brushed the tip of my nose against his. "I don't think you're really that mad about it. It's just your damned pride talking."

"I despise you." His words came out as a hiss, half anger and half pain from the hold on his jaw.

Glancing away, I cocked my head, listening to the way his heart picked up speed. I gave him a dark smile and squeezed his jaw a little bit harder. "Sure you do, pet. I believe every word out of that perfect mouth, just like you believe every word out of mine." I released him roughly. He stumbled backward a step, catching himself against the bookcase. "See you at home, *lover*. Try not to work too late."

With that, I shimmered out of view.

CHAPTER NINETEEN
PHELAN

A wall of information stared back at me on the computer screen.

Am I gay?

Am I bisexual?

Ten Signs.

Things to know.

Take this quiz!

I didn't think it was possible for me to be overwhelmed by information, but at that moment, with my head swimming, all I could do was hurriedly exit the web browser and stare into the distance as if *that* would solve my burgeoning crisis.

Regardless of whatever the computer said I was or wasn't, it didn't matter at the end of the day. Ultimately, I was whatever Remiel said I was. Just like when he claimed he was my boyfriend when Veronica asked. Why, I had no idea. Probably another one of his games.

He'd also switched up his annoying term of endearment, exchanging the possessive and dehumanizing "pet" for the equally possessive but somewhat improved "lover."

I'd say he was even being... affectionate? Was that the right word for it? It had to have been... he could force me to do whatever he wanted at any moment, a fact he proved in Hell time and again. But since I'd been back in Winslow, he hadn't. I wasn't naive enough to think I'd suddenly grown stronger or that his powers were somehow weaker in this realm. He was *choosing* to act like that, just like he chose to come to me when he was hurt.

I couldn't make heads or tails of him. Whenever I tried, he made my head spin, turning what I thought I knew on its head and leaving me even more confused than before.

Pushing away from my desk, I returned to the chained section and resumed thumbing through a German grimoire carefully.

Just like Remiel, finding any information on Hazael was proving to be an impossible task. Historically demons didn't give people their full names, ever since King Solomon found out it was one of the easiest ways to control them. Those demons had already been studied and ranked according to their powers, used by Necromancers throughout time. The ones listed in the Book of Lazarus were entirely different—a subset of demons only Lazarus, or whoever wrote the pseudepigraphical grimoire, seemed to know about. And sadly, Hazael wasn't amongst them.

While having Hazael's (and Remiel's) full name would be ideal, I didn't expect to find it. That didn't mean I couldn't find out how to kill him, though. I'm sure it wasn't all that different from killing any other high-ranking demon, except that it would take much more power.

By the time the bells chimed overhead, signaling the close of the library in ten minutes, I had a crick in my neck and absolutely nothing to show for my efforts. I was no closer to finding a way to kill Hazael let alone rid myself of Remiel's sigil.

Tucking a couple of books into my messenger bag, I headed out the door for the night.

I kept my eyes peeled for any sign of Remiel on my way to my car, but he didn't appear there, or on the drive home.

The unpaved lane to my house was particularly dark. The heavy branches bobbed overhead, forming a tunnel that threatened to scratch the roof of my car with each gust.

After navigating through the split-rail fence, I parked next to the back door and hauled myself out of the car with a sigh, happy to finally be home and give my eyes a break from straining against the harsh glare of headlights in the pitch blackness.

A small spider swung down from the light next to the door and landed on my hand as I inserted the key into the lock.

"I take it there were no problems?" I asked, lifting the spider up to eye level.

It skittered down my hand and launched itself off of my wrist, disappearing into the night.

"Not that it stopped him before," I muttered to myself, stepping over the threshold and flipping on the interior light.

Throwing together a sandwich, I carried my late dinner to the small kitchen table and tossed my messenger bag on the floor. I knew I had more research to do, but after running into nothing but dead ends all day I had a hard time finding the motivation to continue.

Still, I hefted the stack of books up onto the table and flipped through them idly, looking for any breadcrumb I could follow.

The words on the text blurred in front of me until the

medieval monsters on the page ran rampant, like a demented cartoon, dripping in blood from all of the red-ink letters. I shoved the books and my plate out of the way and rested my head on my forearm. I just needed to take a small break and then I could get back to it.

The next thing I knew, I was weightless.

Flying.

Falling.

I crash-landed on the kitchen floor and scrambled into a sitting position, vaguely aware of the fact I wasn't alone.

Pressing myself into the lower cabinets, I followed the strips of long, black fabric upward, past the glittering silver belt and perfect physique, up to Remiel's amused face.

"What are you doing?" I asked, swallowing hard and stealing a glance at my surroundings to make sure I was actually still in my house and that I wasn't trapped in a mirage of some sort.

"Well, I was carrying you upstairs until you flopped out of my arms like a fish."

"Why? Why would you do that?"

"Fine. I'll fuck you right here." He grabbed my biceps and hauled me upward, setting me on the counter like I was nothing more than a sack of flour.

"You're not fucking me anywhere." I tried to shove him off of me, but it only made him bite my neck harder. A shiver rushed down my spine, chasing a spark of electricity that went straight to my toes, even as I hissed through my teeth at the sting.

Remiel straightened, clamping a hand around my throat and squeezing. "You don't tell me no. Do you hear me? You're mine to do with as I please, when it pleases me. I played nice for you at the library so you can keep your pathetic job. Don't get used to it."

I nodded at the same time I groped behind myself on the counter, searching for anything I could use as a weapon.

"Good. Now... kitchen or bedroom?"

"Bed," I gasped with the last bit of air I had.

"After you, pet."

As soon as his grip loosened, mine tightened on the metal beneath my fingertips. I flung my hand forward. Holy water splashed over him from the end of the silver aspergillum.

His skin sizzled and burned beneath the droplets, recreating the way he'd looked when he appeared in my living room. There wasn't enough liquid to do any serious harm, but it was enough of a surprise that I was able to kick him away from me. Able to get a better grip, I grabbed the aspersorium next and hurled the whole metal bucket at him. A wave of holy water doused his face and his bare chest.

Remiel finally screamed, a mixture of fury and pain unlike anything I'd ever heard from him before. His hand hovered helplessly over the flayed skin on his face, wisps of smoke curling around his fingers.

I didn't stick around to see what kind of damage it did to the rest of him or how long it would last.

I sprinted to the end of the room, practically crashing into my supply cupboard while trying to claw the doors open as quickly as I could. Grabbing an armful of crystals, I spun toward him again and threw the hunks of crystal across the floor like a terrible game of bowling. I hoped it was enough to hold him or I'm sure he was *really* going to kill me this time.

Chanting the appropriate prayer, each crystal tumbled to a stop in the worst circular shape known to man. It seemed to do the trick, though, since Remiel took a step toward me, halting abruptly at the edge of the crystals. His skin had already started to heal—the charred black edges fading from red to pink and then vanishing before my very eyes.

"You think a little water and some rocks are going to keep me away from you?" he snarled, testing the barrier again with his hand. It moved farther than his feet before snapping backward like elastic.

Even though I was keeping my distance, I snatched a knife out of the wooden block on the counter to be on the safe side. "We had a deal!"

"Our deal is the only reason you're going to be alive when I'm done with you." He pressed against the invisible barrier again, this time with both hands.

"Forcing me to have sex with you every time we see each other wasn't part of it."

"As long as my sigil is burned into your skin, lover, you're mine to fuck whenever, wherever, and *however* I choose. Your twisted morality has nothing to do with it."

"M-*my* twisted morality?!" I couldn't help but sputter his words back at him. "How delusional are you?"

"Your church, your god, even your own family dictate every aspect of your life and you let them. What do *you* believe, Phelan? What do you truly believe? Not what someone else has *told* you to. Answer that for once in your life."

"So your issue with authority has nothing to do with right and wrong, it's the fact you don't like someone else telling you what to do? Throwing a tantrum like a toddler doesn't make you better, Remiel, it makes you reckless and selfish and—"

"Evil?" he added with a sneer, pieces of his cheekbone melting back together seamlessly.

"Yes! Evil!"

"Just like Necromancers are evil?"

"We do God's work," I countered. "Our power comes *from* God."

"Until a pope said it didn't and burned how many of your kind at the stake? Where was your god then? If you're so important to him, why didn't he intervene?"

"He doesn't interfere with free will. Not like you," I reminded him.

"You don't have any free will *to* interfere with." His lip curled as he raked his gaze over me. For once it wasn't predatory; it was dismissive, inexplicably cutting so deep I flinched. "You gave it all away, always living by someone else's rules, by someone else's decree."

"How is that any different than being your slave?"

"If you were truly my slave, you'd be collared and chained to my bed for the rest of eternity. More importantly, I would have never let you leave the underworld." A dark smile tipped the corners of his mouth as my heart dropped like a rock into my stomach. "What's the matter, pet? Did you think I didn't know? That you managed to one-up me with your magic? I've been toying with self-righteous little witches like you since the dawn of time. I don't have to be inside your head to know what you're thinking."

"For fuck's sake, what do you want from me?!" I inadvertently took a step forward as I shouted the question, every muscle in my body tightening with pure frustration. I could handle a lot of things but not knowing the reason for my continued torment was turning into pure agony.

He didn't answer. Of course he didn't fucking answer. He just stood there, smiling like the cat that ate the damned canary.

I threw the knife on the counter and stormed past him,

edging around the crude protective circle in case he managed to break through the barrier.

"Where are you going, lamb? Going to leave me to rot in your kitchen while you go pray?"

"Fuck you!" I spat over my shoulder.

"I like you when you're angry. So full of fire." His laughter followed me as I strode into the living room, tearing my hands through my hair and pacing out of view. It probably didn't matter, I'm sure he could hear every little thing I was doing. But at least being in another room gave me some space to breathe.

In the midst of my prowling, I caught sight of a spider jumping up and down on the bookshelf out of the corner of my eye. I crossed the room quickly, eyes narrowed on the little arachnid as it scurried up the spine of an old, leather-bound book.

"I don't think it'll be enough," I muttered to the spider, snatching the book off the shelf regardless and flipping through it quickly, hoping to find some sort of inspiration in the Roman Ritual. A normal exorcism wouldn't make him leave. I'd have to use a banishment spell or open a portal, and even then there was no guarantee it would work on a prince. He was too fucking strong and despite all of my training, I wasn't equipped to fight him one-on-one, and I sure as shit wasn't asking anyone from the Congregation for help.

My speed reading was interrupted by the sound of Remiel's wings flapping, banging, and frustrated snarls. Good. Served him right. He could feel what it was like to be held prisoner for a little bit because Lord knew it wouldn't hold him forever.

"Phelan, come back! You need to let me out!" Remiel called from the kitchen. "I'm serious."

I paused, trying to decide what, exactly, I'd heard in his voice. Concern? Fear? Impossible. Just another one of his twisted games.

Shaking my head, I ignored him and muttered under my breath. "Not fucking happening."

"Release me! Now!"

Before I could answer him, something whispered across the floorboards behind me. I froze in place, straining to hear more—more from Remiel in the kitchen, more from whatever it was that made that sound.

A spider leapt onto the book, skittering over my hand and up my arm. I brushed it away, only to find another creeping up around the backside of my bicep.

"Not now," I whispered, dislodging the second spider.

A third dropped onto the back of my neck, darting down my arm before leaping after the others.

The whispering sound was back, along with a faint chattering that was growing louder.

I turned slowly, apprehension bubbling up in the back of my throat with the bitter taste of bile.

A wave, black and undulating, surged over the floorboards, rushing straight toward me. Only, it wasn't water. It was spiders.

"Let me out!" Remiel shouted again.

"*Desistas*," I said, throwing a halting hand toward the advancing spiders.

They refused the command to stop and kept coming.

"Phelan!"

"I can't." I all but whispered it, immobilized by my own fear and the swarm of spiders keeping me pressed to the bookshelf, tiny fangs gleaming. I knew my magic wasn't much, but I'd never lost control over spiders before. They were supposed to help dream witches like me—not turn on us.

A sharp sting pierced my ankle, followed immediately by another and another. In the blink of an eye, the spiders streamed up my legs, biting and pinching every step of the way.

I yelped, trying to swat the arachnids away, but for every few I managed to remove, another dozen gathered in their place. Without even thinking, I bolted for the door, trying to ignore the sickening crunch beneath my feet.

"No! Don't go—" Remiel shouted behind me.

I didn't stop to listen to the rest. Swiping the spiders away from my face and neck, I ran blindly in the direction of the pond.

I was nearly there when the stinging pain suddenly vanished.

Chest heaving, I slid to a halt, looking at my hands in the moonlight.

They were fine.

There were no bites, no spiders.

I ran my hands through my hair and shook it roughly, but no spiders fell from any of their hiding places.

"You really are a weakling, aren't you?" a voice said behind me. It had the same silken tone as Remiel's but it wasn't him. "Chased out of your house by your own familiars? Pathetic."

I pivoted slowly, taking in the man behind me. No, not a man. Another demon, just as beautiful as Remiel and just as evil from the looks of him. Contempt registered in every facet of his face, from his curled lip to the haughty way he regarded me, like I was nothing more than a spider he wanted to crush.

His golden wings spread out wide as he moved closer, blocking off any attempt I might make at running back toward the house. His armor was similar to Remiel's, except his looked bronze instead of black. I didn't see any weapons but since Remiel could conjure them at will, I was sure this one could too.

"I never understood my brother's fascination with witches," the demon continued, looking me up and down with a sneer.

"Well that makes two of us," I replied with a glare of my own, making sure to hold my ground when he stopped directly in front of me.

"Aw. The lamb has teeth." The demon chuckled, skimming his knuckles along my cheek. "Who knew?"

I jerked my head away from him. "Don't touch me."

"Or what? Think Remiel is going to save you?" He seized me by the throat and yanked me closer, so close I could see the inhuman way his eyes glowed in the darkness, like burning embers. "You caged him in a circle, remember? Just listen. You can probably hear him screaming right now, imagining everything I'm going to do to his little pet right in front of him."

"Go ahead. I'm sure your brother has already done it. What else do I have to lose?"

"Maybe I should take you back with me," he mused, turning my face this way and that in the moonlight, considering me the same way a person might assess a piece of fruit before taking a bite. "Watch Remiel lose his mind without his precious toy. Throw a—what did you call it? A tantrum?"

"Go ahead," I repeated with a grimace, trying to wedge my thumb under his hand to give my throat some relief. "Once you get used to the smell, Hell really wasn't that bad."

"Look at the little lamb putting on a brave face. I'd applaud you if you weren't so pitiful."

"If there's one thing I've learned about demons, it's that there's no point in arguing with you people. You're going to do what you're going to do. So go on. Do it. Rape me. Torture me. Whatever sick fucking game you two are playing. It doesn't matter what I say or do, I know I'm just a pawn."

"So eager to die, are you? So eager to escape your bondage?"

"Oh, I won't die. At least not by your hand." I gave him a contemptuous once-over.

"And why do you think that?"

"Because I know your brother. And I know he'll find me no matter what. I can scarcely fathom all the terrible things he'll do once he does."

The demon laughed, squeezing my throat harder. "You think so highly of your master, do you?"

I shook my head as best I could. "No. It's because I don't think much of you. You waited until Remiel was trapped before you made a move on me. If that isn't cowardice, I don't know what is."

"You think I'm afraid of him?" His nostrils flared.

"I know you are."

"You insolent cur."

"You have to be worthy of respect for me to give it, and all I see is some half-ass demon who's jealous of his brother. You're not good enough to forge your own life, so you're trying to steal his—starting with his weak little pet. Now who's pathetic?"

With an inhuman yell, the demon flung me across the yard.

I rolled to a stop with a grimace, pushing myself up

onto my hands and knees. Well, at least he let me go. I suppose that was a plus. And I was infinitely closer to the house now.

"You're lucky I want you alive," the demon hissed, marching toward me.

Silver light shimmered in front of me, completely blocking out my view of the demon. When it faded, a pair of massive white wings stood in its place. White with black edges.

Remiel.

I hated that the first emotion I felt was relief, but I couldn't help it. As much as I despised him, he was still preferable to this unknown demon. Better the devil you know, and all of that.

"And you're lucky I can't kill you outright," Remiel snarled, squaring off against his brother. His wings practically glowed in the moonlight as he unfolded them like a shield in front of me.

I got to my feet slowly, unsure whether I should stay or try and run back to the house. It's not like I was particularly useful in a fight—physically *or* magically. But I was more than curious as to how this was all going to play out.

"Well, well. You really do like this one, don't you?" The red-haired demon scoffed. "Enough to free yourself from a circle, that is. I would be impressed if the sight of the two of you didn't disgust me."

"In that case, I'd be happy to gouge your eyes out," Remiel threw back.

"You just showed your hand, brother." The demon laughed, folding his wings and swaggering forward, arching a red eyebrow. "You can't watch him all the time."

"I don't need to. My little pet was right about you." Remiel matched him step-for-step until they were just out of arm's reach of one another. "You're too craven to attack him again. You lost the element of surprise, Hazael. Time to slither back to your nest and lick your wounds."

I peered over the top of Remiel's wing, taking in the demon in front of us with a new awareness. So *this* was Hazael. But he also said he was Remiel's brother. I shouldn't have been that surprised demons would kill their own family. But Remiel was upset when *we* killed his family... it made no sense.

Hazael's golden eyes flicked to me. The look alone made my skin crawl, like the swarm of spiders was back, creeping all over every inch of me. Somehow I managed to suppress a shudder. Thankfully, he turned and disappeared in a swirl of shadows, taking the horrid sensation with him, though I doubted it would be the last time I ever saw him.

I let out a slow breath and ran a hand over my arm absentmindedly, rubbing away the phantom feeling.

Remiel spun toward me, his lips parted like he was going to say, or snarl, something.

Tipping my chin up, I held his gaze as he marched back to me. I couldn't wait to see what sort of punishment he had in store for me after *this* ordeal. We were probably going straight back to Hell, where he'd make good on his earlier statement, collaring me and chaining me to his bed for the rest of my life.

Curling his fingers around the back of my neck, Remiel steered me toward the house, rather gently considering the way he normally manhandled me. I expected at least a verbal lashing, continuing our earlier fight from the kitchen, but he didn't say a word.

"I have questions," I said, breaking the awkward silence.

"I'm sure you do."

"It'll help with research."

"Well, you're not doing any more research tonight, so it can wait."

Once we reached the front of the house, Remiel opened the door and pushed me through it. "Do not leave this house again. Remember, anything you see is an illusion. It's not real. I'll be back later."

"Where are you going?"

"There's something I need to deal with."

"Remiel, wait," I grabbed his wrist as he turned to go. "Can you stay? Just a bit longer? I don't want to be alone."

His silver brows furrowed, his jaw shifting to one side as he thought it over. After a moment, he nodded once and followed me into the house, shutting the door behind us.

"Will you sit with me?" I drifted to the couch, sinking into one corner and watching him warily.

He stayed where he was, his pewter eyes assessing me in silence.

For the first time since knowing each other, the way he looked at me sent a flutter of nerves through my stomach. It wasn't with his usual hunger, or anger. It almost seemed like... genuine curiosity. I rubbed my palms over my thighs, unsure of what to do with myself while he scrutinized me.

Finally, Remiel moved away from the door and angled himself on the other end of the couch, one of his wings tucked up even further behind the other to accommodate the narrow space.

"Are you ok? Are you comfortable?" I asked, immediately biting my lip when I realized how completely idiotic that sounded. He hadn't cared about *my* comfort at all, why should I care if his wings fit on the couch? Maybe we should have had this little chit-chat in the kitchen, on arm-less chairs. On second thought, that was a terrible idea considering what happened the last time we were in there.

An amused smile pulled at the corner of Remiel's mouth, interrupting my spiraling thoughts. "What's your real question?"

I felt like I was floundering, all train of thought derailed by the rapt attention he was giving me. It wasn't completely foreign, since he usually looked at me like he was a starving man and I was his last meal, but this felt different somehow. "I... um. Hazael?"

His gaze darkened as soon as I said the name, not quite turning black, but it was enough to know I struck a nerve. "What about him?"

"What was that all about back there? What did you mean you can't kill him outright? Is he really your brother? Is that why? But what about the other demons who died? You said *they* were your family. And how in God's name did you get out of that circle?! I mean, don't get me wrong, I'm grateful you did. Somehow. It'd be really good to know how, especially for the Book of Damnation... But what would have happened if you didn't? And why can't I leave the house?" I sucked in a quick breath and exhaled it again, practically deflating. I think those were the highlights, anyway.

Remiel cocked his head, blinking. "You were tricked by his illusion with the spiders and yet you didn't even flinch when he threatened to harm you or to take you captive."

I'm pretty sure I flushed scarlet from my ears to my toes, averting my gaze to the far side of the room. "You heard that?"

"Of course I heard it. The question is—were you lying? About me?"

"I don't lie," I countered tersely.

He leaned forward, lowering his voice. "That's a lie right there."

"Are you going to answer my questions or not?" I glowered, reclining away from him in case he got any ideas.

He rolled his eyes and straightened, giving me my personal space again. "Yes, that was Hazael. Yes, he's my brother but that isn't why I can't kill him. The why has everything to do with Beliar and the oath we swore, a blood oath that cannot be broken."

"What was the oath?"

He drew a breath and looked away, like he was trying to decide how much to tell me. He still looked arrogant and cruel but beneath it, I almost detected a profound weariness. He wanted to trust someone. I could sense it. I just had to show him I could *be* that person if only he'd let me.

"I need to know," I prompted softly, "so I can find a way around it."

"After the war, everything was uncertain," Remiel replied, his gaze fixed on some point on the floor. "We'd been cast out of the only home we'd ever known, forced to hide deep underground to escape those who still hunted us. Angels were made to fly, not cower in caves." His feathers ruffled, as if shrugging off the memory of that earlier time. I wanted to touch them, to smooth them back into place, but I kept my hands firmly in my lap.

"Just as Beliar led us to rebellion, he leads us in Hell," Remiel continued quietly, his silver gaze finally lifting to mine. "He's our king, creating order out of chaos. In the new realm, he made his fellow angels into princes and divided the underworld between us and the rest of the higher-ranked demons with one condition—we could never kill one another. If we do, if we break that pledge, Beliar told us we would suffer a fate worse than death."

"What could be worse than death?"

"For a demon of our stature? Powerlessness. Complete and utter humiliation. We would spend the rest of eternity as a slave. And not just to Beliar—a slave to humans. The demons you Necromancers have been abusing for a thousand years are the result of breaking that oath."

Well *that* certainly explained how Necromancers were able to wrangle some of the most powerful demons into submission. I wasn't foolish enough to think our magic had been enough; their pride was their own undoing and we exploited it to our advantage.

"But why would he care if you kill each other or not?"

"He doesn't. Not really. But he fears another uprising. This way we can't kill him directly, nor can we kill each other in an attempt to consolidate our power. It's impossible to have insurrection without bloodshed, so in theory, Beliar has nothing to fear."

He said "directly" just like he said "outright" earlier, which got my brain working. "If you can't kill each other *personally* then why is Hazael in a war with you? What does he hope to gain?"

"Nothing prohibits his followers from attacking, only him. Lesser demons can kill someone of a higher rank, but it's rare. Very rare. Usually they're too weak. Too unorganized. And if a higher demon allowed themselves to be killed by their inferior, then they deserved it."

"And if your army somehow kills Hazael?"

"Then his dominion falls under my control, along with all of his power."

"So is that what you want? His power?"

"That's what every demon wants. It's the only thing that matters, no matter what realm you're in. But the more power you have, the more of a target you become so you'd better be ready to defend what's yours as ruthlessly as possible." His gaze slid down my body slowly and seemed to stop on my hand—the one with his sigil. "When we die, we cease to be. There is no more Heaven, no more Hell. We disappear into a black abyss from which there is no resurrection."

"That happens to every demon?"

He nodded.

"Like the ones the Congregation exterminated..."

Another nod.

"Were they your brothers too?" I asked quietly.

"In a way. Brothers-in-arms rather than creation."

"I'm sorry." I'd never thought about the ramifications of vanquishing demons before. But now? I had a hard time summoning any sense of pride. Yes, they did terrible things, but could they be faulted when that's all they'd ever known? When that is what their entire world consisted of?

"Why were you killing members of my realm? I checked. No other dominion has reported the same number of deaths as mine."

"I didn't know they were all connected to you."

"Where did you get their names?"

Now it was my turn to hedge, debating how much I should reveal about my family's lineage. If I told him about the Book of Lazarus, would he annihilate the entire Corbin line for their possession of the book? The entire Congregation? Or just every participant he found listed in the Book of Damnation?

Remiel's jaw tightened. "*Where*, Phelan?"

"One of our grimoires," I admitted. "There's a list of demons and their sigils, instructions on how to summon them, control them, and even kill them."

Remiel's eyes flashed dangerously. "Where did you get it?"

I shrugged. "I don't know. It's not my family's book. I'm not even sure if its owner knows the provenance. So many of these things have been handed down through blood and marriage, it's hard to know where any of them came from."

"I want to see it."

I shook my head. "Impossible. You'll never find it. They just got it back after centuries of being gone. They're not going to let *anyone* near it, not even me."

He stood swiftly and stalked to the far end of the room before pivoting and marching back, the angles of his face sharpened in anger. "Someone has been conveniently murdering members of my court for almost a year and yet you claim there is no larger plan afoot. And now you tell me you have a book detailing how to kill the demons who are loyal to me? Either you're lying or you're a fool! Which is it?"

"I swear I don't know anything about any sort of a plan! The only reason we killed those demons was to keep our community safe!"

"Safe from what? From them? What had they done?"

I opened my mouth to reply, but nothing came out—because they *hadn't* done anything. It was a preemptive strike against our age-old enemy. The backlash of paranoia following the murders last year, even though the one pulling the strings had been a witch, not a demon.

Remiel scoffed and pressed on. "So you killed them without provocation?"

My gaze dropped. The weight of what we'd done hung heavily on me because he was right. Demon or not, we'd killed those creatures without cause. And for what? It all stemmed from the fallout of a family feud that'd stupidly lasted centuries. Those demons had nothing to do with what happened in Winslow and yet we made it all about them instead of taking any sort of accountability for our own actions.

Seizing my face between his hands, Remiel hauled me to my feet and kept hold of me even after I was standing. "Open your eyes, lamb," he said between his teeth—metaphorically speaking since my eyes *were* open and locked on his with wariness. "Or I guarantee your faith will be your downfall."

"Isn't that what you want?" I countered, trying to ignore the way my pulse spiked with him holding me so close. "To watch me suffer? I do it so beautifully, after all."

"It is what I want. I want to lead my little lamb astray and corrupt every facet of your soul. I want to turn you inside out; meticulously destroy God's perfect creation." His fingers slid into my hair, twisting until he had enough to wrench my head backward. I grimaced and pressed my forearms against his chest, trying to alleviate some of the pain as he leaned in closer, his lips hovering over mine. "But I want you falling apart on *my* terms, not because your fucking Congregation has broken you."

Anger flared in the center of my chest. For one moment I felt sorry for him, remorseful for what my family had done to his. And within seconds he was back to being insufferable. It was a sharp reminder not to be fooled by any vulnerability he pretended to have. It was all for show. "You couldn't even break me in Hell, what makes you think you'll have any luck up here?"

"Because now I know your weakness, pet." His lips skimmed along my jaw, from my chin down toward my throat, until at the last minute he diverted and nipped my earlobe. I gasped, as much from the bite as from the gentle sucking that followed.

"Do tell," I huffed.

"Me."

My stomach flipped. If his teeth weren't so close to my ear, I would have shaken my head. "You're so arrogant."

"That wasn't a denial."

"Refuting it is a waste of my breath. You only hear what you want to."

"Right now, I hear your heart beating faster." He nuzzled beneath my jaw, pressing kisses to my throat while his wings enveloped me slowly. I renewed my efforts to push him out to arm's length, but it was futile. He was too strong. "Why did you ask me to stay?"

"I told you. I have questions," I said, digging my fingers into his bare chest in the hope it would get him to back up but it only made him hold on tighter, his hands sliding around my ribs, moving up and down my back lazily.

"I'll give you an answer for every article of clothing you take off."

I scoffed. "I thought you wanted my help?"

"I want you, not your help. I never wanted your help and you never wanted to give it, except as a means of removing my sigil."

"A deal's still a deal," I ground out, heaving my elbows against his torso as he yanked my pelvis against his, practically bending backward to try and create more space between us. "Who cares about the reason why?"

He released me quickly and without warning, spinning on the ball of his foot and striding toward the door. "Suit yourself. Just remember, the longer your research takes, the longer you'll wear my mark."

"Wait! Stop!" I ripped my button-up off as quickly as I

could and wadded it in a ball, throwing it at his retreating back. "Accessories count."

He stopped and turned, peering at me over his snowy wing. Even though his face was half obscured, it was nothing short of a smolder that heated me through my core. "First question."

"What's Hazael's true name?"

Padding back to me slowly, his lips curved in a smirk. "You'd have to ask him."

"You don't know your own brother's true name?"

In the blink of an eye, Remiel grasped my white undershirt in his hands and ripped it right off of me. Holding up the tattered remains in victory, he let them drop to the floor as I cursed under my breath. I'd have to choose my words very carefully from here on out. I only had seven questions left.

"No," he replied smugly.

"The wood I pulled out of your back," I continued, unbuckling my belt and tossing it on the floor. "Why did it hurt you?"

His silver brows furrowed, either irritated or caught off guard by the question. Maybe he thought I'd forgotten all about it, but there wasn't a chance in Hell.

"It's a relic," he said at last.

"What relic? Specifically."

One brow lifted slowly, pointedly, as his gaze dropped to my pants.

Rolling my eyes, I took off a shoe instead and tossed it at his feet with a mocking smile.

"It could only have been the True Cross."

"Bullshit."

He canted his head. "You don't believe me?"

I hurriedly took my other shoe off and chucked it after

the first. "How did a demon get ahold of the cross where Christ was crucified?"

"How does a demon get ahold of anything? He stole it. Where is it, by the way? Did you keep it?"

Off came a sock as I pointedly ignored his questions. "Do all relics hurt you?"

"Unfortunately," he replied through gritted teeth.

"Is that the only way to kill a prince?" The second sock landed by the first.

"You're the expert. You tell me."

"That's not an answer. Stop deflecting."

"No," he said tersely, "but it's the easiest way. Magic generally takes too long. Other demons aren't strong enough to kill us by force."

"Unless they ambush you..."

His eyes narrowed. "Even then, they failed."

My mind was already whirling with spells and ideas, ways to get a hold of a relic and incorporate it into a ritual. "How do you summon Hazael without his sigil?" I asked, unzipping my pants and stepping out of them.

Remiel's gaze raked over me. A subtle ripple swept through his feathers. They fluffed and settled again as he took a step forward. I shrunk backward, but he moved with me, his gaze locked on mine intently. "You can't kill him, pet. You don't have the strength, even with a relic."

Holding my ground, I drew myself up straighter despite the fact he was in my personal space again, trailing a fingertip down my bare arm and turning my insides to mush. "Stop avoiding the question."

"What are you planning?" He narrowed his eyes.

"You're the one answering questions here, not me," I shot back. "And I'm still waiting."

"Go to a crossroad, under a full moon, and draw nine

circles. Slaughter a goat and spread the entrails in the last one. Set the skull ablaze in the center and chant whatever little summoning spell you want. Better hope your circle holds him better than it held me or he'll wrench your head from your shoulders before the last word falls from those beautiful lips." He traced my bottom lip with his tongue, giving me a wicked smile when he was finished. "Last question."

"I have everything I need," I replied, swatting his hand away from the waistband of my boxer briefs.

The corners of his mouth turned downward. He was pouting again, which was always better than the angry version, but after the spat in the kitchen, I knew to proceed with caution. His playful moods could turn volatile in the blink of an eye.

"Oh come on," he whined. "You thirst for knowledge. Ask me anything. I promise I won't lie."

"That's not as reassuring as I'm sure you hoped it would be." It also meant everything else he told me could absolutely be a lie. Ultimately I'd have to decide what was real and what wasn't and knowing him, it was probably a very frustrating mix of both.

A flash of genuine mirth sparked in his eyes. "Is that what you need from me? Reassurance? Pretty words whispered in your ear, to soothe the doubt within?"

"All I need from you is to be left alone."

He slid his palm over my heart, tsking me softly. "Whether you admit it or not, I know I have an effect on you."

"Yeah. You repulse me."

"And yet you asked me to stay."

"A momentary lapse in judgment."

"Are you saying now you want me to leave?"

"Yes." My heart tripped over itself a second before a slow smile spread over his lips.

"You're forfeiting your last question?" Remiel asked, arching a brow.

"Yes."

"'Haughty eyes and a proud heart.'" He tipped his chin up regally, looking down his perfect nose with a loftier air than usual. "But your god detests the prideful, Phelan. 'Nothing but sin,'" he purred.

I scowled at him. Quoting Proverbs at me to suit his agenda wasn't going to get me to strip out of my underwear, no matter what he said or how much goading he did. If he wanted me naked, he was going to have to rip them off of me... which I'm sure he'd have no problem doing, so I didn't even know why I thought it would matter.

He regarded me for a moment longer. "Hazael was right about one thing—I won't always be around to watch you," he said at last. "So don't do anything stupid with all of that new information rolling around in your head."

"Heaven forbid something happens to your precious little lamb," I said, folding my arms over my chest. "Whatever will you do with your days?"

"I'd make Armageddon look like a fucking picnic."

I blinked at the seriousness of his tone. When my lashes cleared my line of sight, he was gone.

CHAPTER TWENTY
PHELAN

I didn't believe Remiel as far as I could throw him, especially when I woke the next morning and found the larger piece of wood I'd hidden the other night was gone. His question about its location should have been a clue he'd come back for it, stealing it in the middle of the night like the deceitful brute that he was, but I hadn't picked up on his passing curiosity until it was too late. The story of my life.

Furious, but undeterred, I grabbed the jar of slivers I'd pulled from his back and took it with me to work.

There was one person in the Congregation who could help settle my doubt for me—Samuel Ainsworth. As the Tithing Man, he was the most fair-minded of the bunch, since it was up to him to independently police other witches. But as a scientist, he was as keen to get to the bottom of things as I was. He'd be able to tell me if the slivers actually came from the True Cross, or at least from the same era, or if it was yet another one of Remiel's lies.

Jogging up the steps of Dane Hall, I maneuvered

through the crowd of early-morning students and made my way to the second floor and Ainsworth's office.

I lifted my hand to knock on the door but stopped just as my gaze landed on a dry-erase board with his office hours written on it. Sighing, I turned on my heel and made my way back downstairs, heading toward the laboratory side of the building.

Walking into the massive greenhouse was like walking into a wall of hot, wet air. Two steps into the room and I was already sweating. With all of the plants hanging everywhere, it was like wading through a miniature jungle.

"Samuel?" I called out, hoping to catch a glimpse of him in all the greenery.

"Who goes there?" came the reply, but from where I had no idea.

"It's Phelan." I shifted the strap of my messenger bag on my shoulder, taking another tentative step inside. "Phelan Oliver?"

A curtain of vines parted and Samuel appeared, his short gray hair extra frizzy from the humidity. It made him look like a mad scientist, especially when coupled with his wrinkled lab coat. Although I'm sure I'd be equally disheveled by the time I left the room since my clothes were sticking to every part of me.

"Phelan!" Samuel smiled brightly and gestured around the greenhouse. The vines behind him mimicked the motion, pointing in whatever direction his hands were. "I was actually going to reach out to you, see how you've been. We've missed you at the last few Meetings. But now that you're here, what can I do for you?"

"I was wondering if you could help me with something?" I fished the jar out of my bag and held it out to him. "Can you tell me what that is?"

When he reached for the jar, the vines rushed toward my face so fast I scrambled back a step, eyes wide.

"Enough," Samuel grumbled over his shoulder, slicing his hand sharply at the greenery. Their leaves trembled and the vines drooped, hanging like normal once again.

"Sorry," he continued with an apologetic smile. "They don't get visitors very often, for obvious reasons. Let's go to the lab, shall we?" He tossed his head toward another door, barely visible behind various palm fronds, and set off.

I gave a cautious glance at the pouting vines before following him.

Once we were in the lab, Samuel pulled a handkerchief from his pocket and dabbed his forehead before holding his hand out. "Now, let's see what this is all about."

Without curious plants interrupting the exchange, I dropped the jar into Samuel's hand and watched him get to work.

Holding the jar at eye level, he shook the slivers around, squinting. "Is that blood?"

"Yeah." I scratched the back of my neck, hoping he didn't ask any more questions.

Thankfully, he didn't. He wandered over to one of the microscopes and unscrewed the top, sniffing inside the jar for a minute before shaking one of the larger chunks out and sliding it under the scope.

"It's wood," he said, more to himself than me, and kept turning various knobs. "Looks like an oak."

"Oak?" I furrowed my brow. "Are you sure? Not... cypress? Or olive? Pine, perhaps?"

"No, oak." He straightened and pushed his glasses up the bridge of his nose. "It's too small to tell what kind or how old. I'll have to run additional tests. How soon do you need to know?"

I shrugged. "Whenever. There's no rush. It's just... for curiosity's sake."

"Where did you get it?"

"It, um, broke off of an antique at the house. I was going to try to reconstruct it if possible, as close to the original."

He peered at me over the top of his glasses. "An antique?"

I nodded. "Mhmm. The house is full of them. You know. Waste not, want not."

"Mhmm." He stepped away from the microscope and leaned against the desk, crossing his arms over his chest. "Are you alright, son? I know you're never chatty, but you're even quieter than normal."

I nodded even quicker than before, gripping the strap on my shoulder tightly. "Yep. Fine. Why?"

He shrugged. "I suppose it's because I haven't seen you at a Meeting in a while, which is a first. When I asked Temperance, she said you were under some stress and taking time to process it."

I couldn't help but scoff at her piss-poor excuse. "Yeah. That's all. I'm just... stressed."

"I know I'm not your professor anymore, but my door is always open to you. For anything."

"I appreciate that. And I appreciate your help with the wood."

"I'll call you when I know something."

"Thank you." I inclined my head and escaped out the closest door before he could try and get any more information out of me.

A gust of cold autumn wind blasted me as soon as I exited Dane Hall, chilling the sweat beneath my clothes immediately. I turned my face toward the sun and closed my eyes, taking a minute to try and stop my whirling thoughts while absorbing some of the warmth.

To say things had been tense between Temperance and I was the understatement of the century. In addition to ignoring her and the rest of my so-called family, I had stopped going to Meetings altogether. I dodged their phone calls and refused to open the door when anyone had the bright idea to drive to my house. Marcus, of all people, was the last one to try and reach out. He left a voicemail just the other night asking if I'd join the rest of the dark families for a separate gathering, away from the rest of the Congregation. I swore rather viciously at the recording and promptly deleted it. I could only imagine what the topic of conversation was. Probably me and all the ways Remiel was possessing me, despite the fact I *wasn't* fucking possessed.

I resumed my walk to the library, though I wasn't in any hurry to get there. Maybe it's because I *was* stressed. All I seemed to want to do was turn around and go home, crawl under the covers, and hibernate until spring. I didn't want to think about demons and secret wars and family obligations, but I couldn't focus on the mundane task of reorganizing an entire library catalog either. How was I supposed to care about digitization and record management when my deal with Remiel loomed over every aspect of my life? There was no telling when or where he'd show up and what would happen when he did. And if one prince of Hell wasn't enough to deal with, now I was officially on Hazael's radar.

Fuck my life!

Sighing, I adjusted the leather strap on my shoulder and hurried up the library steps, coming to a screeching halt at the top when I saw the figure leaning against one of the giant stone columns.

It was Remiel, once again barely passing as human,

except this time instead of looking like a model on their day off, he was mimicking an old-school professor. Tweed blazer, collared shirt, tie, the works. He'd left his long hair loose, the silvery blond strands blowing lazily in the breeze. I felt my jaw drop until I snapped my teeth shut and forced myself to move out of the way of two students trailing behind me.

"What are you doing here?" I asked, grabbing Remiel by his jacket and dragging him around the backside of the column, out of view from the quad. "And what are you wearing?"

"Should I go back to the skinny jeans? They're so uncomfortable, but I'll wear them if you want."

"What? No. I don't care what you wear. What are you doing here?" I gestured impatiently, irritated with myself that I even brought up the clothes. In reality, anything was better than what he normally wore... or *didn't* wear, I should say. Although skirts were making a comeback in some fashion circles, it was safe to say Remiel wouldn't blend in in the slightest if that's *all* he was wearing on campus, looking like a mythical god come to life.

"I thought maybe you'd want the help," he replied with a smile. "For real, this time."

I squinted at him, like his true intentions would become clearer the harder I scrutinized him. "This isn't a trick?"

He blinked serenely, not saying a word, and I caved under his apparent sincerity.

"No touching! Do you hear me?" I arched a brow at him. "Me *or* the books."

"I don't know what sort of help I'll be, then."

"It's for your own safety, but be my guest. If one of those books melts your hands off, I don't want to hear about it." I rolled my shoulders back and marched out from behind the column, trying to look totally at ease while walking through the front doors with a demon prince on my heels.

"Is that even possible?" Remiel asked, falling into step beside me.

"Melting your hands off?" I nodded. "Depending on the book. They can blind you, make you go crazy, and even kill you. You have no idea the lengths Necromancers went to to keep their books from falling into the wrong hands."

"Like demons."

I nodded again. "And other witches."

"Who knew being a librarian was such dangerous work?" Remiel smirked when I cut a glance his way. "Is that why you do it? Because the hidden danger thrills you?"

"No," I replied, my spine stiffening.

"Then why do you do it?"

"Why does it matter?"

"It doesn't. I'm trying to understand why you care about this pointless job."

"I don't expect you to understand anything about me."

"And yet you think you somehow possess the ability to understand me?" he shot back.

I scoffed. "I *do* have the ability. It's called compassion. And empathy. Two qualities you lack."

"Because they are also pointless—just like this place." He gestured around the soaring bookcases. "Look at you. You've spent your whole life preparing to destroy someone like me and what good did it do you? I'm no closer to being dead than you are to being rid of me."

"You're pretty callous about my empathy considering it's the only thing that saved your life the other night. If I was just like you, you would have bled out in my living room."

"Perhaps you should have let me then."

"I would have," I snapped, spinning to face him, "if it wasn't for all of the other innocent souls that would die because of it. I couldn't care less about you or me, but those people? They don't deserve that."

"And how do you know that wasn't also a lie?" he asked, the corner of his mouth lifting in a challenging smirk. "What if you're the only one with my sigil?"

I rolled my eyes and continued walking. "I find that hard to believe. You said it yourself, all demons want is power. What better way than to siphon it off of the living?"

"We do want power, but that doesn't mean we mark every creature who crosses our path. It's a two-way street, you know. Demons can draw power from a marked soul, as you said, but we can also be drained in return."

"What?" I jerked to a halt, brows furrowed as I tried to process that new information. Was he serious? Was I the only one he'd truly marked?

"Power is fluid, lamb. If a demon doesn't know what they're doing, or whom they're marking, they can find themselves stripped of their own power and left weakened. Vulnerable."

"How?"

He blinked slowly, languidly, like a cat, and I knew he wouldn't answer. It didn't matter. If it *was* possible to siphon his power, then that was an avenue I needed to explore. Immediately. But I couldn't help the other question niggling in the back of my mind.

"Why me?" I asked before I could help it. "I told you, I don't have any powers that would be useful to a demon. So why waste your energy on me? Why take that risk?"

His gaze raked over me again, with that hungry gleam that made my breath catch in my throat because there was no telling what he'd do next. "You're not a risk to me. One might even say we're perfectly matched."

"Why is that?"

"Perhaps it would interest you to know that I also have a connection to dream magic. Among other things, I used to be one of the beings in charge of gifting 'divine visions' that gullible humans revere so much. You know, *before* I changed allegiances."

My jaw slackened. "You did?"

He nodded, smirking, no doubt pleased with my shocked reaction.

"That's how you got in my head." Somehow that revelation made me feel slightly better about the whole thing, that I wasn't a complete and total failure. If he was one of the angels in charge of dream magic, it was no wonder he could find a way through my defenses.

"And that's how I know you're lying about your power," he said, backing me up against a bookcase and bracing his forearm against the shelf next to my head. "You say you're weak, but I know that's a lie."

"It's not." I swallowed thickly, pressing myself against the books, trying to maintain some degree of space. "And you agreed—no touching."

"I'm *not* touching you." Leaning forward, his breath fanned over my ear, his voice lowering even more. "I'm simply standing here."

"You are *not* just standing there, and you know it," I countered, turning toward him slightly to hold his gaze as sternly as I could while trying to ignore the goosebumps racing down my back.

He reached across me with his other arm, trapping me on both sides, his lips hovering over mine. His eyes shifted color quickly, the pale blue flashing with a silver glow, full of mischief and temptation. "Then what am I doing?"

"You're going to get me in trouble." I stole a glance behind him, but there was no one there. There hardly ever was in this part of the library.

"One kiss and I'll let you run along to your little job."

"No."

Instead of being angry that I had the nerve to refuse him for the hundredth time, his eyes crinkled in amusement. "Why not?"

"Because it's never that simple with you."

"You can trust me this time. I was an angel, remember? There *must* be some good in me. Isn't that what you said?"

"'Was' being the operative word. I don't trust you any more than I trust any other demon."

"You don't trust yourself, you mean."

"I trust myself just fine."

"Then prove it. Kiss me. Kiss me once and walk away."

Damn it! I blundered right into that stupid challenge and now I didn't know how to proceed. Should I kiss him and walk away to prove a point? Or continue to refuse because he was being absolutely ridiculous, which would only lead to more goading in the long run?

Without entangling myself in too much deliberation, I leaned forward and pressed my lips to his. He inhaled sharply, as if I caught him by surprise, but a moment later his tongue slid along the seam of my lips, slipping inside the first chance he got.

Instead of pulling back, I angled deeper into the kiss, stroking his tongue with mine. It might have been my pride at work again, but I was tired of him thinking he had the upper hand in every situation. And unlike him, I was used to punishing myself, denying myself any sort of pleasure, and working through the frustration. So even though I felt my dick hardening behind my zipper and was surprisingly desperate to rub it against something, I knew I'd be able to walk away from this test and not look back. I doubted he'd have the same capability, demon prince or not.

Threading my fingers into his hair, I cupped the back of his head and kissed him harder while my other hand slipped around his waist. Without warning, I whirled him backward, pressing him against the bookcase. He groaned against my lips, wrapping his arms around my waist and dragging me up against him.

The sound of approaching footsteps echoed behind us. I slid my hand down to his chest and pushed away from him. It took a second for his eyes to open. When they finally did, I could hardly see his usual silver or the blue glamor he used, his pupils were too wide, gazing at me with lust and fascination.

Raking my teeth over my bottom lip, I smirked and arched an eyebrow at him before turning and walking away —just as he insinuated I couldn't do. Stubbornness usually wasn't a favorable trait, but today I was thankful I possessed enough of it to outfox a demon at one of his own games.

Before I stepped out of the aisle, I stole a glance in either direction and proceeded to walk as casually as possible with a hard-on across the restricted section to my office.

I expected Remiel to follow me, but he didn't. In fact, I didn't see him again until it was lunchtime when he appeared out of thin air and set a sandwich and a cup of soup on my desk, of all things.

I jumped and closed my eyes, cursing under my breath. "Would you stop doing that?"

"Doing what?" he asked, dropping into the chair across

from me at an angle and draping one leg over the arm of the chair. He was still in his collegiate attire, though he'd pulled the tie loose and undid the top couple of buttons on his shirt.

"Popping in without warning. What if someone had been in here?"

"I made sure there wasn't."

I frowned at him but let it go, turning my attention to the food. "What is that?"

"A pitiful example of that thing you call lunch."

"Yes, I can see that. Why is it on my desk?"

"Because it's too windy to eat outside?"

I spread my hands on my desk, trying to think of another way to phrase it. "Why did you bring me food? I'm more than capable of feeding myself."

"It's an hour past your usual meal break. I assumed you'd gotten so wrapped up in whatever it is you're doing"—he gestured at the stack of books with a painfully bored expression—"that you forgot to eat."

"That was oddly thoughtful." My brow furrowed as I glanced between him and his offering. Was this a truce? Had I proven myself in the stacks earlier and he was waving a white flag? Or was he lulling me into another false sense of security? At the very least, I felt safe in assuming it wasn't poisoned. Despite the torture and the overall maltreatment and complete disregard for personal boundaries, he didn't seem to actually want to kill me. At least not yet.

"You're welcome," he replied with a dazzling smile. It broadened a bit more at the same time my heart spasmed. A coincidence, I told myself, reaching for the sandwich.

Unwrapping it carefully, I fought a smile when I saw what he got me—ham and cheese.

He waggled his brows but refrained from gloating verbally. Leaning forward, he snagged one of the books off the top of the pile and flipped through it the same way unimpressed children flipped through old magazines at the doctor's office.

"Risking life and limb for research? How very unlike you," I mused, taking a bite of the sandwich.

"John Dee couldn't cast a real spell if God himself descended from the Heavens and handed him step-by-step instructions. All he and Kelley cared about was swapping wives and conning idiots out of their money." Remiel shimmied down further into the chair and leaned his head against the other armrest. "Why are you wasting your time with the Book of Soyga?"

"Thought maybe there would be something useful in the Celestial alphabet," I replied with a shrug. "He and Kelley could have been on to something."

"This is gibberish," he said, tossing the book back onto the pile. "The real Celestial language doesn't look like that."

"I don't suppose you'll tell me what it *does* look like?"

"If we actually find some, sure. What do I care?" He shrugged.

I blinked, nearly dropping the sandwich. "Seriously? You'll reveal the Angelic Script? Just like that?"

"Why not?" He shrugged again, looking completely and utterly uninterested in the topic.

"I don't know... usually you want something in exchange."

His pale gaze slid to mine. If he realized he missed his opportunity to strike a bargain, he didn't look put out. He just sat there, watching me with an unreadable expression until heat prickled along my cheeks and the back of my neck.

I looked away quickly, taking another bite of my sandwich to disguise whatever emotion he thought he saw.

"I told you this is all a waste of time," he said, rolling his eyes skyward and staring up at the ornate plaster ceiling. "You're never going to find anything."

"Maybe if you actually provided me with some information, I'd have a better idea of what it is I'm looking for."

"What is it you want to know?"

"I don't know," I huffed. "Something about your oath? Other oaths people have made and how they've broken them? *If* they've broken them. Any weakness I can exploit in Beliar or Hazael?"

"Leave Beliar out of it," he said suddenly, his gaze snapping back to mine. "I don't even want to hear his name cross your lips."

A whisper of dread curled around my throat at his reaction. "Why?"

Remiel glanced around as he stood and circled my desk. I spun to face him, gripping the arms on my chair as he leaned down and pressed his cheek to mine, his lips against my ear.

"He's always listening. Speaking his name aloud is all it takes to get his attention and you don't want his attention, lamb. Demons he ignores, but humans? Witches? He does not remain the king of Hell by his virtue. He kills witches the way hunters kill deer—for sport." He paused, his breath washing down the side of my neck before he continued. "If you believe nothing else, believe this—if he comes for you, you're going to wish I'd killed you."

Swallowing the lump of cotton in my throat, I met Remiel's gaze as he pulled back slowly. His silver eyes were cold and clear, not a hint of amusement or sarcasm to be found. Of everything he'd ever told me, that might have been the first honest thing.

"On second thought, stay away from the Celestial language or anything that purports to be it," Remiel said, his features hardening. "Or don't and see what happens."

"But, I—"

He shimmered in front of me, like a mirage, and vanished.

"Remiel!" I scoffed, slumping back in my chair. So much for turning a corner with him.

CHAPTER TWENTY-ONE

PHELAN

With the full moon aglow overhead, I made my way down Old River Road on foot. It was too overgrown to drive out here, but it was well away from the modern village of Winslow, which was the primary reason for its appeal. I wanted to make sure I had as much privacy as possible for what I was about to do.

A quiet bleating beside me drew my attention down to the small brown and white goat plodding along, unaware of where we were headed or why.

The knife in my pocket suddenly weighed a thousand pounds. I tried to ignore the surge of guilt and tightened my grip on the rope looped around its neck.

Thankfully, the crossroad wasn't much farther. Then I could do what had to be done and leave again, hopefully with the answers I needed. Since my hunt through the library had turned up absolutely nothing, I decided to try another source.

As the trees thinned, the remnants of Millbridge Lane came into view, the skeleton of the dilapidated gristmill off in the distance. The intersection was choked with tall grass and bramble, but if you knew where to look the abandoned roads were visible, practically glowing in the moonlight like a supernatural beacon.

I tied the goat to a low-hanging branch near the road and set my bag down, pulling out the other supplies.

Given Hazael's high rank, the circle needed to hold him would have to be infinitely more complex than the ones I created for average demons. It would have been helpful to know what sort of demon he was, but since I had no idea, I went with a little bit of everything, forming concentric rings out of varying materials—ripped pages from books, chalk, salt, sand, crystals, and candles. The last circle was for the goat's grisly contribution.

Leading the animal to the center of the circle, I staked its lead to the ground and knelt in front of it.

The goat bleated and blinked.

"Don't look at me like that," I said, gripping the handle of the knife but keeping it out of view at my side, in case the creature suddenly had some insight as to what was about to happen.

The goat tipped its head and rubbed its little horns against my shoulder, using me to scratch an itch.

"Stop." I tried to shrug the goat off, but it came back, rubbing its head again. I put my palm on its forehead and pushed it backward, but somehow ended up scratching between its horns anyway.

"I suppose it's the least I could do," I mumbled, dropping the knife and using both hands to scratch along its head and under its chin. "But just so you know, I don't want to do this. If Hazael didn't require such a barbaric summoning, I would have never brought you out here to be killed. Although, now that I think about it, you were probably going to end up someone's dinner anyway.

Some people are destined for misery. I get it. And I'm sorry."

The goat closed its eyes and leaned into my hand as I continued to move it around in small circles, scratching lightly.

"Just know that you're serving a higher purpose than being food," I told the goat, picking up the knife again.

It opened its eyes, gazing up at me with those weird rectangular pupils.

I gripped one little horn and held the animal steady, pressing the edge of the knife to its throat. "I'm so sorry."

The goat bleated and pulled backward, but not enough to dislodge my hold.

Closing my eyes, I turned away, trying to build up the courage to do what needed to be done.

A flash of golden light shone behind my eyelids. They flew open, taking in the sight of Hazael materializing into view before me—not *in* the circle, as he should be, but right outside of it.

"What do *you* want?" Hazael sneered. "And what are you doing to that goat?"

I jumped, dropping my hand from the goat's horn and lowering the knife. "You're here."

"Of course I'm here. I simply *had* to see why my brother's stupid little pet was calling out to me in the dead of night. Out here, all alone... and with a goat?"

"But I..." I glanced around at the circle, trying to piece together how I managed to get him here when I hadn't even called him yet. Unless he was stalking me too. Given his threat the last time I saw him, I shouldn't have been surprised. Either way, I guess it didn't matter. I'd wanted Hazael and now here he was and I *didn't* have to sacrifice a goat along the way. While part of me wondered if Remiel had been lying about that too, the other part was eager to get this over with.

Hazael moved forward slowly, watching me with glowing eyes again. It was unnerving. Even more unnerving than the looks I was used to getting from Remiel. "Does your master know what you're up to? I'm guessing he doesn't otherwise he'd punish you severely. Giving yourself over to another demon when he's already claimed you? The betrayal would shatter him. I can't wait to watch it happen. Maybe we should call him..."

"I'm here to talk to *you*. Leave him out of it." I got to my feet, keeping the knife at my side, like it would do me any good.

Hazael threw his head back and laughed, sounding genuinely amused. "You are strange, indeed, witch. Perhaps you're not as smart as I thought you were."

"I wondered if you could help me," I continued, unfazed by the insult.

"Help you?" He raised his eyebrows. "Why would *I* ever help *you*? I should kill you right now for daring to think you're even worthy of summoning me. Or better yet, take you back to my domain and torture you for a millennium, until I've stripped away every bit of flesh from your bones and turned your mind into a cesspool of hate and misery. Maybe then I'd send you back to Remiel, a creature so unrecognizable he'd kill you on sight out of sheer disgust."

"If you do that, you'll never defeat Remiel," I said, tipping my chin up as Hazael stopped directly in front of me, separated by only a thin line of salt on the ground.

Hazael's eerie golden eyes flashed. "What would you know of it?"

"You can't kill one another without enslaving yourselves in the process, right? The oath you swore is the only thing stopping you. It's the only thing stopping you from killing *any* of the other princes. And the king himself. Right?"

He cocked his head, smirking as his gaze swept over me, obviously reassessing his prior conclusions. "Well, well. Someone has done his homework. Couldn't help but notice you neglected to *name* the king. Go on, witch. Say it. Say his name, if you're so bold."

After Remiel's icy warning and abrupt departure from my office the other day, there was no way I would rise to Hazael's challenge. "What if I could help you find a way around it? The oath? Then nothing would stop you from killing them all and ruling Hell. It's what you want, isn't it? To be king? To have all of their power? Remiel is just the icing on the cake."

Hazael considered me for a moment. "Why would you want to help me? Why not help your precious master defeat Beliar?"

"He's *not* my master," I snapped. "I hate him. He ruined my life and I'd like nothing more than to see him suffer for everything he's done to me."

"And yet you seemed so protective of him the first time we met." Hazael practically purred as he leaned closer to the invisible barrier between us, his dark red hair falling over his bare shoulder like a curtain. "So sure *he* was the superior demon."

I scoffed, shifting backward as subtly as I could. "Despite what you may think of me, I'm not stupid. I knew he could hear us. If I said anything against him, he'd have punished me worse than he already has. I couldn't risk it. I needed to get you alone."

"What is it you want from me, Necromancer?"

"My freedom." I held up my left hand, reminding him of

Remiel's sigil. As if the silver-haired demon knew what I was doing, a flash of white-hot pain stabbed through my palm. Wincing, I cradled my hand against my stomach and glanced around for any sign of him.

Hazael held out his hand, palm up, pulling my attention back to him.

I eyed it warily, making no move to break the circle.

"Give it to me," he said, leaving zero room for argument. "Now."

"Are you going to hurt me?"

"Even if I am, what are you going to do to stop me?"

He had a point. Reluctantly, I stretched my hand across the last ring of the circle.

Hazael seized my wrist and yanked me out of the protective space. Unsteady on my feet, I crashed against his broad chest. I had enough sense, though, to plunge the knife in my right hand into the hollow of his clavicle. I'd meant to hit his heart, but it was too late now.

He tightened his hold on my wrist, practically crushing the bones in his grip until I let go of the knife in a vain attempt to try and pry his fingers off my arm. Wisps of smoke curled around the blade and the smell of burning flesh filled the air, mixed with the herbs and holy water I'd consecrated it with.

Laughing, Hazael pulled the knife out of his shoulder and turned the sharp edge on me, its bloody tip pressing against my carotid. "What did you hope to accomplish just now?"

"You scared me," I said quickly, trying not to even breathe too deeply for fear of cutting myself. "I reacted."

"It was a valiant attempt at bravery. And now I'm going to kill you for it."

"But don't you see? You can use me!" I clung to the

bronze tunic he wore, trying to lean as far away from the blade as I could the second it pricked my skin. "If I can get close enough to stab you, I can get close enough to Remiel. Closer, even. He's infatuated with me. You know he is. You saw it. If you get me a relic, like the one you used before, I can kill him for you."

"And why would I trust you after that little stunt?"

"I told you, you scared me. I didn't know what you were going to do. I don't want to be hurt anymore. I've been tortured enough by Remiel and his henchmen. Please, Hazael. I'm desperate and you're the only one who can help me. Everyone else is too scared of Remiel to make a move against him. But *you're* not afraid of him. Please..."

He didn't look convinced. "Unclench your fist."

Watching him cautiously, I did as he said, opening my left hand again and hoping if I lived through the night, I wouldn't regret it.

He inspected the mark up close, his scowl deepening. "You want me to remove Remiel's mark and in return, you'll kill him? That's it? No other requests?"

I shook my head. "No. Just tell me how. When."

"Well, you've already proven you don't have the speed or the strength," he said, lowering the knife and crushing it against my chest right before he shoved me away from him in disgust. "I suppose you'll have to use whatever intelligence you think you have."

"I have enough, don't you worry about it."

He smirked at my scowl. "Tell me, what sort of magic do you have?"

"I'm a Dreamweaver."

He rolled his eyes and shook his head. "Of course you are."

I made a face at him, strangely insulted by his dismissal. "What is that supposed to mean?"

"It means you have absolutely nothing useful to offer me. You're even more pathetic than I originally thought."

"Pathetic or not, what do you have to lose? If I fail, Remiel will kill me. But if I succeed, you have one less enemy standing between you and all of Hell."

He continued to stare at me, eyes glowing like embers. I shifted from one foot to the other, wondering what the next move was going to be. I, for one, was out of options. Short of Remiel swooping in and murdering me for real.

"Have you heard of the Ring of Eleazar?" Hazael asked at last.

I shook my head.

"Surely you've heard of King Solomon?"

I glared at him and the disdain dripping off every one of his words. "Of course I have. Every Necromancer has."

"Well, then you'll be happy to know there's another ring that can control demons as well as Solomon's Seal. Find that and bring it to me. With it, I'll be able to command Remiel to remove his mark and you can go on living your pathetic little life."

"Where do I find the ring?"

He shrugged, gesturing vaguely. "It was stolen by Vespasian's son and lost to the ages."

"Then how do you even know it exists?"

"Because I was there when God gave it to Eleazar. It cannot be destroyed by anything on this earth, so it has to be here somewhere." A burst of flames erupted in the center of Hazael's hand. When the fire subsided, a small piece of parchment lay there, etched with what I assumed was a rendition of the ring. "Happy hunting, witch," he said, handing me the drawing with a malicious smile.

I took the paper and studied the ring, committing the design of the seal to memory before looking up with a terse nod. “I’ll find it.”

“I’m not counting on it. But it will be so much fun to watch you try.” He laughed and disappeared in a swirl of shadows.

Exhaling a breath, I tucked the paper into my pocket and turned to gather my things. The goat stared up at me, its head cocked to one side.

“Shit. What am I going to do with you now?”

The goat bleated.

CHAPTER TWENTY-TWO

REMIEL

"Why is there a goat in your kitchen?" I asked as I came into view, having grown bored watching Phelan hand-feed the thing a variety of vegetables to try and determine what it liked. As if it actually mattered. It was a goat. They ate everything.

Jumping, Phelan spun to face me with a glare. "Do you *ever* use a door?"

"No." My amused smirk disappeared the moment a revolting odor reached my nostrils. It was one I'd recognize anywhere and it wasn't the fucking goat. "What did you do?" I demanded, stalking across the distance in the time it took Phelan to blink.

"N-nothing!" He backed away from me and darted toward the living room as fast as his feet could carry him. I ran him down like a rabbit, the repulsive smell wafting behind him with each step.

Before he could get too far away, I grabbed his arm and whipped him around again. This close, there was *no* doubt. Hazael's stench was everywhere, like a toxic vapor clinging to his clothes, even his skin.

Rage blackened my vision and my fingers tightened on his bicep. “What did he do to you?”

Phelan winced, trying to peel my fingers apart. “You’re hurting me.”

“Tell me!”

His eyes widened. “What are you talking about? Wh—”

“Do *not* lie to me! I can smell him all over you! What did he do to you, Phelan?”

“Nothing!” His heart hammered inside his chest, tripping over itself when I ripped his shirt open and yanked it off his body in two pieces. “Remiel!”

There were no visible marks on his torso or his arms, but that didn’t mean Hazael didn’t brand him somewhere else. Or do something worse.

Ignoring Phelan’s outrage, I spun him forcefully and scanned his backside, checking along his hairline, down his back to his ass. Finding nothing, I tore his pants off and shoved him face-first onto the couch, despite his continued protests, and checked along his legs.

“Remiel! Stop! Nothing happened!”

He gasped when I ran my hand along his crease and swore viciously as I sank a finger inside of him, searching for any indication Hazael had brutalized him or somehow infected him. There’s no way he had a second encounter with that loathsome beast and walked away unscathed. Not once Hazael knew Phelan belonged to me.

“Goddamn it, Remiel!”

From what I could tell, he felt unharmed, not like he’d been ravaged by anyone or any*thing*. And there were no other sigils to speak of, except my own.

“You don’t have to do this!” Phelan yelled over his shoulder, gritting his teeth and gripping the back of the couch so hard the veins in his forearms popped out.

"Would you stop mauling me and fucking *talk* to me for a second?!"

I granted his last wish and flipped him onto his back, slamming him against the cushions and coming nose-to-nose with him so I could watch his face as he stumbled over each lie. Did Hazael coach him? Tell him what to say? Or maybe he cut out the middleman and decided to possess him directly? Was this even *my* Phelan?

The Phelan lookalike took my face between his hands, stroking my cheek. The tender gesture contradicted the fury in his gaze. "I'm ok. Nothing happened with Hazael. I promise."

"You lie," I growled between my teeth.

"I'm *not* lying." His eyes narrowed. "Look inside my head if you have to. I'm offering it to you."

I immediately seized the opportunity, bursting past his usual mental barricades and tearing through his recent memories like I was destroying the Assyrian army once again. My blood boiled at the sight of Hazael in Phelan's memories, confirming my suspicion.

Seeing him through Phelan's eyes, the way he looked at *my* pet like he was Hazael's next toy, the way his eyes flashed while he held Phelan against him, sent a wave of nausea through my stomach. Fury swelled inside with each passing second, as I could only imagine the thoughts running through Hazael's depraved mind.

My anger abated somewhat when I saw Phelan stab Hazael, but it was renewed when the tables turned and Hazael had the temerity to injure *my* Necromancer.

Phelan ran his hand through my hair, gripping the back of my head gently. "See? I told you."

"Yes, I saw. I saw you conspiring with my greatest enemy," I hissed, wrapping a hand around his throat and pinning him to the cushion, forcibly turning his face to the side to reveal the thin scab on his neck. Phelan might have cleaned the blood away, but there was no disputing the dark red line. "If you're even *you*."

"What are you talking about? Who else would I be?"

"One of Hazael's ghouls for all I know." I squeezed his throat tighter until his breathing came in small gasps. "*Tell me, detestable worm,*" I continued in the Celestial tongue, watching Phelan's face flush a dark scarlet from the pressure, looking for any sign of a demon within him, lurking beneath the surface. "*Was this part of your master's grand plan?*"

"I don't understand"—Phelan choked out, clawing at my hand—"what you're saying."

"*Who are you?*"

"Remiel."

"*Your name!*"

"Please..."

I squeezed harder.

Unable to remove my hand, Phelan wrapped his legs around my bare waist and looped one arm around my neck so suddenly I wasn't prepared when he flung us off the side of the couch. We landed on the hardwood floors and rolled with one another a couple of times, limbs tangled, each fighting to maintain the upper hand.

Somehow, Phelan came out on top, breathing hard, straddling my waist with a knife pressed to my throat. Where he'd pulled it from, I had no idea, but it certainly looked like the one he had earlier when he spoke with Hazael.

"I went there to find a way to kill *him*!" Phelan shouted through a grimace, his voice raspy, the red rings around his pale throat as clear as day. "I've exhausted my resources,

Remiel! So I figured why not go to the source? He's had plenty of time over the years to think of how to kill you. Lo and behold, he had the answer. Only instead of giving it to him, I was going to give it to you!"

I rolled my eyes, not the least bit convinced by his story or concerned with the blade against my skin. "You think that ring actually exists? If you do, you're a fool. It's nothing more than a myth. Demons have hunted for it for thousands of years."

"Yeah, *demons*," he spat back. "Not witches. Do you think God would let something like that fall into a demon's hands? Now, who's the fool? I would bet you anything that ring has more wards and protective spells over it than even the most powerful grimoire. It's going to take a Necromancer to find it, which is probably the only reason Hazael doesn't already have it. How many of us would willingly turn something like that over to our sworn enemies?"

"Do you think I'm stupid?" I growled. "The second you have that ring, you'll use it to kill me."

"I could kill you now if that's what I wanted."

"Unlikely."

As if incensed by the challenge, the muscle in his jaw ticked a split second before he swung the knife downward.

I grabbed his wrist and rolled my hips at the same time, bucking him off of me. Instead of letting go, though, I tumbled with him, pinning him beneath me again.

In the midst of the struggle, the tip of the knife stuck into my chest. From the way pain seared into my flesh, it was clearly not an ordinary knife. He'd done something to it, blessed it somehow with something powerful. Blood trickled down his hand, droplets splattering on his chest, proving my point.

Phelan glanced between the knife and my face, his

beautiful eyes widening with the realization of what he'd done. Wide with fear and genuine concern. The same look he'd had when I collapsed in his living room after the ambush.

In that moment, I knew it was him—not a possessed version. If Hazael had been in control of him, he would have been thrilled with the injury, not horrified by it. But even if Phelan was acting of his own accord, I still couldn't be sure Hazael hadn't warped his mind somehow.

I maintained my hold on his wrist and kept it—and the knife—in place, letting the stench of blood and sizzling flesh permeate the air.

"What are you waiting for?" I taunted. "Push it in."

He swallowed and shook his head.

"Push it in and leave it in. You'll get your wish, lamb." I pulled his hand closer to my chest, sinking the knife in deeper with a grimace. "You'll be rid of me once and for all."

"I won't condemn other people to die just so I can kill you," he said quietly.

My laugh was bitter.

His eyes narrowed. "What's so funny?"

"I lied. You're the only one with my mark."

"How do I know that's not *also* a lie?"

"Guess you'll have to kill me and find out. Hope you made your peace with God."

"I don't want to kill you," he whispered. For once, his heartbeat was steady and strong, not tumbling over itself in the wake of another lie.

Something in his blue-green gaze ignited a firestorm inside of me. This was the closest he'd come to death under my hand and yet he still didn't want to kill me. He was angry, to be sure, but beneath the anger was a myriad of other emotions—confusion, concern, guilt, and maybe even a touch of understanding, like he'd come to expect this sort of interaction and was no longer alarmed by it. Or by me.

Despite the blade in my chest, I leaned forward slowly. My lips brushed across his, questioning his resolve, before pressing against them fully.

Phelan's grip tightened on the hilt, even as he kissed me softly, uncertainly, his body still tense beneath mine.

I shifted between his thighs, sinking down on top of him, trying to eliminate any space between us.

Without warning, Phelan yanked the knife out of my chest and flung it to the side. His bloody hand threaded through my hair, drawing me closer for a deeper kiss. I melted against him, surprising myself when a moan slipped out involuntarily.

He kissed me harder, fisting his hand in my hair and rolling his hips against mine, only a layer of black fabric between us. As much as I wanted to fuck him, I also wanted to lavish as much attention on him as I could, worshipping him from head to toe. *My* Phelan. *My* Necromancer. A treasure that only *I* was allowed to admire, to touch, to find pleasure in. No one else.

Pressing kisses to the side of his throat, I grazed his skin with my teeth now and again, making my way downward. Using my hands and my tongue, I drew abstract designs all over his body, watching him lean in or shy away depending on what I was doing. Making sure there wasn't a spot on him that didn't feel me somehow, my wings danced over the places I couldn't reach with my hands or my mouth.

When my lips closed around his nipple, Phelan's eyes rolled up and he arched against me, like a cat trying to get more contact. I didn't linger long before moving on to the other, toying with it between my teeth and tongue until he whimpered in frustration.

Smiling to myself, I reached between us and stroked his cock gently, languidly, while lapping up my blood from his skin.

"You can't keep doing this," he said, forcing his eyes open.

"Doing what?" I squeezed the crown, palming the glistening pre-cum and rubbing it all over his length.

"This," he sighed, thrusting against my hand without further explanation.

"This?" I stroked him from base to tip again, varying the pressure and the speed.

"Yeah."

"Alright." If he didn't want to do "this," then I'd do "that" instead. Shifting downward, I settled between his thighs. Just the sight of his cock had me wetting my lips in anticipation.

"Remi—" My name ended in a gasp as I swallowed the length of him, gently rolling his balls in my hand and massaging beneath his sac. His hips jerked reflexively and his fingers clawed at the floor beneath him.

Not letting up on his cock, I grabbed his hand and moved it to the back of my head. He immediately threaded his fingers through my hair, pushing the strands of silver away from my face and holding them at bay in his fist.

When I glanced up, I was pleased to see he was watching me, his lower lip caught between his teeth. But he had that pained expression again—the one where his idiotic upbringing stood between him and what he really wanted, making him feel guilt when all he should be feeling was the pleasure of a warm, wet mouth.

I sucked hard, hoping to override his archaic morals.

I must have succeeded since his hand tightened in my hair and his hips chased the pull from my mouth. "Fuck, that feels good," he whispered, more to himself than me.

His words spurred me on, stroking and sucking his cock, his balls, his taint, everything within reach, until his body tensed beneath my hands and he was squirming, on the verge of an orgasm.

Pulling myself off of his cock, I left a trail of kisses along his groin, moving down his thigh with a slow, steady purpose.

Phelan propped himself on his elbows, but before he could ask any questions, I spread my wing over his chest and pushed him backward. He took the hint and laid down, keeping his questions to himself for once.

As his reward, I stroked him with my wings again, caressing over the upper half of his body while I kissed and massaged every inch of his lower half, down his legs to his feet, and up again. I forced myself past his cock to his torso, kissing along his hands, his arms, and back to his lips.

Watching goosebumps race over his skin in the firelight was a pastime I'd never grow tired of. Nor would I grow tired of the sighs and small gasps, sounds he'd only ever made for me—*would* only ever make for me. As much as I loved the way he fought me at every turn, hating me and everything I made him feel, I suddenly saw the appeal in being gentle with him. I couldn't be gentle all the time. It wasn't in my nature. But this one time? I could do it for him.

Once I pulled him back from the precipice of climax, I worked my way to his cock again, swallowing him down to the base.

He moaned my name so softly I almost missed it. I squeezed my own cock beneath the long black shendyt, trying my best not to moan in return. Hearing my name fall from his lips, breathy and reverent, was the sweetest sound I'd ever heard.

"I could do this all night," I murmured against his shaft, licking along the underside before sliding up to suck on the crown and twirl my tongue around it in the pattern he seemed to prefer.

"I can't," he breathed, thrusting into my hand. "We can't..."

"Can't? Or won't?"

His brilliant blue-green eyes opened, settling on me as soon as they came into focus. He didn't speak, but the look in his eyes prompted me to crawl up his body again and claim his lips with mine. He was looking for permission, for someone to tell him it was all right to actually *feel* pleasure—that it wasn't a sin. If that's what he needed, I'd do more than give him permission. I'd give him the out he was looking for; I'd force him to do what I wanted so he could assuage his guilty conscience that the sin was mine alone.

I rolled him onto his side and pushed his upper leg forward so I could straddle the one underneath. A rush of saliva cascaded to the head of my cock before I teased his hole with it. "Tell me you want it."

"No." He closed his eyes and turned away from me.

I leaned forward and grabbed his jaw, forcing him to look up at me again. Defiance and lust filled his gaze in equal measure. "Tell me no again and see what happens."

"No."

"Be good for me, Phelan. You know you want to. You want to be so, *so* good for me." I pressed inside him slowly, keeping ahold of his jaw so I could watch his expressions change.

First, there was his ingrained denial, his stubbornness,

his desire to rebel just because he could. He wasn't submissive by nature—his family, his god, had made him that way. I aimed to undo it all.

As soon as the head of my cock was in, his breathing deepened and came in quicker bursts, his muscles tightening around me. His initial desire melted to uncertainty, unsure if the pleasure was worth that first bit of pain.

And finally, when I sank inside completely, his lashes fluttered and closed, barely hiding the fact his eyes had rolled up in the back of his head. The uncertainty was gone, replaced by hunger, an ache, that only I could relieve because I was the only one cruel enough to torture him like this.

"Is this what you wanted? What you're so scared to ask for?" I released his jaw so I could grip his hip with both hands, anchoring myself so I didn't flip him flat onto his stomach and fuck him senseless.

He had no answer, other than to moan, the muscles in his back tight.

"Doesn't this feel good?" I asked with a groan, rolling my hips slowly to open him up. We didn't need to rush it. I would happily fuck him all night until he passed out from exhaustion, and perhaps even then.

He gasped and reached back, grabbing onto one of my hands. I paused for a moment, studying the crease between his brows, searching for the reason behind the action. Finding none, I slid out and pushed back inside just as slowly, loving the way his fingers tightened on my hand as much as the way his body molded around mine.

"Fuck," he whispered, licking his lips as I thrust as deep as I could go.

"There's my pet," I murmured, picking up the pace little by little.

His fingers remained locked around my hand, but he didn't try to shove me away or slow me down from the steady rhythm we'd settled into.

"That's it, lamb." I slid my free hand underneath him and between his legs, stroking his cock. "Give in to it. I won't stop you this time. Take what you want from me."

Phelan rolled his hips backward, meeting my thrusts as they increased. He twisted in my direction, gazing up at me with the most beautiful expression I'd ever seen, one laden with desire. Desire for *me*.

Leaning forward, I caressed the side of his face and kissed his lips. He returned the kiss eagerly, opening his mouth to me before I had to demand entrance.

He tore away suddenly, panting against my lips. I didn't need to ask what was wrong. I could feel the trembling starting.

"Are you going to come for me? Hmm? Or do I need to fill you up first?" I asked, slowing my thrusting to make each one long and deep, angling my cock to graze that cluster of nerves on the inward strokes. Was it too much to ask that his orgasm be soul-shattering? If I could manage that, I never needed to worry about my lamb going astray. He'd always come back to me.

"I don't… I…" Whatever else he was going to say disappeared in a gasp as I shifted backward onto my ass, pulling him with me. I reclined against the couch and settled him in my lap, his back to my chest. The new position, plus gravity, worked in my favor and Phelan's "Oh fuck!" nearly sent me into my own orgasm.

"You feel so good riding my cock," I mumbled against his ear. "You have no idea."

He slung his arm around my neck and half-turned toward me, pressing his lips to mine. I kept thrusting up into him from beneath, but he met each one, swiveling his hips now and again, adding to the friction.

I slid one hand around his throat, squeezing as I kissed him. A strangled moan escaped his lips before he resumed kissing me, feverish and almost as desperate for my mouth as for the oxygen I was depriving him of.

My other hand drifted to his cock, slicking pre-cum along his shaft while stroking him. He moaned into our kiss, rocking his hips faster to alternate between grinding his ass against me and thrusting up into my hand.

"Do it," I said, grazing my teeth along the faint stubble on his jaw and nipping his neck, just so I could watch the pink blotches spread over his pale skin. "Do it, Phelan. Be a good boy and come for me. I want it. I want to feel you come around my cock. It's been too long."

"I am. I'm—" The first wave of his orgasm rippled through him, every muscle in his body constricting. I tightened the hold I had on his throat, transforming his moan to whimper. He tipped his head back, eyes squeezed shut and mouth slack, as ropes of cum shot over the hand stroking him.

"Fuck, Phelan..." The feeling of him writhing on top of me, my cock buried deep inside, was everything I'd been missing.

As he came down from his high, I licked his cum off my hand, savoring the taste of him. The moment it was clean, I shoved him forward, out of my lap.

"Remiel!" He sprawled on his stomach in front of the hearth. In the time it took him to look back, blinking with a furrowed brow, I was on him, sliding between his legs and sinking inside him again. His surprised gasp melted into a sigh.

"I can't help it," I said, slamming my cock into him

again and again, giving in to the primal urgency he unleashed within me. "I need you."

"You have me," he moaned, resting his head against his forearm.

I covered his body with mine, threading my arms through his and bracing on the floorboards beneath him. "Do I?"

Pushing up onto his elbows, he reached behind him with his left hand—his *marked* hand—and grabbed the back of my neck, pulling my face into his hair. I breathed in the scent of him, thrusting harder and harder until I buried myself one last time, spilling my release with a grunt into the back of his neck.

I stayed there for a moment, trying to catch my breath, before rolling Phelan and I onto our sides. He was still twitching. I kept my cock inside him as long as I could, curling myself around him and draping a wing over us.

He sighed softly, folding his arm on top of the one I had wrapped around his waist. I caressed his flushed cheek before laying my hand over his heart, enamored with the steady rhythm as it slowed, along with his breathing.

"So fucking perfect," I whispered to myself once he was asleep. "And you're all mine. Forever."

CHAPTER TWENTY-THREE

PHELAN

When I woke the next morning, I expected sore muscles from a night spent on the floor being a demon's personal plaything. Needless to say, I was surprised to find I was in my bed. Even more surprised to see I was alone.

"Remiel?" I sat up, looking around, but he wasn't there.

Flopping back into bed, I exhaled a breath and rubbed a hand over my face.

Last night had been... interesting. I guess. I didn't know what else to call it. Terrifying? Remiel had scared the shit out of me, that was for certain, more than Hazael managed to. And after everything Remiel put me through in Hell, I didn't think it was possible to reach any new levels of fright.

His eyes, for one, were unlike anything I'd ever seen from him. They'd changed color in Hell when he thought Melech might have come around, uninvited, but last night they were black through and through, like a true demon. It was obvious he was beyond pissed but the reason behind it remained a mystery. I got that I was "his." His "pet." And he hated Hazael. But he didn't get that mad when Hazael showed up the first time and launched me across the yard like a lawn dart.

Speaking of manhandling—I was used to Remiel tossing me around like a toddler with a new toy, but last night was different. It was almost... frantic. At one point, I didn't even think he was talking to me. In addition to the strange language, he was literally trying to strangle me to death—and nearly succeeded.

Swallowing thickly at the memory, my hand drifted to my throat.

If you're even you.

Did he think Hazael had actually possessed me? I suppose it would explain a lot. Although, I didn't even know how I managed to convince him I *wasn't* possessed. I mean, I accidentally stabbed him, but I don't know why he would consider that to be a good thing since he was taunting me to kill him. Plus, I'd blessed the blade and dipped it in so much anointing oil that the scar was bound to be worse than the first time I stabbed him. Yet, *that* was the moment his eyes cleared and returned to a gleaming silver, like the clouds parting after a violent storm.

He was so fucking confusing!

First, he tried to kill me, justifiably or not, and then he spent the rest of the night practically smothering me with attention. I didn't understand it—or him!

I tried not to think about it as I forced myself out of bed and into a cold shower. Since his handprint was beyond obvious around my throat, I disguised the red marks as best as I could by turning up the collar on my button-up shirt and throwing a sweater over the top to look like a fashion choice. Maybe I could justify wearing a scarf all day, too.

Once the goat in the kitchen was fed, I made a mental

note to look up building plans for some sort of lean-to that I could attach to the side of the house. I suppose I could have returned him to the farm where I bought him, but I wasn't in the mood to try and explain why I was bringing him back instead of eating him, never mind that whole sacrificing bit.

I had one goal in mind as I headed into work—to find out as much as I could about the Ring of Eleazar. At first, I wasn't necessarily inclined to believe Hazael, but given Remiel's reaction to what he saw, I figured there had to be some kernel of truth to it.

A brisk wind pushed me along as I made my way across campus, brown and yellow leaves swirling around my feet before tumbling down the sidewalk.

I stuffed my hands in my pockets and darted up the library steps, casting a quick glance to the column where Remiel had been lurking the other day. To my surprising disappointment, only a trio of freshmen stood there, coordinating a schedule for their study group.

Shaking it off, I ducked inside, avoiding the ornate Tennebrose seal in the floor as always, and headed toward my office.

It was a slow morning, thankfully, so I could fly through my regular tasks before diving into research on Eleazar. Well, attempting to dive. It was like doing a cannonball from a diving board into the shallow end of a pool.

Within an hour, I had come up blank in my usual sources for necromantic information. It was like searching for Remiel or Hazael's true names. Apparently, Eleazar wanted to be just as elusive.

Except, there *was* one place left that I hadn't tried, for any of their names...

The Combermere Codex.

I grabbed my set of keys and headed for the basement,

ignoring the way they jangled in my hand before I gripped them hard enough to leave indents on my palm. Offhand, I didn't know if this constituted a valid reason to consult the book or not, but considering it was under my purview as part of the rare books department, who was going to stop me?

Descending into the basement via the elevator, I hesitated, nevertheless, when the doors slid open.

The basement was bright and airy, having been renovated to accommodate modern technologies and preserve as many of our books and primary documents as possible. Still, each step I took toward the vault at the far end felt like I was slogging through knee-deep mud.

The protective wards pricked my skin the closer I got to the vault, but I pressed on. Punching in my security code on the outside of the giant metal box, the heavy steel bars disengaged and the door slid open. I sorted through the keys, looking for the biggest of them all—one three times the size of a normal key, with a complicated tooth design on both sides. Slipping it in the old lock on the second door, I turned it until the mechanisms inside clicked.

Hauling the heavy iron door open, I waited outside of the room until the motion detectors activated the lights overhead.

I clutched the keys and stepped inside, approaching the book in the center of the room warily.

Trapped beneath an iron cage, chained to a black stone pedestal, sat the Combermere Codex. The large book practically hissed as I approached it, malevolent whispers flitting around the vault in a myriad of tongues. Some were curses. Some were promises. Others pleaded with me to open it.

It was the last request that bothered me the most because that's exactly what I was there to do.

Selecting a small iron skeleton key from the ring, I unlocked the heavy padlock and removed the old cage from over the top of the book.

A soft sigh circulated the room.

Next came another key, this time to unlock the actual cover of the book from where it had been chained shut decades ago.

The yellowed pages trembled as the clasp disengaged.

The cover flung itself open, an unseen force flipping through the pages at warp speed.

"*Desistas*," I snapped, throwing a hand over the top of the book.

The pages stilled but the hissing returned, slithering around to different parts of the room like a snake.

Clearing my throat, I tucked the keys into my pocket and extended both hands over the book, careful not to touch the pages, even if they happened to turn on their own.

"*Show me*," I commanded in Latin, thinking of nothing but the Ring of Eleazar.

A low growl reverberated around me, but the book obeyed and shuffled through the pages again, stopping at a drawing that looked eerily similar to the one Hazael gave me, as if he'd somehow drawn them both.

Unfortunately, the text beside the ring was brief. It documented an event called "Eleazar's Miracle," which read like any other ancient exorcism we had on record. A man named Eleazar was summoned to the Roman emperor Vespasian to perform a ritual. Eleazar laid a ring with a seal on it upon the person and exorcized the demon inside.

And that was the extent of the entry, save for a string of strange markings at the bottom of the page. It looked like a combination of the Hebrew and Greek alphabets, though the letters were either intentionally misshapen or they were pure nonsense.

My shoulders slumped. That wasn't the least bit helpful, except to confirm Hazael hadn't been lying about the ring existing at one time or another. But Remiel also wasn't wrong to think finding it would be impossible. With next to no information to go on, how was anyone ever supposed to track it down after nearly two thousand years?

A sinister laugh floated past me, as if the book could sense my disappointment.

"Show me Vespasian," I said, glaring at the old book.

The pages refused to turn, so I could only assume there was no reference to the ancient emperor inside.

I tried again. "Show me Hazael."

And again, the pages refused to turn.

I knew better than to command the book to show me anything about Remiel. It would only end up amusing the cursed tome and frustrating me all the more. Just like demons, Necromancers had to be extremely careful with the Combermere, for the book was learning as much about us as we were about it. More than one witch had lost their mind simply from reading it and I was *not* going to fall prey to the same fate.

Still, I had one last query for the book.

"*Show me the last page Bridget Oliver looked at,*" I ordered in Latin, steeling myself for the revelation of what, exactly, drove my mother to insanity.

An awful croaking echoed through the room, like a death rattle.

The lights overhead flickered, buzzing loudly. Right as I looked up, the fluorescent bulb exploded. Dust and shards of glass rained down.

I swore and covered my head with my arms.

One by one, the rest of the bulbs shattered. The vault was plunged into total darkness.

"Phelan..." a voice whispered, drawing out my name. It was too garbled to tell if it was male or female, but it definitely wasn't human.

Crossing myself quickly, I took a step forward, glass crunching beneath my feet. I couldn't chain the book shut in the dark, but I could at least slam the cage on top of it until I could get replacement bulbs.

"Such a good boy," the voice continued in a soft hiss. "Mommy's good boy."

Gritting my teeth, I ignored the damned book and took another careful step.

"You want to be good for me, don't you?"

I stopped dead in my tracks, the hair standing up on the back of my neck. I couldn't exactly ignore that. It was the same thing Remiel said to me the night I gave in to him. The night I escaped. Or, the night I *thought* I escaped, as he later pointed out. But how did the book know that? I didn't feel it in my head and the iron should have prohibited it from using any sort of magic.

"This is what you wanted, isn't it?" the voice growled, not at all the silken tone Remiel used when he came to me at my house after my escape, prolonging my torment under the cover of darkness.

"It was a nightmare," I said out loud, my stomach twisting into knots. "It doesn't mean anything."

"So good," the voice continued, "when you're being so bad." It laughed darkly, the sound scratching at my skin like claws. "Just like mommy. Sweet little sinners."

"Show me what she read," I snapped, taking the final step so I was directly in front of the book. "And you might see the light of day again."

A dozen different hushed voices whispered frantically, arguing and pleading with one another, steadily growing louder until they swelled into a cacophony of sound, shouting and snarling and hissing. I covered my ears with my hands and squeezed my eyes shut, trying to block it all out.

As suddenly as it started, the noise stopped, prompting me to open my eyes slowly and lower my hands.

Something was glowing in the center of the book, moving across the page in swirling motions.

"Eternal Father, I offer Thee the merits of the Most Precious Blood of Jesus," the book whispered, luring me closer.

The fact the codex was quoting the Prayer of the Seven Offerings of the Precious Blood wasn't necessarily alarming. It was the image coming into view on the page that propelled a wave of nausea through me.

Sacrificium.

The same image I saw in Remiel's mind stared up at me from the pages of one of the most evil books ever created.

And it was the same thing my mother had looked at, the very last page she saw before her mind snapped. Right about the time she was pregnant with me.

My vision blurred.

My head swam.

The cloth around my neck squeezed tighter, strangling me. I couldn't breathe.

Abandoning my quest, I turned and sprinted to the vault door, glass crunching underfoot. I heaved my weight against the heavy door, slamming it shut. The key shook, scraping at the lock before I finally shoved it in and turned it. Slumping against the cool metal, I slid down to the floor and inhaled air in gulps.

Beads of sweat trickled along the back of my neck.

Swallowing thickly, I raked a hand through my hair and exhaled a shaky breath. I had no idea what happened or what the fuck was wrong with me. I wasn't prone to panic, but when I saw the spell in person I went to pieces. Because of Remiel? Because of my mother? Because of what was on that page?

By the Middle Ages, Necromancers had prohibited the use of human sacrifices. They had been common enough practice in the ancient world, but over time, we'd turned to other sacrifices—animals, mostly, along with simple offerings of food, drink, special objects. If there was blood to be shed, usually it was our own, mimicking the ultimate sacrifice of Christ.

But there it was, a forbidden spell, right there in the Combermere Codex. Not just human sacrifice, *infant* sacrifice, complete with a prayer and a diagram of how to properly flay the child open.

I'd hoped the ritual I saw in Remiel's mind was something obsolete in our world, something only demons did. I never expected to stumble across it in a Necromancer's manual, no matter how diabolical the codex turned out to be, or that the woman who gave birth to me had any interest in killing babies.

As if the mere thought conjured him, Remiel appeared in front of me in a crouch. He was wearing modern clothing again, back to the t-shirt and skinny jeans ensemble.

"What's wrong with you?" he asked, looking anything but concerned. Instead, he looked annoyed, with a furrowed brow and pursed lips, like harassing me at work was some great inconvenience to him.

"Nothing." I cleared my throat and glanced behind him,

even though I knew we were alone in the basement. “What are you doing down here?”

“I thought you called.”

“I didn’t.”

He shrugged, his brow remaining furrowed. “Well, I’m here now. Is this where you’ve been all day? And why are you sweating?”

“Not feeling well,” I mumbled, getting to my feet slowly and using the vault for support.

He mirrored my rise, hands slightly splayed like he was waiting for me to fall. Once we were both upright, his gaze darted to the door behind me. “What’s in there?”

“Books.”

“Dangerous books.” It wasn’t a question, but if he thought I was going to tell him, what, exactly Tennebrose had stowed away, he was mistaken.

“Was it all the iron that clued you in or the wards?” I glared at him.

His eyes narrowed in return. “You’re different today. What happened?”

“Nothing. Not like you’d care, anyway.” I sidestepped him and pushed the outer door closed, locking it securely.

He promptly shoved me against it, blocking my retreat to the elevator. “I told you not to lie to me.”

“Or what? What are you going to do?” I threw my hands wide, suddenly itching for a fight. “Are you going to torture me right here in the basement of the library? Go ahead. See how that works out for you. Security will be down here in minutes. Better be quick about it!”

His jaw clenched a little more with each word out of my mouth. Without warning, he yanked the keys out of my hand and pushed me out of the way so hard I stumbled over my own feet.

"What are you doing?" I made a grab for the keys, but he shoved me backward like I weighed nothing and jammed the first key in the outer door, bypassing the security code.

"Seeing what your problem is."

"You can't go in there!"

He yanked the door open with ease and moved to the second. "Seems like I can."

"Remiel! Don't!"

He didn't listen.

A second later, the iron door groaned and we stood in the opening, side by side, staring into the pitch-black vault.

The book had ceased glowing and the room was eerily silent. Part of me was relieved the whispering and howling had stopped, but then doubt began to creep in. Had I imagined it all? Was it some sort of... reaction to inexplicable anxiety? Or pure insanity?

Remiel moved forward slowly, like he was testing the ground with each step. Glass crunched under his feet and he stopped, sliding a curious look over his shoulder.

"It's the lightbulbs," I said lamely from the doorway. At least I hadn't imagined *that* part. And the ceiling was too tall for me to reach on my own, so there's no way I could have somehow inadvertently knocked them down. Something *else* had made them all shatter.

Remiel flung a hand toward the ceiling. Wisps of luminous green circled the top of the vault, illuminating the codex below.

"What is that?" Remiel asked, taking another step forward.

I glared at his back, refusing to answer. After all, it should look familiar since he had one of its spells locked away in his head. Did he read it? Write it? Or simply inspire the Necromancer who did? Either way, I was tired of his lies. I didn't want to play his game today. I had too much work to do.

Remiel circled around the backside of the pedestal, studying the book from every angle.

I kept waiting for whispers or screaming or anything, but the book remained dark and silent, non-threatening in the presence of true evil. Perhaps Remiel was the key. It was behaving because it wanted to be taken from its iron prison and returned to the Hell from which it came. God only knew what kind of havoc *that* would bring.

"I've seen this book before," Remiel said, squinting at it as he leaned closer.

I snorted, crossing my arms over my chest. At least he was admitting it. *That* was a first.

He shot me a glare from across the room. "Something to say?"

"Yeah. Are you about done? I need to work on book returns and then lock up."

"Not until I figure out what's going on with you." He reached for the book.

"No, don't!" I took a step toward him, my hand lifted like I could stop him from ten feet away. "Don't touch it!"

His gaze flicked up to mine, his hand hovering over the page. "Why not?"

"It'll drive you insane. I swear."

"If you touch it?"

"Maybe. I don't know. This is only the second time I've ever seen the book. We're not supposed to be in here. No one is. No one is supposed to use what's inside that thing."

"Because you think it'll make you go insane?" Remiel blinked at me, clearly not believing a word I was saying. "Did *you* read it?"

"Briefly." I straightened, squaring my shoulders under his suspicious gaze. "I have the training. Few do."

He circled to the front again, canting his head to read the text. It was still open, laying flat on the pedestal, presumably on the page with the sacrificial spell since I hadn't bothered to close the book before I ran out of the room.

"Phelan," he said quietly, holding a hand out to me even though his gaze was still fixated on the book.

I didn't move. "What?"

He beckoned me forward, not even bothering to turn and look at me.

I still didn't budge. Even if Remiel was there, I didn't want to go anywhere near that book. It might not have seemed as intimidating before, but maybe that's because I'd seen demons cower before him. Besides, I didn't think a grimoire would have much, if any, effect on him.

Remiel turned slightly, raising an eyebrow, his impatience as palpable as my trepidation.

Swearing under my breath, I walked forward. As I drew closer to Remiel and the cursed book I glanced at the page quickly. Sure enough, it was the same spell from earlier—the same one from his memory. A detailed drawing of a flayed infant on display, surrounded by sigils in some sort of evil ritual.

"You wanted to see the Celestial alphabet? There it is." He rested his hand between my shoulder blades and guided me forward so I was at his side, right in front of the book.

"Those are sigils," I countered, refusing to look down again. I kept my gaze focused on the iron wall across from us, listening intently for any foreign whispers in the dark.

"These are," Remiel said, gesturing to the page. When I didn't look, he gripped my chin and forcefully turned my face toward the drawing. "But *those* are Celestial letters."

"I don't believe you." He furrowed his brow at me as I ripped my chin out of his hand, glaring at him. "Why is the Angelic script written on a spell with instructions on murdering children?"

"Still believe your god is good?" Something of a smirk twisted his lips as he returned his gaze to the book. "Did you forget the story of Passover? The Binding of Isaac? Murdering children is what he does and yet you, his blind faithful, never question it."

"This isn't a sacrifice to God."

"Isn't it?" His eyes flashed dangerously in the strange green light. "The god you worship sacrificed his own son. What makes you think he cares about anyone else's child?"

Frustratingly, I didn't have an answer for him. How do you argue with a fallen angel about faith? He knew more about God and Heaven than I could ever hope to and he vehemently rejected the whole of it for reasons I would probably never understand. But the God I loved couldn't have condoned this...

"What I want to know," Remiel continued, "is how you can stand there, full of self-righteousness, when I saw this very same ritual laid out in your head? Why would a godly little Necromancer like you study this spell only to turn around and act affronted?"

Gaping at him, I searched his face for any signs of deception, trying to suss out if it was another lie. Though I had no evidence to support my suspicion, I decided it was. "Don't try to deflect this onto me. The first time I saw this spell was in *your* head! While you were passed out on my floor. Big surprise that it's included in one of the darkest grimoires to ever exist!"

"Funny because it was the *only* thing I could glean from *you* during our first time together. The one time I managed to break through your mind, this was all I saw. Imagine *my* surprise. All of those old stories about Necromancers were suddenly true! You got your power by slaughtering babies and eating their precious fat. All the better if they're unbaptized, right?"

I shook my head, nauseated all over again. "You're lying."

"Am I?"

"It's not possible. I told you, I've never seen it before. Not before you."

He turned to face me completely, arching a brow. "You let me inside your head to prove a point, so have at it. Poke around wherever you want in mine. This is your one free pass."

"So you can trap me there? No thank you." I sneered at him.

This time it was Remiel who crossed his arms, scrutinizing me with a curled lip. "How would I trap you? More importantly, *why* would I trap you? I can already take you back to Hell whenever I want. What good are you to me if you're locked inside my head?"

"I don't know!" I threw my hands up, on the verge of screaming. "*You're* the demon! Do you need a reason to do a fraction of the evil shit you do?"

Beside me, the book made a broken sort of hissing sound—like it was giggling.

I spun to face it, hands clenched at my sides. "Stop it!"

"Who are you talking to?" Remiel asked.

"The codex! Didn't you hear it?!"

He unfolded his arms, glancing between me and the book. "No, I didn't."

"You're such a liar!" I turned my anger onto Remiel again, squaring off with him. "Everything out of your mouth is a goddamn lie! I don't know why I ever thought I could reason with you! You're the most unreasonable creature to ever exist! I thought maybe there was some good left inside of you, *somewhere*, underneath all of that hate and contempt and depravity, but I see now what an idiot I was to ever give you the benefit of the doubt!"

The book giggled again, its laughter growing louder. Bolder. The whispers returned, excitedly hissing to one another.

"*Desistas*!" I slammed my fists on either side of the codex, practically nose-to-nose with the fucking thing.

But the book didn't stop. It started howling in glee.

Remiel's hands encircled my biceps from behind, tugging me backward.

"Don't touch me!" Anger surged through me so hard and fast I actually managed to shrug him off, returning my narrowed gaze to the awful ritual on the page. "I hear you! And I know what you did to her. What you're *trying* to do to me! It's not going to happen a second time."

"Isn't it?" The book snickered.

"I'm going to find that ring and then you're going to wish you'd helped me!"

"The dead know nothing." The book's whispered insult trailed off into another giggle.

"I'm going to rip your spine out and burn every fucking page!" I lunged for the damnable thing, clawing for the faded vellum despite the fact I wasn't getting anywhere. Remiel's arms seized me from behind, crushing me in a bear hug, as he dragged me out of the vault. The heavy iron door slammed shut of its own accord, but the book's awful laughter continued to ring in my ears.

"Let me go!" I thrashed as best I could, but he carried me as if I weighed nothing. "Remiel! Put me down!"

"Not on your life."

"I swear to God, if you don't put me down, I'll—"

"You'll what?" Remiel growled in my ear, squeezing me so hard the air wheezed out of my lungs. "Hmm? I didn't quite catch that. What do you think you're going to do to me?"

If I could have sworn at him, I would have. If I could have kicked or punched, I would have. As it stood, all I could do was grimace and pray he let go before I had permanent brain damage from the lack of oxygen.

"I don't know *what* your problem is," Remiel snarled, continuing toward the stairs, "but we're leaving."

"I can't leave. I have work to do. Remember? That pathetic little job of mine that you despise so much? It's my responsibility to close tonight. Not that you would know anything about responsibility. You shirked your duties the first time someone came along claiming they had a better offer. How's that going, by the way? Enjoying Hell? It's quite the view from what I recall."

"You smell different. You sound different. You're certainly *acting* different," Remiel muttered, dragging me up the side stairs instead of taking the elevator. "Until you tell me what's going on, I'm not letting you out of my sight."

He shouldered open the emergency exit, ignoring the shrieking alarm, and dragged me across the side yard of the library. Somehow it was already after nightfall. I had a clear memory of going downstairs before lunch, and yet, the world was now dark. How long had I been down there with that thing? Or could Remiel manipulate time? I wouldn't put it past him.

"Oh, I'm going to have a demon stalker again? Really? Can't wait," I tossed back with a snort, deciding I didn't care about pushing my luck with him anymore. The wrought iron lamp posts that lined campus didn't extend to this side of the building. He could have murdered me right then and there and no one would have seen unless they were almost on top of us. The highlight would be that I'd finally get away from him, forever. "What are you going to do this time, Remiel? Stop the clocks? Change the temperature? Molest me in my sleep? Kill Kevin?"

"Who's Kevin?"

"My goat. The one I'm now stuck with since *you* told me I needed to fucking behead one and set it on fire to summon Hazael. Another lie. Surprise, surprise! It's lie after lie after lie after lie."

Remiel scoffed behind me and stopped walking, spinning me to face him.

"What?" I snapped. "What do you want now? Gonna fuck me right here? Humiliate me? Burn more fucking marks into my skin? Go ahead! I don't care anymore! I'm done!"

His eyebrows slanted sharply, his scowl deepening. "Sleep."

My brain registered the word a second before my legs gave way, my lids slamming shut.

CHAPTER TWENTY-FOUR

REMIEL

I paced back and forth in Phelan's bedroom while he slept. My wings dragged along the bare floor behind me, the only sound in the room, along with his even breathing.

He wasn't dreaming—I made sure of that. But his mental barriers were still firmly in place, which was fine for a change. It meant he wouldn't be susceptible to whatever had affected him so badly at the library.

Almost as soon as I'd returned him to his family's house in the woods, I sensed the change. His heartbeat slowed from its panicked state, his smell returned to normal. Once he woke up, we'd see if he'd regained his usual personality or if he was still under the book's perverse influence.

He finally woke near midnight, jerking awake with a start, his eyes wide in the moonlight. "What are you doing here?"

"Sleep well?" I gave him a small smile, staying perched in my corner by the fireplace while he eased himself into a sitting position, holding the side of his head.

"I'm not in the mood to argue with you," he muttered,

throwing back the quilt and standing. He glanced down at himself, still dressed for work, and attempted to smooth the wrinkles out of his shirt on his way to the door.

"Oh really? Get all of that out of your system earlier?"

He glanced at me from the doorway, his confusion appearing genuine. "What are you talking about?"

"You have no recollection of our earlier conversation?" I asked, trailing after him.

"No." His brow furrowed for a moment and he shook his head. "What happened?"

"If I tell you, you'll scream at me that I'm a liar again. Perhaps it's better if I show you."

"Show me... what?"

I tossed my head to the interior of the room, indicating the warm bed he'd just abandoned.

"I have to feed Kevin," he said lamely.

"I already gave it its nightly garbage," I huffed. "It wouldn't shut up without it."

"You fed my goat?" If I wasn't paying attention, I might have missed the flash of a smile on his face.

"You're lucky I didn't kill it. Now go sit down."

Nodding, he turned obediently and made his way back to the bed. He sank onto the edge of the mattress, swallowing thickly as I sat next to him.

"How do you get inside someone's head?" I asked, keeping my tone neutral. After that little display at the library, I didn't know what sort of mood he'd be in and I didn't want him any more defensive than he already was. I liked him fiery, not spiteful.

"I, um..." He cleared his throat, glancing around, like he wasn't sure if he should answer or not. "They have to be asleep. Then I can enter their dreams. Memories. Everything is open to me if they haven't learned to lock it all down."

"Good." I slid behind him and laid on my back carefully, closing my eyes. "I want you to look inside my head and see for yourself."

"You were the angel of dreams," he said quietly. "I know you can alter visions. Why would I believe anything I see over anything you tell me?"

My eyes flew open again, narrowing on his as I swung my feet over the side of the bed. "You want gaps in your memory? Fine. But just know you've lost your one and only chance to—"

He scooted forward suddenly, laying his hand on the center of my chest to keep me from leaving. "No, wait. I'm sorry. I'm... I'm just tired. I don't know what's going on. I feel so drained."

Of that, I was sure. Shadows clung beneath his eyes. With his mussed hair and wrinkled clothing, he looked even less like his usual self. Like he was more fragile in the moonlight. That book had tainted something inside of him. I wanted to know why. *How*. Especially since he was terrified to even touch it.

"I'll try," he continued. "I'm just..."

"Tired," I said flatly. "So you said."

His gaze drifted downward. I realized his fingers were moving back and forth slowly over my sternum, almost in the same way he stroked my wing, running his fingertips along the edge of the feathers so lightly, yet the sensation still reverberated through every cell in my body.

I closed my hand around his, pressing his palm flat against my chest. His eyes flicked up to mine, silently questioning.

Laying down again, I pulled him with me, enveloping

him in my wings as he settled on top of me, his cheek pressed to my shoulder.

"Go back to sleep," I whispered into his hair. It wasn't a gentle suggestion; it was a command and this time I made sure he *did* dream.

The second he fell back into an enchanted slumber, his body relaxed and his full weight settled on top of me.

I gave him a moment to get his bearings before I joined him inside his own dreamscape. Since he was still suspicious of me and my intentions, it seemed safer to take a look at what was really on *his* mind than try and recount what had happened at the library.

Except, the inside of his head looked more nightmarish than Hell itself.

We were standing in the middle of an old farmhouse. It was reminiscent of his current house, but it wasn't the same. It was technically newer, but falling apart from neglect. The longer I looked, the stranger things became.

A molding pig's head hung from a beam overhead in what was supposed to be the living room, its rotten eyes clustered with black flies.

An old, wooden cradle near the large hearth moved on its own, rocking back and forth. A strange rattling emanated from inside, rolling this way and that.

I made my way to it silently and peered down.

Instead of a baby, the grinning skull of a cat stared up at me. As the cradle swayed from side to side, the bones skittered from one end of the tiny bed and back again.

Phelan stood in the center of the dirty, rundown living room with his hand held aloft. Black spiders ran up and down his arm, encircling his wrist, and rushing along his fingertips, like a glove that moved.

"What are you doing here?" he asked quietly, preferring

to play with the spiders on his hand instead of looking at me. “I thought I was supposed to be looking inside your head?”

“You are. Since the proverbial door was open, I wanted to see inside yours first,” I answered truthfully, making my way to him. “What are you doing here? What is this place?”

“I don’t know. I haven’t dreamt of this house in a very long time.”

“But it’s so... charming.” It made my palace in Hell look positively cozy. At least there it was clean. And warm. This place was cold and dank, covered in a layer of grime that made me wrinkle my nose and lift my wings off the rotting floorboards. Even without looking through the dirt-crusted windows, I knew we were deep in the woods. Everything inside had a mildewy smell, like the forest was trying to reclaim the house.

The spiders jumped from his hand and descended to the ground on silken strands, disappearing in the cracks of the old, uneven floorboards.

As soon as they were gone, Phelan gave me his attention, not even acknowledging my sarcasm. “You didn’t answer my question. Why are you here? Am I dead?”

“You’re not dead, I assure you.” I walked away from him to give him some space, studying the severed pig’s head up close. A maggot fell at my feet, writhing on a pile that formed where putrid chunks kept accumulating as they rotted away. “Call me curious. Why is *this* the first place your mind went to when you fell asleep? I pictured you dreaming of dirty old books or the quarry or something.”

“I don’t know.”

Except something in his tone sounded off. It sounded like he knew *exactly* why this is where his subconscious led him. And *that* is the reason I invaded his dreamscape—to see what he was hiding from me.

I turned and stared at him, arms crossed, waiting.

"I was thinking about my mother," he said quietly, hanging his head, like the admission was somehow shameful.

"Your mother? What about her?"

"It's the strangest thing. I remember researching the Ring of Eleazar at work, clear as day. And then the next, I was thinking about Bridget. But it's all so... I don't know. *Un*clear. I feel like I'm forgetting something. Like I'm blocking it out." He looked up again, his brow furrowed. "Is that why you're here? Did something happen? Please, just tell me. I need to know."

I crossed the room to him again slowly, examining the various sigils that formed a ring around the center of the room. Phelan stood in the middle, whether he realized it or not. "Do you remember that book? Beneath the library? The one you have locked in a cage?"

His puzzled look remained. "How do you know about that?"

"Because I saw it today. And I saw this diagram in its pages," I replied, pointing at the circle of symbols beneath our feet. "Just like I saw it in your head the one and only time I was able to break through in Hell."

He blanched. "But I..." His gaze dropped, roving over the dirty floorboards, following the circle of carved symbols. "I've never seen these sigils before. I don't know what they mean."

"You accused me of writing it."

"I... did." He blinked hard, touching his forehead. "Didn't I? I screamed at you. And that fucking codex." His hand fisted at his side. "I asked it what my mother was researching. This is what it showed me, right before it began taunting me."

Nodding, I strolled over to the hearth, perusing the array of photographs on the mantel. None of them were of Phelan. Most looked like his ancestors from various eras, predating his birth. "This place belongs to the Olivers, I take it?"

"Um..." I glanced over my shoulder, waiting for more, but Phelan was also looking around, his brow creased. "I don't know. I think maybe it was the first house I lived in. The one Bridget set on fire. So... yeah. I guess."

"Why would she set her house on fire?" When he didn't answer right away, I turned to face him, my head cocked.

"She was trying to kill me," he replied quietly, so low I could hardly hear him. "When I was a baby." He continued just as quietly, not meeting my gaze. "Some say the pregnancy drove her mad. Others say it was magic. Either way, after I was born, she did all sorts of strange things. Spoke in tongues. Ate insects. Did things... violent things... to me." He exhaled a slow breath, shoving his hands in his pockets. "The thing that finally put her away was burning the house down. And leaving me inside."

"What did she do to you before that?"

"I-I don't know. I obviously don't remember and no one will tell me. Temperance said she took her aggression out on me. One of the only stories she divulged was that one night Bridget took me into the North Woods and left me there, at the old village. Like some sort of... of... I don't know..."

"Sacrifice," I concluded.

Phelan's pale eyes swept to mine. They darted away just as fast, but not before I caught a glimpse of tears.

"Where is your father?" I asked, noting the absence of any male in the more recent photographs.

"I don't know." He dashed the dampness from his cheeks quickly, clearing his throat. "She never told anyone who he was. There's nothing on the birth certificate. There were rumors that she was raped at Tennebrose, but no one could say for certain except her... and that's not happening."

"You don't talk?" I arched an eyebrow at him. "I thought you're all about forgiveness? Or is that only when it suits you?"

For once, he didn't rise to the challenge. "After the fire, I didn't see her for several years. She didn't want to see me and I didn't even know she existed. She wrote me letters as I got older, but I never read them. Just threw them in a box and tried my best to not end up like her. But here I am. Losing my mind like she did."

"You're not losing your mind." Closing the distance, I cupped his cheek, smiling softly when he leaned into my hand. I'd started to develop a theory about his need for touch a while ago, but it became clearer with each new encounter. He was so isolated from everyone that he sought it out whenever he could, even from his sworn enemy. His head told him to resist, that he shouldn't want it. But deep down he *needed* it. All creatures did. And if touch was what he needed, I'd gladly give it to him, as much as he wanted.

"But the book—"

"Did not make your mother crazy." I laid my other hand against his cheek, holding him in place so he couldn't look away from me. "And it's not going to make you crazy. It's evil, yes, but you're stronger than a damn book."

"Then why am I dreaming about spells to murder babies? It's forbidden in Necromancy. Even if it wasn't, I could never do that sort of magic. I couldn't even kill a goat."

"It's not a dream, Phelan. It's a memory."

"I don't understand. How can I have a memory I don't actually remember?"

"You of all people know the powers of the mind." I let him go and reconsidered the symbols around us. "Your mother went to Tennebrose?"

He nodded. "All Winslow witches do."

"Did she also have dream magic?"

"Some. I think. Her main power was bibliomancy—divination with a book."

I smirked at him. "And I bet she used that big ol' Oliver family bible, didn't she?"

Another small, sheepish nod. "Officially, she studied theology."

"Of course she did." Using the tip of my wing, I swept a few brittle leaves out of the way, revealing another Celestial symbol. "Did she have visions?"

"I don't know. I honestly don't know much about her. Everything I've gotten is second-hand and, I'd bet anything, highly redacted."

"She was also looking for the ring," I said, walking between the symbols and trying to make sense of their chaotic order. "Right here." I pointed to a series of Celestial letters. "This says 'Eleazar.'"

"But this was the ritual to sacrifice a child. I'm sure of it." His eyes widened. "Was that what she was doing?! Sacrificing *me* for a fucking ring?"

I didn't answer, because I didn't have to. He knew the truth the moment the words left his lips.

Phelan drew in a ragged breath and turned away from me.

Abandoning my study, I made my way over to him once more. I hesitated behind him, listening to the way his heart hammered and his diaphragm trembled. He was holding in the little puffs of air he took, trying so hard not to lose it.

Rather than touch him with my hand, I unfolded one wing and curled it around to the front. Stroking his cheek delicately, I waited until he pivoted, forcing himself to meet my gaze.

His eyes were red and blurred with tears, but he refused to let them spill. "I'm twice the scholar she was," he said quietly through his teeth. "If she thought she could find that fucking ring, then it's only a matter of time until I do."

A dark smile curled my lips. He was utterly beautiful in his sorrow. But in his quiet, seething rage? He was absolutely divine.

CHAPTER TWENTY-FIVE

PHELAN

It was a beautiful October morning in Winslow, the kind that made tourists flock to the town in droves and budding photographers whip out their cameras. Mist rolled across the fields and hugged the ditches along the curving road as I headed toward Tennebrose. The brightly-colored leaves hung overhead, a myriad of scarlet and saffron against the dark trees and gray landscape below.

Autumn was my favorite season. I should have found peace in the moody atmosphere and delighted in the smell of damp leaves and woodsmoke. But I couldn't. Not anymore.

In the light of day, I felt... irrevocably changed.

Being in the dreamworld with Remiel was strange, but his presence had a comforting effect, like it had in the vault beneath the library. Maybe it was the knowledge that once upon a time he was the angel of dreams, meaning he was more than competent to handle anything that might go awry on the other side. Or maybe it was the fact I'd grown stupidly comfortable in his company, more than I ever thought would be possible.

Either way, I couldn't dwell on Remiel, not while the specter of Bridget's madness dogged my every step.

The first thing I did when I got to work was to log into the student records.

She might have attended the university thirty years ago, but I had no doubt I'd be able to track down Bridget's pertinent information. We witches were nothing if not excellent record keepers.

In a short while, I'd managed to compile a list of every book and document Bridget had checked out or requested from the library. Some of the titles I could easily rule out due to their irrelevancy. But the deeper I dove into her theological studies, the more I paid attention. Most of them came from the rare books section, which meant they *couldn't* be checked out.

Once I had my list, I grabbed an empty cart and headed out into the stacks, pulling down volume after volume.

Rather than stand around and read some of the texts in the chained section, I unlocked the precious books and added them to the pile.

Rolling the heavy cart back to my office, I closed the blinds and got to work retracing her steps from the very beginning. I could have started with the last book she ever referenced and worked backward, but I wanted to get the full picture of her research, as she did, and piece everything together for myself. On the most basic level, I hoped it would also lead me to the Ring of Eleazar. But, in the darker part of my brain, I hoped it would help me understand how my mother ended up the way she did... if I was really the cause of her insanity or if something else was to blame.

The minutes ticked by. Page after page after page.

Medieval manuscripts. Ancient Hebrew. Alchemy. Roman memoirs. Her research was all over the place. She'd focus heavily on the English Renaissance only to turn around and spend an inordinate amount of time on the Hebrew Bible. More than a few Necromancers' manuals were also consulted, but I couldn't find anything about Eleazar.

It was all beginning to feel like a wild goose chase.

Around lunch, Samuel called with an update on the wooden slivers I'd asked him to test—and subsequently forgotten about.

"It's fascinating," Ainsworth said in a rush. "Between the science and the magic, I was able to determine these oak slivers are from the first century, Phelan! This is more than an antique. It's priceless."

"You're sure it's really that old?" I asked, rubbing my forehead. Not that I didn't believe Remiel, exactly, but it was truly a miracle *anything* wooden had survived for a millennium let alone a piece of the True Cross.

"Quite. And the blood that came with it? Not anything of this world, my boy. I know that wasn't part of the assignment, but I couldn't very well test the wood without cleaning it first. This wouldn't have anything to do with the reason you've been missing so many Meetings lately, does it?"

Oh shit... could Ainsworth tell it was a demon's blood? Or maybe since Remiel was one of the fallen, it was beyond the scope of anything Samuel was used to.

"I hate to backtrack," I continued quickly, ignoring his question. "But you said oak? I thought for sure it would be... cypress or pine or something more common to the Holy Land, especially given its age?" Although the jury was still out on what the True Cross had been fashioned out of, none of the scholars I'd kept up with over the years mentioned oak. Then again, a few still insisted it was olive wood, which would have been a terrible choice for crucifying anyone, let alone a full-grown man. Not that I knew much about Roman torture and execution methods, but the haphazard structure of the olive tree's branches and the fact it was seen as an important food source would have meant ancient people wouldn't be very likely to chop it down just to kill a few criminals.

"Oaks are quite common to the Holy Land," Samuel replied, "or they were. What sort of object did this come from again?"

"I, um..." Floundering, I cast about for something believable. "A reliquary, I think." I winced, hoping it sounded halfway convincing through the phone.

"Explains the blood, I suppose."

"I suppose it does. Can you tell me anything else about it? The blood or the wood? Anything that would stand out to you?"

"I'm afraid not. It's old and there's a latent power in it, but I'm not sure if that's from the blood or the wood itself."

"Would it be possible to graft the wood into a new tree? To make more of it?"

"Anything is possible with enough determination." And Ainsworth sounded like he was *very* determined. He loved a magical mystery as much as anyone, especially if it involved plants of some sort.

"Wonderful. I can't wait to see the end result."

"I'll let you know when I have something."

I disconnected with a sigh and leaned back in my chair, rubbing my hands over my face. If Ainsworth could pull this off and regrow the True Cross into a renewable source, then maybe I could use *that* to kill Hazael. At the moment, it seemed like a better solution than tracking down a ring that had gone missing in the annals of history—if it ever existed in the first place. It wouldn't be the first time historians fell for ancient or medieval hoaxes. And if the Combermere was the only book that referenced the ring, however briefly, there was no way to test its veracity.

"Oh, good. Are we done for the day?" Remiel's voice asked out of thin air.

I dropped my hands, fighting the urge to smile as he came into view, wearing his standard "human" disguise again, a white t-shirt and skinny jeans, with his long blond hair gathered in a messy ponytail.

"Not even close," I replied, pushing one stack of books out of the way and dragging another closer.

Remiel swaggered around the side of the desk and straddled my legs, seating himself directly in front of me on the desk. "I'm bored."

"Don't you have something demonic to do to pass the time?" I reached past him for a book, but he intercepted my hand and redirected it to his thigh. I managed to yank it away before he could lay it against the outline of his cock, barely concealed by the denim.

"There are still people here," I said, glancing behind him at the main section of the library. Even if the blinds were closed, someone could still come barging in at any moment.

"You act like that's supposed to stop me."

"Can you not think about sex for, like, two seconds?"

He folded his arms over his chest and cocked his head, arching an eyebrow. "There. I thought about how annoying you are. Now back to sex." He slid off the desk and into my lap, despite my objections. Raking his fingers through my hair, he pulled my head back and dragged his tongue along my throat.

"Remiel..." I turned my face away when he leaned in,

trying desperately to ignore the fact my dick was perking up behind my zipper. "Please. I have—"

"Ugh. Work. Yes, I know, you have work. Fine." He groaned and climbed off of me, turning to the stack of books. He snatched one off the top and thumbed through it before throwing it back on the desk. "Nope." He did the same thing with the second. "Nope."

"You can't possibly be reading that quickly."

"If you only knew what was possible, lamb." He sped through another book and looked up at me. "Are you going to sit there and watch or are you going to help?"

Shaking my head, I rolled up to my desk again and resumed scanning my own pile of books.

For once, Remiel kept his hands to himself. He dutifully flipped through every book I put in front of him, annihilating my workload in no time at all.

He even came in handy a few times as a walking ancient dictionary. The first time I encountered a misspelled Greek word, Remiel took the book from beneath my nose, translated it correctly with a huff, and resumed his own task without even blinking.

"Thank you," I murmured, watching him work.

Either he didn't hear me, or he didn't care about my gratitude, because he continued reading with the same bored expression he'd had since he started.

Studying his profile, I twirled my pen idly between my fingers. Despite the fact he was in his human form, he still radiated an ineffable mystique. His sharp jawline, his plush mouth. Perfectly sculpted brow. Even "disguised," he was so beautiful. I could only imagine what he'd looked like as an angel, illuminated with an ethereal glow. Perhaps with a real smile instead of the scowl he typically wore. And far fewer scars—inside and out.

As if he could read my thoughts, Remiel scoffed and rolled his eyes. "What?"

Caught in the act of staring, I nearly sputtered out some lame defense, but the Psalter in my other hand saved me. I shoved it at him quickly, hoping I looked sincere and not guilty. "Can you make out what this says? Just there, in the margin."

He took the book and squinted at the faded letters. "It's Aramaic."

"I don't know Aramaic."

He gasped in faux scandal, a sly smile curving the corner of his mouth. "You don't? A dutiful scholar such as yourself? Say it's not so!"

I responded with a glare.

His smile turned genuine and he set the book in front of me before leaning down, propping himself on an elbow on the edge of the desk. Trailing a finger beneath the small script, he read it out loud in what I presume was Aramaic, but I honestly didn't hear a word of it. From the second he leaned over me, I was enveloped by the cinnamon musk that was uniquely his, immobilized by his closeness. For once he wasn't touching me or forcing himself on me in one way or another and rather than be happy, some primal part of my brain was screaming at him to grab me and make me submit.

"Phelan!"

I flinched, blinking hard. "What?"

"Are you listening?"

Clearing my throat, I looked at the book again, gesturing vaguely at the cramped handwriting in the margin. "Of course. Is that helpful? The, the marginalia?"

He straightened and crossed his arms over his chest,

looking enormously pleased with himself. "You weren't listening at all, were you?"

"I was."

"Then what did I say?"

"It was in Aramaic. How am I supposed to know?"

A brow lifted slowly, adding to his smugness. "I said it in English too."

"Forget it." I slapped the book shut and stood, adding it to the discard pile to be shelved later. When I turned around, Remiel was right behind me.

Grabbing my waist, he lifted me easily and set me on the desk, sliding between my legs.

"Do you mind? We're in public." I glanced at the transom windows at the top of my office, trying to listen for any patrons out in the library, but all I saw was darkness. I hadn't realized it was already so late. But just because the library was technically closed, it didn't mean we were completely alone. Other librarians, security guards, who knew who might wander through? The lascivious part of me, on the other hand, rejoiced.

"We were in public the other day when *you* kissed *me*. Right out there, if I recall," he purred, dipping his hands beneath the hem of my shirt and sliding them along my ribcage. "Besides, I've been waiting to do this for hours. I think I've exercised considerable restraint by not fucking you on your desk."

"You can't," was all I managed to spit out before he bit the side of my neck, making me gasp and twist my fingers into the front of his t-shirt.

"Can't I?"

"You'll ruin the books."

"Does it look like I care about your precious little books?" He laced his fingers through mine and forced my hand downward, slipping it between us and molding my palm to his hard cock. "I don't care about anything except being inside of you, lover."

"We're not finished... with th-the books. And research." Try as I might to keep my hand still, to fight following the hard, bulging line, I found my palm moving along his length, rubbing and stroking him until he groaned.

"We're finished when I say we're finished. You work too hard." He ground himself against my hand and wrapped his fingers around the back of my neck, sealing our mouths together. His tongue pushed past my lips, sweeping along mine and making my toes curl.

I moaned into the kiss and gripped his cock just to hear him inhale sharply, his hips flicking against me.

"I'm going to fuck you right here," Remiel growled, biting my lips and working his way down my throat.

I knew I should protest. I knew I should shake my head or try to push him away. But the greedy part of me was too busy leaning backward, giving him greater access to my belt buckle, which he tore open with little effort.

"Remember," Remiel said with a sudden seriousness as he pulled me to my feet, "there's no talking in the library. Which means no screaming."

We lunged to kiss one another again, but the distinct sound of heavy boots on the tile floor had me reeling backward.

"Security," I gasped. "You can't be here. They're all witches, Remiel."

Remiel opened his mouth to argue, but I grabbed his hand and hauled him out of my office, hurrying through the restricted section to the side door. I keyed us out of the old employee entrance and circled around the side of the building, where the lights didn't reach.

Collapsing against the stone wall in the library's sunken garden, I laughed while also trying to catch my breath. "You are going to get me fired one of these days, I swear."

"And I won't be sorry about it," he murmured, planting his hands on either side of my head and running his lips along the underside of my jaw.

"You're not sorry about anything." I tipped my head back, resting it against the stone while he left kisses up and down my throat.

"No, I'm not." He bit the curve of my neck and sucked the tender flesh so hard I actually moaned.

"Remiel," I breathed, clawing at the back of his jacket and pushing my hips against his. His hard-on pressed against mine, stoking the flame in my lower abdomen I'd tried and failed to extinguish.

"Phelan," he shot back before pressing his mouth to mine and plunging his tongue inside to take what he wanted.

Gripping both of my wrists in one hand, he pinned them above my head, stroking my cock with his other on the outside of my trousers.

I tore my mouth free, turning my face to the side. "We can't."

"We can," he replied, squeezing my balls before flicking open the button on my pants and shoving his hand inside the fabric. "You just have to be quiet. Do you think you can manage that?"

I shook my head, trying to ignore his persistent strokes. "I can't. You have to stop."

Dropping his hold on my wrists, he clamped a hand over my mouth and pushed my shirt up, swirling his tongue around my nipple. Between the shock of cold air and the wet heat of his mouth, I couldn't help but gasp beneath his hand. He did the same thing to the other side, scraping his teeth over the peak as he dropped to his knees, raking his blunt nails down my abdomen on their way to my pants.

"Just stand there and hate me, pet," he said, hooking his fingers around the waistband of my underwear and pulling it down slowly. "Because this is happening one way or the other. I've been without you for too long."

"Can't we at least go home?" I asked, stealing a glance down at him. His hair looked silver again in the moonlight and when he met my gaze, his eyes flashed like a cat's. He continued to watch me, even after he freed my cock, gazing up with those luminous eyes as his lips caressed my length.

I shivered from the cold and impatience. With each soft kiss he pressed to my crown, the more I wished he'd hurry up and touch me the way he knew I wanted.

He was still holding my gaze when he sucked the head of my dick into his mouth and continued to swallow me whole.

I swore under my breath. My head tipped back against the wall again and I tried to remind myself that I hated him. I did. I hated him and everything he was doing right now. I said no, and he did what he wanted, as always. He was a selfish, arrogant, piece of—fuck!

My hips jerked forward, my body reeling from whatever he just did to me. It felt like he hit that one spot again, but his fingers were still on the outside, alternating between massaging my balls and rubbing my taint. It was almost like the time he'd fucked my thighs; I felt those weird, toe-curling tingles every once in a while that time but only when he added pressure at a certain angle. But every time he did it, he sucked harder, humming in satisfaction around my cock, which only made my hips chase the sensation until I was clinging to the dormant ivy on the wall, praying it would be enough to keep me upright.

"You have to stop," I whispered with ragged breaths. My balls were *so* tight. I knew stopping before a climax would hurt, but I had to try. Right? I wasn't a prisoner anymore and I wasn't trying to assuage his murderous paranoia. I couldn't willingly give in to him even though the heat coiling along the base of my spine didn't give a shit about the religious high ground.

Apparently, neither did Remiel.

Instead of stopping, he stroked my shaft in tandem with his mouth. The wet heat, the firm pressure, it all felt so good. Too good. I might as well have been back in Hell—Remiel was dragging my soul there anyway with his wicked mouth.

"Oh, God. I'm going to—" I didn't even have enough time to warn him before my orgasm hit like a tidal wave. My abs tightened and my legs trembled. I slapped a hand over my own mouth to muffle the sounds that were trying to escape as Remiel continued to wring the very life out of me.

Once my dick stopped pulsating in his mouth, he stood and took my face between his hands, pressing his lips to mine. When I opened my mouth for his tongue, a burst of tangy saltiness rushed in instead. I recognized it immediately as my own release, something I would have never tasted had he not forced me to all those weeks ago. I should have been disgusted by it. And maybe some part of me was because it was dirty and lewd. But I swallowed it all and sucked the rest off his tongue.

Remiel groaned and thrust against me, about to burst out of his pants from the feel of things. He pulled back with a literal growl and slid one hand to my throat, squeezing just enough to tilt my head back and force me to look at him. "My little blasphemer. From now on, you have no other god but me. My name should be the only thing on those lips. Yes?"

"Yes," I rasped.

"Good. Now get on your knees." He didn't even give me a chance to move before he shoved me downward by my throat. I grabbed his thighs to steady myself, gazing up at him from a clear position of submission. The moonlight illuminated him from behind in a soft glow. It was easy to forget he was a prince of Hell when he looked like an angel, beautiful and terrifying all at once.

He ran his hand through my hair, gripping it at the back and guiding my face to his hard-on. Even through the dark denim, I could smell him, that spicy musk I'd once associated with Church and now only related to him—to memories of being in his bed, in his arms, his wings wrapped around us.

"Phelan Oliver!"

I startled and whirled toward the sound of Peregrine Northrup shouting my name, scrambling to tuck my clothing back into place while he was still too far away to see clearly.

"You have to go," I whispered to Remiel. "Now."

There was no reply.

Getting to my feet, I looked behind me and spun in a circle.

Remiel was gone.

When I returned my attention to Peregrine, I was disheartened to see he'd brought a small army with him. Directly behind the Deacon was Thomas Treadwell, the chief of Winslow PD, and Samuel Ainsworth. Eileen Green,

George Hewitt, Nathaniel Dane, Marcus Ambrose, and Temperance rounded out the bunch.

"What's going on?" I asked. My gaze darted to each of them before landing on Temperance. Her arms were crossed over her chest and she shot a nasty look at Eileen.

"I didn't tell anyone about the teddy bear," I said, directing my gaze to Eileen as well. "Maybe I should have."

Samuel slid a curious look in Eileen's direction, meanwhile Peregrine came to a stop in front of me.

"It's too late to blackmail your way out of this," Peregrine said, his tone icier than usual. "You need to come with us this second to the meetinghouse. If you resist, we will use force."

"How about you ask nicely?" Temperance snapped at the Deacon. "Unless 'innocent until proven guilty' went out the window because Eileen Green had a so-called 'vision.'"

"Don't even start, Temperance," Eileen shot back. "We all know where your loyalty lies."

"What is going on?" I interjected. "Why are you all here?"

"We'll explain at the meetinghouse," Treadwell said with a sigh. "But in the meantime, I need you to put these on." He lifted a pair of iron shackles into view, similar to what Remiel had employed in Hell and for the exact same purpose. To prohibit me from using magic of any sort.

"You've got to be kidding me." I was frozen in place, staring at the lot of them while I tried to process what the fuck was happening. "I don't have an active power!"

"Your demon does!" George Hewitt shouted back.

All I could do was gape at him. How did they know about Remiel? The other Necromancers made it perfectly clear they weren't telling the rest of the Congregation about what happened to me. So what, exactly, did Eileen see?

Using my stunned silence to his advantage, Treadwell crossed the distance and hooked one cuff around my wrist. I didn't fight him. I couldn't. Fighting would only make me look guiltier than I was.

Once the second cuff was locked into place, he gestured me forward.

I already felt like a dead man walking. Moving through the small crowd, feeling the weight of each of their stares, I did my best to keep my chin up even though on the inside I was screaming.

CHAPTER TWENTY-SIX

PHELAN

"This is unacceptable!" Peregrine shouted, pointing a finger at me. "And to think you kept it from us!"

"It doesn't affect the rest of the Congregation," I replied tersely, gripping the arms of the chair I'd been shoved into the moment we entered the meetinghouse.

"When one of our own has been marked by a demon, it most certainly affects us!"

One of our own? I snorted and rolled my eyes, but refrained from commenting.

Peregrine wasn't done, anyway. "And I suppose you knew about this?" he shouted, turning toward the rest of the dark families who'd clumped together to stare down their so-called "good" counterparts across the aisle of the building.

"More secrets! More lies!" Eileen Green interjected right as Caius Corbin opened his mouth to answer Peregrine's charge. "Another perfect example of why *none* of them can be trusted, especially after last year!"

"That's fucking rich coming from you," Peter Simms snapped. "I'm sure the rest of the Congregation would love to hear how you gave my daughter a possessed teddy bear! Who the fuck does that, Eileen?!"

A murmuring erupted on both sides, with many confused looks darting back and forth. Amber, meanwhile, stood with her husband, shooting daggers at her mother. She didn't look surprised by what Peter said, which meant he probably told her the truth at some point. Or she figured it out once Isla's sleep magically returned to normal. Either way, I was glad to see they were in a better place.

"Phelan has never done anything to harm the Congregation," Caius said above the din. "All he's ever done is serve us when we ask. That's why he was targeted. The demons know how important he is to the Necromancers and they aim to deprive us of him. We should be grateful he's only been marked and not killed or possessed. It's a testament to his strength and it gives us time to undo—"

"Marking is the first step," George Hewitt snapped. "Or that's what you all would have us believe after what happened with Marian! Never mind the fact it was your own daughter who forced my wife to do her twisted bidding!"

"That was an entirely different situation and you know it!" Caius threw back, taking a step in George's direction. Cassius and his fiancé, Graeme (ironically, George Hewitt's only living son), both moved forward and subtly grabbed onto the back of Caius's coat, drawing him away from his lifelong nemesis. Their sons might have found peace with one another, but Caius and George would never see eye-to-eye on anything.

"Can we please focus on Phelan?" Temperance asked, moving to the center of the room and staring Peregrine down. "He is the reason we've been dragged here, after all.

And now that he's here, what do you plan on doing with him?"

Peregrine was about to reply when George Hewitt thundered, "Kill him! It's the only way to keep us safe!"

"Over my dead body!" Temperance shouted, stepping in front of me and squaring off with the much bigger and much more powerful Hewitt.

Ainsworth hurried forward and squeezed her arm, pulling her back a couple of steps. On the other side of the aisle, the nature witches secured George and likewise forced him to retreat to safety.

"The Selectmen will decide," Ainsworth said, ever the peacekeeper, as he glanced around at the gathering. "We'll do what's best for the Congregation *and* for Phelan."

"There's no need," Peregrine said sharply, his gaze darting to the southern door as it swung open.

All eyes turned to the late arrival.

It was Hester.

The blood drained from my face, leaving me cold and nauseated. I should have been relieved as my grandmother strode down the aisle, but a lifelong dread buoyed to the surface in her presence. All she'd ever done was try to keep me from following in her daughter's footsteps and here I was—marked by a demon and keeping secrets.

She cut an impressive figure as witches on both sides of the aisle parted and shrunk back. Her gray hair was swept up on her head and twisted into place with an elaborate pin, meanwhile, her dark-lined eyes flicked across each face dismissively before she came to a stop in front of me.

"Grandmother," I said, forcing myself to swallow the lump in my throat.

"Phelan." She looked at Treadwell and cleared her throat pointedly. "The chains, if you please."

Treadwell nodded and moved forward, unlocking the cuffs from my wrists. Even if I was technically freed, I remained seated, rubbing my sore skin gingerly.

"What are you doing?" Diane Tenney cried, gaping at Peregrine. "You're going to let him go?"

"It's her family," Peregrine replied, gesturing toward Hester. "She decides his fate."

"You're the Deacon!" Someone in the back cried. "You can't let him go!"

"He'll kill us all!"

"They're going to hide him, like they did Bridget!"

I closed my eyes and bowed my head, as if it would help me drown out the noise or the bizarre theories about my mother. My heart hammered in my chest, waiting to see what Hester would say. Given what she did to my mother, there was no reason to hope she'd be any more lenient with me. I *was* probably destined for the same fate—locked up at Hester's mercy. A slave in Hell. A slave in Winslow. A slave to God, if Remiel was to be believed. Where, then, could I be free?

"Since all other methods have failed to remove this mark, we are left with one choice," Hester said calmly.

There was a quiet rumbling from the nature witches, speculating what that choice was. They all concluded it was my death or lifelong imprisonment.

"Execution?" Diane Tenney asked, louder than the rest.

"Exorcism," my grandmother spat back.

That time both sides of the aisle erupted. The families on the east side gasped and exchanged wide-eyed glances while the families on the west side decried Hester's decision.

I, on the other hand, balled my hands into fists, not

knowing who or what I should even pray to for guidance, let alone assistance.

"You can't do that to him, Hester!" Marcus shouted.

"He's not possessed!" Temperance exclaimed at the same time.

"It's not about possession," Hester countered, looking at Temperance with a brittle smile. "But it is about removing the hold this demon has over him before it's too late."

"I am not his puppet," I said, glaring up at my grandmother.

"Of course you would say that," George said. "Lying for your master just as you and your family lied to the Congregation for months about what you've been up to!"

"He is *not* my master!"

"Enough!" Peregrine said. "Hester has decided. Take him to Middlewich."

"Middlewich?!" Temperance practically shrieked. "You want to take him to the same barn where our ancestor was sentenced to death for the same goddamn thing?! Unjustified fear and hysteria?!"

"It makes sense. It's away from town, in case something goes... wrong," Ainsworth said softly, as if the logic would appeal to Temperance's anger.

"Like they murder him in cold blood?!"

"That is *not* going to happen," Caius said hotly. "Nathaniel and I will be there to make sure nothing 'goes wrong.'" He shot a disapproving look at Ainsworth.

I wished I had the same faith Caius did, but it seemed the well had finally run dry.

Undergoing an exorcism in the center of Middlewich barn, strapped to another chair like I was awaiting my death sentence, was *not* how I imagined my night going.

We were all exhausted. I didn't even know what time it was or how long Hester had been at it. All I knew was she kept asking the same questions, over and over, like Melech and Remiel had in Hell, demanding demons leave me despite the fact there weren't any in the first place.

"Who are you?" Hester repeated. "Give me your true name."

I'd long since given up trying to answer her honestly. Instead, I exhaled as my shoulders sagged. She thought she was speaking to Remiel through me, but she was wrong. Remiel had abandoned me at the library and now I knew why. This wasn't his fight and he knew I was a lost cause.

"I'm telling you, he's not possessed," Temperance said for the twentieth time, rubbing her temples in small circles.

Hester ignored her and turned to Marcus. "The mark."

Marcus and I furrowed our brows at each other and then at her. He was primarily a fire witch. At this juncture, there was only one reason she'd want his involvement.

"What about it?" Marcus asked warily.

"Burn it off."

"No!" I shouted, jerking upright in my chair. "You can't!"

"Demons are preternatural, not supernatural. Their power is dictated by the same order as ours. So if the mark was made by a demon's fire, it can be removed by God's fire," Hester replied firmly. "Once it's gone, we can tend to your hand."

"You can't burn my fucking hand off!" I shouted, yanking against the leather strap around my left wrist as two of the strongest members of the Congregation came forward to assist with the barbarism, holding my arm firmly in place against the arm of the chair and leaving my hand hanging off the end.

"First of all, watch your language," Hester snapped. "And secondly, you leave me no choice, Phelan. If the demon won't identify itself or obey commands, then ridding you of the physical link is your only hope."

"Or I could give him what he wants! Then he'll let me go."

Hester blanched, her hand drifting to the brooch at her throat. "You struck a deal with a demon?"

"In order to save my soul? Yes! And I'd do it again!"

"All you've done is condemn yourself for eternity, whether you give that thing what it wants or not! The damage to your soul is done, Phelan. Only God can forgive you now." Hester took a step back and nodded to Marcus.

I sought out my cousin's face in the crowd, my last hope since no one else would stand up to Hester on my behalf. "Temperance, don't let them do this! Please!"

"Why don't we all go home and get some rest? Start again tomorrow?" Temperance said quickly, trying to block Marcus as he moved forward, his jaw set in grim determination. "Take him to the witches' jail. Or keep him here! We can stand watch! Right Samuel?"

Ainsworth nodded quickly in agreement.

Marcus moved around her, but he cast a glance back at Hester, like he was hoping she'd change her mind.

"I agree with Temperance," Caius said. "This is all happening so quickly. We need to be rational, Hester. Not like—"

"Like last time?" She threw back with a sneer. "No, I don't think so. I already lost my daughter. I refuse to lose my grandson as well."

"You haven't lost me! I'm right here and I'm begging you not to do this!" I tried to see through the bodies of the men as they tightened their holds on me, but it was impossible.

"Marcus," Hester said—a final command to proceed no matter what I had to say on the matter.

A single flame sparked in Marcus's palm as he turned toward me, resignation in his dark eyes.

I shook my head. "Marcus, please don't. I'm not possessed. You know I'm not possessed. The holy water. The crucifix. The prayers. None of it had any effect on me!"

"It's the demon talking," Hester said. "Do it."

"It's for your own good," Marcus said softly before raising his palm beneath mine.

The flame in his hand flared brightly. I felt the heat a second before the searing pain engulfed me.

I thought the initial process of marking me was the worst pain I'd endured, but this was a thousand times worse. The stench of my own flesh burning filled the room. I didn't bother trying *not* to scream. Screaming was the only way I knew I was still conscious and that I hadn't passed out from the excruciating pain.

The weathered clapboards of the old barn rattled against each other, as if God himself was shaking the very foundation of the structure.

Marcus took a step back, glancing around.

I slumped forward as much as the restraints would let

me, my head hanging as I drew in ragged breaths. I couldn't even look at my hand, to see what damage they'd done.

Hester moved forward and doused me with holy water again, commanding the evil in my body to take its leave, along with another Latin prayer for my safe delivery.

I vaguely registered when her footsteps walked away from me and then my left hand was consumed by fire once again, burning even more intensely than before.

Another scream ripped out of me, echoing the winds that must have been howling outside.

The clapboards started shaking again, along with the rickety floorboards. Up above, the hay loft door swung open and slammed shut. Banging again and again, adding to the clamor inside my head.

Sweat dripped from the tip of my nose as I pitched forward, bracing against Marcus's body as his flames continued to ravage my hand. The world spun. If I could have breathed, I was sure I'd vomit.

A pair of hands slammed me back against the chair and held me there.

The heat in my left hand faded, but I continued to sweat and gasp for air, staring up at the mass of cobwebs in the corners of the barn rafters, high overhead. The spiders were gone, but evidence of their hard work remained. Hard work that wasn't appreciated by society at large. They were shunned; dismissed as nothing more than disgusting or evil creatures. Now I knew why they were my familiars. After tonight, there was no way I *couldn't* know. The similarities were glaring.

Hester started in with the Litany of the Saints, rattling off each of the holy defenders while the other Necromancers repeated the key parts in a murmur, a sick mimicry of Mass.

For hours now, I'd avoided thinking of Remiel, partly because Nathaniel Dane was there and I didn't need the doctor reading my mind but also because I didn't want to run the risk that somehow Hester's magic might summon Remiel through my thoughts alone. I'm sure Nathaniel was there to be an actual physician, to assist Caius if needed, but he also had some of the strongest telepathic abilities in the whole Congregation and right now, I didn't trust any of the people in front of me—even the ones I shared blood with.

Without a single ally to turn to, I couldn't help but wonder where Remiel was. He let Melech torture me. Ordered it, in fact, and took advantage of my weakened state to try and worm his way inside my head. But he stopped Hazael from whatever fate *he* had planned and nearly lost his mind when he thought Hazael had done something the second time after our meeting at the crossroads. Why, then, would Remiel let the witches do this to his precious little pet? To show me he was right all along? But wasn't he the least bit concerned they might actually succeed in severing our link? Or kill me in the process?

Temperance rushed over to Hester and whispered in her ear, gesticulating emphatically at the barn once all of the rattling stopped.

Was that Remiel? Was he warning them off without making his actual presence known? Seemed a little understated for him, personally, but maybe he was cognizant of the fact I was inside and if he ripped the building down entirely, I might be crushed in the process. Maybe he did care. Or maybe I was fucking delusional.

Hester brushed past Temperance and marched up to me, skipping over the Gospels and going straight for the words of the exorcism. Planting a hand on my forehead, she consulted the book in her hand and began the next prayer.

I tried to shake her hand off, but she held firm, the tips of her nails digging into my skull. Halfway through the prayer, she nodded to Marcus.

"Fear Him, who in Isaac was offered in sacrifice, in Joseph sold into bondage," she said, shifting to the side while keeping her hand on my head so Marcus had more room. "Slain as the paschal lamb, crucified as man, yet triumphed over the powers of Hell—"

I didn't hear the rest.

As soon as Marcus set my hand on fire again, I threw my head back and screamed, but the sound that came out was far from human. I writhed beneath all of the restraining hands. The pain spread from the mark throughout my body, twisting and stabbing like a thousand razor blades slicing through me.

Green and black flames erupted around the perimeter of the barn. People screamed and shouted at one another. Unseen hands tore the boards off the skeletal structure of the barn and hurtled them across the room. The boards crashed into the bystanders, knocking them to the ground in the best of cases. One jagged board, however, slammed into a woman's midsection, skewering her to the opposite wall while the people around her tried to dislodge the broken wood from her body. Another tripped a man as he tried to get out of the way, only to have his skull smashed by a third.

"Remiel," I whispered, forcing my gaze skyward again. Did God answer my prayer by sending a demon to rescue me? Or did the Devil work miracles of his own?

Marcus stumbled backward, dragging Hester with him

as the infernal fire surged forward, creating a barrier between me and the rest of the Congregation.

"Not again," Treadwell said, pulling Ainsworth away from the unholy fire. "Don't touch it!"

The roof above me exploded. Shingles and heavy beams rained down in the center of the barn, pelting everyone —except me.

Through the haze of dust and eerie green light, a pair of massive, glittering wings emerged.

It was Remiel.

Dressed in his armor, he looked every bit like an avenging angel minus the flaming sword. Surprisingly, his hands were empty. But the look on his face more than made up for it. It wasn't just fury. It was apoplectic.

He threw his hands toward the flames and they surged forward under his command, lashing out at whatever witch happened to be nearby. A female shrieked in pain. From the frantic yelling around her, I knew he'd set her on fire.

"Kill it!"

"A demon!"

"Peregrine, do something!"

Some witches were trying to move to the flanks, but Remiel was relentless. The green and black flames flared brighter, leaping forward at anyone who tried to come closer. Every time he threw his hands in a new direction, the flames moved with him, engulfing people and spreading out to the walls of the old barn. But it wasn't just fire. Every ball of flames unleashed another demon, until the barn was swarming with them, their unholy shrieking and cawing sounding above the roaring fire, jeering at the witches who were helpless to fend them off.

Half of the Congregation tried to battle the blaze, while

the strongest tried to subdue Remiel and his horde from afar.

Gradually, the heat became unbearable. Sulfur and smoke choked me where I sat. I couldn't breathe, nor I couldn't see anything beyond the wall of demon fire.

Turning to me at last, Remiel ripped the leather straps off of me. He hauled me to my feet and secured his arms around my torso before leaping upward without warning. His wings flapped hard, blowing gusts of toxic air toward the crowd as we climbed higher.

I buried my face into the side of his neck and closed my eyes as he spun in a circle and shot through the giant opening in the roof.

As soon as we were in the open air, he hovered for a minute, nuzzling the top of my head. "Wrap your legs around me."

I didn't argue. I couldn't. I couldn't speak. I could barely breathe, even with the fresh air rushing over me.

I shimmied up him until I could get both legs around his waist and hook my feet behind him. He tightened his arms around me and leaned forward. I hung on like a koala while we set off over the trees, away from Winslow.

Thankfully we didn't go far.

Right when my legs started to tremble from exhaustion, he drifted downward and landed softly on the ground.

"Oh my God," I exclaimed when Remiel released me. The world was still spinning. I stumbled backward before dropping to my knees, pressing my hands together in prayer and squeezing my burning eyes shut. "Please help me. Please help me understand why this is happening. How could they do that to me, knowing what they know?"

"He's not going to answer you," Remiel said behind me.

I ignored him. “Please, merciful Lord. Give me some sign as to what I should do. I’m so lost right now.”

“I don’t know what kind of a sign you’re looking for, but your god just let you get tortured by your own kin. I’d say there’s only one way to interpret that.”

“Oh, and you’re somehow better than God?” I snapped, glaring up at him as he circled in front of me. He furrowed his brows, but I didn’t let him get a word in as I got to my feet and continued my tirade. “You let me get tortured as well! And I’ll never forget what it was like in Hell. To be burned and whipped and violated for no reason other than your fucked-up desires! And now, instead of saving your precious pet from further suffering, you yourself stand by and do *nothing* while they tortured me for hours!”

“I beg your pardon?” He crossed his arms over his chest, the metal bracers clanking against his black breastplate. “I came as soon as you called!”

“I didn’t call you! I purposely didn’t even think of you until the very end, when I couldn’t help but wonder where the fuck you were! If I’m so fucking special to you, how could you let them do that?! How could you stand by and do nothing until the last second when you oh-so-helpfully tried to kill the whole Congregation?” He squinted at me, but before he could get a word in edgewise, I thundered on. “Do you have any idea what a disaster this is?! I swore up and down you weren’t a threat, that your mark wouldn’t affect the Congregation as a whole. And then for you to attack them with demons and hellfire, or whatever you call it? Now they’re going to be hunting us both!”

“Hellfire? You think that was me?” He laughed, uncrossing his arms and waving his armor away so he was only in a black skirt again, despite the fact our breath clouded in front of us in the cold autumn air. “Are you in that much denial about what you are?”

“A sacrificial lamb? Yeah. Got it. That doesn’t mean I’m going to die for *you*.”

He canted his head, watching me with an amused look. “*You’re* a demon, pet. Can’t you see that?”

“What?” I froze to my core at the unthinkable accusation.

“That green fire? You know, the one that was in full effect *before* I got there?” He shook his head, gesturing from his bare chest to where I stood, gaping at him. “That wasn’t me. That was you.”

“You’re lying.”

“For once, I’m not.”

“You always lie,” I said, taking a step backward as he came closer. “Stay away from me.”

“Or what?” He shoved me in the chest and kept shoving me every couple of steps. “Hmm? What are you going to do? Going to finally embrace your demonic side? Explore those new powers you claim aren’t yours? Come on, Phelan. Fight back. You fought off your Congregation without my help. And now I’m pretty sure you’re the one who set that fire when you were a baby. You were defending yourself against your psychotic mother before she could turn you into a filet! So surely you can summon enough anger for one little flame. We both know you have more stamina than you pretend to.”

I stumbled backward, trying to keep the distance between us and ignore every single lie pouring out of his mouth. “Stop!”

“Stop what? Lying? Telling the truth? Doing this? What do you want me to stop?” Another shove, this one even harder. My head cracked against something rough and solid. A tree, which he promptly curled his wings around, trapping me there. "Come on, lamb," he said through his teeth, slapping my cheek in order to grab my jaw viciously, heat blooming under his hand. "You hate me so much? You think I'm lying? You want me gone from your life? Then get rid of me!"

He turned suddenly and flung me through the air like I was no more than a toy.

I landed hard, tumbling through the dirt and the leaves before finally sprawling out on my back. My hip and shoulder screamed in pain, but I forced myself to my feet and started running. I had no idea where I was going. We were in the North Woods, but that was all the information I had. Still, I'd rather take my chances in the wilderness than spend one more minute in his loathsome presence.

I ran into something unyielding and bounced off of it, the air in my lungs rushing out. Landing flat on my back again, I sucked in a ragged gasp while the world above me spun. A sharp metallic taste flooded my mouth; I must have bitten my tongue on impact.

Remiel materialized in front of me, straddling my lap. Both hands encircled my neck and he lifted me up by it, squeezing harder than he ever had before, even when he thought I'd been possessed by Hazael. "I thought I tasted it before, that undeniable essence in your blood, but it was so faint I couldn't be sure. Until now." His mouth covered mine and he forced his tongue inside, licking greedily. A primal growl rumbled in the back of his throat as he pulled away, his lips coated with my blood and saliva. "I didn't think you could taste any better, lover, but you proved me wrong. Wickedness suits you."

I clawed at his hands, trying to get them to loosen from

my throat so I could get even half a breath, but it was no use.

"What did they do to you?" he asked, lowering his face to mine again, but never letting up on the pressure around my throat. "How did they shield that part of you from me? It must have been a long time ago, for you to be in such denial. If you'd tasted this power when you were young, there's no possible way you could have ignored it the way you have."

A tear slipped out the corner of my eye as I shook my head, trying to tune out his voice and focus on not losing consciousness. He was lying. He had to be. This was another one of his games. Another way to torture me. I was already so weak from their failed exorcism. All he was doing was trying to confuse me more, like he'd tried to do in Hell.

Releasing the hold on my neck, Remiel seized a handful of hair and yanked my head backward at a painful angle. "Stop denying what you are and fight me!"

I closed my eyes, too busy coughing and sucking in oxygen to worry about trying to escape anymore.

"No? Ever the pacifist? The good little lamb? It will be the death of you. I'll tear you apart piece by piece in the middle of these fucking woods." He slammed me back to the ground and ripped my shirt open with both hands.

Once the canvas of my skin was laid out before him, a knife shimmered into view in his palm and he twirled it between his long fingers. "Where should I start?" he asked, dragging the tip down the center of my sternum.

My chest heaved up and down beneath the blade. Part of me hoped he'd do it already and end this twisted thing between us. Like all Necromancers, I'd accepted death in order to embrace my power. But tonight, I longed for it.

Anything was better than this so-called life I was living. I realized that now.

"If anger won't trigger you, and fear won't trigger you, maybe pain will," Remiel said thoughtfully. I'd barely had time to comprehend what he meant before a searing pain sliced across my chest. "Bridget was going to cut your heart out for a ring. Maybe I'll give it a go."

I bit my lip, stifling myself from crying out.

"Use your power," Remiel snarled, dragging the knife across my skin again as slowly and as deeply as possible, until I was sure he was slicing into the bone.

"I'm not a demon!" I shouted.

"Yes, you are!"

"Liar!"

"Face it, pet—your beloved Congregation spellbound you. *They* lied to you. *They* hid what you truly are. And for the first time in your life when you needed them, they turned their back on you. They tried to break you! And when that failed they would have done what Necromancers *always* do to demons—they would have killed you!"

"I'm not a fucking demon!" I took advantage of his momentary surprise and threw my hips up, bucking him off. As soon as his weight cleared me, I ducked under his arm and pushed past his wing. As soon as I was on my feet, I took off again.

I didn't stop running and, for some reason, Remiel didn't chase me.

CHAPTER TWENTY-SEVEN

PHELAN

Going back to Tennebrose was a risk, but I had to take it. If I was going to truly escape this town, once and for all, I needed my car. After what happened at Middlewich Barn, I knew I needed to get away—and fast.

Darting through the mostly-empty parking garage, I was nearly to my car when something shoved me hard in the back.

Expecting Remiel, I whirled around, jaw already clenching. "What do you—"

It wasn't Remiel.

It was, however, someone else I equally despised—Kevin Treadwell, my childhood nemesis and the one who'd inspired the damn goat's name. He stood flanked by his two cronies, Hunter Tenney and Dave Green. It was like the high school bully reunion I never wanted.

"You need to come with us," Kevin said. "The Committee wants to see you. Now."

"No." I shook my head, assessing the three of them. It was exactly like that time on the playground when they cornered me behind the slide and left me in a pile of blood and snot. Not much had really changed in the twenty years since then, except we were all older and even more firmly entrenched on opposite sides of the magical line. I'm sure standing in front of them with blood soaking my torn shirt did little to convince them of my innocence, even though it was *my* blood.

"It's not a request, demon," Hunter snarled.

"Grab him." Kevin lifted his hands toward me and a second later something strong encased my torso, like invisible chains.

His two lackeys surged forward, while Kevin held me in place with his magic.

My heart beat wildly with each step. Heat blazed across my palms. Not just my left, from Remiel's unscathed sigil, but *both* hands. Green and black fire erupted from them, engulfing Hunter right as he reached me.

The other two screamed and rushed to their friend, knocking him to the ground and trying to smother the flames. Their efforts only made the hellfire burn brighter until it latched onto all three of them, turning them into human torches.

As soon as the invisible chains let up, I sprinted to my car and dove inside, peeling out of the parking garage.

"Fuck, fuck, fuck!" I slammed my shimmering hand on the steering wheel and shook it wildly, hoping it would make the iridescent flame go away. It didn't. I didn't know how he did it, but it had to have been Remiel, just like at Middlewich. Somehow he was able to manifest magic *through* me and now I'd most definitely killed three of my fellow witches. There would never be peace for me in Winslow after this.

No, not me. *Him*. Remiel. *He* was the demon prince, I was merely his pawn, like Peregrine said. But after tonight,

I'd find a way to sever our link once and for all, even if it killed me.

I made it to Boston in record time and threw my car into park outside the old church.

"Please, for the love of God." I pounded at the rectory door. "Somebody! Open the door!"

My hands wouldn't stop trembling. They'd been like that since Winslow, shaking and shimmering with the eerie green and black flames, refusing to extinguish no matter what spell I shouted at them. It didn't melt anything in my car, thankfully, but it was unnerving all the same.

The door to the rectory creaked open at last. Instead of a face peering out, a silver cross thrust through the opening, narrowly missing my face.

"Be gone, demon."

"I'm not a demon, Father. Please. I need your help." I didn't know this priest like Father Sullivan, but I knew this church had a resident exorcist. If anyone could help me outside of my own people, it was him.

The door opened slowly, the cross lowering. The priest stepped into the light, assessing me from head-to-toe. "You've been touched by a demon, then. I can sense it."

Swallowing thickly, I held my left hand out to him. The black sigil on my palm practically glowed underneath the flames, proud of its mastery over me. "Can you help me remove it?"

He shook his head sadly. "There is no removing it."

"Surely if you can exorcise an entire demon from the

body of the possessed, you can remove its mark? My deacon seemed to think so."

The priest stepped back and gestured into the dim interior. "Come in."

I hurried inside the church, tucking my hands beneath my arms as if that would snuff out the hellish green flames.

"I've only seen a mark like this one time," the priest said, leading the way to the altar. He motioned for me to stay where I was while he fetched a large black bag from one of the cabinets. "I am sorry to tell you, it ultimately killed the woman who bore it. She was too far gone to be saved."

"I'm not afraid of death, Father."

"Good. That's good. Kneel."

I did as he instructed, pressing my hands together in prayer and hoping for a miracle.

Kissing the end of his stole, the priest draped the red silk around his shoulders and finished a prayer before turning to me. He dipped his thumb in anointing oil and blessed me with the sign of the cross, murmuring in Latin as he worked.

Prayers and invocations and pleas filled the heavy silence of the nave as statutes of saints and angels looked on. The priest sprinkled holy water on me, smeared me with more oil, and lit candles so the smoke would carry our words to God.

Throughout it all, my hands never ceased glowing, nor did I feel like Remiel's hold had lessen. The black mark remained as vivid as ever against my skin.

Placing the end of his stole against my neck, the priest covered my head with his hand and continued the Roman Ritual in an attempt to exorcise Remiel from me.

Just like with my grandmother, it didn't work. A man of

the cloth had had no more success than a witch with a personal interest in saving my soul. I didn't want to believe God had turned his back on me, or that my soul was beyond saving, but I couldn't see His larger plan for me no matter how hard I tried.

By the time he was done, the old priest was winded and hunched over. "I am sorry, my son."

"Please, Father, that can't be all. With all the mysteries of the Church? You must know something else, or some*one* else, that can help?"

"There is one thing we might still try," the priest said solemnly. "But it requires a sacrifice."

"What sort of sacrifice?"

"Your hand."

My spine stiffened. Sacrificing my hand wasn't merely the loss of motor function—it was virtually the loss of my magic. Some magic could be worked without the use of hands, but typically they were a necessary part of any ritual, used to conduct power and direct the energy of the spell. In my case, it was the only way to induce sleep so I could enter someone's dreams.

"After it's removed," the priest continued, "I would perform the exorcism again to ensure the link is severed for good."

"Do it," I said quickly.

"Are you certain?"

I pushed my sleeve up and slammed my hand flat on the altar. "Do it! If it's the only way to free me, then do it! Now. Before he finds me." *And before anyone else dies...*

The priest nodded and disappeared into the sacristy to retrieve whatever he needed.

The candles in the votive stand flickered as a gust of wind swept through the large, empty church.

The hair along the back of my neck stood up.

I spun in a slow circle, searching for the shimmering ripples that indicated Remiel was near.

Another breeze churned around me, extinguishing all of the candles in the blink of an eye.

"Stay away from me. Please," I said under my breath. I closed my eyes, concentrating on detecting where he was. He felt so close, I would have sworn he was right behind me, his lips brushing the nape of my neck. A shiver crept along my spine—more wind or his dark magic? I didn't dare turn around to see which it was.

"Phelan." The voice wasn't Remiel's. It was the priest's. "Come here. Now."

I turned toward the sacristy and took one step before the priest's large silver cross was in my face again.

"*Vade retro daemonium*," the priest hissed. He held out his hand to me, beckoning me forward while holding the cross out like a weapon. It was only then that I realized my hands were no longer covered in flames. They were normal again—finally! God hadn't abandoned me after all!

I darted forward, seizing the priest's hand. He whipped me into the sacristy and slammed the door shut behind us.

"Go!" He shoved me toward another door at the far end as he bolted the lock.

Rushing through the second door, my knee slammed into something hard and unyielding on the other side. In the colored shafts of moonlight pouring in through the stained glass, I saw we were in one of the smaller side chapels.

Wood shattered behind us. Once. Twice. Two doors obliterated.

We circled back into the transept and out into the nave. I dove into a pew, dragging the priest down with me.

"Do it now," I said, shoving my wrist at him.

The priest nodded, whispering a prayer in Latin as he unsheathed a large knife from inside his frock.

"*In nomine Patris et Filii, et Spiritus Sancti*," the priest concluded, raising the blade.

"Amen," we said in tandem.

The knife flashed downward.

I braced for the onslaught of pain.

The blade sliced across the top of my wrist, enough to draw blood but not nearly deep enough to sever my marked hand.

The priest swore as the blade turned in his own hand and plunged into his chest.

"No!" I reached for him as Remiel materialized behind the old man, one hand wrapped around the priest's, while the other had a hold of his throat. Since stabbing him wasn't enough, Remiel forced him to carve out his own heart as he choked on blood and unanswered prayers.

"Do you finally see? God doesn't care about you," Remiel sneered, flinging the bloody knife away. "*Any* of you, even his so-called mouthpieces." He reached inside the giant hole he'd created and ripped the priest's heart from its cavity, squeezing it until the blood ran dry and it turned black, crumbling to dust.

Seizing the momentary distraction, I jumped to my feet and sprinted down the aisle for the front door.

Remiel didn't let me get far. He appeared in front of me, throwing his giant white wings out wide. "Where do you think you're going? I told you, you are marked, Phelan. You can't escape me. I don't know why you're still trying."

"You killed a priest," I said pathetically, stumbling backward.

"I've killed many priests."

"Why?"

"Because I can."

"He was only trying to help me. He didn't deserve to die."

"He was trying to take you away from me, so *yes*, he did deserve to die." Remiel's bloody hand shot out. He seized me by the throat and jerked me forward, so close our noses brushed together. "You belong to me, body and soul, until fire rains down from the sky. No power in Heaven *or* Hell will change that."

Before I could so much as think of a reply, he crushed his mouth to mine. It wasn't gentle. It was teeth and tongues and a continuation of our never-ending battle.

His hands raked across my body, slotting mine against his as tightly as he could, sliding beneath my shirt and digging into my skin like he couldn't get enough.

I pushed, he pulled.

Struggling against one another, there was never more than an inch between us. As much as I tried, I couldn't escape him. His arms, his wings, his thighs. He used them all to maneuver me backward, trapping me between himself and the altar.

The second my back hit the rigid edge, his hands dove for my pants, tearing open my belt buckle.

I knew he felt the bulge straining behind the zipper, but I shook my head regardless. It was a struggle I was used to by now—my body doing whatever Remiel wanted despite my head telling it not to.

I still had a voice, though, even if he refused to listen to it. "No."

"Yes."

"Not here."

He spun me roughly and shoved me forward, yanking

my pants down past my hips. His hand pressed against the small of my back, forcing me to arch for him. "Yes, here. Here in front of God and all the fucking angels, so everyone and everything in this universe knows you are mine once and for all."

"Remiel." I meant it as a warning, or even a plea, though I knew neither would get me very far. Instead, to my horror, it came out like a prayer, ending in a gasp as his cock pushed inside of me without warning.

He exhaled against my ear, running his hands down the lengths of my arms to intertwine with my fingers. Together, we both gripped the green velvet vesperale covering the altar and its cloths beneath, joined in the unholiest of unions in what was supposed to be one of the most sacred buildings on earth.

"Don't I make you feel good?" Remiel asked, thrusting into me in smooth strokes. He punctuated his question by nipping my earlobe and sucking away the sting. "Haven't I shown you you can be so much more than the life you have here?"

My fingers tightened around his, each thrust sending a damnable wave of pleasure through my body. A warm tingling seemed to spread from him into me. Magic, manipulation, or my own madness—I couldn't be sure what it was anymore, but it was the closest thing to euphoria I'd ever felt, even better than the time I'd seduced him. Every sensation was magnified, probably compounded by the sin of what we were doing and where we were doing it.

"I want God to hear your screams," he said, pulling my arms behind me. Folding them across my lower back so I was forced to lay flat on top of the altar, he kept one hand locked around my stacked wrists. The other gripped my hip, holding me steady as he pounded into me, faster and faster, so hard I couldn't even catch a full breath.

My gasps turned to moans muffled against the velvet cloth and full-on whimpers, adding to the staccato of our bodies slamming together. I squeezed my eyes shut, not wanting to see the statues up above or the saints in the stained glass, all bearing witness with nothing but cold condemnation.

"How much longer are you going to fight what you are?" Remiel asked in short breaths, panting between every other word.

How long was a lifetime? An eternity? I'd never accept being a demon. I couldn't, even with the evidence he presented. It was more of his mind tricks that I had to ignore, just like I had to ignore the swell of heat rising in my groin.

"Embrace it, Phelan."

The way he whispered my name sent a shiver down my spine, so full of yearning, making him and the feelings inside impossible to discount. How could someone so evil make me feel the things I did? Things I didn't want to. Things I never imagined for myself in a thousand years. I hated him and I hated what he did, but there was no denying my body's response to him. Maybe because I really was a demon…

Without warning, without even thinking, I pulled my hands out from behind my back. Bracing one against the altar again, I wrapped my hand around my shaft and stroked myself in tandem with him, a new wave of pleasure coursing through me. "Oh, fuck…"

"Yes! That's it!" Seemingly renewed by my active participation, Remiel's hands gripped my shoulders and held me firmly while he drove into me again and again.

My thighs quivered. Each pass his cock made over my prostate had my balls drawing up tighter and tighter. I hated him. I hated how he made me feel. I hated what he'd turned me into, that the sin of what we were doing would never wash away. I hated that I wanted the release he was offering more than anything else.

But I took it anyway.

"Remiel!" It was too late to clue him in as to what was about to happen. I came with a cry, my cock throbbing with each rope of cum that painted the side of the vesperale. The trembling spread from my legs to the rest of me as Remiel also came, collapsing against my back, his chest heaving and his silvery hair tickling the back of my neck.

Gradually he stood straighter, dragging me upright with his arms and wings locked around me, his cheek resting against my temple.

I expected him to gloat, to relish his victory over my shattered moral compass, to try and further degrade me about how futile it had been to resist him.

He didn't.

"What are we going to do now?" I asked, my voice barely above a whisper. Somehow, in the still aftermath of what happened, it seemed better to stay quiet—like somehow speaking too loudly in the house of God would be the proverbial straw that made Him finally decide to smite us for our reprehensible wickedness.

Remiel turned his head, quirking a brow. "We?"

"I can't go back there... Besides whatever happened at Middlewich, I think I killed three other witches at Tennebrose."

"You did."

"How do you know?"

"I followed you, of course." He stooped and picked up

my pants, sliding them up over my hips for me before wrapping his arms and wings around me once again.

"So it *was* you who killed them."

"No, pet," he said softly. "That was you. I swear. What were you thinking about before you used fire magic?"

"I..." I exhaled, shoulders rounding. "I don't know. I don't remember, really, except that I was afraid. Afraid they were going to take me away and kill me this time."

"Interesting."

That wasn't the reaction I was expecting. I turned slightly in his arms, glancing back at him. "What is?"

"I tried to get you to tap into your power in the woods earlier and yet you didn't. Were you not afraid then?"

The cuts on my chest stung as I recalled everything that transpired only a few hours ago, though it felt like a lifetime. The way he threw me around, taunting and trying to provoke me. I *should* have been afraid, but deep down I wasn't. "I guess I didn't think you'd actually hurt me."

"So much trust for someone who says they hate me."

"I *do* hate you," I said, even though my words lacked any venom.

"As much as I hate you, I imagine," he murmured, kissing the side of my neck.

I didn't know what to say to that.

Thankfully, he didn't press and I allowed myself a much-needed moment of silence to try and get my thoughts in some sort of order.

We stood there for a while, staring up at the stained glass windows. Droplets plinked against the colored glass, slowly but with increasing speed. Every time lightning flashed outside, it looked like the statues in the church were crying, streaks of light and shadow darting down their marble faces.

"Do you miss it?" I asked quietly, returning my gaze to the windows and fixating on a scene of St. Michael in the midst of slaying a dragon, his sword held aloft, preparing for the kill.

"Being an angel?"

I nodded.

"No." His wings opened and his arms dropped from around me. By the time I turned around, he was already halfway up the center aisle.

I followed after him, pausing when I reached the priest's broken body. "What should we do with him?"

Bright green fire erupted from the center of the priest's chest and spread over him in the blink of an eye. I jumped back, wide-eyed, and stared at Remiel's retreating form. "Remiel!"

He didn't answer. Bursts of green and black flames ignited all over the church—pews, banners, the altar he'd just fucked me against—until no amount of water or magic would be able to extinguish it.

I stared in horror as the flames spread, eating everything in their path and turning it to ash. The marble statues wept for real, except this time their tears were made of blood before they, too, were blackened and consumed by the fire.

Choking on the acrid smoke, I chased after him and burst into the cold, rainy night, gasping for clean air.

"Why?" I managed to spit out, jogging down the front steps and yanking on his wing when he refused to stop.

He whirled toward me, his eyes solid black as he thrust an accusatory finger at the burning church. "This world could do with one less shrine dedicated to that egotistical maniac!"

"Is this because I asked you one stupid question? Then punish me! Not the people who belong to this church!"

He canted his head, the black fading from his eyes until they were silver once more. "You still think he cares about you? He doesn't care about anything except power! And as long as there are fools like you who believe in him, he'll always have it."

"Where should I put my faith, then? In the Devil? In you, my heretical god?"

"In yourself," he snapped. "Try that for a change, lamb. It might get you farther in life."

"You talk as if I'll have a life after all of this. If I'm truly a demon, there is no life for me. And no afterlife without God's forgiveness for everything I've done."

Remiel scoffed, shaking his head. I could have even sworn I saw a flicker of hurt buried beneath his incredulity. "You're *still* fighting what you are. What will it take to convince you?"

"I need to know what really happened to me when I was little. What happened with my mother. And who my father really is."

"Then it sounds like we need to talk to your mother."

CHAPTER TWENTY-EIGHT

PHELAN

"And you have the nerve to condemn us," Remiel murmured as we made our way down the sterile hallway, his nose wrinkled.

I couldn't bring myself to answer him. He was right, of course. Mental institutions were never cheery places but at least we'd come around as a society and actually treated the patients like human beings, even when they acted like anything but. I couldn't exactly say the same for the souls in Hell.

That wasn't to say I didn't see my mother get slammed to the floor, tranquilized, and physically restrained with leather straps over the years. I did. In fact, it was the very first memory I had of her.

Hester brought me to see her when I was still a child, the woman I'd only known in stories. As soon as Bridget saw me, she started shouting in a strange language and clawing at her own arms until the blood flowed freely. Then she started tearing out chunks of her own hair, shrieking and screaming. I know now it was Latin. Over the years, most of the words faded from my memory, but one word stuck out—*daemonium*.

That word haunted me for years, as did another: hagborn. Child of an evil witch.

I first heard it on the playground at King Street Academy when I was in first grade. That was the year Kevin Treadwell started taunting me about my mother and called me stupid for not knowing what it meant. I might have been smaller, and scrawnier, but the rage I felt was unlike anything I'd ever experienced. I punched him so hard he fell flat on his back. And then I kept punching him until my knuckles were bloody and bruised and the headmaster physically ripped me away.

Rubbing my knuckles absentmindedly, I tried to take control of my breathing in the wake of all those memories. Yet another reason I hated coming here. It brought out the worst in me.

"What's wrong with you?" Remiel asked, elbowing me.

"I hate it here," I admitted. "The smell, the sounds. All of it."

"Well, the sooner we find her, the sooner we can leave."

"Her room is this way." I turned down the next hall.

Each step closer made my heart thud louder in my chest. I clenched my hands, willing it to stop. I didn't want to face her. I didn't want to try and ask her the questions burning the tip of my tongue. Who knew if she'd answer? And even if she did, there was no guarantee the answers would be intelligible.

I was somewhat relieved her room was empty when we arrived.

"She's probably at lunch or a group activity or something," I said, turning to go.

Remiel, on the other hand, swept inside the small

space. One wall was covered in rough sketches, random bits of paper taped on top of one another in no sense of order. Some pages had writing on them, a mix of ancient Hebrew and Latin. Others were merely covered in symbols. Some looked like demons' sigils. The rest looked awfully similar to the icons Remiel said were Angelic Script.

"Can you read it?" I asked quietly, afraid if I spoke too loudly I'd wake the sinister presence lurking in the text.

"This looks like that book," he replied, just as quietly. "Like she's trying to recreate the ritual."

"Why would she do that?"

He shrugged. "She's your mother. Go ask her."

I shook my head. "Probably not a good idea, considering that spell is what landed her in here."

"Oh, right. So you're going to lead by asking which demon raped her? That ought to go over well."

I glowered at him. "That was only a theory. There's no proof."

"Right." He smirked. "I'm sure they had a long, swoon-worthy courtship. In case you haven't noticed, we're not exactly the romantic type. A demon takes what they want. Period."

"Is that supposed to excuse what you've done?"

"Are you asking me, or was that rhetorical?"

I shook my head, turning my attention to the Bible on the desk. There was no point in pressing for any sort of apology or recognition of wrongdoing. Remiel would never give one and, at this point, I didn't need it. I'd already forgiven him. It didn't excuse *any* of the horrible things he'd done, but after spending so much time with him, I think I understood why he did them. And somehow understanding is what gave me peace in the absence of an apology.

"What *are* you going to ask her?" Remiel continued, folding his arms over his chest and cocking an eyebrow at me.

"I... wasn't," I hedged, flipping through the Bible and taking note of the passages she'd underlined. "I thought you could read her mind." When he didn't answer, I glanced over at him. "What?"

"You want me to read her mind?" he repeated, with a slow blink to accompany it. "And you'll, what? Take me at my word? Trust whatever it is I say I saw?"

I nodded, not sure what sort of answer he was looking for.

He made a face and stalked out of the room. "Let's go."

We continued down the hall to the nurse's station. She directed us to the dayroom, where Bridget was.

I thanked her and then headed in that direction at a glacial pace. At one point Remiel seized my bicep and physically moved me forward, shoving me against the glass wall separating us from the patients inside the bright, spacious recreational area.

"Which one is she?" Remiel asked, his pale gaze raking over the people on the other side.

Suddenly, I was ashamed of the entire situation. I didn't want to tell him who she was. I didn't want to point her out. I didn't want him knowing anything else about her beyond the embarrassing history he already knew. It was entirely driven by the fear he'd forever equate me with her, that *her* crazy would become *my* crazy, that I'd no longer be the person I was, but a broken reflection of *her*.

"This wasn't a good idea," I said, turning to flee as quickly as I could.

Remiel's hand flashed out, his palm landing in the

center of my chest, keeping me right where I was. "What's wrong?"

"I can't. I can't do this. I don't want to know anymore."

"We both know that's a lie," he murmured against my ear, turning me toward the window. "She's over there, isn't she?"

My gaze shifted to the woman by the window, scribbling over a pad of paper with red chalk. She looked twice her age, not even a fraction of the woman Hester showed me in pictures. Her oversized pink pajamas did nothing to hide the fact she'd gained weight over the years, thanks in large part to the slew of antipsychotics and lack of activity. There weren't as many scabs on her arms, so it looked like the clawing had mostly stopped... except for the chunk of dark hair missing from the side of her head.

Unaware of her audience, Bridget continued to scrawl on the paper with the chalk, stopping now and again to side-eye people when they got too close to her.

Remiel said nothing.

I don't know how long we stood there, watching her through the glass.

No matter how much I willed it, I was unable to bring myself to move. I couldn't leave. I couldn't go in and see her. I was just... frozen, suffocating under the weight of guilt and obligation and a desperate need to know the truth.

"I know this isn't easy for you," Remiel said, clearing his throat softly and shifting beside me.

"How could you possibly know? You don't have parents." I winced the second the words left my tongue. I hadn't meant it like that... or at least not so viciously.

"No, I don't. But I know what it's like to wish for a love that will never be returned."

"Is it possible for a demon to love?" I glanced over at him in time to see him look away. He drew himself up straighter, his jaw set in a hard line. Any tender moment or hint of vulnerability was gone. Even disguised as a human, he was surrounded by a regal air, unaffected by something as trifle as emotions. I could have kicked myself for ruining such a rare moment.

"Don't be ridiculous," was all he said, refusing to look at me.

"You want to know the truth? I look at her and I don't see my mother," I said, turning my gaze back to the dayroom. "I don't even see *a* mother. I see... a waste. Someone who should have never brought life into this world when they were so recklessly irresponsible and unable—or unwilling—to care for it. Even if my conception wasn't her choice, her treatment of me afterward most certainly was. She could have gotten rid of me before birth, given me up, sent me away. But no.

"I don't feel love when I look at her. I feel pity. And disgust. And fucking anger. And then I feel guilt for only seeing her wretchedness and how utterly pathetic she is. Weak. Undisciplined. Helpless. And, of course, underneath all of that... there is the seedling of fear I'll end up just like her."

"Regardless of your feelings toward demons, you should know by now that will never happen. You're too strong, Phelan. I sensed it long before that side of you was unbound."

"You sensed it?" I squinted at him.

He nodded and sent a smirk my way. "I'd never had so much trouble getting in someone's head before."

"I guess that's saying something."

"Excuse me?" A nurse appeared next to us. "Are you waiting for someone?"

My mouth turned into the Sahara and sealed itself shut.

"Bridget Oliver," Remiel said in the wake of my silence. "Her son is here to see her."

She nodded. "I'll go get her."

After the nurse left, Remiel lifted my chin with the tip of one finger. "You don't choose your parents, the same as I didn't choose my creator. She's a necessary means to an end. That's all. You don't owe her anything. Now go get what you came for."

The nurse was finally able to persuade Bridget to set down her chalk and hobble out of the dayroom, into one of the smaller rooms families used to visit.

Remiel might have literally faded from view as I crossed the threshold into the private room, but I sensed him near me all the same.

Bridget sat in one chair, more or less curled in the corner, glaring at the floor.

I didn't know whether to sit or stay standing.

Remiel decided for me, laying an invisible hand on my shoulder and pushing me down into a chair.

I shot a glance at the empty space beside me and cleared my throat before returning my attention to my mother. "How are you?"

"Why are you here?" she replied, still not looking at me.

"It's been a while. I thought I should come check on you."

"I'm not talking to you." Her gaze shifted past me, staring at where I imagined Remiel would be standing. "*Daemonium*."

The doctors said not to play into her delusions. Even if she was right, it seemed better to follow that advice than admit I had a prince of Hell currently running his fingers along the nape of my neck, drawing abstract designs on my skin.

"I came to ask you about my father," I said, trying to keep my tone as even as possible.

"You have no father," she bit back as her gaze darted to me, only to glare contemptuously. She'd never been so hostile before. Then again, I'd never come to her with a demon beside me, either.

Nevertheless, I bristled at her lack of empathy. A lifetime of shame and anger burned my cheeks. "Unless you're claiming to be the Blessed Virgin, we both know that's impossible."

"*May Jesus Christ, the King of glory, help us,*" Bridget murmured in Latin, pressing her hands together in prayer and looking in the opposite direction again, "*to make the right use of all the suffering that God sends.*"

My heart skipped a beat. The memory of a demonic summoning hit me hard. The fire demon. It's what she said before chaos erupted that night. Before Remiel took me.

"Where did you learn that?" I asked, my voice hollow.

Remiel cupped the back of my neck, his palm a burst of warmth against my skin when I suddenly felt like a block of ice.

She didn't turn toward me, just continued muttering to herself.

"I heard it from a demon," I continued, my hands balling in my lap. "Right before I was dragged to the pits of Hell."

Pivoting slowly, she glared at me again. "It's where you belong."

"Because my father was a demon?" I tossed back.

"Father of Lies."

“That’s not an answer.”

“Prince of Darkness.”

“Is Lord of Flies next?” I rolled my eyes. “This was a bad idea...”

“Angel of enmity,” she said through her teeth. “Isn’t that right, angel of destruction?” Once again, her gaze shifted past my shoulder.

“Can you—” Remiel’s fingers dug into my shoulder and I cleared my throat quickly, amending the question and the hostility in my own tone. “Do you see something, Bridget?”

She looked away again, wrapping a lock of hair around her finger and twirling it tighter and tighter until she was pulling on her scalp.

I stood, crossing the small space to stop her. Before I could even touch her, she shot out of the chair and practically threw herself into the corner, standing with her forehead pressed to the wall.

“Go back to the abyss you crawled out of,” she said, raking her fingernails down the wall, chips of pale blue paint flaking off in their wake. “You don’t belong in this realm.”

“Who are you talking to?” I didn’t want to think she was talking to me, but how could she possibly see Remiel? Decades of heavy medications should have suppressed most, if not all, of her magic.

“Phelan,” Remiel’s voice sounded against my ear, his hands sliding around my waist. “Let’s go.”

“Wait. One more thing. Were you really looking for the Ring of Eleazar? The Combermere—”

Without warning, Bridget whirled away from the wall and lunged at me, screaming like a banshee. If Remiel hadn’t been standing behind me, she would have surely toppled me to the ground. Her fingers clawed wildly at my face and neck, like she couldn't decide if she wanted to strangle me or shred my skin to pieces.

I caught her wrists and wrestled her backward, shoving her down into a chair even as she continued to thrash and kick.

It wasn't long before the staff rushed in, shooing me out of the way.

I didn't stick around.

Retreating out of the room, I hightailed it down the hallway, swallowing the lump in my throat.

"That went as well as I expected," Remiel said, morphing into view leisurely, matching my strides.

"How could she see you?"

"She couldn't."

"She was looking right at you. Speaking to you."

"Do you remember where we are? She probably 'sees' people all the time."

"She saw you. I know it. How is that possible, Remiel?"

He sighed. "Another demon could have gifted her the sight, if she didn't have it already."

"Why would a demon do that? Especially for a Necromancer? Seems like handing your enemy a map straight to your own forces."

"I have no idea. A countermeasure, perhaps?"

"Against other demons?"

"Naturally. If you want to keep your pet safe from other predators, it helps when they can see them coming and not be blinded by the glamour."

"Are demons so thoughtful?" I shot him a look out of the corner of my eye, unsure if I meant it as a joke or not.

Remiel smirked. "You mean, are demons so paranoid? Yes."

"Then why haven't you given me the sight?" I arched an eyebrow at him.

"You have no need of it," he replied blithely.

"Why is that? Because I'm a demon?"

"Because I'm not letting you out of mine."

There was a flicker of something in his eyes, a faint glimmer of the real silver color showing through the pale blue glamour. My chest squeezed uncomfortably, knowing he wasn't kidding. As long as I bore his sigil, I was going to be his for the rest of my eternal life and for some reason, that didn't bother me as much as it once did.

I cleared my throat, looking away from the intensity in his gaze, the predatory look that always sent my nerves aflutter. "So now I suppose it's a matter of figuring out which demon took an interest in her."

"Do you have anything of hers? From before you were born?"

"At the house. Why?"

"Let's go. I have an idea."

I nodded and set off down the hall with a renewed purpose.

"Phelan..." A phantom voice whispered, followed by a giggle that was neither masculine nor feminine.

I stopped suddenly, that sound as piercing to my ear drum as a needle. It was haunting and eerily familiar.

"What are you doing?" Remiel asked.

"Such a good boy," the voice hissed. "Mommy's good boy."

"Do you not hear that?" I whispered, my fingers curling around Remiel's sleeve. If we were in the library, I would have assumed it was the damn Combermere. But it couldn't be the grimoire all the way in Boston... could it?

Remiel frowned at me, but I didn't dwell on it. Instead, I kept glancing around the hallway.

A flash of movement at the far end caught my attention.

A tuft of brown fur. One black, button eye.

The teddy bear.

"No," I whispered in horror, the blood in my veins turning to stone. "It can't be."

"Catch me if you can, witch!" the teddy bear shouted with glee. Breaking into a run, the raggedy toy fled down the hallway.

"*Desistas!*" I shouted, chasing after it.

"Phelan!" Remiel yelled behind me.

I ignored him.

Rushing down the hallway, I grabbed the edge of the wall and swung myself around the corner, screeching to a halt before I almost face-planted on the floor.

Saw horses, tools, and various buckets littered the hallway, like a construction worker's obstacle course. Heavy, plastic tarps fluttered up ahead.

Hopping over the mess, I sprinted after the bear and barreled through the plastic, almost tripping over an extension cord stretched across the peeling linoleum in the near-dark.

This part of the hospital was even worse off than the last hallway. The paint was an unsettling shade of green, made all the more unpleasant by the fact there were no lights overhead. The only illumination came through a few dirty windows, slicing through the dusty air between the slats boarding them up.

There was no sign of the teddy bear.

I picked my way through the renovation area carefully, whirling to face every shadow that moved or whisper of sound.

"I banished you!" I yelled into the empty corridor. "How did you come back?"

That haunting chortle echoed all around me. "You're not the only one with friends in low places."

"Laugh now. When I catch you, I'll do more than send you back to Hell."

"No, you won't. You don't have it in you, witch. And I don't see your pet spider this time."

"Don't underestimate me. I'm not the same Necromancer as before."

A shadow moved behind one of the plastic tarps. I studied it for a moment before ripping it down. My reflection stared back at me in a new pane of glass. Crumpling the dirty plastic, I threw it aside and kept moving.

"Mommy's good little boy isn't so good anymore, is he?" The demon laughed. "I told you. You're going to go insane, just like your whore mother."

"What would you know about my mother?" I threw a door open, glaring into the old padded cell.

It was empty.

"Everything," the voice whispered right behind me.

I spun quickly. Something hard slammed into the center of my chest, sending me flying backward into the room. The heavy door swung shut and latched on the outside as my back crashed into the padded wall.

I pressed myself against the pads, yellowed and stained with age and only God knew what, searching the area in front of me. I had no idea if the demon locked me in here alone... or if it was still with me. That sight Remiel was talking about would have been real fucking useful right about then.

"Phelan!" It was Remiel's voice, echoing down the hallway. "Phelan, where are you?"

I opened my mouth to answer, but my throat seized, unable to form a response.

"Answer him, Phelan," the demon's voice whispered, taunting, invisible claws digging into my neck. "Unless you don't *want* him to find you. Do you? Do you *want* him? Do you want him to swoop in and save you from yourself? *Again*? Or do you want to crawl back to God and beg for forgiveness for all the naughty, naughty things you've done?"

The sigil on my hand burned suddenly. I couldn't help but yelp as pain flashed across my palm, cradling it against my chest.

"Uh-oh. Someone's mad," the voice cackled.

"Shut up," I hissed into the empty room, relieved to at least hear my voice again.

"Oh, you're right. You're *not* the same Necromancer as before. You've been"—a frantic sniffing sounded right next to my ear—"tainted. Your soul is bound for Hell no matter what you do. Sinner."

Green and black flames erupted on my hand. I shook it in the vain hope it would extinguish, but all it did was send unholy fire arcing across the small space. The flames latched onto the old padding and flared brighter, licking their way up the wall.

The demon's laughter echoed in my head. "Uh-oh. Now what are you going to do? Call out to your prince? Go ahead. See if he'll make it in time before you burn. A little taste of what's to come."

I backed away from the flames, coughing against the smoke and stench of sulfur. As much as I wanted to call out to Remiel, I couldn't. Between the smoke and the return of the strange strangling sensation, I couldn't speak. The demon managed to stifle my voice, probably the same way he prohibited innocent children from screaming in terror for their parents.

"This is what should have happened all those years ago," the demon said. "You should have choked to death on your own magic, you disgusting halfbreed."

Halfbreed?

I'd barely had time to process the thought when the cell door was ripped off its hinges.

The hellfire dissipated immediately in Remiel's presence, both from my hand and the walls of the cell. Apparently he wasn't trying to pass for human anymore since he'd returned to his demonic state, complete with black armor and wings that practically filled the room.

His silver eyes swept over me, an utterly lethal look on his perfect face. In the blink of an eye, he closed the distance on me, his hand flashing outward.

I turned my head, bracing for the impact.

But it never came.

An inhuman shriek sounded behind me as Remiel's fingers dug into unseen flesh. Black blood gushed over his hand as he dragged the creature forward, away from me. With each step, it howled, finally revealing itself.

It was a horrendous, misshapen thing, with black leathery wings and a forked tongue that darted in and out.

Remiel crushed its shoulder with a snarl, shoving it to its bony knees. "Tell me, what is a servant of Hazael doing in a place like this?"

"I go where my lord bids me," the demon hissed.

"Hazael brought you back?" I asked, though my voice was raspy from the remnants of smoke. "Why?"

"I don't answer to halfbreeds." The demon's initial growl turned into another shriek of pain as Remiel stepped behind the creature and started ripping its wing from its gaunt body.

"You answer to me," Remiel shouted over the top of its wailing, "and I command you to answer his question!"

"To pay my respects," the demon said between gasps, "to your filthy whore of a mother!" The demon's vicious laugh was cut short by another howl. Remiel ripped the rest of the wing off and flung it to the side. Black blood arced across the wall, pooling steadily at his feet.

I pressed on, strangely unperturbed by the violence for once. "Why would Hazael care about my mother?"

"The only thing he cares about is watching her suffer unimaginable horrors. Day after day after day. The same as you, you filth."

I looked at Remiel, expecting him to clarify, to give some sort of answer or insight into his so-called brother's thinking.

"She's already insane," Remiel snapped, grabbing ahold of one of the demon's horns and yanking its head backward. "Why do you continue to torture her? What is it he really wants?"

"*Anulum Lazari,*" the demon spit out.

"The Ring of Lazarus? What's *that*?" Again, I looked to Remiel for the answer.

His lips pressed into a hard line before he turned his gaze to the demon. "Your master thinks she has some sort of magical ring?"

"When he finds it, he's going to send the hounds of Hell after you," the demon said, craning its head to glare at me with yellow eyes. "And I get to watch them tear you apart, again, and again, for all eternity."

Its malicious giggle ended in a scream as Remiel seized its head between his hands and gouged his thumbs into the creature's bulbous eyes. They burst under the pressure, oozing black and yellow down its disfigured face. But rupturing the eyes wasn't enough. Even as the demon bellowed and thrashed, its black nails clawing at Remiel's hands, Remiel sank his thumbs deeper, until they could go no further, and he kept crushing. Bone cracked. Skin split. The demon's head collapsed between Remiel's palms, dripping chunks of something black and gelatinous, presumably its brain.

Flinging the ichor off his hands with a sneer, Remiel disposed of the rest of the carcass with a burst of green and black flames. Somehow I knew the demon was gone for good, though it did little to comfort me.

"Why did you do that?" I asked quietly. "He could have given us more information."

When Remiel looked up at me at last, something warmed the center of my chest. Stepping over the flaming corpse, Remiel closed the distance, fixing me with another one of his predatory stares. "No one threatens you."

The depth of his possessiveness was still baffling to me, but also comforting, in a way. He might torture me, abuse me, and use me for his own desires, but at the same time, I knew he wouldn't let anyone else harm me ever again. He was a demon, without a doubt. But he was *my* demon, as much as I was his.

"Hazael sent me after the Ring of Eleazar," I said out loud, forcing my thoughts back on track and away from Remiel and his confusing motivations. "But he told this demon he was after the Ring of Lazarus. Are we to believe there are two rings?"

Remiel shook his head. "They're one and the same. It's a matter of which translation you prefer—Hebrew or Latin."

"Latin," I said, my voice hollow as pieces of this ever-growing puzzle shifted in my head. "Like the language of Necromancers."

"I know that look." His silver eyes narrowed. "What aren't you telling me?"

"The name Lazarus is well-known to my family. One of our grimoires is called the Book of Lazarus. It's the book that contains all the information on your demons, the ones we've been killing since last year."

"Then we need to get that book, along with your mother's belongings."

CHAPTER TWENTY-NINE

REMIEL

I left Phelan at the edge of the pond while I approached his house under a cloak of invisibility.

Once I was sure none of his fellow witches were laying in wait, I returned to claim him, depositing us safely in his living room before he'd fully exhaled a breath.

He swayed on his feet, clinging to my shoulder to steady himself.

"You better get used to that," I said, splaying my fingers along his waist. "If I get one inkling of another witch nearby, we're leaving."

"It's all in the attic." He cleared his throat and took a step away from me, straightening his shirt before striding to the stairs.

I followed him up the narrow staircase, holding back so I could admire the way his ass flexed with each step. When we arrived at the top, he gave me a disapproving look but, for once, didn't waste his breath scolding me.

In the dusty old attic, he retrieved a cardboard box and blew a decade's worth of dust and cobwebs from the surface before opening it.

"This was everything she left at my grandmother's house, along with whatever letters she sent me. There wasn't anything else left after the fire."

I picked up one of the yellowed envelopes and turned it over, surprised to see the seal was still in tact. "You never opened them."

"No, I didn't," he admitted quietly, leafing through a notebook filled with girlish doodles and loopy cursive.

"Not the least bit curious about what she had to say for herself?"

His gaze cut me to the quick and I managed to withhold a smirk as I ripped open the first letter. Rambling drivel and nothing else. I discarded it quickly.

"These are some of her papers from university, it looks like," I said, pawing through the box and handing a stack of manuscripts to Phelan. "Why don't you read that while I start with these?" I held another letter aloft. It was clear he didn't want anything to do with his mother on a personal level, so I'd spare him the task of reading whatever nonsense she sent him.

He nodded and started flipping through the research papers while I began decoding the mind of a lunatic.

Some letters were perfectly legible, polite questions you'd send to a pen pal, while others looked like they were written by an entirely different being. Between the varying handwriting and word choice, Bridget also liked to mix in ancient symbols and phrases. It would be a novice sleuth's dream to try and crack, except it was all gibberish, much like the Voynich Manuscript and its pointless text. There was no rhyme or reason to Bridget's correspondence through the years. If she *was* under the influence of a demon, she didn't seem to be aware of it.

"This whole paper is on the *Ars Notoria,*" Phelan said with a disgusted scoff.

"You act like that's supposed to mean something to me," I replied, tearing into another envelope. If he honestly expected me to be intimately familiar with *every* religious book ever written, he'd better be prepared for disappointment. I had more important things to do with my time than read bad fanfic of a book I hated with my entire being.

"It's a medieval grimoire in the Solomonic tradition. You know, *that* King Solomon, the one who commands demons?" He gave me a fleeting smirk, though he didn't wait for my reply. Nor was he affected by the glare I shot in his direction. "Anyway, some of the Necromancy inside requires a sacrifice to the dead, despite the fact it's a mortal sin and the Church had already prohibited it. Guess it goes to show she already had a predisposition to child sacrifice by the time I came into the picture."

"How many times did she try to sacrifice you, I wonder?" I shook a dry, brittle leaf out of a letter and cocked an eyebrow at it.

"I would assume twice—once in the woods and once in the farmhouse."

"And at least once after she was locked up." I extended my palm so he could see the back of the leaf. Though the mark was faded, she'd written a Celestial symbol on the back, along the spine.

"What is that?" Phelan took the leaf from me, careful not to crumble the fragile thing as he studied it.

I consulted the letter it came from. "Well, according to her, you're supposed to crush it into a powder and drink it. She claimed it would protect you."

His pale gaze snapped to meet mine. "'Claimed.' So what does this symbol really mean?"

"Death."

"But it's a regular maple leaf. They aren't poisonous in the slightest." He turned it over again, his brow creased as he tried to make sense of it all. "Remiel, what is this? It looks like your sigil."

I took the leaf back from him, glaring at the nearly-invisible mark beneath the Celestial word. The graphite had rubbed away over the years, but there was enough left to get a sense of the sigil. And there was only one demon whose sigil was *that* similar to mine.

"Hazael," I growled, crushing the leaf in my palm.

"You don't... he's not... Do you think he's my father?" Phelan asked, blanching an even paler shade of white.

"No. I don't. It's not his style."

"But how can you be sure?"

"Would you like to call him up and ask him?"

"I would like to know why he's so fixated on my mother and why she knows his sigil enough to write it on a spell intended to kill me. I would like to know how she knows the Celestial language at all and how she could see you when she's supposed to be drugged out of her goddamn mind. I would like to know what the fucking point of my existence is!"

"The point is to suffer, Phelan. That's it. That's God's whole plan. Suffer for him until you die and then you suffer some more. Knowing who spawned you doesn't change that."

"Spare me your warped ideology," Phelan sighed, turning back to the box of papers.

"Says the one who lives like it's the fourteenth century because some stupid little book written by men told him to."

"I don't want to fight with you. I just want answers. Can we please focus on that for once?"

I held my hands up in a motion of surrender and resumed reading Bridget's letters, keeping my eye out for anything else related to Hazael or any other demon.

A little while later, Phelan shoved a paper at me with a gasp. "Remiel, look. She wrote about it. She wrote about Eleazar. She was trying to find it as a student."

"Well that was a stupid thing to do," I replied, skimming through the paper. "It's asking for trouble from everyone—demons, witches, God himself."

"Why should God care?"

"Imagine creating an all-powerful object and bequeathing it to mankind to fight their—and your—greatest enemy only to have some moron lose it along the way. I think it's safe to say your benevolent god would be more than a little irate with his pet gerbils. He'd have no problem sending an angel down here to snatch it back up and leave the lot of you to your fate, demons and all."

"We're not gerbils."

Ignoring his pouting, I continued. "But an angel wouldn't make your mother insane and they wouldn't compel her to kill you. That part is Hazael's doing, at least somewhat. Maybe she was already crazy and he tipped her over the proverbial edge. I have no idea. But he wouldn't waste his time giving her the sight, teaching her the Celestial language, giving her the tools she might need to actually find the damn thing only to turn around and scramble her brain."

"Ok. So two questions then: who *would* take their time to do all of that and where are they now?"

"I have no idea, on either account." That was a lie, a double lie, actually, but he didn't seem to notice.

He scowled, his molars grinding together as his jaw shifted. "What's Hazael's end game? He still wants the ring badly enough to send me after it, since Bridget apparently failed to find it. So why torment her?"

"To punish her."

"But why, if he's not the one who set her after the ring in the first place? You said he's not the kind to take their time and help a mortal along the way. So he wouldn't care about punishing her. But he *would* care about other demons." He brightened, rushing forward with his idea. "Demons are inherently distrustful, you said so yourself. If Hazael couldn't have the ring, he would make damn sure no other demon could either. That's why he made Bridget go insane, so she couldn't finish what she'd started but also so she couldn't tell anyone else where it was—whether that's me or whoever my father was.

"Other than you, are there any other demons Hazael has a long-standing issue with? Any other princes he'd go to these lengths to spite? Any other demon with an interest in necromantic magic like this?"

Only one name came to mind and I grimaced as it settled on my tongue, refusing to come out. I had my suspicions, but Phelan's line of questions left no room for doubt.

"Paimon?" Phelan asked. "Asmodeus? Loray? Please, Remiel." He reached out and squeezed my wrist, his blue-green eyes pleading. "I'm not asking for their true names or sigils. But whichever prince got close enough to my mother to teach her the Angelic Script must have been one of the fallen. There are only so many of you left. And whoever that was is probably the demon who fathered me, which means if I know that, then I'll at least be able to understand what sort of magic to expect now that that side of me was apparently unbound during the exorcism."

I snorted and got to my feet, stalking away from him and his pleading gaze and pouty lips. My wings scattered the letters on the floorboards, sending them swirling around the dusty space like brittle leaves. If the house wouldn't have gone up like kindling, I would have set the lot of them on fire. "What to expect. You know what you can expect, lamb? Power! Unbridled power. For the first time in your life. If you can think it, you can do it. Fancy green fire that burns everything it touches and nothing can extinguish except the will of the demon who summoned it. You'll be able to read the minds and desires of any mortal you encounter, unless they've trained themselves as you did. You can call a host of lesser demons to you just by snapping your fingers and they'll have no choice but to obey because, even being the so-called halfbreed that you are, you're still more powerful than they'll *ever* be."

"You know who my father is, then...?" Phelan watched me warily as I paced back toward him, waiting for him to come to the conclusion for himself.

"There's only one demon who fits the parameters you've deduced and he's not a prince."

Phelan got to his feet slowly. "A duke? Is he a duke?"

I gave him a pitying look. "Stupidity doesn't suit you."

He shook his head, the color draining from his face once more. "No. Not... It can't be."

"Beliar," I said the name so he wouldn't have to, although my earlier prohibition against speaking his name was all for nothing. Being half-demon, Phelan's voice was unlikely to garner his father's attention, especially now that the witches' spell over that part of him had been broken. Beliar didn't acknowledge demons' attempts to summon him, even if they shared his blood.

Phelan shook his head harder, as if that would suddenly

make it all untrue, or somehow erase the name from his brain.

"The king of Hell," I continued. "Father of Lies. Prince of Darkness. And every other epithet your mother used. The answer was in front of us the entire day. She knew who he was, *what* he was, and she knows what *you* are. I don't know if you were part of their original plan or not, but she *was* going to kill you to find that ring and give it to him until Hazael stuck his nose in. Maybe I should thank the bastard."

"I..." He exhaled a shaky breath and pushed past me, stumbling toward the stairs. "I need some air."

I let him go. My feathers ruffled, but I refused to budge from that spot, even after I heard the stupid goat bellowing in the kitchen and the back door opening and slamming shut.

He couldn't get far and nothing, short of another prince, would be able to hurt him now. So I'd let him process this revelation in peace and then spend the rest of eternity distracting him from it by whatever means necessary.

CHAPTER THIRTY
PHELAN

Beliar.

The king of Hell.

The personification of evil on earth.

My... *father*.

I raked my fingers through my hair, pressing against my skull from both sides to try and stop the spinning. It didn't help. Nor did the deep breaths I inhaled to the point of hyperventilation.

My brain continued to race, examining everything about my life, every oddity, every bad little thing. He was to blame for all of it. As was I. By existing, I continued to spread his wickedness through the world. But there was a way to remedy that.

Slipping the knife out of my pocket, I turned it over in my hands, studying it through a bleary haze. How many animals had it sacrificed over the centuries? How much blood had it spilled? It didn't matter now. It only had one creature left to kill.

"What are you doing?" Remiel voice sounded behind me.

I didn't bother turning around. I kept my gaze forward, staring out over the abandoned quarry. I didn't think he'd find me here, but then again, Remiel swore he'd find me anywhere I went. Halfbreed or not, I was stupid to think I could outrun him. Stupid. Evil. I didn't know which was worse. Like an idiot, I saw myself as intelligent and pious. How wrong I'd been. About *everything*.

"Thinking," I replied stiffly.

"Dare I ask?"

Even though he couldn't see me, a faint smirk pulled at the corner of my mouth. "You wouldn't want to know."

"If it's about anything other than destroying Hazael or you writhing against me, then no, I don't."

"You don't care about Beliar?"

His feathers rustled behind me, meaning he probably shrugged. "I'll deal with him if he decides to push the issue."

"The king of Hell?" I turned slowly, pivoting on my heel and keeping the blade hanging at my side. "You'll 'deal' with him? Who do you think you are, Remiel? You're nothing! Nothing! You're a speck of dirt beneath his heel. You have such derision for God, yet you think you can poke your finger at the only being who has ever challenged God's authority and lived to tell about it? Your ego is astounding."

His silver eyes narrowed, flicking from my face to the knife and back again. "What are you doing, lamb?"

"I know I'm not your first pet," I said, ignoring his question and the way his jaw shifted to one side. "Am I your first halfbreed? Is that what really drew you in? You could sense the detestable corruption inside of me? You just wanted to stick it to Beliar by literally fucking his son?"

"I could sense *something*." Moving forward a step, he paused again when my grip tightened on the hilt. "But I didn't know what. It wasn't until the witches inadvertently unbound you that I finally knew the truth. I told you that. I didn't know about your father until just now, after you pieced it all together, combined with what Bridget said."

"I see."

"What is it you think you see?"

"It's me. Bělīya'al," I said in Hebrew. *Worthless.* "I am a true son of Beliar after all. Worthless as a Necromancer. Worthless as a demon."

"What worth do you aspire to? Is there some achievement that would finally fulfill you? Is there some sign from your god that would grant you a modicum of peace? Because you'll never get it, lamb. Never. God doesn't acknowledge anyone, doesn't praise anyone. All those fools who think God talks to them are just that—fools. You are worth a hundred of them."

I rolled my eyes before I could help it. "I don't want your flattery."

"No, of course not. You only want that if it comes from God or your fucked-up Congregation."

My glare darted back to him. "As if you would understand. You turned your back on your Creator and your fellow angels and for what? To live in perpetual sin? To forgo your honor?"

"To have freedom!" he yelled, taking another step toward me, his wings unfolding but not completely expanding, like he was holding himself back. "Freedom which *you* have and spurn every day! Freedom you were *born* with! Instead, you bemoan *your* creator for giving you something others have fought and died for. You're not worthless, Phelan, but you're ungrateful and short-sighted. Everything you do is for the promise of salvation. Be a good little boy and God might finally love you, might finally grace you with his presence. Except real love doesn't come with strings attached!"

"You speak of love as if you know anything about it!"

"And you mock freedom like the clueless mortal you are!"

"I don't need freedom in this life, as long as I have it in the next." My gaze fell from his furious face, staring at the empty space between us. "I only pray God can forgive me."

"For what? Existing? Either by his grace or in spite of it?"

I tried to blink away the tears, but a sudden wave of fear rushed through me. My hands trembled and my breathing hitched. "For breaking the covenant. The unforgivable sin of destroying what He created."

Remiel stood straighter, his head tilting slightly. His voice took on the silken purr he used when he wanted something from me and was seconds away from taking it. "Phelan. Come to me." To emphasize the demand, no matter how nicely he put it, he held his hand out to me, palm up. "Please."

I shook my head and took a deliberate step back. "No."

His face hardened. "I won't ask you again."

"You won't have to."

"Do not—"

"*Mors ad caelos.*" If the knife in my hand wasn't enough of a clue about my intentions, my parting words were —*through death to heaven.*

"No!" Remiel's eyes flew open and he lunged forward, his hand outstretched. If I didn't know better, I would have sworn it was fear etched on his face and not rage.

I gave him a faint smile and jammed the blade into the side of my neck, ripping it across the front of my throat as fast and as hard as I could.

The last thing I saw was my blood spraying out in front of me, an arc of crimson staining Remiel's flawless face.

Coldness surged through my body as I collapsed to the ground, victorious in the ultimate penance.

God forgive me.

CHAPTER THIRTY-ONE

REMIEL

"Phelan!" I caught his head before it cracked against the stony ground.

His eyes were glassy, lids half-closed as blood gushed from his throat. I made no move to staunch its flow. It would only prolong his suffering and I'd make sure he suffered plenty when this was all said and done.

"Damn your pride," I growled, as the light dimmed in his eyes. Laying him flat on the ground, I got to my feet again, rolling my head from side to side and sending a series of cracks down my spine. Conjuring my sword, I unsheathed it and turned in a tight circle. I twirled the blade in my hand, waiting to see which creature would come for him first.

It wasn't long before Allu made their presence known, tearing through the earth and erupting not far from Phelan's body like a giant worm. Despite being faceless, it snuffled around, following the trail of blood straight to the source. Claws outstretched, the monstrous form lurched forward, stopped only by the point of my sword at its throat.

"Not this one," I said, angling myself between them and spreading my wings to their full expanse, shielding Phelan from its sightless view. "He's mine."

A deep, unnerving chuckle rumbled in Allu's chest. Even without a mouth, it still managed to rasp out a reply. "He's a suicide. He belongs to Beliar."

"I told you he belongs to *me*. Crawl back to your master and tell him I said as much."

A dark reptilian tail whipped around from the side, lashing at my face.

I spun toward it, ducking beneath the razor-sharp barbs. As soon as I was clear, I sliced downward as hard as I could. The barbed end fell away with a gush of foul-smelling ichor. Allu's unearthly scream flooded the woods, echoing through the quarry, alerting every demon within a thousand miles that a servant of Beliar needed help.

Before I could lift my sword again, the demon's talons ripped through my shoulder, forcing my sword arm downward. I immediately regretted not conjuring my armor as well, but it was too late now.

I let go of the sword and hurled a mass of green and black flames at the demon with my other hand.

They exploded in the center of its chest, knocking it backward, but not for long. I snatched my sword off the ground and leapt upwards, my wings buffeting as hard as I could to get away.

Allu pivoted in a circle, clawing at the space I'd just been occupying. When it realized I wasn't there, it huffed the air and swung for my feet, floating overhead.

Aiming the sword for the back of its head, I let my wings collapse and fell from the sky. I drove the sword into the base of its neck and twisted roughly, rocking the blade in every feasible direction as I severed as much bone and sinew as possible.

The demon crashed into the earth, convulsing and oozing black blood. Ripping my sword free, I wiped the sticky blood off on my thigh and resheathed it, keeping the weapon with me instead of sending it away.

Movement in my periphery had me whipping toward it, sword half-drawn, preparing for another attack.

Phelan's spirit, glowing with a translucent light that was bound to attract every other devil in the dark, floated there, his ghostly eyes wide with terror.

"You have no idea what you've done," I seethed as I stalked forward.

"What was that thing?"

"The least of my problems." I grabbed his spirit by the throat and dragged him with me as easily as if he were still alive.

"No! You can't do this!" He tried digging his phantom heels into the earth, but I didn't slow my steps. Since that failed, he tried prying my fingers open, also to no avail. "I'm dead! Just let me go already! I'm no use to you!"

"You're lucky you *are* dead because I have half a mind to kill you myself!" I stopped next to his corpse and dragged his spirit's face closer to mine. "It's bad enough I have Hazael after my crown and now you've gone and set Beliar's sights on us! He will know what happened here and he will come for what he thinks is his."

"I'm not scared of him or any other demon," Phelan spat back, defiance flashing in his translucent eyes. "I just want peace, Remiel. Let me go!"

"So you can spend eternity being torn apart by that?!" I shouted, shoving him toward Allu's rotting carcass by the back of his neck. "You think that is the only one of its kind?

This place will be flooded with them in moments. And when they've grown tired of you, a few millennia from now, you will truly belong to Beliar and God certainly won't save you no matter how loudly you beg for forgiveness."

"I don't care! Let those things rip me apart. I deserve it. At least that way I won't be able to hurt anyone else."

"If you're about done with this pity party, we need to get out of here." Dismissing my sword, I grabbed his spirit with both hands. Even though he had no corporeal form, he still tried to free himself, struggling and thrashing as I forced his spirit back into his body, cursing me the entire time.

As soon as we were back in Hell, in the safety of my castle, I slapped Phelan in manacles and chained him to my bed. Naked and weaponless. Even though all four of his limbs were restrained, I conjured a thick iron collar for him as well.

"What are you doing?!" Phelan yanked against the cuffs, his face darkened with rage and his body contorting to try and find a way to free himself.

"Making sure you don't do anything stupid," I shot back. "*Again*."

"Remiel! Unchain me! Now!"

"No." I folded my arms over my bare chest and glared at him.

He gave up thrashing after a few minutes, his chest heaving and his skin flushed from the exertion.

"I can't live like this," Phelan said, so quietly it was like he was speaking more to himself than me. His eyelids drifted shut, a deep crease forming between his brows as the anger slipped away, leaving despair in its place.

"You've been living like this your whole life," I reminded him, sauntering to the edge of the bed and crawling up next to him. "*'This'* changes nothing about you, except now you have full knowledge of what you are. What you can do."

His lashes parted, revealing two glassy wells of the most beautiful shade of blue-green known to ever exist. "I am the spawn of the most evil creature to have ever lived. I am the thing I hate more than anything in this world. Please, Remiel, I'm begging you. If you feel anything for me at all, any ounce of compassion… don't make me live on this earth another second."

I swung my leg over his waist, straddling him, and ran both hands through his hair. Holding the back of his head, I pulled him upward toward my face. The chains on his wrists and ankles disappeared, but the collar remained firmly in place—protecting the area he'd already attacked once. Given how stubborn he was, I wouldn't put it past him to try again.

"No," I said softly, pressing my forehead to his and cocooning us in my wings.

"Why not? Because you want to see me suffer? Is that it?"

"No."

"Then why won't you let me go?"

"Because you're mine. You're not your mother's son or Beliar's scion or some Necromancer at the beck and call of your Congregation. You, Phelan Oliver, are *mine*. Until the end of days."

A tear splashed onto his chest, trickling through the valley of his muscles.

He buried his face against the side of my neck, wrapping his arms around my waist. Every once in a while, I could feel him stroking my feathers at the base of my wings.

I pressed kisses to his temple, his cheek, moving down to his neck. He tipped his head back, exposing his throat to me. If he was hoping I'd take off the collar, he was going to be disappointed. Instead of removing it, I kissed the pale skin above the iron. Threading my fingers through his hair, I held him in place gently as I worked my way from one side to the next.

It didn't take long to feel his cock harden beneath me. I swiveled my hips, rubbing myself against it and taking full advantage of the fact he got hard on his own without me instigating it. His fingers tightened on my waist momentarily before his lips parted and he exhaled a small sigh.

I cupped his face between my hands, sucking on his lower lip gently.

Laying him down again, I left a trail of soft kisses down his body. Caressing his chest, I swirled my tongue around his nipple before flicking it across the hardening peak. No biting or pinching this time, just thorough, gentle attention.

"Why are you doing this?" Phelan whispered, his voice rough.

"Because I want to," I murmured, kissing my way across his chest and palming his pec. "Because *you* want me to."

I didn't give him time to argue. I closed my mouth around his other nipple, letting my hand drift down his abdomen, straight to his cock. He rolled his hips, thrusting against my hand with a soft curse.

Sliding downward, I wasted no time taking his cock in my mouth, licking and sucking every inch of him. His little sighs and twitches spurred me on, seeing what new technique I could try that would make him shiver until he was on the verge of climax.

Once he was close, I shifted up on my knees again, straddling his waist once more and dipping down to kiss him.

I licked into his mouth hungrily, sucking on his tongue. Even though he responded in kind, I took him by the jaw and pushed him backward into the pillows before scooting upward, my knees on either side of his chest and my cock right in front of him.

I didn't even have to say anything. As soon as he was presented with it, he leaned forward and sucked me into his mouth, taking it as deep as he could into his throat. The way his gaze raked up my body made me shiver, as if he'd touched me the entire way instead.

"Perfect," I sighed, running my fingers through the top of his dark hair and thrusting in and out of his mouth slowly, savoring the heat and the suction and the way he looked beneath me. "You're so fucking perfect."

By the time I pulled my cock out of his mouth, we were both breathing hard. His lips were even redder than normal, glossed over with saliva and pre-cum. I kissed him greedily, sucking the taste of myself off of his luscious mouth.

When I pulled away, he chased after me. It took a moment for his eyes to open, his brows dipping as he watched me back up.

I let a mouthful of spit fall to his cock, stroking it languidly to disperse the saliva.

Just like the first time, I rose up on my knees and angled his cock beneath me, sinking down on him slowly. Except this time, he was actually free to touch me—which he did. Hesitantly. His fingers skimmed along my thighs, creeping higher, over my hips. He stroked my chest, grazed his thumb over my nipple, and traced the outline of my abdomen back down to my cock, exploring me like he did the night he first yielded.

Swiveling my hips against him, a burst of satisfaction rippled through me when his eyes rolled back in his head and he grabbed onto my waist.

"Do you like that, lamb?"

He forced his eyes open, meeting mine as I rocked against him. There was no denying the lust there. The pleasure. The sin. And, oh, how he looked now that he finally embraced it. "How could I not?"

I picked up the pace, balancing on his chest while riding him harder.

He slid his fingers into my hair and pulled me down, kissing me. Once I was flat against him, caressing his tongue with mine, he surprised me by thrusting into me from below.

It felt good, naturally, but the fact he was once again a willing participant thrilled me to no end.

I didn't even hesitate when he rolled me off of him and onto my back. Perhaps I should have worried he'd try and exact some sort of revenge, but something told me he wouldn't.

"Is this ok?" he asked, glancing behind me at my wings

"It's perfect." I cupped the back of his neck and kissed him again in case he didn't believe me.

He thrust into me slowly, finding his rhythm. I caressed his face and the flush in his pale skin, trailing my fingers down his throat to the iron collar. As far as I was concerned, he could wear it for eternity. For once, it wasn't meant as a punishment. I wanted to protect what was mine, even if it meant protecting him from himself.

Once he settled into a steady pace, he reached between us and stroked my cock, squeezing and sliding and twisting the way I'd done to him countless times.

I grabbed his ass in both hands and pulled his pelvis against me, hard.

From the hungry gleam in his eyes, he got the hint. I took over stroking my own cock so he could balance himself, picking up the tempo and driving into me as hard as he could. Heat gathered along my spine, curling through my midsection as my pleasure rushed toward its apex.

"Fuck, Remiel," Phelan panted. "I'm going to come."

"Yes, do it."

A few thrusts later, he buried himself deep with a moan, his hips jerking now and again. I could feel his cock pulsing, emptying inside of me. That thought, that feeling, was all I needed.

I clenched around him, stroking my cock as my release jetted out onto my chest.

Phelan gasped, nearly collapsing on top of me. His hips gave little involuntary flicks as my body wrung the last of his orgasm from him with my own.

Breathing hard, I swiped my thumb through a droplet of cum and held it out to him.

He leaned forward and took my finger in his mouth, sucking it off. His dark brows furrowed. Before I could say anything, his face dipped downward and he licked another splotch of cum off my skin.

A wicked smile spread over my lips. "Find something you like?"

He didn't answer until he'd cleaned off every drop, lust and confusion radiating through him in equal measure. "Is it always like that?"

My smile remained as I arched a brow at him, nodding slowly.

"When the Bible talked about milk and honey, that is not what I pictured," he murmured, looking away suddenly, a fresh stain of pink on his cheeks, as if he'd just realized what he'd done and the eagerness with which he did it.

"Had I known you would enjoy it so much, I would have shared it sooner."

Wordlessly, he climbed off and lay beside me, staring up at the stone ceiling overhead. His brow creased again and I wondered what he was thinking about. What he was truly feeling beneath his satiated bliss. He was such a complex creature. No longer a simple Necromancer, but half-demon. By all rights, he *was* another prince of Hell, whether he accepted it or not.

So many sons of Beliar had come and gone through the ages, not knowing what they were, why chaos followed them. But Phelan was different. He *knew* what he was. He knew, on a basic level, what he could do with those newfound powers. The question now was, would he? Would he stay in Hell, embrace a dark title, and rule a realm of his own? Or would he keep fighting for the "normal" life he'd never have?

When his breathing deepened, I curled my arm and wing over him, cradling him against me.

Even in sleep, he laid his hand on my wing and ran his fingers along the edge of the feathers. At this point, I didn't think the gesture was meant to soothe me in the slightest—I think it was solely to comfort himself.

Either way, I craved the feeling. I craved *him*. Everything about him. And I didn't want him to leave Hell ever again. Beliar and Hazael be damned.

CHAPTER THIRTY-TWO
REMIEL

It didn't take long for Beliar to call for me. The mere act of cursing his name coincided with a summoning inside my head so loud my temples throbbed.

I cursed him again for good measure and gave Phelan's sleeping face one last look before answering the rude bidding.

Appearing before Beliar, dressed in armor as a precaution, I pressed my fist into the center of my breastplate and bowed my head.

"Your majesty," I murmured.

The king of Hell stood at the base of his oversized throne with his back to me. His massive black wings stretched out wide, shimmering in the green light, like a wild animal making themselves appear even bigger before their enemy. On first glance, it appeared we were the only two in the room, but Beliar's servants were never far.

He wasn't in armor, but that didn't mean anything. As devious as I was, Beliar had more tricks up his sleeve than a hundred princes combined. One didn't remain the king of Hell through goodwill alone.

"I am most disappointed in you, Remiel," Beliar said, his feathers ruffling with palpable anger.

My spine stiffened, but I refrained from commenting.

"Did you think I would make an exception because it's you? That I would give you something for nothing?" Beliar turned without hurrying, descending the steps like ink spilling in slow motion. With his long black hair and unsettlingly bright green eyes, he still looked every bit like an angel, but I knew better. And now knowing his connection to Phelan, I was even more surprised I hadn't realized it sooner.

"I'm sure I have no idea what you're talking about," I sighed, feigning boredom with the entire conversation.

"You know the rules. Suicides are *mine*." Beliar stopped in front of me, his nostrils flaring. Either he didn't know who the suicide in question was, or it was another means of testing me. I opted to leave Phelan's name out of it, to see if Beliar would reveal himself, and doubled down on my irritation.

"As I told that worthless slug right before I killed it—that one belongs to me. He was trying to circumvent my hold on his soul. I wasn't going to let him win that easily."

"You think your claim supersedes my own?" He arched a black eyebrow.

"It does, hence the reason I maintain my claim even now."

"And if I were to take it from you anyway?" His green eyes flashed dangerously in the dim light. "What would you say, then?"

"I'd say nothing, which would have you wondering about my loyalty until the end of days." I gave him a bitter smile, refusing to back down. "Tell me, majesty, is that something you want to concern yourself with? Spiting one of your most powerful princes, only to question every move I make henceforth?"

Beliar's hands remained at his sides, but I didn't miss the green sparks dancing there, partially hidden in the folds of his long, black shendyt. "Do you seek to overthrow me, Remiel? After all this time?"

"I have no interest in ruling Hell."

"Which is exactly what one would say if they *did* have an interest."

"Have you been speaking with Hazael again?" I cracked a smile, purposely lightening my tone. "I'm surprised you've been so lenient with him considering the lengths he's gone to in order to thwart your plans."

Beliar squinted, trying to see through my bravado. "What plans?"

"The Ring of Eleazar." My smile broadened at the faint twitch on his lips. "Yes, I know you used a witch to try and find it all those years ago. And I know Hazael tormented her until her mind broke. Yet you didn't kill him—or her, for that matter." *Or the baby*, which I wouldn't mention unless absolutely necessary. I'm sure he'd fathered a hundred children since Phelan was born. There was no reason to set his sights on one wayward offspring.

"It seems you've been busy digging up the past." It *wasn't* a compliment, despite the smile Beliar tried to pass off as pleasant.

"Retracing Hazael's footsteps, is all. He hasn't given up on his quest."

"You think I don't know that?"

I shrugged, spreading my hands. "I would never presume to claim any insight as to what you do and do not know, majesty."

"Here is some insight for you, then." Beliar's smile

twisted, just shy of an actual sneer. "Find that ring before Hazael does and I'll forget you took a soul from me. If you fail, I'll take you in its place and send that suicide you want so desperately to Hazael as an olive branch."

I schooled my features into a mask of apathy, but inside I was screaming at the threat. "You would enslave me and reward Hazael instead of forcing him to turn over such a powerful artifact?"

"The Ring of Eleazar will command any demon," he said slowly, like he was speaking to one of the brainless imps used to clean his palace. "The one who wields it will have power second only to God."

"So the stories go," I replied with a sneer of my own.

"Therefore it's in my best interest to make peace with the demon who possesses it. Wouldn't you agree?"

"I wouldn't," I replied loftily. "I would find a way to kill him and take it. At the very least enslave him for the audacity of even entertaining the idea of claiming your throne."

"And that is why you'll never be king of Hell." He gave me a contemptuous once over, as if I'd failed to meet some standard he was measuring. "Not every enemy needs to be killed immediately. Some of them are far more useful alive. Like you."

The muscle in my jaw was starting to ache from being clenched so tightly. "Once again, majesty, I have no interest in your throne—only preserving what is rightfully mine."

"We'll see about that. Find that ring, Remiel, or watch as Hazael takes everything you hold dear while you waste away as a slave until the apocalypse."

Rage flared inside of me, but I knew a dismissal when I heard it.

Inclining my head, I took a step back and disappeared from view, retreating to the safety of my realm as quickly as I could before I broke my oath to Beliar right then and there by ripping out his fucking heart.

CHAPTER THIRTY-THREE

PHELAN

The iron collar sat heavily around my throat, making it hard to swallow or even turn my head. I glared at it in the polished mirror in Remiel's bedroom, trying once again to pry the stupid thing off. A bent metal comb lay discarded on the table in front of me from my fruitless attempt at picking the lock.

Since Remiel stripped me of my clothing and I couldn't conjure new ones with the iron around my neck, I ransacked a trunk at the end of Remiel's bed looking for something I could wear. Unfortunately, none of his human clothes were there, only piles of skirts and elaborate belts.

"When in Rome, right?" I muttered to myself, wrapping the black fabric around my waist and triple-tying the knot. The thin material did virtually nothing for my modesty, but adding the wide, silver belt on top at least gave me another layer to work with.

After thoroughly investigating his barren room and finding nothing useful or entertaining, I crept to the door and tried the handle. To my surprise, there weren't any guards there when I peeked out. With nothing else to do, I seized the opportunity to explore outside his bedroom.

I knew which direction led to the outside world and I knew which direction led to a torture chamber. Opting to venture down a third hall, I moved silently on bare feet and prayed I didn't meet anything else along the way. Although, with the iron collar still in place, maybe they'd inherently know to leave me alone, kind of like last time. At least, I hoped.

The hallway twisted and turned, green flames illuminating the way. I didn't pass a single creature until I came to a pair of massive doors. Huge, minotaur-looking guards stood on either side, swords hanging from their belts and their spears crossed in front of the entryway.

Neither of the demons looked at me, but from the deep, inhuman growling that suddenly filled the hallway, I got the feeling they'd acknowledged my presence.

I expected them to storm away from the door and drag me back to Remiel's room, but they maintained their posts.

"Is Remiel in there?" I asked, glancing between the two, unsure if they could even understand me.

The growling got louder from the one on the left.

I took a step forward. "Open the door."

The demons exchanged a look over the top of my head before the one on the right snorted loudly, like a bull, and moved out of the way.

Equal parts surprised and relieved that that went so smoothly, I strode into the room, scanning the impressive interior for any sign of Remiel.

The ceiling vaulted overhead like a cathedral, black stalactites glittering in the eerie hellfire. A black throne dominated one wall, carved into the rock face itself. Silver banners hung on either side of the throne, Remiel's sigil emblazoned on them, in case you somehow didn't know whose castle you were in.

The room was empty, but curiosity still got the better of me as I walked further into the space. A long table stretched across the far side of the room, covered in scrolls and papers and books. I wandered over to the table, examining the stack of books.

Unsurprisingly, I couldn't understand a word. They were all in the Celestial language, including the documents. The only thing I could make sense of was Remiel's seal—a more elaborate version of the sigil that marked my palm—at the bottom of some papers. It was also centered on a map, with a very similar sigil marking the land to the north. Hazael's sigil. Pools of silver and bronze moved back and forth over the map every now and again, ebbing and flowing, the border between their realms shifting as it appeared one side gained strength and the other lost it. This wasn't merely a throne room, then—it was a war room, proof of his eternal battle with Hazael.

"What are you doing in here?" a deep voice rumbled behind me.

I whirled to face it, pressing myself against the table in the face of the horned demon. "Melech."

His snake eyes skimmed along my body before flicking upward again, his tail lashing behind him. "You're a halfbreed."

"How can you tell?"

"I can smell it. But you didn't smell like that before." He took a step forward, his meaty hands curling into fists at his side. "So what is a filthy halfbreed doing in the prince's castle?"

"You'd have to ask Remiel."

"Do not speak his name! You are not worthy."

"Oh yeah? What are you going to do to me?" I tipped my chin up as he stomped closer, a growl reverberating through his massive chest. "Did *Remiel* tell you to torture me this time?"

Melech's tail whipped back and forth, but he didn't say anything.

"I bet he didn't," I continued with a smirk. "But go ahead. Hit me. Whip me again. Because I can't wait to see what he does to you when he gets back."

"One day he will grow tired of you and then he'll let me do whatever it is I want with you."

"What do you want to do to me, Melech?" I cocked my head and gazed up at him, the picture of innocence. If Remiel were here, I knew how he'd take my question. Would Melech interpret it the same way? Remiel seemed to think it was a concern once upon a time. Was that simply his demon paranoia, or was there validity to it? I needed to know only to ensure my own survival. There was no way I could fight Melech, especially bound in iron. That left one avenue of defense without Remiel.

Melech's clawed hand shot out, stopping a breath away from grabbing my jaw. "You're playing a dangerous game."

I threw a pointed glance at his hand, a smile stretching over my lips as he clenched it and withdrew it slowly. "You can't touch me, can you? Is it the collar? Or orders from your master?"

His lip curled, but he refused to answer.

"I wonder if I can touch you, though?" I asked aloud, lifting my hand toward his face. "Or if the collar prevents that too."

Instead of flinching away, he loomed over me, his black eyes flashing a warning. "You think you have some sort of power here, halfbreed?"

"I know I do." I grabbed him by the back of the neck and yanked his face closer to mine. He gripped my biceps, steadying himself, but the more I talked, the deeper his claws sank. "Because one word from me and Remiel will rip your fucking heart out. Your insignificant little demonic life is in the hands of this filthy halfbreed and I am sick and fucking tired of people looking down on me. The next time you address me, it better be with the same respect you show your master."

Melech's growl turned to a yelp as his head snapped backward. In the blink of an eye, he was jerked away from me and slammed onto the floor so hard the room shook and the stone beneath his back cracked.

Remiel knelt in the center of his chest, his fingers clutching Melech's throat and digging deep. "I warned you."

"Remiel, don't!" I hurried to his side and dropped to my knees, using both hands to pull on his arm, even though I knew it wouldn't do any good. It was like trying to bend steel.

For his part, Melech didn't try to offer any sort of defense or fight back, even though every part of his face was lined with fury.

"I goaded him," I said quickly. "He followed your order. He didn't touch me."

"Then explain that!" Remiel snarled, pointing at the bloody claw marks on my biceps with his free hand.

I couldn't—at least not in any way that would satisfy Remiel's bloodlust. At the very least, maybe I could distract him from it.

"You've been away from me all day," I said softly, taking his free hand in mine and pressing it to my face. "And now instead of being with me, all you want to do is kill another one of your soldiers?"

The hand around Melech's throat loosened before Remiel stood, pulling me to my feet. "He made you bleed."

"I made myself bleed by yanking him off balance."

Melech eased into a sitting position on the ground, touching his neck gingerly.

"On your feet," Remiel snapped, his silver eyes boring into Melech's. "And do not move."

The demon did as he was told, clasping his hands behind his back and planting his feet. For once, his tail lay still instead of whipping back and forth.

"And as for you." Remiel's furious gaze slid back to mine, the irises as black as night. "Is that the kind of demon that appeals to you? Finally embracing the darkness within?"

I couldn't help but glare at his insinuation. "Don't be ridiculous."

"Then what is it you wanted from him? Did you expect him to kill you? Is that it?"

"It was nothing, Remiel. A battle of wills. That's all."

"That's all?" He raised his eyebrows at me in mock disbelief, the onyx color overtaking the whites of his eyes. "Once again I observe you in the embrace of another and you tell me 'that's all'? Don't you *ever* forget to whom you belong! Until your bones turn to dust, you are mine! And no one, angel or demon, will take you from me!"

I had barely processed what he said, and the paranoid rage with which he screamed it, when he shoved me against the table and spun me roughly.

"What—Remiel, no!" It was the church all over again. His wrath was palpable and only God knew why.

"I will fuck you in front of my entire legion if I have to," he growled, grabbing my arms and forcing me to bend over the table. Iron manacles appeared from nowhere, securing my wrists to the damn table and leaving me completely defenseless.

"Fine," I sputtered quickly, hoping my compliance would calm him down. "Fuck me. Here. In bed. Wherever. Just send him away."

"No. I want him to see what will never be his." He ran his hands up my thighs, pushing the black skirt up over my hips and exposing me for Melech—and whoever else stumbled into the room—to see.

Remiel bent my knee and shoved it up on the table, spreading me wider before his mouth descended on me. Even though I knew it was coming, I still jerked against the restraints when his tongue probed inside, as hard and demanding as his cock tended to be.

"Remiel." I hated the way it came out as a whimper instead of the furious way I'd intended, but my body was warring with me once more, desperate for the vile things he was doing despite the fact we had an audience. It was humiliating for so many reasons, but even as my stomach churned, my cock hardened.

Melech's gaze was as hot on my flesh as Remiel's had been; I could feel it from across the room and fuck if *that* didn't leave me even more confused. I'd never been any sort of exhibitionist. In fact, the whole concept normally made my skin crawl. But now? Guess it was a good thing I was already in Hell, since I was destined to end up here after all the wicked things Remiel had done with me.

Remiel pulled back and spat at my hole before pressing the pad of his thumb inside. I gasped once, then again when his mouth slid down the length of my shaft and enveloped the crown of my dick.

Not being able to see him (or Melech, for that matter) made the whole experience that much more vivid. Each swipe of his tongue, each scrape of his nails, not knowing where he was going to lavish attention next, made each sensation a hundred times more potent.

By the time I felt Remiel shift behind me, his cock rubbing against my ass, I didn't care who was watching. He gripped my hip with one hand, holding his shaft steady with the other as he pressed inside of me without warning.

"Fuck." I gritted my teeth and squeezed my eyes shut. I knew I could accommodate him, even when he was being forceful, but it didn't take the initial sting away.

"Isn't this what you wanted?" Remiel asked, sliding in the rest of the way with a satisfied groan. "To be with me?"

"Not like this," I replied, pressing my forehead against the table.

"Then you wanted *him*?" Remiel seized a handful of hair and wrenched my head back, angling me so I had no choice but to meet Melech's burning black gaze.

"No!"

"Liar." He slammed his cock into me again, punctuating the snarl in his voice.

I couldn't stop the yelp that escaped. It didn't slow him in the slightest. His thrusts continued hard and fast, like he was punishing me as much as Melech for a transgression that didn't occur.

Just like the church, when he said the priest was trying to take me away, which is why he deserved to die.

And what did he say moments ago?

No one, angel or demon, will take you from me.

I didn't know what happened in the time we were apart, but *something* had set Remiel off and I had a feeling it had nothing to do with what he may or may not have witnessed between his soldier and I.

"Unchain me," I said, trying to look at Remiel instead of Melech.

"So you can try and escape again?"

"So I can touch you. Please." The intimacy worked once before. Hopefully it would work again. Not to escape, as he assumed, but to calm him down and remind him I wasn't a *thing* to possess, no matter what he thought.

Remiel's laughter was dark. He raked his fingers along my scalp before yanking back on the heavy collar, practically strangling me with it. "Who do you belong to?"

"You," I gasped, sure that at any moment I was about to be literally bent in half. "Only you. And I only want you."

The iron around my wrists disappeared a split second before he tossed me onto my back like a rag doll, thrusting into me again before I'd so much as gotten my bearings.

"Kiss me," I said, wrapping my legs around his waist and trying in vain to hold him in place. "Remiel, please, kiss me."

He obliged my request with all of the gentleness I expected from him at that moment—which was none. His kiss was as rough as his fucking, angry and raw, with more than a dash of paranoia.

Still, I took it. Tangling my fingers in his silken hair, I held on, keeping him close, continuing to kiss him whenever he tried to pull away.

Eventually, my efforts paid off. His thrusting slowed and his kisses deepened. He even pulled me closer, settling me on the edge of the table in an upright position, his hand roaming over my back and shoulders in gentle caresses.

"You're mine," he whispered against my lips.

"I'm yours," I reassured him, pressing kisses to his face

and down the side of his neck to his shoulder. "I'll always be yours."

He wrapped his arms around me tighter, holding me, not even trying to fuck me anymore even though his cock was still inside.

I smiled to myself, nuzzling the curve of his shoulder.

His wings shifted and stretched, wrapping around us.

My gaze flicked to Melech, not the least bit surprised to find the look on his face had changed. Instead of disgust, or hatred, all I saw was the beautiful sign of my victory—the realization that I was right. I *did* hold all the power and Melech fucking knew it.

Before I could bask in the glory, Melech shimmered from my sight. In fact, the whole world around us tilted and swirled for that split second as Remiel returned us to his bedroom.

He laid me on the bed wordlessly, but instead of resuming what we'd started in the throne room, he settled between my legs and wrapped his arms around my waist, using my stomach as a pillow.

I ran my fingers through his hair, toying with the silver strands while trying to figure out what was going on inside that head of his.

"Where were you earlier?" I asked softly.

"It doesn't matter," Remiel replied, though his tone sounded weary for a change and not like he was being difficult out of principle. *Something* had happened, but what, I had no idea.

"It matters to me." I tugged the ends of his hair, hoping he'd look up at me. He didn't. I wasn't about to give up, though. "Do you remember that day you showed up at my house? Injured?"

"What about it?"

"You never told me what happened."

"You know what happened."

"I know you were attacked. But... how?"

"What do you mean 'how'? It isn't some great mystery. Hazael sent a message as a ruse and the ones who carried it are all dead."

"Are you sure they belonged to Hazael?"

Remiel finally sat up, quirking a brow at me. "What are you driving at?"

I wet my lips quickly, my gaze darting away while Remiel scrutinized my face. His eyes may have returned to their usual silver color, but I didn't want to set him off again.

Using the tip of one finger under my chin, he turned my face toward him again. "Tell me."

"Whoever it was, they came really close to killing you. You assume it was Hazael's order and it probably was. But how would he know where you'd be? Specifically? You could have been in any realm at the time."

"He has his spies, as do I."

"How close do your spies get to their target?" I asked quietly.

"You think someone betrayed me?"

"Are you that surprised?" When he didn't answer, I continued, making sure to keep my tone even and as neutral as possible. "But there's more... I've been thinking about the Book of Lazarus. You said all of the demons the Congregation eliminated were from your realm. So how would we have gotten all of that *very* specific information? It's a guidebook on how to systematically kill your people."

The likelihood of God or one of his archangels bothering themselves with a list of demons was slim to none. The answer, then, was obvious.

"Another prince," he replied tightly. "Or the king himself."

"Exactly. I think it's time we borrowed the Corbins' grimoire. Maybe there's another clue in there that can help us."

CHAPTER THIRTY-FOUR

PHELAN

"Hopefully they're out in the woods for All Hallows Eve. We usually do a big ritual on nights like tonight, when the veil is the thinnest," I said as we approached one of the back doors to the Corbins' massive house, my breath clouding and hanging in the night air. I was grateful Remiel had conjured one of my normal outfits for the journey, instead of making me wear the skirt I stole from him. I'd also managed to convince him to remove the collar, promising I wouldn't do anything rash again. He reluctantly agreed, with the threat it would go right back on if I did anything that even made him remotely suspicious.

"And if they're home? What's your big plan, then?"

"Ask nicely to borrow the book?"

Remiel snorted but managed to keep his opinion to himself.

"You're probably going to have to wait here," I said, gesturing to the doorknob.

"Why?"

"The house is warded and Caius's magic is ten times stronger than mine."

Holding my gaze defiantly, Remiel leaned forward and twisted the doorknob with a tad more force than normally required. The mechanism inside the lock snapped. He pushed it open and gestured inside with a sweeping bow. "After you, lamb."

I moved across the threshold cautiously. When I wasn't struck down by lightning, I turned and watched Remiel do the same—although he strode through the doorway with zero hesitation and no ill effects at all.

"How is that possible?" I asked. "This house is even older than mine. You shouldn't be able to get in."

He gave me an all-knowing smirk. "Princes go where they please. All wards do is keep away lesser demons. Kind of like praying."

"Good to know."

We made our way through the silent house, winding through the rooms and halls. Even though I'd been here countless times over the years, it was still odd to sneak around in the near dark. Once I found the entrance to the basement, Remiel yanked open the locked and magically sealed door as if it was nothing and followed me down the stone stairs.

The deeper I descended into total darkness, the more my vision shifted, taking on an eerie green hue. I blinked a few times, but it always came back. There could only be one reason—my demonic powers were growing, testing their limits after being restrained for nearly thirty years.

On the one hand, it was deeply unsettling. But on the other... being able to see in the dark was a pretty useful ability. Even if that's the only power I used, it gave me a considerable advantage.

"You can see now, can't you?" Remiel asked after I successfully navigated the large table in the center of the pitch-black room.

"I suppose so," I muttered, approaching the giant armoire set back against a wall. When he didn't reply, I glanced over my shoulder. There was no mistaking the self-satisfied smile on his face or a flutter of pride that stirred in my chest. "Look for a book. Small. Unassuming."

The moment gone, Remiel rolled his eyes and drifted to the shelves, pawing through skulls and crystals and stacks of paper and not being the slightest bit careful to put anything back the way he found it. Scolding him wouldn't matter, so I let him be. Hopefully the Corbins would blame it on an angry spirit.

I, on the other hand, worked my way neatly through the large armoire, but the book wasn't there.

"The only other place they'd keep it is the crypt," I said, more to myself than anything. "Come on."

I took a step toward the stairs, but Remiel grabbed my hand and pulled me against him.

"I have a faster way you know."

Suppressing a groan at the idea of astral travel, I linked my arm around his waist and held on for dear life as he teleported us out of the basement. I'd no more than braced myself for the journey when something jarred us from every angle, like we were caught in a wind tunnel, being buffeted against one another. Remiel's arms tightened around me, crushing me until I couldn't breathe, but I didn't have the air to tell him to let go.

The sensation didn't last long.

When we reappeared, we weren't in the Corbin crypt. Nor were we outside of it.

We were in the midst of a burned-out barn, charred

support posts clawing upward through heaps of rubble that had been cleared away from the center and piled up around them. A large, jagged opening tore through the very middle of the roof, allowing the moonlight to filter into the open space.

Middlewich.

"Remi—"

An unseen force ripped me out of Remiel's arms and threw me backward, while Remiel remained rooted in place. No, not rooted. Chained around his wrists and ankles, by thick, heavy iron like he'd used on me.

A series of different colored crystals ringed the floor around him—nine rings total, the necessary number to contain a prince.

I landed hard on the dirty floorboards and scrambled to get up again, but hands seized me from both sides, holding me where I was.

The whole Congregation filtered out of the shadows, some carrying crosses, others small bottles of what was probably holy water.

"Let me go," I snarled, trying to shake off my human shackles. Two more men joined the task, their rough hands clamping down on me from behind.

Remiel, meanwhile, stood as still as a statute, despite the manacles around his wrists and ankles. His wings stretched to the limits of the invisible barrier. Even though he hadn't been able to manifest his armor or any weapons, his calm visage was terrifying enough, like he was surveying a room full of dead men. "I suggest you do as he says."

"You have no power here," Peregrine said, marching to the front of the crowd and locking eyes with Remiel. Caius stood beside him, holding the Book of Lazarus, while

Hester held the Book of Damnation. Off in the corner, old Bob Winslow sat with the Book of Transactions balanced on his lap. It seemed everyone wanted to document their encounter with a real demon prince.

"Where's Temperance?" I asked, searching the faces in the crowd.

"Your cousin has been detained until we can get this mess sorted out," Hester replied. "I'll not lose her too."

"What did you do to her?!" I surged forward, breaking free of the hands that held me.

Peregrine threw his hand out. A gust of wind knocked me back the few steps I'd claimed. "Stay where you are, Phelan! This is about him, not you."

"Where is she?" I repeated once the wind had died down.

"She's with Ainsworth," another voice answered. There was shuffling in the crowd and Cassius appeared, his face drawn. "She's ok. They didn't do anything to her. They just want the demon."

As soon as I saw Cassius, I seized the opportunity presented to me. There would be no reasoning my way out of this or talking to any of them like civilized adults. If Remiel and I were going to make it out alive, this was the only way.

Throwing a hand toward the younger Corbin, I snared him in a ring of green and black fire.

Caius shouted and took a step toward his son, restrained at the last moment by Marcus.

"Phelan, let him go!" Hester yelled. "Cassius is innocent!"

"Release the demon," I snapped back, "or watch the Corbin heir burn in front of you."

Hester squeezed her hand into a fist, aiming it in Remiel's direction.

Before I even knew what was happening, he fell to his knees inside the circle, holding his head. An inhuman scream ripped out of him, piercing my soul as sharp as a knife against flesh.

The green fire surrounding Cassius flared brighter with my wrath. Remiel could handle whatever it was she was doing to him, I was sure of it. There's no way I was going to back down.

"Let him go!" Graeme Hewitt screamed, but not at me. His mismatched eyes were narrowed at Hester, a look of pure hostility on his face, so much so that even Peregrine hurried forward to lay an arm on Graeme's bicep before he did something reckless, like electrocute her. "Now!"

"You're not yourself, Phelan," Hester said. "Once we kill this creature, we can restore you to your sensibilities."

"My sensibilities have never been better," I shot back. "For the first time in my life, I see things as they truly are."

"You see them the way *he* has manipulated you into seeing them!" Hester threw an accusatory finger at Remiel with her free hand. "Everything he's told you is a lie, Phelan!"

"He's not the one who spellbound me!" I took a step toward her, propelled by a lifetime of frustration and resentment. Another burst of green and black flames erupted on the floor, this time around Hester.

"I'm not going to talk to you when you're like this," Hester said coolly, not the least bit concerned I'd trapped her as well.

"And I'm not negotiating. You have three seconds to let him go. Or I'll burn what's left of this barn to the fucking ground with everyone inside of it. I hear I did it once before and I was just a baby then. I wonder how much stronger I am now."

Hester's eyes widened, confirming Remiel's theory. Bridget might have been trying to sacrifice me, but *I* was the one that started the fire that ultimately got her locked away. I'm guessing Hester bound me shortly thereafter, keeping my demonic powers a secret from everyone while watching me like a hawk and imposing as much strict religious discipline as she could get away with, waiting to see if I'd end up like my parents—either insane or pure evil.

Apparently she had her answer now and I certainly didn't want to disappoint.

The hellfire lurched toward Cassius, burning brighter and growing taller. Each second that dragged by, weighed down by her indecision, was another second closer to roasting Cassius alive. It wasn't fair to him, I knew that, but what did Remiel say to me? All's fair in love and war.

"Dad!" Cassius shrank back from the flames, his gaze darting between his father and his fiancé. "No! Don't!"

Graeme yelled for Cassius, yanking against Peregrine's restraining hand, but unable to throw the older man off.

"Phelan, please!" It was Caius' turn to beg. "Don't do this! He's all I have left. He's innocent. If you want to punish someone, punish me!"

"This isn't about punishment," I replied tightly. "That's the difference between demons and witches. Witches are the ones who punish. They curse. They hex. They kill. Demons let your actions dictate your fate. 'Be careful what you wish for,' and all of that. I get it now. You call them liars, but they're only telling you the truth. It's not their fault the truth is fucking ugly."

"You're right," Caius agreed. "You're absolutely right. We have lied to you, and I'm sorry. We knew Bridget was floundering. We knew her search for the ring had taken her down a dark path. But I promise not all of us knew you were spellbound. We just found out. Like you did."

"For the love of God, Caius." Hester's eyes narrowed and she jerked her closed fist, knocking Remiel off his knees and onto his back. "Use the knife and end this nonsense once and for all."

Remiel's screams renewed and turned deafening.

Since the witches didn't seem to be taking me seriously, I conjured another ring of fire around Graeme and Peregrine. It might have been dangerous to stretch my newly-found magic so much, but it was a risk I had to take.

The rest of the Congregation yelled, unsure how to proceed with their Deacon and future Deacon trapped by hellfire. George Hewitt summoned a burst of water to splash on the flames around his son, but all they did was splatter and spread, like napalm.

"You would murder innocent people to free this monster? After everything you've been taught?!" Hester yelled.

I met her glare with one of my own. "Absolutely. Don't believe me?" The green flames lunged at Graeme. They caught his pant leg and raced up his body in the blink of an eye.

Cassius screamed, unable to help his fiancé while Peregrine tried desperately to pat the flames out. Despite his best efforts, they wouldn't extinguish, and soon his sleeve was on fire as well.

Peter burst through the crowd and ran toward the circle containing Remiel. Before anyone could stop him, he kicked crystal after crystal out of the way, breaking each ring.

As soon as the magic holding him was gone, Remiel shot upward with a furious roar. The chains snapped and his massive wings flapped hard, lifting him higher. Each gust of wind was strong enough to knock the bystanders over, save for those contained in demon fire.

I ran forward and snatched the Book of Lazarus out of Caius's hand. As soon as I had it, I sprinted to Remiel. He continued to hover for a moment, just out of reach, a look of pure contempt on his perfect face, as if I had been the one to chain him in the first place.

Finally, he lowered his hand. The moment I grabbed onto him, we blinked out of existence, leaving Middlewich behind us.

When we reappeared, I was surprised to see he hadn't taken us back to Hell. Instead, he took me back to my house, depositing me rather unceremoniously on my ass by the pond. But more than that, I was surprised to see the irate look was still on his face.

Remiel ripped his hand out of mine and spun, striding toward the dark woods.

"You're welcome!" I snapped, scrambling to my feet.

He laughed, a dark, derisive snarl of a sound, and whipped around to face me. "I'm supposed to thank you for that? For nearly getting me killed?"

"That wasn't *my* doing!"

He gave me a contemptuous once over, shaking his head in disgust. "Go back to your people, Necromancer. I've no further use for you in this life."

"What?" The air rushed out of my lungs. "What are you talking about?"

"I never want to see your face again! Is that so hard to comprehend? The sight of it sickens me. You, and all of your blinking, doe-eyed innocence. To think there was a time when I doubted your ability to lie."

"I'm not lying! And I didn't set you up, if that's what

you're getting at! I had no idea they'd summon you tonight!"

"So they figured out how to trap a prince all on their own? After all this time? Didn't have anything to do with that damned book they had in their possession? The one *you* record everything in?"

I didn't have a comeback, because he was right. For all intents and purposes, the Book of Damnation *was* my book. My notes. My record of every demon we'd summoned and slain and step-by-step instructions on how we did it, including the night I more or less summoned Hazael at the crossroads. While I might have grudgingly accepted that I was half-demon, apparently my Necromancer half was still naive, especially when it came to my family.

"That's what I thought," he sneered, shaking his head. "Stupid little lamb. Still so trusting of the ones who hurt you the most. No wonder you're a Catholic. You're a glutton for punishment. You think it makes you a martyr. All it does is make you easier to manipulate. Zealots always are."

When Remiel walked away from me a second time, I threw up a wall of black flames directly in his path, my hands clenching at my sides to keep from aiming the fire at him.

He halted abruptly and whirled on me. "Either you're proving my point, Necromancer, or you've lost your ever-loving mind. So which is it? Stupid? Or insane?"

I met his glare head-on. "You don't get to throw me away like I'm nothing. Not after everything you put me through. And not after I chose *you* over my entire Congregation. Do you understand what this means, Remiel? I have nothing! I *am* nothing! There is nothing left for me in Winslow. No family. No Congregation. No fucking job at a university for witches! In the blink of an eye, I gave up everything—for you! Because for reasons I will never understand, I somehow mean more to you than I do to any of them. Stupid lamb or not, I trust *you*, Remiel, not them. And now I have this"—I held up the Book of Lazarus for emphasis—"so I can fulfill my promise to you. I'll find the ring and kill Hazael once and for all. For *you*. You ungrateful, self-centered, psychotic asshole!"

Remiel's face was devoid of any discernible emotion. If he was moved at all by my angry declaration, it didn't show. Nor did he seem particularly offended by the ending and my heap of insults.

"Are you going to say anything or are you going to keep glaring at me?" I asked with a huff.

"Why didn't you let them kill me?" His voice was a step above a growl, which didn't mean anything as far as his moods went since they were so damn capricious. "After everything I've done. It was your first real opportunity to get away from me, to escape my mark."

"I don't know," I answered truthfully. "I should have. God knows I should have. But I couldn't. You're everything I hate, everything I shouldn't want. But..." I shrugged, unable to find the words to explain even a shred of what I felt. Not just for him, but for the entire situation we found ourselves in. Maybe *this* was insanity. Maybe this was the very same thing Bridget had gone through with Beliar, warring with this cognitive dissonance and unable to make heads nor tails out of it.

Remiel stared at me for a moment, his head tilted like a cat's. "You're not at all concerned about what your grandmother said? That I've been lying to you. Manipulating you."

"Of course you have," I scoffed. "You're a demon. Not only that, but you're a prince. I think I'd be more concerned if you weren't constantly manipulating me. But how is that any different than what they've been doing? Right? Hasn't that been your point this entire time? That everything they've said, everything the Church has said, has all been one giant manipulation? I don't know what any of this means. I don't know who's right or who's wrong. But for once, I'm trying to figure it out on my own. I'm trying to listen to my intuition and see where that leads me."

"You are a curious creature, Phelan Oliver."

"Is that a step up from a stupid lamb?"

"Time will tell." Remiel held a hand out to me.

I glanced at it before returning my gaze to his, trying to discern any emotion in his pale eyes as I crossed the short distance and slipped my hand into his palm. A sense of relief washed over me the moment his fingers curled around mine and he pulled me in close. As soon as his wings enveloped me and his lips brushed along my cheekbone, I knew I'd made the right choice—stupid lamb that I was.

CHAPTER THIRTY-FIVE

PHELAN

Back in the safety of Remiel's bedroom, I shed my heavy coat and withdrew the Book of Lazarus from inside one of the large pockets. I held it in both hands, taking note of its new size and shape. After the Corbin family folios has been successfully located last year and the two halves of the Book of Lazarus were reunited once more, someone took it upon themselves to bind the book back together. It was a simple black leather cover with no markings to indicate what it was. Even if I'd been able to find it at the Corbins' house, there was a good chance I would have overlooked it entirely since I was looking for the old version of the book. If there was one silver lining to Remiel being summoned and trapped by Hester, then this was it. We had one more piece of this never-ending puzzle.

Aside from the cursed Combermere Codex, I'd never been nervous around books before. They were my living, after all. I knew how to handle them magically and in terms of preservation. But knowing *this* book had been instrumental in tracking down Remiel's people and murdering them? It made me hesitate to open it, especially with him pacing in front of me.

"I wonder," I said out loud, finally giving voice to another thought that had been niggling in the back of my mind. "Do you think this is the same book they used to bind me when I was a baby?"

Remiel's silver eyes flashed, darting from the book to my own. "You're the expert. You tell me."

I shrugged off his iciness and flipped open the first page. It didn't matter if it was or wasn't. Caius said he hadn't known and I was inclined to believe him. Next to Ainsworth, he was one of the more trustworthy members of the Congregation. And he was one of the only people who tried to stand up to Hester before the exorcism. That had to count for something.

As I read, I could feel Remiel hovering, creeping closer with each page I turned, trying to see for himself but not wanting to admit it.

"Would you like to sit?" I asked, patting the bed beside me. "You're going to give yourself a crick in your neck if you keep it up."

Remiel hmphed at me and spun away with a snarl, his feathers ruffling. "I have no interest in any of your Necromancy books."

"Remiel, please. Your pacing is driving me up a wall. And there might be something in here you recognize that I don't."

Grudgingly, he returned to the bed and sat beside me, glaring at the book in my lap. "You don't know where that came from?"

"I have no idea. Honestly. I suppose we could always go steal the Book of Damnation and see if there's any sort of reference to it, but you know as well as I do that magic practitioners in that era didn't ascribe their names to their works for obvious reasons."

"I don't need a history lesson, thank you very much."

I ignored him and kept reading.

While turning through the pages, scanning each methodically for any nugget of inspiration, one name jumped out at me from an entry in the early 1700s—my ancestor, Gyles Oliver.

It was such a brief note at the bottom of an exorcism prayer, I might have overlooked it, if not for the name.

"*Ex terra, arcana nostra,*" I read aloud, squinting at the rest of the text and turning my head to the side, like it would make the faint letters somehow more legible, or the meaning more clear.

"'From the earth, our secrets' what?" Remiel asked.

"I don't know. Can you read the rest of this?" I shoved the book in his hand and leaned into his shoulder, staring expectantly at the page, like an impatient child waiting for a bedtime story.

"Can't *you* read it?"

"Apparently not as well as you in this light. Now read. Please," I added as an afterthought.

He huffed and repositioned the book, holding it in both hands. "It says, 'The cords of Sheol entangled me; the snares of death confronted me.' Standard biblical bullshit. Happy?"

"Sheol?" I frowned at him, an unsettling feeling creeping into the back of my mind.

"The Hollow. The ancient Hebrew afterlife. Often conflated with Hell, Hades, and Gehinnom—since you feel the need for a deep dive into theology all of a sudden," Remiel said, tossing the book on the bed when I refused to take it back.

"I know what Sheol is." I shot a glare in his direction. "But that is not what the Vulgate Bible says. Even the King James Version uses 'Hell' instead of Sheol. So why did they write that particular word? And what secrets are they talking about?"

Remiel shrugged. "You're supposed to be the expert, remember?"

"Not helpful." I stood and started for the bedroom door.

"Where are you going?"

"I need my Bible."

Remiel snapped his fingers, loudly enough that it echoed around the room. A second later a loud thunk sounded behind me, like something heavy slamming.

I turned slowly, scanning the room for any sign of what he'd done. The only thing different was the giant black Bible laying in the center of the floor—the Oliver Family Bible. "Did you just summon that?"

"No, I've been lugging it around this whole time for some light reading." Remiel rolled his eyes.

"How did you get it out of the house?"

"After all this time, you still doubt me?"

"I don't doubt you. I'm just trying to understand how we've managed to survive this long if you're capable of coming and going at will. First my house, then the Corbins'."

"Because contrary to what you people think, I have more important things to address than slaughtering witches in their sleep. It's much more fun to convince the humans to do it for me." He gave me a wicked smile as soon as I glared at him. "And what is it you're looking for in that decrepit old thing?"

"The family tree," I replied, flipping through the pages as I carried the book back to the bed, resuming my seat beside him. "I don't remember where Gyles Oliver is in the grand scope of the family."

The branch I was looking for was buried in the seventeenth century, with Gyles's name squeezed amongst more prominent members with one tiny little offshoot.

Due to the limited space, there wasn't much information to go on. According to the genealogy, Gyles Oliver married Margaret Corbin and had one child who survived to adulthood: Eliezer Oliver, who went on to intermarry with other Necromancers in Winslow.

"What are the odds of that?" I brushed the tip of my forefinger across Eliezer's name.

"A biblical name for someone born in the wake of Puritanism? It's not much of a stretch."

"But look at the other child listed here: Salamon. Close to the original, but just slightly obscured. Do you think that was intentional?"

"If only you could talk to the dead." Remiel smirked, clearly amused with himself.

"The dead know nothing," I murmured, too lost in thought to worry about his snarkiness.

Another piece of the puzzle shifted in my brain and my eyes widened as I turned to Remiel.

Remiel arched an eyebrow, the mirth leaving his face. "Didn't you say that right before you lost your mind at the library?"

"The Combermere said it," I replied. "When I asked about my mother… when I accused it of trying to make me crazy. I thought it was a taunt about Necromancers, since we seek counsel from the dead, but what if *that* was the actual answer? 'The dead know nothing,' from Ecclesiastes? What if *that* is what Bridget found? What if the Combermere gave her the answer, coupled with that fucking sacrifice?"

"So? What does that have to do with us? Or Eleazar, for that matter."

"It's another reference to Sheol—not the afterlife version as you so helpfully pointed out, but the gathering place for family. What if they meant a literal gathering place? Like a cemetery?"

"You think the Ring of Eleazar is in a cemetery?"

"Why not? It's sacred ground. Until just recently, I was under the impression demons couldn't penetrate our wards. So perhaps my ancestors thought it would be safe there."

"Well, let's go desecrate some graves and find out, shall we?"

"I wish you wouldn't phrase it like that," I sighed, only to have him laugh.

The Old Burying Grounds were dark and quiet. Despite my family's interest in death and spirits and the fact it was still All Hallow's Eve, I had no reason to think they'd set up camp here. I'm sure they were too busy trying to recover from their wounds—literal and figurative—after what they'd tried to do to us at Middlewich. A twinge of remorse slithered through me for any lasting damage I might have inflicted on Cassius or his fiancé, but had they been in my position, I had no doubt they would have done the same thing.

The only thing we had to worry about now were idiot

kids partying in the historic cemetery or the police who tried to keep them out.

"So where is this ancestor of yours?" Remiel asked. The wind ruffled his feathers, though his bare skin showed no signs of being cold.

"Given the date listed in the family tree, he should be over here," I said, leading the way to the oldest part of the cemetery, struck by a sudden thought. "Unless they dug him up and cremated him. That might pose a problem..."

"Not very Catholic of you, cremating your corpses."

"They've let up on that restriction, thank you very much. And besides, we've been pretending to be Protestant since the sixteenth century."

"Glad to see they've finally admitted defeat. After all, who cares if your body burns when your immortal soul is going to be roasted for all eternity for every little thing?"

"Do you have such a low opinion of all organized religions, or just Catholicism?"

"They're all morons. I've just been forced to endure Catholics longer than the rest. Besides, you've apparently accepted you're half-demon, so why are you still getting so defensive about your precious Church?"

"My faith is what's kept me alive."

"Your strength is what kept you alive. Faith has nothing to do with it."

Thankfully, Gyles's headstone came into view, giving me an excuse to end the argument.

Cracked and weathered with age, the letters carved into the old slate were barely visible, but it was the right one. Beneath a winged death's head, read:

Here lyes the body of Gyles Oliver of Bayfield. Husband to Margaret. Who departed this life Apr 30th Anno Dom 1705 in the 93rd year of his age. Mors omnibus.

"I don't suppose you brought a shovel?" Remiel asked with a dazzling smile. He might have been charming if he wasn't such an asshole.

"No. I didn't." It was my turn to roll my eyes as I stepped up to the foot of the grave. What did Remiel say about accessing my demonic magic? Just will it into existence? Something like that.

Exhaling a steadying breath, I held my hands out over the grave and willed the dirt to dig itself out.

Nothing happened.

Not a blade of grass stirred, nor a speck of earth moved.

I cleared my throat and tried again, well aware that my single audience member was watching my every move with the utmost fascination.

Why was it so much easier with fire? Probably because each time I'd used fire magic, I was angry. Or scared. This time, what emotion did I have to tap into? Desire? A desperate need to find this ring?

As if sensing the issue, Remiel sidled up behind me, sliding his hands underneath my shirt and across the front of my stomach. "What's wrong, lamb? Having difficulties?"

"Just... trying to figure this out. Do you mind?"

"Go ahead," he murmured. "I'm not stopping you." Each exhaled breath warmed my neck as his lips moved from one side to the other, leaving a trail of kisses along the top of my shirt collar.

"You're not helping, either."

"I'm not?" His hand snaked up my chest and seized my jaw, forcefully turning it to the side to expose more skin to his mouth. The minute he sank his teeth in, sucking hard enough to leave a mark, I let my eyes drift shut.

"Think about what you want," he whispered against my ear, his thumb and forefinger exerting just enough pressure on my arteries to make my head spin. "You don't have to beg the universe or praise god to access your magic. The power is already yours. *Make* it happen."

For once it sounded like he was actually trying to be helpful, except I could barely concentrate on any of it with his cock hardening against my ass and my own twitching in anticipation. When did I lose all sense of self-control? When did I stop resisting him? More importantly, why? Even if I was half-demon, Remiel still represented everything I stood against. He was vile and malicious. And every time he put his hands on me, my heart spasmed in my chest.

But I couldn't think about any of that right now. Right now I needed to focus on getting six feet of dirt off of a three-hundred-year-old corpse through willpower alone.

"Do you need more motivation?" Remiel asked, his free hand drifting to my cock and curling around it over the top of my pants. "Do you need me to fuck you right here in this cemetery? Clear your mind?"

I tried to shake my head, but he squeezed my throat tighter. "No," I gasped out.

"Then do it already. Dig out the grave. We don't have all night."

I squeezed my eyes shut tighter and focused on the task at hand... not Remiel's hand. The *real* task. The real reason we were here. Not how good he was making me feel. How relaxed, but wound up in another way, a way that only he was able to make happen. He was a paradox, as always. My tormentor and my salvation, who made sinning feel like a dream.

Remiel's husky laugh broke through my concentration. "I knew you could do it, lover."

I blinked quickly, staring at the yawning grave in front of us, a mound of dirt piled neatly on one side. "Holy shit."

Remiel stepped away, leaving me on unsteady legs and suddenly cold from the loss of his infernal warmth.

Adjusting my hard-on as discreetly as I could, I moved to the edge of the grave and stared down at the rotten coffin. Now for the unpleasant part.

With a wave of my hand, the nails wriggled themselves loose and the lid moved to the side, exposing Gyles. Or what was left of him.

Unfortunately, that's as far as my demonic magic would be able to help me. It wouldn't be able to summon the ring, which meant if it was there I would have to find it the old-fashioned way. By hand.

Hopping down into the pit, I winced as something crunched under my boots. "I'm sorry, Gyles."

"You realize you're talking to a pile of bones, right?" Remiel asked overhead.

"It's habit." Carefully lifting the corpse's skeletal hands up into view, I frowned at the gray bones. No ring. I groped along the edges of the coffin carefully, feeling through the worm-eaten fabric for any metallic hardness or circular-shaped objects.

"It's not here," I said after I'd thoroughly searched the corpse and the coffin, taking far longer than I'm sure Remiel wanted. "Damn it! Do you think it's in Eliezer's grave instead?" I glanced at the graves nearby, hoping one might stick out as being more important than the others.

Remiel sighed, studying his nails in the moonlight while he lounged against a taller gravestone nearby. "I told you, the ring probably doesn't even exist. Hazael and Beliar are chasing their tails and this has all been a giant waste of time."

I hated that he was right. Again!

Climbing out of the coffin, I replaced the lid and assessed the dirt walls around me, wondering how the hell I was going to get out again. Even stepping on the closed coffin didn't elevate me that much and there was nothing to grab onto up top.

I was about to ask for a hand out of the grave when my foot plunged through the old wood and I pitched forward. Throwing my hands up in time before I smacked my face against the freezing earth, I came face-to-face with Gyles's headstone.

"You could've asked for help, you know," Remiel said, still not making a move to lend any assistance. He muttered something about "pride" under his breath, but I wasn't paying him any attention.

Almost as unreadable as the name was the town in which Gyles Oliver was born, staring me straight in the face—Bayfield. *Not* Winslow.

Family history and lore rushed back to me, situating Gyles within the larger Oliver saga, like I'd been trying to do earlier with the Bible. Despite the fact he was an Oliver, he wasn't a *Winslow* Oliver.

Escaping East Anglia and the history of witchcraft persecutions, the founders of Winslow came to the New World to build a sanctuary for our kind. But they still had family in England. Family that stayed for one reason or another... until local politics threatened the next generation and either forced them underground or abroad.

Gyles was welcomed with open arms in Winslow because he came bearing one particularly important gift for his American kin—the Bayfield Manuscript.

"Oh shit," I said out loud as the imaginary lightbulb clicked on above my head. "It's a riddle! Bayfield. Open land. Earth. Break down the etymology. *Ex terra, arcana nostra. That's* the secret Gyles had. From Bayfield, from the open land, otherwise known as the fucking earth, our secrets. Our family secrets are all in that book! Remiel, help me out." I waved my hands impatiently at him, my body practically buzzing with the realization.

"What are you babbling about?" Remiel asked, hauling me out of the grave but not letting go of my hands.

"We have to get to the university. I think I know how to find the ring."

CHAPTER THIRTY-SIX

REMIEL

"The Combermere was actually telling the truth by giving me that hint about Sheol, I just didn't have enough of the pieces to put it together. I thought it was talking about *my* family and the cemetery. But the book was talking about its *own* version of Sheol," Phelan said excitedly as we hurried across campus, avoiding clusters of late-night party goers stumbling down the illuminated sidewalks. I didn't even bother trying to hide my true form. In the middle of a drunken university town on Halloween, I blended right in.

"A cemetery for books?" I asked, trying to follow Phelan's leaping logic while giving a giggling she-devil an unimpressed stare as she teetered along with her friends on spiky heels. The red horns and pointy tail wouldn't win her any favors with the real Devil, nor with his son, who had zero interest in the cleavage she flashed his way. He was too entranced by the real love of his life—books.

"Not like a genizah. You know, where Jewish religious texts are stored before proper disposal? I think what it meant was the library. Think about it. What else would constitute a gathering place for a grimoire's family?" Phelan continued, completely oblivious to the coeds as he stepped off the sidewalk and headed for the darkness along the side of the library.

"A family of... books?"

"Yes! Exactly! And one of those books has been missing this whole time but it should be back by now."

Phelan keyed us into the library through the side door and all but ran to his office. Logging into the computer, he typed quickly, scrolling through various screens until he sprang up from his desk again. "It's still in archives! Come on."

He was too excited to even wait for the elevator, preferring instead to take the basement stairs two at a time. Never mind the fact I could have transported him down there in the span of two heartbeats...

"Is this book going to make you crazy, too?" I asked as Phelan cut across the basement and unlocked another door to a room clearly labeled "Archives and Preservation."

"No. The Bayfield isn't that kind of book."

"Then what kind is it?"

"It's a history of our people. Yes, it's a grimoire, but it's nothing like the Combermere."

"Wonderful. Let's get it and get out of here."

Phelan strode up to a large, brown book set out on a table and lifted it from its archival box carefully. Running a hand along the thick spine lovingly, a genuine smile flitted across his face. "They fixed the binding. It's beautiful."

A sense of unease prickled along my skin. I ruffled my feathers, trying to ignore it, but the longer Phelan stood there, fawning over a damn book, the more persistent the feeling became. "We don't have time to entertain your book fetish. Let's go."

"I can't take it out of the library," he replied with a scoff, carefully turning the pages and scanning the illuminated text. "It's too delicate."

"I don't care how delicate it is!"

"Why are you being so pushy all of a sudden?"

I couldn't name the feeling crawling through the pit of my stomach, so I merely flexed my wings and spun away from him, stalking to the office door and peering out at the darkness across the rest of the basement.

"Remiel?" Phelan's voice changed. I was tempted to turn and look at him, but the shifting shadows at the far end of the substructure kept my attention, though I couldn't make out anything in the distance. His footsteps sounded behind me, soft and unsure. "Is everything ok?"

"Are you finished?" I asked, though my gaze remained narrowed at the darkest part of the blackness, waiting to see if the shadows would move again.

"No, I—"

"Then stop talking and find it already!"

Phelan cleared his throat and I heard him retreat. A moment later, the thick pages resumed turning.

Leaving him to it, I set off for the darkest part of the basement to assuage my gut feeling. Stalking through rows of old bookcases and empty filing cabinets, I strode toward the shapeless shadows, pausing now and again to listen or smell for anything foreign. The whole university reeked like witches and their potions, but I was more concerned with something demonic.

The weird iron vault came into view and the unsettling feeling within me surged. I'd been here before and it had no effect, but this time, an unusual sickness twisted along my insides, like I'd swallowed a snake. Perhaps that's what Phelan had been talking about before when he was trying to warn me about the dangers of these magical texts.

"Release us," a serpentine voice whispered. "Take us with you."

Both doors to the vault were standing open. The last time I was here, I'd needed a series of keys to unlock them. Keys that were currently with Phelan, since he'd used them to access the building and the archival room.

The heavy doors groaned as I pushed them open even farther, my gaze sweeping the corners of the giant iron box as I stepped inside.

The grimoire sighed audibly on its pedestal as soon as I came into the room.

"You didn't speak to me the last time," I said, eyeing the book. It wasn't caged and the chains that normally bound it dangled freely. After I dragged Phelan away, I hadn't bothered locking it up, but I knew damn well I'd closed those doors behind me. So who, or what, had opened them?

"Apologies," the book hissed, the pages trembling.

"What do you want?"

"Freedom. A sentiment you can understand."

"And in exchange?"

"We'll tell you where it is," another voice chimed in, slithering around in the dark like it was dancing.

"Where the Ring of Eleazar is?"

"Yes."

"So it *does* exist. On this plane?"

"Yes."

"Did you tell Bridget Oliver where it was?"

The book sighed again; wistful, annoyed, I couldn't tell. "Release us, please. Before it's too late."

"Too late for what?"

"If Phelan finds it, he'll destroy you."

I shook my head at the mere thought. "No." Perhaps once upon a time I would have been inclined to agree, but things had changed between us. Even after his family managed to capture me, Phelan proved his loyalty. He wouldn't betray me now. I could feel it in my bones.

The Combermere tsked me like a patronizing schoolmarm. "Your lust for him is your weakness. First, he will bind you. Then, he will enslave you. After that, he will destroy you. Free us. We can stop him."

"And what would you do with your freedom?"

The book hissed. "Whatever the master wants."

"Really?" I took a step closer, head tilting to the side as I studied the book and the way the pages fluttered, like it was breathing. "And which master do you truly serve? Hmm? Beliar? Or God?"

"Remiel!" Phelan's voice rang out in the dark, even more alarmed than it had been a few minutes ago. Turning toward the doorway, I met his bewildered gaze and raised my brows at him, waiting. "What are you doing in here?" He glanced between the book and myself, his keys clutched tightly in his hand. "How did you get in?"

"The door was already open." Plucking the iron cage from the floor, I nestled it on top of the pedestal and secured the padlock again. Some other librarian could wrestle with the chains if they wanted; Phelan had more important matters to tend to.

The voices wailed from inside their prison, pages flapping in frustration.

"The ring is real," I said, walking back to Phelan and pushing the first door shut. "The book just told me."

"I know. And I know where it is."

"Don't let him reach it!" the book screamed behind me,

its inhuman voice seeping through the seams of the vault. "Kill the usurper before he destroys us all!"

Phelan's eyes darted to the door, his throat constricting with a hard swallow. I took him by the chin and forced him to look at me, running my thumb over his lower lip. There was the familiar uptick in his heartbeat that I craved, the hitch in his breath. The way his pupils widened as his gaze zeroed in on me like prey who'd been caught by a predator.

"If I find out you've betrayed me, you will suffer like never before. The collar will be the least of your worries. Do you understand me?"

He nodded mutely.

"Liar," the book whispered through the cracks.

"Then it's the moment of truth, lamb. Show me what you found."

He nodded again, but made no move to leave. In fact the only movement was his heart hammering in his chest. Fear had wound itself through his usual scent, disrupting the citrusy herbal smell with a sharp bitterness I hadn't detected from him in a while—at least not because of me.

"What are you afraid of?" I asked quietly, lifting his chin up when it started to fall.

"I know what the Combermere did to me when I was near it."

"And you think it had the same effect on me?"

"I don't know." Liar, just as the book said.

"Phelan..." I let my hand fall from his chin to his throat, stroking downward to his chest and flattening over his heart. One little push, two steps backward, and he was pressed against the outer doorframe. "Take me to the ring and forget everything that execrable book said."

"But it told the truth before, in its own twisted way, and now you think I'm about to betray you." His pale gaze lifted from my mouth, a small crease between his brows. "So what did it say to you?"

"Trying to see which of your lies is about to be revealed?"

"I've never lied to you."

The hand on his chest fisted, clutching his shirt and yanking him closer. "Stop pretending to be good. It's gotten you nowhere."

"I'm not—"

"The next words out of your mouth better be a location to that damn ring, or you begging me to fuck you right here."

"Upstairs. The foyer."

Disappointment ebbed between us; each failing the other's test. I'd refused to be honest with him and he'd refused to give up on his mission. If the Combermere told the truth, even in a convoluted way, then he *was* destined to betray and enslave me. I'd hoped that if he gave into me and forgone his pursuit of the ring for just a moment, that maybe he'd prove the book wrong.

Releasing my hold on his shirt, I waited until he moved out of the way before slamming the outer door shut.

Rather than waste time by taking the elevator or the stairs, I simply grabbed his hand and transported us to the lobby of the library.

Phelan expelled a breath and turned away from me, unsteady on his feet for a moment. I resisted the urge to assist him and hung back while he stopped at the edge of the giant tiled seal in the library floor.

"It's here," he said, almost breathless. "They hid it inside during construction, knowing it would be guarded by witches without us even realizing it was here."

"Is there a key, or do we simply smash our way in?"

"No, I think I need a knife." He held his empty hand out in front of him, staring at it. It took a moment, but eventually a knife wavered into view, dimming a couple of times before it solidified in his hand. "It worked!" Happiness burst through him like sunlight in a storm cloud. Thrilled as I was that he was getting a firm grasp on his demonic magic, a pang of trepidation hit me when he laid the edge against his forearm.

"Phel—"

Before I could even finish, the knife flashed across his skin. Droplets of red rushed out, spattering over the ornate seal at his feet. A blood offering, not another suicide attempt.

The moment the blood touched the tile, the drops pooled together and ran through the crevices, slick as mercury, before filling the O in "Tennebrose" and disappearing into the floor.

Something loud clanked underfoot.

I grabbed the back of Phelan's shirt and yanked him away from the seal a moment before the entire thing shifted. The seal lowered and slid out of sight, beneath the floor.

The floor rumbled. More metal clanked and groaned, protesting its use after centuries of lying dormant.

A small iron box ascended into view from beneath the seal, no bigger than my hand. That didn't stop someone from scratching sigils and spells all over the blackened metal, though. And not just spells—curses.

"Maybe this isn't a good idea after all," I said, pulling Phelan back as he reached for the box.

"You want to back out? Now? When it's right there?" Phelan stared at me, as confused by my sudden concern as I was.

"You don't even know if it's *in* there. It could be a trap."

"It's not a trap. The seal can only be opened with the blood of a Necromancer. It said so in the Bayfield Manuscript. After the upheaval of the English Civil War and the terror in Salem, my family decided it was safer to hide the ring than risk it falling into the wrong hands. Some artifacts, they felt, were best left unused. At least, that's what they wrote."

"And now you're going to break over three hundred years of family secrecy to hand over your greatest weapon to your sworn enemy?" Was this all a ruse? Was I the one falling for a trap? Was this the moment of his betrayal? Or had Phelan really strayed that far from his beliefs that he was genuinely willing to help a demon?

His gaze was earnest as it met mine, not a trace of subterfuge anywhere on his countenance.

"I'm not afraid of you anymore, Remiel," he said softly, refusing to look away, even when I glared at him.

"That's not what I asked."

"What *are* you asking?" He cocked his head, his brow furrowing. "Are you asking if I still hate you? If I'm actually in league with Hazael? If I'm going to eliminate you from existence the second I get my hands on that ring?"

My jaw clenched with indignation because yes, that's exactly what I was asking. What would his first command be? Make me remove my sigil? Kill me? Keep *me* as *his* pet?

A frown touched his lips, even more disappointed than when we were in the basement. "Can I say anything that would convince you? Or does your mistrust of witches run too deep?"

"I'm choosing to trust *you*," I said quietly, hating how thick my voice sounded.

"Then trust me." He held my gaze, his blue-green eyes

pleading, until I gave a slight nod. Turning back toward the box, he knelt beside it and murmured a Latin prayer. Once the wards were removed, he pushed the lid back.

Nothing happened.

Neither of us combusted into flames.

He didn't lose a hand.

God didn't get down off his throne to reclaim what was his.

Phelan threw a glance over his shoulder, either to gloat or to make sure I wasn't sneaking up on him. I wasn't. I was too interested in the thing that had inadvertently drawn us together.

A single ring sat inside the box, the silver tarnished with age. A modest, oval-shaped stone was placed in the center, its dark russet surface carved with a sigil. Carnelian, if I had to guess, one of the ancients' favorite stones for protecting the wearer and warding off evil. All in all, everything about the ring spoke to its authenticity as the Ring of Eleazar, though the real test would come later.

Phelan drew in a breath and held it, reaching out for the magical jewelry as if he was afraid it might come alive and take his hand off.

Before long, I was also holding my breath and I didn't let it out until he successfully plucked the ring from the box and stood slowly.

"Can you feel that?" Phelan asked in hushed tones, the ring laying flat on his palm. "All of that energy?"

"No. I'm not sure I want to." I'd already poked a finger at God once and barely lived to tell the tale. I didn't need to be caught redhanded playing with his toys.

Phelan glanced up, a grin splitting his face. "Don't tell me you're afraid of a ring."

"I'm not."

"Then take it. I'm giving it to you, as I said I would." He held his hand out in offering, the innocent-looking ring laying flat on his palm. "It's safer with you than it is with me."

He might have had a point, but I still rolled my eyes as I reached for his hand, but my fingers swiped through the air.

Phelan yanked his hand back at the last second as another form materialized in front of us.

It was Melech.

"Sire," he bowed his horned head. "Hazael is attacking the realm with his entire army. And the witches are on their way here."

"What?" I looked at Phelan, as if he might confirm the truth.

"It could be security," Phelan said. "Or maybe the Congregation did some sort of spell to alert them when I'm back in town. I have no idea. But we can't stay."

"No, we need to go," Melech said. "Now."

I nodded, extending my hand to Phelan.

As he reached for me in return, Melech's tail lashed out and snatched his wrist like a whip, jerking my Necromancer away from me and straight into his arms.

Phelan yelped as he crashed against Melech's armor, immediately freezing when Melech's claws pierced either side of his throat.

"Have you lost your fucking mind?" My own armor shimmered into place, though I didn't bother with a weapon of any sort. I planned on ripping the demon apart with my bare hands and reassembling the pieces into something even more monstrous just so I could do it again. "Unhand him."

Melech's black eyes locked on mine. "Too long have I

toiled and suffered by your side. And for what?"

"You want my gratitude?" Anger spiked my pulse. Even my wings seethed with outrage, the feathers spreading with each second that passed until my wings stretched to their full extent. "I raised you to the position you have now. The general of my army. My second in command. It's more than you deserved."

"I should have been made a duke with a realm of my own," Melech growled. "Not Jabez. He wanted your crown more than Hazael and you were too blind to see it!"

"It was you, wasn't it?" Phelan whispered before I had a chance to tear into my general. "You gave the Necromancers those demons' names. How long have you been betraying your master? Centuries? Millenia?"

"As if you know anything, halfbreed," Melech snapped, squeezing Phelan's throat until he winced.

"Let my Necromancer go and I might be persuaded to end your wretched life quickly," I said, taking a step forward. Even if I could have made it across the distance in the blink of an eye, that's all the time Melech would need to pop Phelan's head right off like a dandelion. "If you don't, I promise I'll do more than crucify you."

Melech shook his head, his nose wrinkled. "You don't deserve your crown."

"Come and take it, then, if you think you're able."

"No need. Beliar will take it soon enough and reward me justly. Now give me the ring," he said, jerking Phelan up on the tips of his toes.

"Fuck you," Phelan spat.

"Maybe one day," Melech mused, "after Hazael is done passing you through his legion like the halfbreed whore that you are."

Keys turned in the lock at the front doors of the library,

halting me from lunging forward and disemboweling the ungrateful traitor where he stood. A series of silhouettes moved in the frosted glass, the voices murmured but urgent.

The witches.

"Well, I didn't lie about that," Melech said, cocking his head with a smug smile. "So now you have to wonder, did I lie about Hazael attacking your precious realm? Who is there to defend it? Certainly not me. And not you once the witches get inside here with their spell books and their iron chains and everything else they need to subdue a mighty prince."

Was he lying? I couldn't tell. But if Hazael managed to breach the castle walls and claim my throne in my absence, I'd be powerless. None of that mattered if Melech gave Beliar the ring, though. Which was the worse fate? To be free, but powerless and a target for every imp and ghoul with a grudge? Or maintain my abilities to an extent, but face the humiliation of enslavement to Beliar and Necromancers for the rest of time?

"You know what happens when a prince loses their throne, but does he? Does he know what happens to princes then? I've heard it's so unbearable that more than one of them begged God for forgiveness and tried to go back. Can you imagine? Crawling up to those shining gates on your belly, begging God himself to take you in?" Melech held his free hand out to Phelan expectantly.

"Here," Phelan said, lifted his hand up at an awkward angle, trying to show it to Melech. "Take it."

A sinking feeling in the pit of my stomach made my mouth run dry. "Phelan, don't. He'll kill you the second he has it."

"I already lost it all," Phelan replied, looking at me with

a somber expression. "Even if he does kill me, I can't let you go through the same thing."

"A bleeding heart until the end. I can't wait to watch Beliar rip it out." Melech snorted, digging his claws into Phelan's palm. There was a flash of silver and Melech disappeared.

Phelan stumbled forward, holding his bloody throat.

The locks on the front door turned.

"We have to go," Phelan rasped.

It wasn't the time to argue, but I wasn't gentle as I snatched his hand and swept us across time and space, landing right in the middle of his living room. The second we were in the safety of his house, I threw his hand back at him and stalked away to the opposite side of the room before *I* ripped his fucking heart out. "I can't believe you would be so stupid! You gave him the ring! You fucking *gave* it to him! Do you have any idea what you've done?!"

"I bought us time so you could get away from my family and go save your throne!"

"There *is* no more time!" I thundered, whirling on him. "You've condemned us both!"

He flinched but held his ground. "What are you talking about?"

I didn't care he was completely bewildered and more than a little hurt. I didn't care he *thought* he was doing the "right" thing. Fury raged through me, uncaring about anything except the fact we were both destined for the unthinkable. "Beliar!" I shouted, as if that would clear up Phelan's confusion. "He knew what Hazael was up to. He knew we were trying to find the ring. And as soon as he gets it, I'll be enslaved and you'll be gifted to Hazael to keep the peace between them. All you've done is hasten our unspeakable fates!"

The color drained from his face. "What? When did you see Beliar? When did all of this happen?"

"It doesn't matter! So whatever time you think you bought by handing over that damn ring, you can forget about it. The only weapon you have left, Necromancer, are your prayers."

A thought occurred to me, popping up in the midst of my wrath like a glimmer of light. Perhaps Phelan had more than prayers. He said he lost it all, but he still had his family. His so-called bleeding heart could be used to his advantage. Any evil-doing could always—*would* always—be blamed on me. They already thought he was possessed. If he could prove he wasn't, they'd do everything in their power to take him back and protect him. It wasn't ideal, but it was better than life as a pawn in a game controlled by demons.

"Come here," I snarled. Ignoring his startled yelp, I grabbed his left hand and yanked him to me. I closed my eyes, concentrating on removing my mark while he asked a slew of questions and tried to pull himself free.

"What are you doing? Remiel! Why does that feel weird? What is happening? Ouch! That burns! What's happening? Remiel! For fuck's sake, answer me!"

I held on tight until I felt all traces of myself removed from him, then I released his hand without answering his questions. "Go back to your family, Necromancer. Hell is coming to Winslow and they need you more than I for the inevitable battle ahead."

Phelan's eyes widened. But instead of worrying about his stupid town, or his precious Congregation, he turned to his hand. Flipping it over and back again, he was undoubtedly looking for any lingering sign of my mark, his jaw slack.

"It's gone," I said, grinding my molars together to keep from saying anything else on the matter. I didn't need to. In time he'd figure out why I did it, so there was no need to tell him now. It would only make leaving that much harder.

"Remiel. I, I don't understand." His dark brows drew together, searching my face for the real reason. "What are you doing?"

Gripping the nape of his neck gently, I pulled him forward, pressing my forehead to his. I wanted to hold him but I knew I was too selfish to let go, so I kept myself at a distance, allowing only those two, small points of contact, before taking a pointed step backward.

"I want it back." He hooked his fingers around the edges of my breastplate, turning me to face him again. "No, don't leave. Not until you fix it."

I shook my head, refusing to meet his entreating gaze. I didn't have time to placate him. I needed him as far away from me as possible, before Beliar or Hazael reached us. Since demons had all the time in the world to torture their victims, to make the anticipation of agony as bad as the eventual pain itself, I knew they weren't in any particular rush. But none of that was a comfort. I wouldn't find peace until I guaranteed Phelan's safety for the rest of his natural life, until he could finally be with that god of his he adored so damn much.

"I have to go," I ground out. "I have to defend my throne before Hazael takes that too."

"Mark me. Please, Remiel. I'm asking you to." A wave of tears spilled down his cheeks and his voice hitched with the request. "Give me your sigil again. Claim my soul. It's yours anyway."

"It can't be. Not anymore."

"But I love you."

"No, you don't." I tried to turn away again, and once again he yanked me back to him with a surprising strength.

"I do. I love you. I didn't want to, but I do. So please don't do this. Don't go. Whatever you think is going to happen, we'll deal with it. Together." He slid closer, his fingers tightening on my armor as tears continued to well in his beautiful eyes. "Please, Remiel. I'm begging you. Mark me. Take me with you. Make me yours until the end of days. I can't do this without you."

I wanted nothing more than to do as he asked, to return my sigil to his skin and claim him as mine for the rest of eternity. But I also knew there wouldn't *be* an eternity for either of us now that Beliar had all but sided with Hazael. Phelan was a weakness they exploited, so our connection had to be severed for his own good. Without my mark, his family would keep him safe if only to keep themselves safe from whatever demons came looking for him.

"You're so strong," I whispered, my nose brushing his, his breath warm on my face. "You've survived so much already. You'll survive this, too."

"I don't want to survive. I want to live. With you. Please." He dragged me closer, as if clinging to me would get me to change my mind. When that failed, he peppered me with desperate kisses, anywhere he could. My face, my throat, my lips.

I could only ignore him for so long before I yielded to one last desire. Pressing my lips to his, I tried to kiss away the sadness and the saltiness of his tears. But with every second that passed, my resolve weakened. And weakened...

Ripping myself out of his grasp without warning, I strode across the living room. Before he could ask any more questions, I closed my eyes and shimmered out of view.

The last thing I heard was him screaming my name.

CHAPTER THIRTY-SEVEN
PHELAN

No matter how much I screamed, Remiel didn't come back. I cast about for something to get his attention, some way to draw him back to me, but there was nothing. Without his sigil and without his real name to command him, I had no more connection to him.

Except, I did.

Against all odds, I fucking did!

Remembering the feather in my bedroom, I sprinted up the stairs, taking them two at a time. I burst through my bedroom door and all but crashed into the mantel where the decorative box was still sitting.

I snatched the whole thing and rushed downstairs again to the kitchen. Tossing the box in the center of the floor, I ran to the supply cabinet and grabbed armfuls of candles, crystals, and herbs—anything I could possibly need for a spell.

Dumping it on the floor next to the box, I dropped to my knees and picked up a piece of white chalk, hastily drawing a circle around myself complete with a mixture of protective symbols and the best approximation of Remiel's sigil that I could manage. Before I finished setting up the candles and crystals at alternate points, I summoned the Book of Lazarus to me, hoping I had enough power to reach it all the way in Hell.

Like the knife at the library, the book flickered into view before dropping with a thud on the floorboards. I could have cried from happiness, but I had more important things to do than celebrate having an active power for the first time in my life.

Turning my attention to the box, I cracked the lid and stared at the feather inside. It was as beautiful as the entirety of Remiel's wings, gleaming white and pitch black. I just hoped it would be enough.

With a wave of my hand, I sent the pages in the Book of Lazarus flipping, ordering it open to the binding spell. As it obeyed, I sifted through the heap of supplies in front of me, but I couldn't find a knife. With the circle in tact, there was no way I was going to break it and waste more time or magic by starting over.

"Fuck it," I growled, snatching a piece of obsidian off the floor. I held it at an angle and bashed the marble pestle against it, shearing off a large flake.

Muttering a prayer under my breath in Latin, I picked up the shard and dragged it over the meatiest part of my palm. Hissing through my teeth, I squeezed my hand into a fist and let my blood drip over the feather.

While that soaked, I assembled a pile of basil, bay leaves, rosemary, and cinnamon sticks and wrapped them together quickly with a piece of twine, consulting the book once more to make sure I had the spell right.

"Whatsoever is bound on earth," I whispered, moving quickly, "shall be bound in Heaven." God only knew what

Remiel was doing. I couldn't think of a single reason for him to remove his sigil. Not now. Not after everything.

Unless...

He was going to kill Hazael. Fuck!

Why, why *now*, I had no idea. But I couldn't stand by while he threw away everything that he was, damning himself for eternity as a slave to the whims of humans. They were beneath him. He was a dark angel, a demon prince, who had fought God for his freedom—and won. He fought for *my* freedom! It was because of him that I'd finally learned the truth behind my lineage, behind my powers. No matter how furious I was at his sudden sense of nobility, I couldn't let Beliar and Hazael win.

Working as fast as I could, I laid the bundle of herbs on top of the bloody feather and wrapped them together with more twine. Dripping white candle wax over the knots, I crossed myself and pressed my hands together in prayer, using whatever power I had to send my will into the universe and keep Remiel safe wherever he was. "Come back to me, Remiel."

Something loud banged against the front door.

I held my breath, trying not to hope and failing miserably. How many times had I scolded him for *not* using a door? Was he finally listening?

A scraping sound came next, quiet rustling against the old wood.

Still, I didn't move from the circle in case it was another demon's trick.

"Phelan?" Temperance's voice called out as the door creaked open. "There were demons at the library! Treadwell called and he said—hello? Are you home?"

Deflating at the sound of her voice and not my demon's, I curled up into a ball in the center of the circle. A fresh flood of tears blurred the chalk beneath me, smearing the edge of his sigil.

"Oh my God!" Temperance's feet sprinted across the floor and she slid to a halt, her hands outstretched. She pulled back at the last second, knowing better than to reach across the barrier of a circle. "What happened? Were you there? Are you ok?"

"Remiel's gone." I made a point of opening my left hand to show her my bloody, sigil-free palm. The thing I'd wanted to get rid of so desperately ever since Remiel branded me with it was now the thing I'd give my life to have back. "I tried to stop him, to bring him back. But—" I choked on my words, unable to give voice to my failure. My necromantic magic wasn't enough. My demonic magic wasn't enough. *I*, simply, wasn't enough. Bĕlīya'al. *Worthless*. Just like my father. Just like my mother. They were a match made in Hell.

"Maybe it's not too late," Temperance said, digging into her purse.

"It is. Wherever he's gone, my magic can't reach him."

"But God's can."

"What?" I sniffed and blinked through my tears, looking up at her hazy form and the paper she was holding up, nodding emphatically and waiting for me to put it together.

"I found him, Phelan. Remiel! I found his true name." She held the sheet of paper closer for me to see. It was a scan from an old book. Another grimoire. At the top of the page, she'd written *Bayfield Manuscript, page 382.* The very same book I'd held in my hands not but an hour ago.

"What!" I dashed the tears from my face and sat up. She held it as close to the circle as she could. I squinted through my damp lashes, trying to concentrate on the line she was pointing to.

And there it was. There was his name in Hebrew, clear as day, along with his Latin name in a book that *should* have been in the library this whole time. If it had been there when Remiel first kidnapped me, Temperance could have ended this all. She would have saved me, just as she promised.

But if she had, things wouldn't have turned out the way they did. And despite the fact Remiel insisted I was wrong, I still believed God had a plan. He *had* to. Suffering at the hands of an archdemon, finding forgiveness, falling in love... only the Almighty could have devised such an undertaking because it's not the life I would have ever chosen for myself. Not in a million years.

"Jeremiel," I breathed, a bloom of hope unfurling in my chest. "Come back to me."

CHAPTER THIRTY-EIGHT
REMIEL

"Hazael!"

I wasted no time swooping down to where he was, my sword leading the way. It turned out Melech hadn't been lying about Hazael, either. His legion had indeed stormed the gates, laying siege to my castle. To my surprise and never-ending choler, it was defended by less than half of my regular army since Melech had apparently been recruiting from within my ranks.

Hazael threw his arm up, deflecting the blow. It was enough to save him, but I still knocked him to the ground. He rolled to the side and sprang to his feet as I landed behind him. Charging at him as fast as I could, I leapt into the air at the last second and drove the sword downward again, angling it for the top of his breastplate.

He disappeared in a flash.

My sword bit deep into the stony ground.

"Coward!" I whirled in a circle, looking for any sign of him amongst the battling demons. "Were you and Melech in this together? Or was it merely an opportune moment?"

A hard kick to my back sent me flying forward. I tucked

into a roll and came up swiftly, just in time to block his sword from plunging into my chest.

"You'd really kill me? For *him*?" Hazael snarled. "A filthy halfbreed Necromancer?!"

I threw my arm to the side, knocking both of our swords out of position before punching directly into the side of his knee.

He howled and dropped to his uninjured one, giving me enough time to get to my feet.

"I've wanted to kill you since time began," I said, leveling my sword at him. "He has nothing to do with it."

"I expected you to be a better liar by now," he sneered, standing slowly.

I feinted left and then swerved right, slashing straight across the top of his thigh. Spinning quickly, I thrust the sword at his midsection. He parried and followed it by hurling a sulfurous ball of fire at me.

Disappearing from view, I reappeared after the flames had passed and lunged for him.

Flapping wings and scrabbling, clawed feet grew louder around us. The battle was shifting. Hazael's ghouls were coming to his aid now that a real opponent had shown up to challenge their liege.

Something sharp sliced across the back of my thigh.

I hissed and darted away from it, hurling a streak of black flames to where I'd just been standing.

A small, taloned creature caught the brunt of the fire, screaming in agony as it turned to embers and ash.

I spread my wings out wide, blood-stained sword in one hand, swirling green and black fire in the other.

The rest of the minions who had been approaching slowed their advance.

"Kill him," Hazael commanded. "Whoever brings me his head shall wear a crown on theirs."

They rushed me as one, a wave of overeager, inexperienced creatures who had probably never fought in any serious battle in their lives.

I made short work of them, my sword slashing and thrusting as unholy fire flashed from one imp to the next.

Ducking and dodging more attacks, I tried to keep my focus on Hazael as he dispatched creatures from my own legion. He beheaded one of my counts and moved on to a knight, slicing off his scaly wings before running him through like a sack of grain. With each of my demons he killed, I felt my power wane that much more.

Pain ripped through my abdomen, right beneath my armor. I'd barely had time to register it when something stabbed through my wing.

Wincing, I disappeared, only to crash land a few feet away.

When the horde descended, I endured their vicious attacks, summoning my rapidly diminishing power as fangs and claws ripped into me from every angle.

Using all my strength, I unleashed a wave of hellfire. It spread out around me in an ever-widening circle, destroying every creature it touched—mine *and* Hazael's.

Once I was cleared of all the little imps and goblins doing their worst, I got to my feet, facing Hazael once more.

I ripped pieces of bone and bits of wood out of my body one by one, slivers of relics they'd used to try and tip the odds in their favor. "You always had a penchant for trinkets, didn't you? Where is your precious ring, anyway? Oh, that's right. Beliar must have it."

"No thanks to your disgusting little halfbreed and that revolting thing you had as your general," he shot back.

"So you *did* know what Melech was planning." A fresh wave of wrath crashed over me. Melech's betrayal was one thing, but to have him colluding with Hazael? If I somehow managed to evade enslavement, I would make them all suffer in the most horrific ways possible.

"Who do you think gave him the idea?" Hazael smiled.

Letting out an angry snarl, I charged across the distance, my sword leading the way.

We continued to dance around each other, slashing and hacking, trying to inflict damage wherever possible. Trading blows with fists and swords, bursts of hellfire augmented the battle.

Time slowed. My muscles weighed ten times what they normally did. Even Hazael was feeling the effect of the fight, as each of his movements became sluggish.

Our swords clashed together again, metal shrieking against metal, as we both heaved our weight behind them.

I slumped against Hazael, exhausted but not even close to defeated. My hatred wouldn't let me give up.

Hazael grappled at my armor, hauling himself upright, breathing as hard as I was. "When Beliar gets here, you're going to wish you'd succeeded in killing me."

"I'm not going to wish for anything," I snapped. "You'll be dead soon enough."

"You can't kill me, you fool," he panted, blood dripping from the corner of his mouth from a punch I'd landed what felt like eons ago.

"Can't I? Beliar already threatened me with enslavement. My castle is in ruins. My army's all but obliterated. I have nothing left to lose." I tightened my grip on my sword. He shifted just so, exposing the narrow gap along his ribs where his armor was split into two pieces. From inside one of my armguards, I unsheathed the jagged piece of wood I'd stolen from Phelan weeks ago, after he'd pulled it from my back. Without hesitating, I drove the remnants of the True Cross straight into the opening of Hazael's armor, through his black heart, and gave a vicious, fatal twist, snapping it off inside his ribcage.

Hazael's eyes bugged out.

Blood perfumed the air around us, mixing with the stench of gore and sulfur from the battle.

I held Hazael close in a mocking embrace, my hand tangled in his long red hair so he couldn't escape my final taunt. "I win, brother."

He crumbled to ash in my arms, his agonized screams echoing in my ears.

Without him keeping me upright, I collapsed, hitting my knees before keeling backward and sprawling on my back. My sword and the remainder of the relic bounced out of my hands; I didn't bother reaching for them again.

The screams of Hazael's minions reverberated across the distance as they fell, one by one, turned to dust with their master's defeat.

Secure in my victory, I closed my eyes and thought of Phelan as Hell's infamous flames erupted across my own skin. The pain was excruciating. Agony racked every inch of my body. I writhed on the ground, engulfed in the fire I'd used against so many others. Beliar's wrath stripped me of my autonomy, rendering me vulnerable to his will—and that of all Necromancers. A slave for all eternity. Worse than serving an ungrateful god, I'd serve spiteful devils and malicious humans. But first, I'd be subjected to indescribable pain and torture for breaking my oath.

Still, as I was swept away from the battlefield to my own personal prison in the deepest pits of Hell, I could hear Phelan's voice over my own tormented screams. Maybe that was as close to Heaven as I'd ever be again. To have been loved by him, against all odds.

"Jeremiel, come back to me."

He found it... my true name.

If only it wasn't too late.

CHAPTER THIRTY-NINE

PHELAN

With my hands clasped in prayer, eyes squeezed tight, I rocked back and forth, issuing the same command in every language I knew—English, Latin, Hebrew. Over and over until the words blurred together.

Jeremiel, come back to me.

Ieremihel, come back to me.

Ra'amel, come back to me.

"I'm sorry, Phelan," Temperance said quietly. "If only I'd found it sooner, maybe this..." Whatever else she said trailed off.

Somewhere in the back of my mind, I heard her, but I didn't give any indication that I did. Nothing except God himself would get me to stop praying.

Temperance must have known it was a lost cause because she gave up trying to comfort me. A little while later, she got to her feet again and slipped out of the house, leaving me alone with my denial and my mounting grief.

"Jeremiel, come back to me!"

A second later, the spell ingredients flew across the kitchen, propelled by nothing more than my magic and my rage as I let out a frustrated scream at the sky. Green and black flames erupted around me, scorching the floor outside of the protective circle. I didn't even try to put them out. I let them surge with my anger and my helplessness, spreading out across the floor and creeping up the cabinets. The whole house could burn down around me and I wouldn't care. I wasn't leaving that fucking circle until I knew the outcome of my spell.

Pages flipped beside me and a silver light sparked in the growing darkness.

I turned to the Book of Lazarus, watching as an intricate sigil manifested itself in the pages. Along with a name, written twice, so he could be commanded in whatever language a Necromancer preferred.

Jeremiel.

Ieremihel.

A demon prince with power over dreams, souls, and warfare.

"No!" I nearly collapsed over the top of the book, my hands slamming the ground on either side of it. The words blurred in front of me as I dragged it closer, hugging the page to my chest. "How could you do this?"

He'd become the one thing he hated more than anything. A slave. In one stupid moment, he gave up everything he'd fought for, everything that he was. And for what?

Wiping the tears from my cheek, I summoned the Book of Damnation with a flick of my wrist. The book thumped to the floor in the other room and slid across the floorboards, resting by my thigh, the page already open to what I wanted.

And there sat Hazael's name and sigil, waiting for a Necromancer to fill in the details of the demon's demise.

"All so you could finally kill him?" I exhaled a sharp breath.

Then it dawned on me.

Remiel was now a slave... to Necromancers.

Getting to my feet, I dispersed the green flames steadily gnawing their way through my house and assembled another circle quickly.

"In the name of God and by His grace," I said, making the sign of the cross in the air, "I call thee hither, Jeremiel, Prince of Hell."

My breath caught in my throat.

Glancing around the room, I searched for any ripples in the air, any fleck of silver.

Nothing.

The longer I waited, the more I began to despair, until I noticed the temperature in the room had risen—was still rising. Little by little. A bead of sweat trickled down the back of my neck.

I closed my eyes and pressed my hands together in prayer, continuing to command Remiel's presence.

At last, he materialized into view on bended knee, his head bowed and lusterless gray hair obscuring his face.

I ran to him and dropped to my knees, taking his face between my hands.

When he lifted his gaze, a jolt of pain slammed through me. Gone was the exasperating, ruthless, beautiful demon I'd grown to love. In his place was a shell of that former being. His eyes had dulled to a dark gray, but they were nothing compared to the vacant stare that met me.

Brushing his hair behind his ear, I gasped when my fingers touched metal.

A thick iron hoop had been pierced through his left ear. Like a nail. A mockery of the stigma of Christ... and the mark of a slave.

"You called?" he asked, his voice hoarse and ragged, like

he hadn't spoken in a century. Or he'd lost it screaming. I knew all too well how differently time moved in Hell and there was no telling how many lifetimes he'd suffered while mere minutes ticked by on the human plane.

"What did they do to you?" I caressed his face gently, searching desperately for some spark of remembrance, some feeling of warmth inside of him.

"I knew my fate," he replied, his gaze as hollow as his voice.

"Did you kill Hazael?"

"Yes."

"Did Beliar do this?"

"Yes."

"I command you to take me to him."

Remiel blinked slowly. "That is impossible."

"No, it's not. I command you, Jeremiel, to obey the power of God and answer the charge of His vessel before you," I said as gently as possible. While it *was* a command, I didn't want to order him around as such. Even though the tables had officially turned, I didn't want to exploit this sudden shift in power between us. Despite everything, it didn't feel right.

"It's impossible, as I said," he growled. "No human can reach Beliar's kingdom."

"I'm not fully human," I reminded him.

"He'll kill you." Remiel forced his flat gaze to mine. "Do you understand that? He won't care who you are or how you came to be, because you're nothing to him."

"I understand it perfectly. And I don't care. I demand you take me to him. Now."

"As you wish," he whispered. Holding his hand out to me, I tried not to flinch when I touched his palm and the scabby bumps there. Without even looking, I knew a sigil had been burned into his skin, one I could only presume belonged to Beliar.

"Wait," I said quickly.

He looked up glumly.

"Take me to the university first. Then to Beliar."

Remiel closed his fingers around mine and hung his head. The world around us shifted and blurred, darkening as we left the safety of the house.

Beliar's kingdom was nothing like Remiel's. While Remiel's was dark and foreboding, full of stone and shadows, Beliar's was everything I expected Hell to be.

Inhuman screams echoed for miles. Rotting corpses hung from everything and anything—trees, rocks, crosses. Even those who appeared alive, or at least animate, had some level of decay. Some bodies were missing limbs, or flesh. Others looked like they'd been torn apart by wild dogs and haphazardly stitched together.

Remiel and I stood atop a rock formation, above it all, but hands still clawed at us—to solicit help or to drag us down, I wasn't sure. Meaty hands. Bony hands. Hands with claws. Hands missing fingers. One half-skeletal looking thing managed to haul itself over the top of the rock, only for Remiel to kick it back down into the pit it crawled out of.

"The only way in is through there," Remiel said, unmoved by the suffering all around us, and gestured to an opening in the black and red mountain that loomed overhead.

"Fly me up there then."

Remiel's jaw shifted, like he wanted to say something, but his bondage prevented it. Instead, he opened his arms to me and unfurled his dirty, ragged wings. Blood and soot stained his white feathers and more than one was broken or missing. Did it hurt? I wanted to ask, but I didn't know if I wanted the truth.

Holding me close, Remiel lifted off and flew toward the crevice, dodging wraiths and other shrieking spirits as they floated above the carnage below, looking for something to torture.

Swooping inside the gaping opening, we touched down on a polished black floor inside the cavernous structure. As soon as we landed, Remiel released me, though he didn't go far. He drifted just behind me, out of sight, his head bowed again, and I had to wonder if the deference was to me or the massive black throne dominating the center of the room.

Much like Remiel's palace, Beliar's, too, had been built into the rock and this entry point was the only visible way in or out of his throne room. A pair of red banners hung overhead with a black sigil in the center of each. The lines looked like they were moving, slithering over one another like a heap of serpents. A shudder rippled through me and I forced my attention to the perimeter of the room, looking for any sign of another demon.

"Well, well," a deep voice boomed in the darkness. "It's not every day a mortal comes to me. Normally I find them quivering in their beds or clinging to their crosses."

"Yes, I'm sure you're terrifying," I scoffed, channeling as much of the Remiel I knew as possible. I had a feeling Beliar could smell fear like a dog, and that I'd be better off setting the tone for this meeting rather than letting him dictate how it was going to go.

A rumbling laugh sounded before the Devil himself

appeared like a mirage, his huge, black feathered wings spread wide. I swallowed thickly, watching as he descended the carved stone steps at a leisurely pace. While we weren't identical by any means, there was enough of me in him to make my stomach turn. The question remained to be seen —did he know who I was, and if so, did he even care?

"So, you're the one who finally found it. The Ring of Eleazar." Beliar spread his hands for dramatic effect and stopped in front of me, tilting his head to the side. "I knew it would take a Necromancer, just as you said. Far be it for God to make it easy for us. I had hoped your mother would have found it first, but, all good things to those who wait, I suppose." Rubbing salt in the wound, he lifted his hand and studied the ring on his index finger, completely glossing over the giant elephant in the room.

I tried not to dwell on it. After all, I wasn't here to catch up on family history. Knowing he was the one who fathered me had zero impact on what I was here to do. "And you think that ring is enough to guarantee your throne?" I smirked, glancing around the empty room. "Maybe you should reread some of those holy texts you look down on."

Remiel, who'd slowly circled to the side of me while I was too busy gawking earlier, shot me a look out of the corner of his eye, the muscles in his jaw tightening.

Beliar stared at the ring on his hand, his bright green eyes flashing as if he was suddenly seeing it in a new light, or at least doubting the stories he took as gospel.

A smile stretched across my face. "Have you figured it out yet? I don't think you have. I don't think you've even tried to command your fellow demons with it. I think you've been too cowardly to test it out, because what if it doesn't work? What if you've been searching for that ring for centuries only to find out it's worthless? Just like you, Bĕlīya'al."

Beliar's nostrils flared and his lips hardened into a thin line. "I let you live this long to see if you could be useful to me. But now that I have this..." His narrowed gaze flicked to Remiel. "I command you, Remiel, to rip out your lover's tongue."

I, too, looked at Remiel and cocked an eyebrow. Seconds ticked by as I made an open perusal of his body. He didn't move. Not a finger twitch. Not a blink. Nothing. I wasn't even sure he was breathing at that point, he was as rigid as stone. "I'm waiting, *lover*," I said with as much sarcasm as I could, spreading my hands.

Remiel's silver eyes crinkled slightly at the corners. It was the only movement he made.

"Remiel!" Beliar shouted, pointing at me with the same finger that bore the ring. "Rip out that halfbreed's tongue!"

"He won't be doing that," I said, my smile widening as I strolled forward, closing the distance between my prince and I. I stroked his cheek gently, my chest warming at the smirk tugging at the corner of his mouth. Despite everything Beliar had done to him in our time apart, he wasn't gone. My Remiel was still there.

"You see, it's right there in the name," I said, turning back to Beliar. "El ʿāzār. '*God* has helped.' Demons can't call on the power of God, can they? Which means the ring will *never* listen to you or any other full-blooded demon. It will, however, listen to a Necromancer. Even a filthy halfbreed like me." I crooked my finger and prayed with every fiber of my being that I'd interpreted the text in the Bayfield Manuscript correctly.

Deo adjuvante—by the help of God—had been carefully annotated in red in the marginalia of the Bayfield. While

Remiel was arguing with the accursed Combermere, I had what felt like an epiphany, a rush of euphoria and a sense of *knowing* Hazael would never control the ring. Even when I offered it to Remiel, it was purely for the ring's safe keeping, though I hadn't had time to explain that *or* why I handed it over to Melech. If Remiel had shared his conversation with Beliar, I wouldn't have given up our leverage quite so easily, but I couldn't do anything about that now.

The three of us stared at Beliar's hand. My breath caught in my throat.

The ring disappeared.

Remiel inhaled sharply while Beliar's face twisted into a snarl. His eyes were no longer green. They'd turned pitch black as they narrowed on me once more, zeroing in on my right hand and the Ring of Eleazar that had manifested on my index finger.

Thanking God, I released the breath I'd been holding and crossed myself. When I opened my eyes, it was to see Beliar storming across the throne room toward me.

"*Desistas*," I snapped, throwing a hand out toward him. He halted immediately like he'd run into an invisible wall. Chest heaving and teeth bared, he looked nothing like the composed king he was a moment ago. Part of me wanted to gloat—the demon part. The Necromancer part wanted to take my prince and leave this horrible nightmare behind us as fast as I could.

"Now," I said, keeping my hand aimed at Beliar, "release Remiel from bondage."

Beliar sneered. "He's a slave to Hell. As long as it exists, he'll always be in its snare."

"That's your sigil," I countered, "so remove it."

"That's the mark of Hell," he shot back. "And as its king, I command you to come forth and take them away." He yelled the last part over his shoulder, motioning to unseen servants. A group of demons in various horrifying forms appeared from the shadows, as if they'd seeped through the walls. Sadly, Melech wasn't among them. But no matter, I'd deal with him as soon as Remiel was free.

I held my other hand up at the demons charging us. "*Desistas*."

They all slid to a stop, looking at one another uncertainly, struggling against the unseen force holding them at bay, just as their master had. I offered another thankful prayer to God and whatever angels might still be watching over me—or the ring.

"I said take them away!" Beliar shouted, throwing an impatient hand toward Remiel and I.

"Better yet," I said to the gathering of demons. "Seize *him* and remove his wings." I withdrew a tiny branch from my coat pocket, the slivers of the True Cross that Ainsworth had managed to regrow. It stretched and morphed, elongating itself and growing thicker as it floated through the air. By the time it settled on the floor, it had transformed into a giant cross. "And then I want you to crucify him and put him in the courtyard so everyone can see what happened to their king. How he was bested by one of the filthy halfbreeds he sired."

As much as I may have wanted to, I knew I couldn't kill Beliar outright. Killing him would kill Remiel. While crucifixion was a slow, agonizing death for humans, I figured it would be even slower for demons and that would buy me the time I needed to figure out how to remove the marks of bondage from Remiel before ultimately dispatching the king of Hell.

"Do not touch me," Beliar snarled as the demons

grabbed him, dragging him to the center of the room and shoving him face-first onto the stone floor.

Two slices were all it took to rid the massive black wings from his body. Thunder boomed overhead as each wing fell, rattling the mountain all around us. A rock chipped and fell away, crashing to the floor.

Dripping blood, the demons dragged Beliar to the cross I'd conjured for them and forced him down onto it, restraining him while one of the others positioned the first nail in his wrist. Iron, of course, to negate his magic while he suffered as he'd made so many suffer before him.

"You have to kill him, Phelan," Remiel said, making me jump. He'd approached so silently I hadn't even realized he moved. "You'll never truly be safe until he's dead, even with the ring. You might control him in his presence but once you leave here, he'll be free to rule again."

"I can't kill him, Remiel."

"Fine, I'll do it." The muscle in his jaw tightened as he took a step toward the king.

"You'll die too," I whispered, grabbing his arm and yanking him to a halt. "Killing him means damning everyone he's marked. Right? You'll *all* cease to exist..."

Beliar's screams echoed throughout the chasm, following each heavy thud of the hammer driving the iron nails into place. Finally, they hit the last nail home.

"Is this your pride talking?" I continued, tightening my grip on Remiel's bicep in case he tried to shove past me. I didn't want to use the ring against him, but I would if it meant keeping him alive. "Because you don't want to live as my slave? I won't treat you like a slave. I promise. And I promise I'll never leave Hell, so you don't have to worry about falling victim to some other Necromancer. I'll stay here, with you. For as long as it takes to remove that mark."

He shook his head slowly, as expressionless as he was when he stood in my living room and removed his mark. "This isn't pride."

"Then what is it?" I snapped.

He didn't answer.

The realization hit me so hard it nearly broke me.

Love. Love, the only way a demon knew how.

"*Ubi amor, ibi dolor,*" Remiel said as tears crested my cheeks. *Where there's love, there's pain.* "It's a lesson God teaches us all. You, of all people, should know that, lamb." He brushed the salty droplets away with his thumb, offering me a small, sad smile before he turned and headed toward Beliar.

I couldn't watch him walk away from me again. Each step he took echoed around us. My heart hammered inside my ribcage and my throat constricted. Remiel was walking toward his own death and his steps never faltered.

The ring weighed heavily on my finger. My heart screamed at me to use it, to stop him. But my head chided me sadly, reminding me I'd just promised him I wouldn't. He'd be furious if I betrayed him anymore than I already had.

I didn't care.

I could live with his fury. I could live with the punishment. I could live with anything he did to me, because it meant he would still be alive too.

His footsteps stopped and I turned, throwing out a hand to stop him. "Remiel, don't!"

But it was too late.

Remiel's fist punched through Beliar's chest. Muscle tore. Bones snapped. Beliar's screams reverberated through the vast room, rolling out into the wasteland beyond. A stalactite fell, smashing against the polished floor. Then another and another, until I was sure the whole mountain was going to crash down on us.

After the Devil's heart was ripped from his chest, it continued to beat, thumping slowly in Remiel's bloody palm. He crushed it slowly until the defiant muscle burst. Black blood ran down his forearm, dripping over the floor.

Beliar's skin turned to black, sulfurous sand. It swept across his body like a wave, reducing him to a pile of nothing.

Demons in the palace and the realm beyond shrieked and bellowed. One by one, they began to burst into flames and evaporate before my very eyes.

My gaze darted to Remiel.

He dropped to his knees, clutching his marked hand to his chest and screaming.

I ran to him, my hand outstretched.

With each step I took, he faded a little bit more. I stretched farther. Praying. Begging.

I was almost there.

My fingers clawed through the empty air where he'd been as he disappeared from sight.

I collapsed on the floor, unleashing my own scream.

Remiel was gone. For good.

He'd killed the king of Hell and sacrificed himself along the way. For *me*.

I didn't know what would happen now. I didn't know who the next king would be or what dangers lay ahead. I didn't care. The Necromancer in me should have been celebrating. Not only was the Devil dead, but I had the Ring of Eleazar, one of the ultimate weapons against demons. From here on out, I would be untouchable. But none of that mattered. Nothing mattered.

Remiel was gone.

A sob tore through me. Helpless. Furious.

All around me was death and destruction. I had no idea how I would get back to my plane or how I would even get out of this disgusting palace to start with.

I didn't care.

Remiel was gone.

Suddenly everything I'd stood for seemed pointless. Everything I had sacrificed paled in comparison to the loss of my prince. He was everything I hated and everything I didn't know I wanted. We didn't agree on... anything. He pushed me, challenged me. But he also accepted me for who I was, *what* I was, before I knew what any of it meant. And now, I was alone, with only his illusive memory for company.

As illusive as dust motes twirling in a ray of light. Like those dancing in front of me.

Except, the dust motes turned blinding, burning my eyes. Even with my hand shielding my face, it was impossible to see anything.

When it finally dimmed, I lowered my hand.

"Remiel?"

I gaped at the figure before me. It looked like him, except... different. He was glowing. Like an angel. A true, Heaven-sent angel.

Getting to my feet slowly, I approached the being with caution.

He extended the tip of one wing and stroked my cheek, despite the fact I jerked backward, caught off guard. Its feathers were no longer marred with black edges. They were a brilliant, shimmering white, from root to tip, gleaming like an opal.

"Hello, lover," the angel said. As soon as I was within arm's reach, he grabbed me around the waist and yanked me against his chest, crushing his mouth to mine. The way he kissed, smelled, tasted. It all screamed that it was him, but a part of me didn't want to believe it. I was still in Hell, after all. *Everything* was meant to torment you and I knew nothing was ever as it seemed.

"How are you here right now?" I whispered, touching his face, trying to determine if he was an illusion or if he really was real.

"*Mors ad caelos*," he said softly, pressing his forehead to mine. *Through death to Heaven*. The same words I'd uttered before I took my own life, hoping for divine forgiveness.

"I thought demons didn't go to Heaven?"

"We don't. But a curious thing happened. After I disappeared, I was... trapped. Apparently I was in limbo, since a witch went and did something utterly stupid and bound themselves to me." He gave me a knowing look, a smirk toying over his lips. "I was supposed to disappear forever but I was stuck there, in between. And while I waited, trying to find a way to reach you, Heaven came to me."

"*God* sent you back?" I stared at him, afraid if my eyes opened any wider they might pop out.

"With a message." I held my breath, waiting for him to continue. "He sends his regards to the new king of Hell."

"What?! You mean *me*?"

A smile tipped the corner of his mouth, but he didn't offer any further commentary on the news.

"I can't be the king of Hell, Remiel. You do it."

"I can't. He's got a thing for bloodlines," he said, flicking his gaze upward. "You're the son. You inherited the throne."

"I'm not a full-blooded demon!"

"It doesn't matter."

"It will when some archdemon comes and rips my head off!"

He took my hand, the one bearing the ring, and lifted it between us before kissing each knuckle slowly. "You always said God had a plan. Who better to test the faith of humanity than a man who has dedicated his life to it?"

"I don't know the first thing about any of this..."

"Of course you do. It's in everything you've ever been taught. Evil cannot exist without God's permission and God *needs* evil to exist, to tempt his precious little humans so he has something to feel good about when one of them actually makes it to Heaven. Therefore, as the insufferable Catholic that you are, it's your duty to honor God's will by serving as his counterpart."

"I suppose..." That was all I could muster, since the concept of speech seemed to fail me. It was, in a twisted sort of way, an honor to be tasked with something as divinely important as this, but I still felt woefully inadequate and not up to the task at all. "Will you help me?"

A soft smile curved his lips and he slid his hands over my hips, pulling my pelvis against his. "I'm sure we can come to some sort of arrangement."

"Good. There is something I want to do."

He arched an eyebrow.

I held up my left hand. "I want it back."

Remiel frowned. "You're the king now. You can't wear my mark."

"Says who?"

He gave me an exasperated look.

"If I'm going to do this, I need to know you're with me. Always," I said, lacing our fingers together and pressing my palm against his as tightly as I could. "God already recognized our bond. I want all of Hell to recognize it too."

He considered it for a moment, his face as solemn and

unreadable as ever. When he finally decided, his eyes tightened at the corners. "This is going to hurt."

"I know. I'm ready."

Nodding, he squeezed my hand tightly and summoned a swath of green and black flames. They engulfed our hands. Even though I knew it was coming, the shock of pain still stole my breath. But at least this time, I undertook it willingly. I could grit my teeth and bear it, like I had with flagellation, knowing it was for a reason. A divine reason.

Even after the pain subsided, Remiel didn't let go. "Now I want yours."

"My what?" I blinked.

"Your mark."

"I don't have one. Do I?"

"Of course you do. And I will be the first and *only* one to ever wear it."

"Well, now, that's awfully presumptuous of you..."

He jerked me closer by the hand, wrapping his other arm around my waist to draw me in even more while his wings closed around us. "Do I need to pledge myself to you, your majesty? Swear on all that's unholy that I will gouge out the eyes of any creature who so much as looks at you? Because I will. I will be as ruthless as I need to be to ensure the world trembles at the mere thought of being in your presence. I want them too terrified to even whisper your name. I don't care if you wear the king's crown, you're as much mine today as you were the first time I laid eyes on you. I didn't break my oath to lose you now, to some lesser being who doesn't deserve you."

"And you think you deserve me?"

I might have been teasing, but he shook his head, as serious as ever. "No. No one does. But you're mine all the same. And once you mark me, you'll know I'm yours. Until the end of days."

My fingers tightened around his as I leaned up, pressing my lips to his. I closed my eyes and willed my sigil into existence, burning my love for him into his palm as he'd done to me. That's all I saw his mark as—irrefutable proof of his love and loyalty. Once upon a time, it might have meant servitude or ownership, nothing more than a way to stake his perverse claim. But I think it became more than that, for both of us. It was the only way to explain why God gave him a second chance. Remiel might never say the words out loud, but his sacrifice was all the proof I needed. After all, Christ's sacrifice was the greatest testament of his love for mankind.

"There," I whispered once the flames subsided from our hands. "Now you're mine."

Remiel studied the sigil on his palm, a series of circles and triangles reminiscent of his own. "Well done, lamb. Now can we officially christen your new palace?"

"Palace?" I blinked at him and glanced around warily. "You mean I'm living here?"

"Of course, your majesty." He gave me a wolfish grin and kissed me again.

I pushed him back gently. "Wait, wait, wait. What about Melech? And the other princes? What if they come here?"

"As soon as you sit on the throne," Remiel said, tossing a nod toward the towering black chair, "all of Hell will know there's a new king. They'll come alright, if only to see who has succeeded Beliar. You can make them swear the same oath to you, or an entirely different one. It's up to you. And as far as Melech is concerned, as soon as you're settled, I will hunt that traitorous wretch to the ends of the earth."

I nodded along as he spoke, processing the words even though I still didn't understand how any of it worked. "Ok. Let's get this over with, then." Stepping away from Remiel, I swallowed thickly and walked up the smooth, stone steps to the platform where the throne sat. The closer I got, the more the chair seemed to dwarf me, like each step made it triple in size. Shadows loomed behind it and voices whispered in the dark chasm beyond the throne.

At the top of the platform, the voices stopped.

The throne was still large and exquisitely carved, but it was appropriately sized.

Steeling myself for whatever was about to happen, I turned and braced my hands on the arms of the chair, lowering myself downward.

A swirl of shimmering green and black particles rushed down the throne and dispersed as soon as it hit the floor, shooting off in a thousand different directions.

"All hail the king." Remiel smiled and covered his heart with a closed fist, bowing his head.

I couldn't help but send a glance to Heaven. They always said God worked in mysterious ways. Never in a million years did I think *this* was the path He would have laid out for me. But here I was and with Remiel by my side, I'd be the best/worst Devil I could be.

CHAPTER FORTY
PHELAN

"Are you sure you want to do this?" Remiel asked, his silver eyes serious. "You have emissaries now. You don't need to speak to these people ever again."

I nodded, trying to ignore the bone-deep chill slipping down the back of my neck. It was already well into the new year and a fresh layer of snow had fallen in Winslow, blanketing the world in glittering white. I'd never minded the cold before, but after spending the past several months in Hell according to the human calendar, I'd grown accustomed to the heat. Remiel was still able to be half-naked in the freezing cold, but I think my human DNA precluded that ability, so I'd conjured normal winter clothing for the occasion.

"I will rip this building apart if they so much as breathe in your direction," he said, his silver eyes glinting like the moon overhead.

"I know." I touched his cheek, offering a small, reassuring smile. "They won't. This is their one and only opportunity for peace. They're going to want to hear what I have to say for once."

Nodding grimly, Remiel turned to the meetinghouse and literally blew the door in with a wave of his hand. He swept inside with a gust of cold air and swirling snow, his wings snapping open as soon as they cleared the doorframe.

The Congregation inside started to panic, screaming and shouting to one another and climbing over the walls separating their boxed pews, until I entered the doorway behind Remiel. Then, I could have heard a pin drop.

Chin lifted, I strode down the aisle, well aware of every pair of eyes that followed me.

Graeme and Cassius grabbed onto one another with a combination of fear and anger on their young faces, like I might try to separate them with another ring of fire. Caius wrapped his arm around both of their shoulders, pulling them closer like little ducklings.

Ainsworth and Treadwell exchanged concerned looks at the front of the meetinghouse, while Peregrine blanched about five shades of white.

"What is the meaning of this?" Peregrine asked, stepping away from the pulpit.

"I'm here to talk. I suggest you listen." I swept past him and turned, facing the Congregation with a smirk and steel in my spine. I'd never addressed them like this and to see everyone's rapt attention focused on me brought me a perverse sense of joy. For so long they'd overlooked me or dismissed me outright. After tonight, my name would be whispered with reverence or I'm sure Remiel would see to it that their tongues were ripped from their skulls and nailed to the meetinghouse door.

"Phelan," Temperance said by way of greeting, breaking the silence from where she sat next to our grandmother in the Colburn box. "Where have you been?

We've been looking for you for... months. Ever since Halloween."

"I know. I heard you calling. I've been busy."

"Do you have the Ring of Eleazar?"

"I do," I replied, not bothering to hide my hand or the carnelian ring that sat on it. "But that's not why I'm here."

"It's not?"

"No. I did, however, bring the Book of Lazarus. Although, I took the liberty of making some amendments." I turned to Caius and held the book aloft before levitating it to him slowly.

The elder Corbin took the book and flipped through it carefully, his dark brows knitting together. "The demons' names are all gone. Except... Melech?"

"The last demon this Congregation will ever hunt," I replied evenly. "Unless I appear in person and give you more names. In return, they'll steer clear of Winslow and its witches."

Warren Simms snorted. "Why would we agree to that? If we kill them, they'll leave us alone anyway."

"Because as the king of Hell, if one more of my subjects is killed without justification"—my gaze cut to Warren—"I will hold you personally responsible."

A murmur erupted through the meetinghouse.

Hester cried out, covering her mouth with her hand. Temperance shushed her, patting her forearm gently.

"Yes, the rumors are true," I sighed. Even if I was expecting this sort of pearl-clutching reaction, it didn't mean I wasn't annoyed by it. "I am half-demon. Beliar was my father. Remiel killed him." I gestured to the smirking prince at my side, watching his beautiful white feathers ruffle like a proud peacock. "And God appointed me as his successor. Now you have the opportunity to make peace.

Kill Melech and I'll know we have a deal. Don't, and Remiel will seek vengeance on behalf of the demons you've already slain. You have until the next full moon to decide."

I took one step toward the door when a voice stopped me.

"Wait!" It was Peter. He stood slowly, holding Isla, who in turn was happily clutching her pink, crocheted spider. "What are you... are you leaving? For good?"

"It's better if I do. Demons belong in Hell. I've served this Congregation as faithfully as I could. Now it's time to fulfill my obligation to God."

"How can you speak of God and turn around and proclaim you're the king of Hell?" Eileen shouted. "It's blasphemy!"

I gave her a dark smile. "I don't expect you to understand. Nor am I going to waste my breath explaining it."

"You have some nerve coming here!" George Hewitt shouted, getting to his feet.

I motioned him back down with a sigh as my magic slammed him into the pew. "No one wants to hear your blustering, Hewitt, least of all me."

Behind me, Ainsworth snorted.

"Will we ever see you again?" Temperance asked.

"Time will tell," I replied with a tight smile.

She nodded grimly, tears welling in her pale eyes. As far as we were concerned, this was goodbye without labeling it as such. She knew it. I knew it.

With nothing left to say, I looked at Remiel. He gave a slight nod. Swallowing, I pushed my shoulders back and made the walk back down the center aisle. I may have been king for months already, but it was still new to me—the deference. Not from Remiel, but from *other* people. Other witches. After a lifetime of being discounted, it was strange to have people looking at me with awe. And fear. I'd be lying if I said it didn't give me a thrill of power each time it happened.

Remiel fell in step behind me, his wings expanding to form a shield as we exited. As soon as he crossed the threshold, the meetinghouse erupted into chaos again. He slammed the door shut on the noise, rattling it in its old hinges.

"Could you *not* destroy this building, please?" I asked, my exasperation only slightly exaggerated. "It's historic."

"You started the fire in that decrepit old barn, not me," Remiel shot back with a smirk.

"You annihilated the roof!"

"It was going to collapse anyway because of the fire."

"Seems like you're splitting hairs."

"Seems like you're still trying to be a good little lamb." He slipped his hands under my shirt and around my waist, pulling me closer. "We both know you're not as saintly as you like to pretend, your majesty."

"If God's divine holiness is his eschewal of sin, and Hell is the inversion of Heaven, doesn't it follow that my pursuit of sin is integral to my divine *un*holiness?"

He pretended to consider it but could barely contain a smirk. "For once, your theological argument holds weight."

"Then let's go home. I feel the urge to sin again." I wrapped my arms around his neck and kissed him while he took us back to Hell and straight to my bedroom.

After I'd taken my place on the throne of Hell, the palace around me had shifted and transformed with no more than a passing thought. Gone was any trace of Beliar and the desolate abyss he'd created. I modeled my choices after what I saw in Remiel's castle since I had no idea what constituted diabolical tastes in interior design.

Remiel seemed to appreciate the bed the most, since that's where we spent the majority of our time together. Not that I was complaining.

Stripping me of my modern clothing, he growled as he ripped open my belt. "This damned thing."

"I'll be back in the skirt thing tomorrow," I assured him, helping him shove my pants to the floor.

"Or you could go naked." He raised his brows, as if it was a tempting offer.

"I might be the Devil now, but I still have to uphold some modicum of decency."

"Right now, I want you to be anything *but* decent."

"Then stop talking and start worshipping." I bit my lip and sat on the edge of the bed, spreading my legs open.

He smirked and dropped to his knees, kissing his way from my neck down my chest, taking his time to tease my nipples, before finally dipping down to my cock and enveloping it in his wicked mouth.

I slid my hands into his hair and pushed the silver strands away from his face, tightening my grip now and again, just enough to let him know how fucking fantastic he felt, in case he couldn't tell from my moans and sighs.

Pulling off of my cock, he pushed me onto my back and spat at my hole, rubbing the pad of his thumb in small circles around my rim. I angled my hips for him, trying to give him better access to both areas while guiding his mouth back to my dick.

He sucked me in deep, sliding a finger inside at the same time. My eyes rolled up in the back of my head and I arched my back, chasing the dual waves of pleasure.

Sucking harder, he took my cock all the way into his throat and swallowed around it at the same time he crooked his finger inside, brushing the cluster of nerves he knew would make my whole body tremble.

"Fuck, Remiel." My fingers twisted in his silver hair so hard he groaned.

He ran his free hand up my abdomen, up to my chest, raking his nails across my skin and leaving fiery trails in their wake. I hissed at the sensation, even as his feathers caressed the same path, easing the pain.

Pulling off my cock, he licked it from root to tip, gazing up at me with luminous silver eyes. "You like that, lamb?"

"You know I do. I like everything you do to me."

He twisted his finger inside of me, adding a second as he kissed my cock and balls, teasing them with his teeth and tongue. "Tell me what you want."

"Fuck..." I ground against his hand, trying to take his fingers deeper. "I want it all. I want you to fuck me, but I want to fuck you too."

"Whatever you wish." He gave one last lick to my crown and crawled into my lap, kissing me as our cocks rubbed together.

I wound my hand through his hair again and tugged his head back, forcing him to break our kiss. "I want you on your knees."

He arched an eyebrow with a smirk but climbed off, assuming the position he'd forced me into more times than I could count. Spreading his wings, he arched his back and slid a smoldering look over his shoulder. "Like this?"

"Just like that." I shifted onto my knees behind him, running my hands down his back, between his wings, and over the curve of his ass. I wet one of my fingers quickly before slipping it inside of him, just so I could watch the muscles in his back tighten.

He was perfect in every way and the fact he was mine? I

felt my own heartbeat quicken. The sense of possessiveness gave me an indescribable feeling of… freedom. As odd as that sounded. We could be as wicked and vile and sinful as we wanted with one another and it was never too much.

Being in Hell with Remiel was a kind of Heaven I never would have imagined. I had the freedom to do whatever I wanted, whenever I wanted. I didn't have to pretend everything was alright. I didn't have to keep up appearances. I could revel in his toxic infatuation and be equally crazy about him and who could possibly tell us it was wrong? We were demons, for fuck's sake. *Everything* about us was wrong and that's what made it so unexpectedly right.

Adding more saliva to my cock, I rubbed it against his hole. "Are you ready?"

"I'm always ready."

Grasping his hip with one hand, I held my cock steady with the other and pushed against him. I exhaled a breath as I sank inside of him, enjoying every second of the tight heat enveloping me. A quiver rippled through his feathers. I smiled to myself and stroked his wings with both hands, thrusting in and out of him slowly. His feathers fluttered again and a soft moan escaped him.

"Do you like that, lover?" I asked, my voice sounding husky in my ears as I ran my fingers through the downy feathers at the base of his wings. It seemed the tables had turned in more ways than one.

He didn't reply. Instead, he rocked his hips back against me and sent another one of his lust-soaked glances over his shoulder.

I wrapped a hand around his silver hair and jerked his head backward, thrusting my hips into him hard enough to make him gasp. "Answer me."

"Yes," he hissed, arching his back even more to alleviate some of the pressure. "I like it."

"And if I hold you by the wings and fuck you senseless?"

"I'd like that too."

"Good. Because that's exactly what I'm going to do." Releasing his hair, I gripped the base of his wings and held on tight, snapping my hips as hard as I could to drive into him over and over. The harder I fucked him, the louder he moaned and gasped, cursing my name in a series of languages. All of it fed my desire to see him come undone completely. It was one thing to watch him get off on fucking me, but it was something else to know that *I* was the one doing it to him for a change.

When his hand disappeared between his legs, I seized a handful of his hair again, wrenching his head back so I could growl directly in his ear. "Don't even think about it."

"But it feels so good."

I slid my hand around his throat and pulled him up on his knees, pressing myself against his back as firmly as I could between his wings, and took over stroking his cock for him with my other hand. "But it'll feel even better when I'm riding you." I squeezed the head of his dick so hard he flinched. Instead of being turned off, he reached behind him and grabbed the back of my head, pulling me closer. The moment my lips touched his, he ravaged my mouth with his tongue, as hard and fast as I thrust into him. This is what we truly were—not simply demons, but hellfire and preternatural lust, coming together in an explosion of sin and I relished it. I relished *him*.

Sliding out of him suddenly, I rocked back on my heels, giving the base of my shaft a couple of quick squeezes to stave off my own building orgasm. "Lay down."

Remiel turned with a mock glare but laid on his back

nonetheless, spreading his wings out to get more comfortable. "I don't know if I like taking orders from you."

"You know you love it," I shot back, straddling his lap as soon as he was settled. "You love seeing how far I've fallen."

"You are my greatest achievement, lover."

I eased myself onto his cock slowly, drawing out the pleasure we both got from the change in positions and the dynamics. As good as my cock felt inside of him, there was something about him fucking me that unlocked my true depravity.

"Fuck, just look at you," Remiel whispered. He cupped my cheek gently, rubbing the pad of his thumb across my lips. I took it between my teeth and sucked on it hard, swirling my tongue around the tip. The carnal heat of his gaze radiated into me so much so that I felt the warmth flare in my cheeks.

He thrust into me from below, his mouth dropping open in a silent gasp when I swiveled my hips against him, taking pleasure from him as much as he was giving.

Riding him like this gave me another burst of satisfaction, knowing I was the one he took pleasure in. The *only* one. Sex might have originally been a weapon he'd wielded, a means of alternately seducing and tormenting me, but now? It was pure, hedonistic rapture.

He sat up and grabbed the back of my neck, pulling me down, straight to his lips. While he kissed me, exploring every inch of my mouth with his tongue as if he hadn't mapped it out a thousand times before, he rolled us to the side so he was on top, my legs wrapped around his waist tightly.

"I want your cum," he panted when he tore himself away from my mouth.

"I want yours."

He nodded and resumed thrusting in long, smooth strokes that hit so deep I had a hard time keeping my eyes open. I fisted my cock and jerked in time with him, pushing myself closer and closer to the edge. Our breathing turned ragged and sweat glistened on our bodies.

"Fuck, I'm going to come," I ground out approximately two seconds before the first wave of climax rushed down my spine and pulsated over my hand. What I didn't catch ended up on my abdomen. It didn't matter. Remiel snatched my wrist and brought my hand to his mouth, lapping up the drops, never once slowing his hips.

It wasn't long before Remiel's jaw clenched and his brow furrowed. I watched the muscles in his chest tighten a moment before he pulled out and surged forward, his hand flying up and down his shaft. A few strokes were all he needed before he gave a strangled cry and shot his release on top of the mess I already made.

Instead of conjuring a towel, he leaned down and licked and sucked everything off of my skin until it was clean. When he lifted his lips to mine, I opened my mouth and happily accepted the mouthful he gave me. I'd barely swallowed the salty, honey combination before his tongue swept inside and caressed mine languidly.

We kissed for what felt like hours until my lips were raw and swollen. Remiel didn't seem to care, but after a while, he laid beside me and draped his wing over me in lieu of a blanket.

In the quiet aftermath, I stroked his feathers gently, admiring their shimmering, iridescent quality. I kind of missed the black tips, but I would never tell him that.

"I love you, Remiel," I said, so quiet it was almost a whisper. I didn't even turn to look at him. I didn't want to risk seeing his disapproval or disgust at anything sentimental. "I just want you to know that. I know I said it before, but I wanted you to know I meant it. It wasn't something I said because I was trying to manipulate you into staying."

He didn't move at all in my periphery. As desperate as I was for him to say something, I knew better than to ask what he was thinking. So I continued.

"I think He"—I glanced up at the ceiling pointedly—"sent you to me. I didn't understand it back then. I don't know if I really understand it now, to be honest. But you saw something in me no one else ever did. And I love you for that. I don't expect you to say anything. I just wanted you to know that's what I feel."

"I know," he murmured against my ear, nuzzling closer and laying his left hand—the one branded with my sigil—over my wildly beating heart. "I've always known."

"Am I that transparent?"

"From the moment I first marked you, I've had an insight into what you were feeling. Remember what I told you in the library? Wearing my sigil meant so much more than forfeiting your soul."

"What does it mean now? Do I even have a soul anymore?"

"Of course you do. You're still half-witch." His hand shifted to mine, pulling it out from beneath his wing so he could trail his fingertip over the Ring of Eleazar. "It's what gives you the power to command this, remember?"

"Have two demons ever marked each other before?"

"No."

"So what does that mean?"

"I have no idea. You're writing a new chapter in that detestable book as we speak."

"You mean the Bible?"

He scoffed. "Not the one you're used to—the one used

to record everything, on everyone, on every plane of existence."

"The Book of Life?" I tried my best not to gape, but I couldn't help it. "It's... real?"

"It's very real," Remiel replied with a sigh. "And no, you can't see it because it's in Heaven. There is another book you *can* see, though—the Book of All Souls. Anyone not included in the precious Book of Life ends up in that one. It's the Devil's Book. Your book."

I expelled a slow breath, trying to wrap my head around the fact the Book of Life was real and the Devil really did keep records on everyone too. I used to think it was like the Boogeyman, just a tall tale used to scare children into behaving. "There's still so much I have to learn."

"Good thing you have the rest of eternity, then."

"Yeah..."

Silence pressed in around us. I toyed with the edge of Remiel's wing, trying to slow my racing thoughts and focus on his steady breathing, hoping I'd be able to match it.

"Let me guess. You're not going to sleep until you see it," Remiel said flatly.

"Come on!" I pushed his wing off and climbed out of bed, conjuring a black skirt as I moved. Skirts might not have much use in the modern world, but down here? They were certainly preferable to "normal" clothing.

Groaning, Remiel hauled himself out of bed. By the time he stopped in front of me, he was dressed in a matching "outfit," if a long skirt and bejeweled belt could even be called that.

"I knew I shouldn't have said anything," he mumbled, wrapping his arms and wings around me before sweeping us through time and space. Since I had *no* idea what I was supposed to be envisioning in order to teleport successfully, it was safer for everyone to let him continue to be my tour guide.

Depositing me outside a set of heavy, oversized doors, he gestured to them with a weary expression. "Your library, lamb."

As giddy as a child at Christmas, I pushed the doors open with my magic and darted inside. Green fire sparked to life in each of the torches lining the walls. On and on it went, down row after row after row, until the green dots disappeared entirely in the aisles of soaring bookcases.

I walked to the edge of the railing, overlooking the endless books, and grasped it before I fell over.

Ancient scrolls, papyri, and tablets filled bookcase after bookcase. Eventually, real books appeared on the shelves, varying in size and shape until they became more or less standardized in what looked like nineteenth-century binding. Down below, in the center of the room, were a series of large books on display. As I watched, black ink appeared on the pages, written by invisible hands, though it was too far away to see what, exactly, was being recorded.

Remiel stepped up behind me and wrapped his arms around me, kissing the curve of my neck. "Are you happy, lamb?"

I leaned back against him, folding my arms over the top of his and holding him tightly. "You know I am. And now I know you can feel it."

He hummed against my skin, kissing here and there lazily.

"I can feel your happiness too," I said quietly, making sure to keep my tone light. "Among other things."

"I'd hope so." His teeth sank into my neck right as he pressed his cock against my ass. It wasn't hard yet, but I'm sure it wouldn't take long. It never did with him.

“That’s not what I meant,” I sighed, mostly out of pleasure but with a dash of annoyance.

“I know what you meant.” He spun me to face him, his lips brushing over mine before his tongue traced my lower lip. Licking inside my mouth, he teased me with his tongue until I was breathing hard again, clawing at his bare skin and trying to pull him as close to me as I could. I wanted to feel every part of him, be it his physical body or the emotions radiating through the bond of our sigils.

As impossible as it was, for the first time in my life, I felt like I was *exactly* where I belonged—with Remiel, until the end of days.

THE END

And Kevin lived happily ever after

ACKNOWLEDGMENTS

Stefka — Girl, there aren't enough words to thank you for all of your support, not just with this project, but with everything. You've helped me so much as a friend and fellow author and I'm *so* grateful for you. You read this manuscript a dozen times, in various stages of hot garbage to a full-on dumpster fire, so I hope with every fiber of my being that you love the end result.

Kendra — You also got to experience *Igni* as a dumpster fire in the early days and I cringe to think how many spastic voice messages I left for you while I was brainstorming. How many times did I change the direction of this story? I lost count. But you also stuck by me and kept encouraging me. So thank you!!

Nisha, Julia, and Lori — They say it takes a village... I mean, that's about raising kids, but *Igni* is my book baby, so I'm going with it. I wouldn't be where I am today without your encouragement, your endless patience, and you all being the voice of reason when my crazy brain gets to be too much. The fact that Phelan and Remiel meet your high standards also makes me stupidly happy.

Gloria — thank you so much for inspiring the name for the creepiest book ever, the Combermere, and not even batting an eye when I asked to use it. I love that fictional grimoire so much!

And last but certainly not least, Kat, Stacey, Anna, Mari, and Amy — my awesome beta readers. You took my OK-ish draft and made it amazing! Whether it was an outright suggestion, a clarifying question, or "I want more of this!" feedback, you guys helped make this book the incredible story that it is today. So thank you for taking the time to read a less-than-perfect manuscript, looking past its flaws, and seeing the potential. It means so much to me!

ABOUT THE AUTHOR

International best-selling and award-winning dark romance author Ashlyn Drewek has always been a hopeless romantic. She's also fascinated by the dark, macabre things in life such as Halloween, murder, cemeteries, and witch-craft. Not necessarily in that order.

Most of her time is spent making up stories in her head or researching obscure historical topics. The results of those efforts usually end up in a book as some sort of weird Easter egg or symbolism. Anything to make Edgar Allan Poe proud.

ALSO BY ASHLYN DREWEK

The Leander Welles Series:

THE MYSTERY OF LEANDER WELLES — a dark, psychological romantic suspense about a criminal psychiatrist who falls in love with her patient. *Finalist for Suspense in the 2021 Next Generation Indie Book Awards.*

THE RATIONALE OF LEANDER WELLES — a dark, psychological romantic suspense about an alleged murderer who falls in love with his psychiatrist... or does he?

THE DAMNATION OF LEANDER WELLES: OR, THE DEATH & LIFE OF BENNETT REEVE — a dark MM friends-to-lovers romance about a cutthroat lawyer and an enigmatic millionaire and what happens when two dark souls join forces. *A prequel to Book 1 and 2.*

THE WRATH OF LEANDER WELLES — a dark, MM romantic suspense about love, revenge, and how far a psychopath is willing to go for both.

The Solnyshko Duet:

THE KIDNAPPING OF ROAN SINCLAIR — a dark MM romance about an American college guy who is kidnapped by a Russian criminal.

THE VENGEANCE OF ROAN SINCLAIR — a dark MM romance

about love in the aftermath of trauma and finding your new normal.

Paranormal & Dark Fantasy:

MALUM DISCORDIAE — a dark academia MM enemies-to-lovers paranormal romance about witches, Necromancers, and a blood feud that has lasted centuries.

THE COVENTRY CAROL — a darker MM Christmas novella with hot Santa smut, anti-Christmas feels, and a cannibal hitman.

PER SANGUINEM — a slow-burn paranormal MM romantic suspense standalone about vampires and cops with commitment issues and what happens when you fall in love with your partner.